The HUSKY & His WHITE CAT SHIZUN

ERHA HE TA DE BAI MAO SHIZUN

6

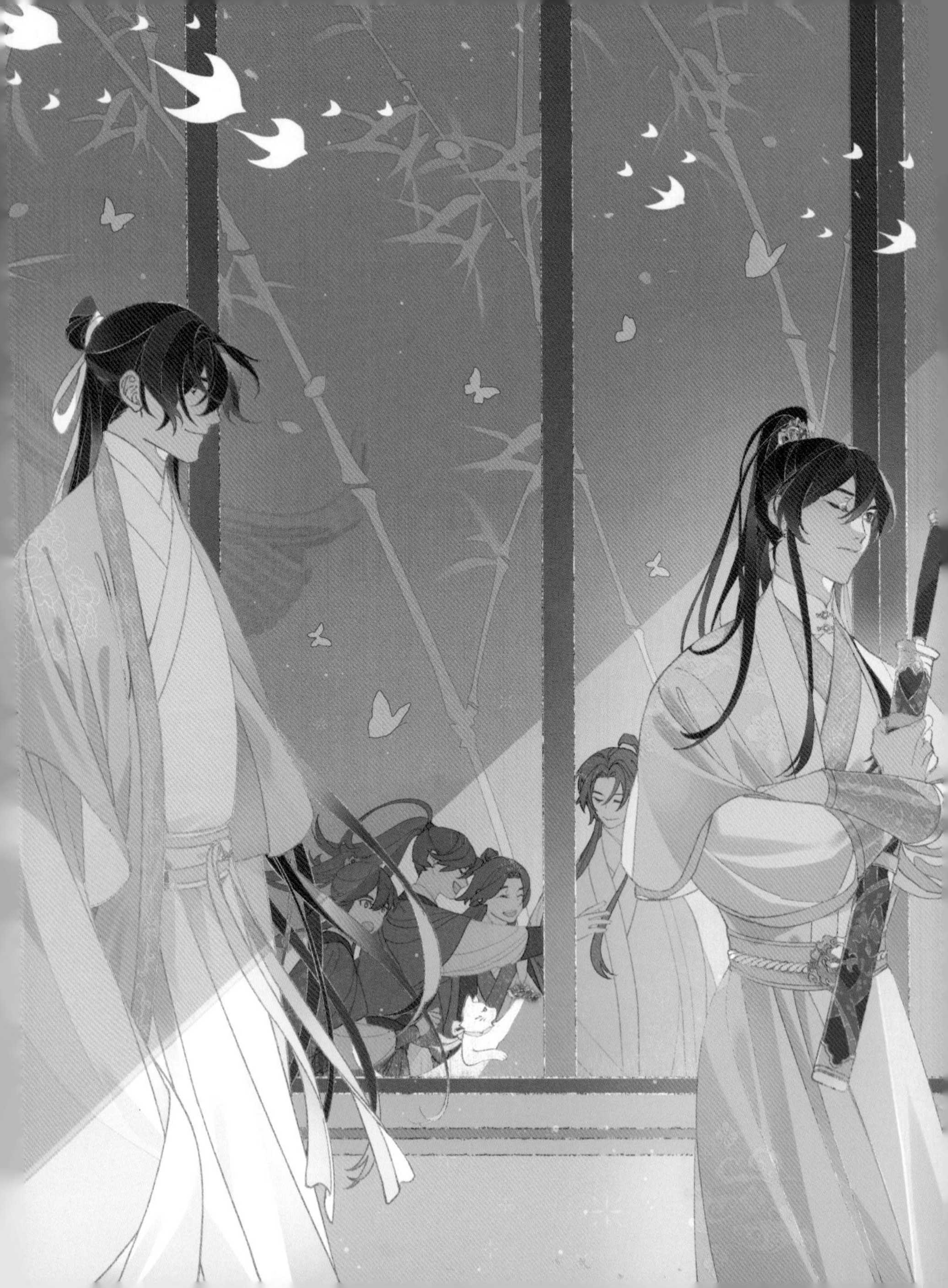

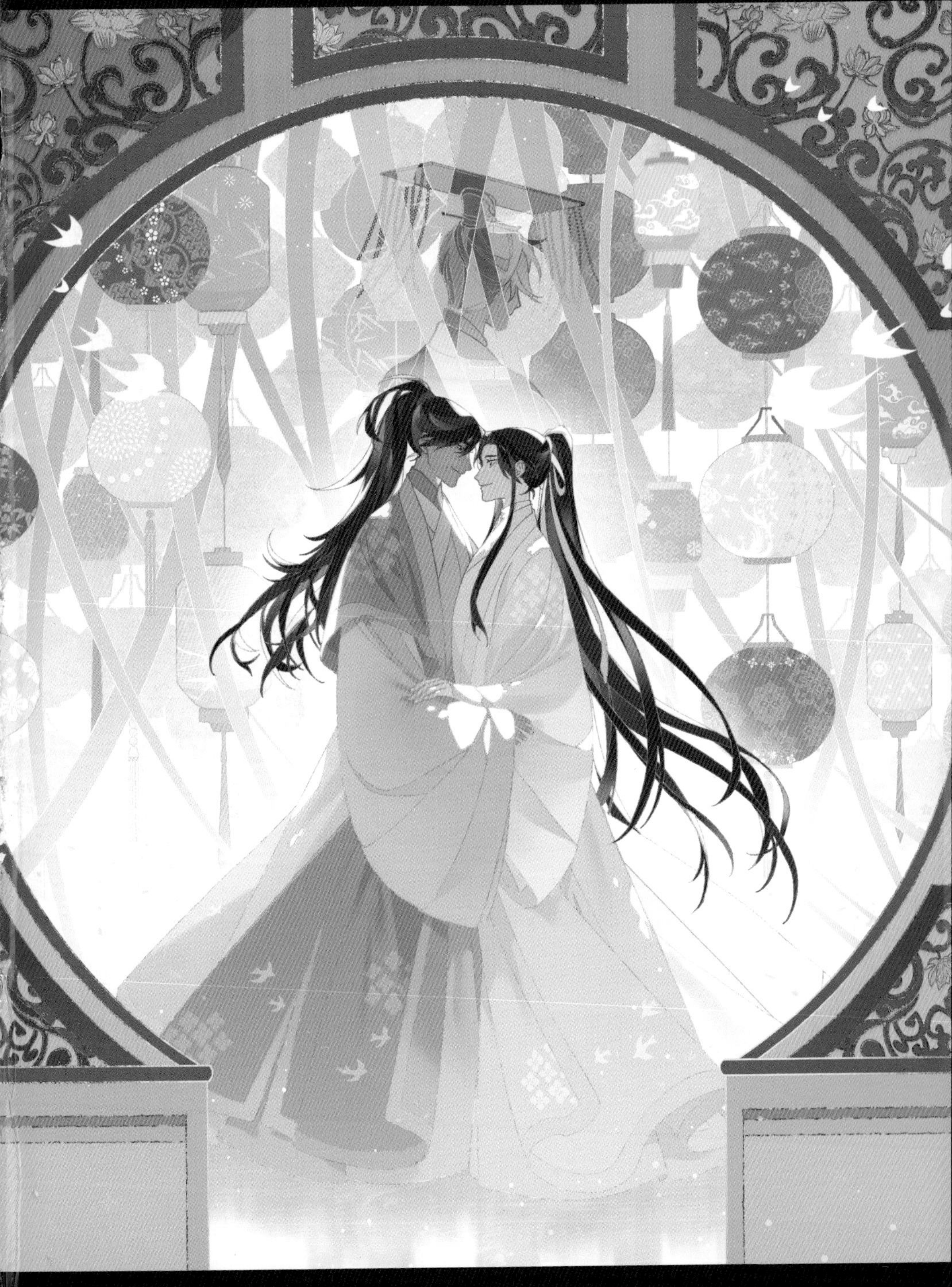

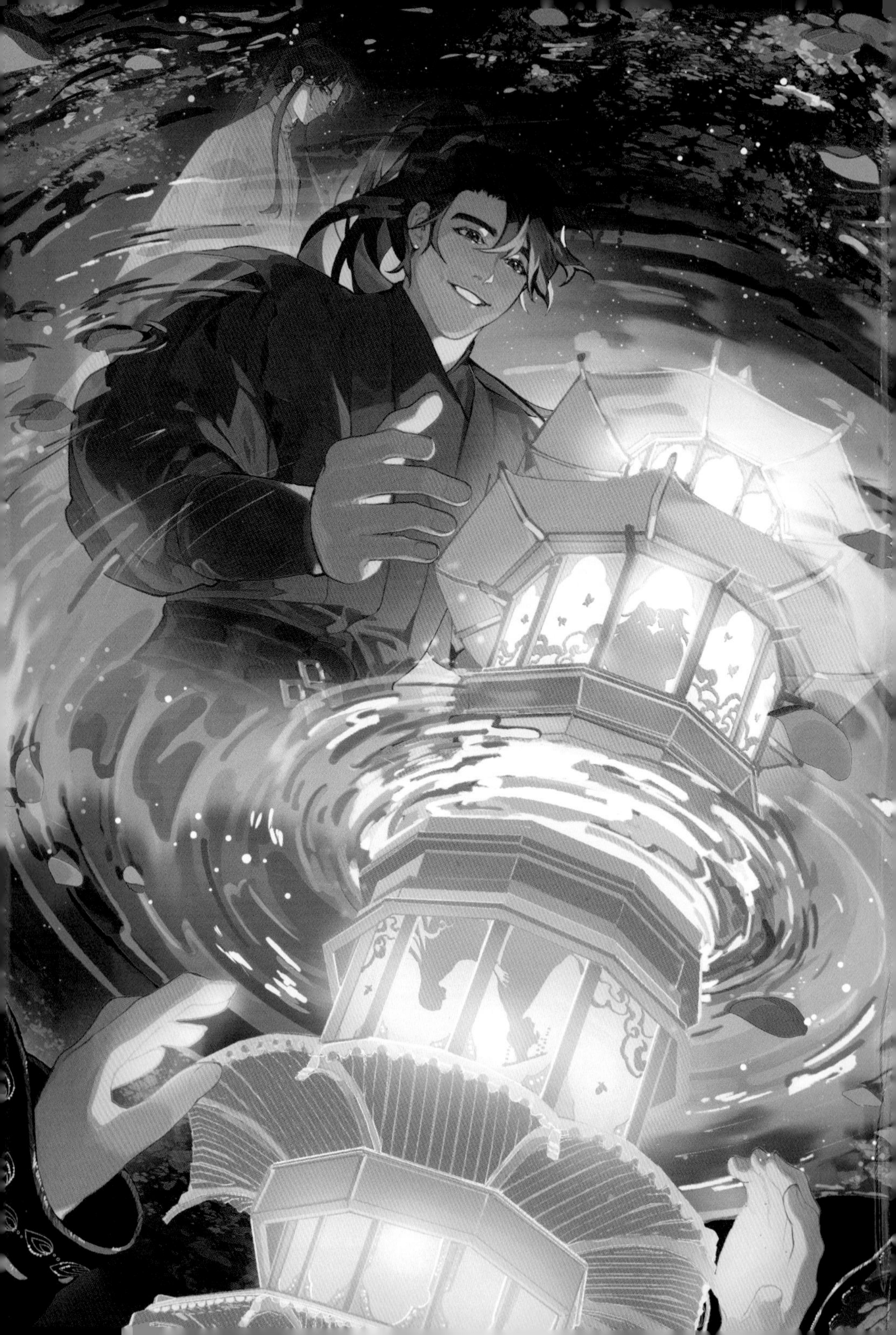

The HUSKY & His WHITE CAT SHIZUN

ERHA HE TA DE BAI MAO SHIZUN

WRITTEN BY
Rou Bao Bu Chi Rou

ILLUSTRATED BY
St

TRANSLATED BY
Jun, Rui, & Yu

Seven Seas

Seven Seas Entertainment

THE HUSKY & HIS WHITE CAT SHIZUN:
ERHA HE TA DE BAI MAO SHIZUN VOL. 6

Published originally under the title of 《二哈和他的白貓師尊》
(Erha He Ta De Bai Mao Shizun)
Author © 肉包不吃肉 (Rou Bao Bu Chi Rou)
English edition rights under license granted by 北京晋江原创网络科技有限公司
(Beijing Jinjiang Original Network Technology Co., Ltd.)
English edition copyright © 2024 Seven Seas Entertainment, Inc.
Arranged through JS Agency Co., Ltd
All rights reserved.

Cover and Interior Illustrations by St

Seven Seas press and purchase enquiries can be sent to Marketing Manager Lauren Hill at press@gomanga.com.
Information regarding the distribution and purchase of digital editions is available from Digital Manager CK Russell at digital@gomanga.com.

Seven Seas and the Seven Seas logo are trademarks of Seven Seas Entertainment. All rights reserved.

Follow Seven Seas Entertainment online at sevenseasentertainment.com.

TRANSLATION: Jun, Rui, Yu
ADAPTATION: Neon Yang
COVER DESIGN: M. A. Lewife
INTERIOR DESIGN: Clay Gardner
INTERIOR LAYOUT: Karis Page
COPY EDITOR: Jehanne Bell
PROOFREADER: Stephanie Cohen, Hnä
EDITOR: Kelly Quinn Chiu
PREPRESS TECHNICIAN: Melanie Ujimori, Jules Valera
MANAGING EDITOR: Alyssa Scavetta
EDITOR-IN-CHIEF: Julie Davis
PUBLISHER: Lianne Sentar
VICE PRESIDENT: Adam Arnold
PRESIDENT: Jason DeAngelis

ISBN: 978-1-68579-763-8
Printed in Canada
First Printing: August 2024
10 9 8 7 6 5 4 3 2 1

TABLE OF CONTENTS

181

Shizun's Memories

THE MORNING AFTER the confession, Chu Wanning woke early. He didn't get up. He could see Mo Ran through the canopy, still asleep on a simple pallet of straw on the ground beside the bed.

It was difficult to see through the gauze of the curtain. Chu Wanning hesitated a moment before reaching out to lift it—yet before he even touched the thin fabric, he curled his outstretched hand into a finger, pointing. Using that single fingertip, he parted the veil the merest crack, as if it wouldn't count as peeking were it only through that gap.

The light of dawn streamed through the paper of the window. Cut into thin beams, the rosy glow gilded Mo Ran's handsome features.

Chu Wanning couldn't remember the last time he'd seen his sleeping face. He watched him quietly and carefully for a long time—so long he began to recall when Xue Zhengyong had first brought Mo Ran back to Sisheng Peak. Mo Ran had been a bashful youth, yet he seemed to shine with a fiery enthusiasm when he was happy. He spent his spare moments clinging to Chu Wanning, determined to become his student no matter what Chu Wanning said or how Chu Wanning tried to shake him off.

He looks the gentlest, I like him the best. Mo Ran's declaration back at the Heaven-Piercing Tower had been so absurd, so unbelievable, it left Chu Wanning without any intention to take him as a disciple. In the end, he'd left Mo Weiyu hanging for two whole weeks.

In that time, he heard Mo Weiyu had asked Xue Zhengyong, Madam Wang, Shi Mingjing, and Xue Ziming in turn for advice on how to become his student. Which of these Mo Ran ultimately got the idiotic notion from, no one knew, but he took to lurking outside the Red Lotus Pavilion like it was Cheng Yi's door,[1] waiting for Chu Wanning to appear. When Chu Wanning left in the morning, he greeted him and begged to become his student; when Chu Wanning returned in the evening, he greeted him and begged once more. He continued in this vein, rain or shine, with the persistence of water wearing a hole in a rock.

Each time, Chu Wanning had huffed and walked away, as if Mo Ran didn't exist. He didn't like this kind of fervent pursuit. As someone who was himself indifferent, he preferred others to approach him with emotions that were equally mild.

But the boy was keenly observant, surely a result of the environs in which he'd grown up. He only pestered Chu Wanning this way for two days; sensing Chu Wanning's coolness, he stopped chasing after him to beg for his tutelage. Yet he still came to the Red Lotus Pavilion every day without fail to sweep the fallen leaves from Chu Wanning's courtyard. Once Chu Wanning emerged, he would stand with his broom and smile, scratching his head as he said: "Yuheng Elder."

No *good morning* at dawn, or *rest well* at dusk. Only the simple greeting, *Yuheng Elder*, and a smile to go with it. Chu Wanning would barely spare him a glance before striding off, but Mo Ran wasn't fazed in the least. As Chu Wanning left, the rustling sounds of swept leaves carried on behind him.

---

1   A well-known idiom, "程门立雪," about two disciples who waited for hours in the snow at the door of Cheng Yi, a Song dynasty philosopher, requesting to be taken on as his disciples.

Ten days peacefully passed in this manner.

The dawn of the eleventh found Chu Wanning in unusually high spirits. It was a particularly fine morning, which contributed to his mood; nearly a dozen lotuses had bloomed in the pavilion overnight, filling the air with their sweet fragrance. When he pushed open the doors, he saw the young Mo Ran on the winding mountain path. Mo Ran was sweeping the fallen leaves as he slowly made his way up the steps, head bowed in concentration. One leaf seemed stubbornly caught in a crack in the stone; he bent to pick it up, intending to toss it into the bushes.

As Mo Ran glanced up, he saw Chu Wanning standing before the gate. He stared in stunned silence; then his face split into a grin. Arms bare beneath rolled-up sleeves and that leaf still in his hand, he waved at Chu Wanning. "Yuheng Elder."

His voice was clear and sweet as fruit from the vine. Though it wasn't loud, it seemed to echo between the mountain peaks. A pristine expanse of clouds drifted on, and sunlight poured past the boughs of the trees. A breeze sang through the bamboo forest. Chu Wanning stood for a moment, squinting into the dazzling sunshine that turned his eyes to liquid amber. In that sunlit instant, the dead leaf in the young man's hand seemed no longer so mournful, but took on something of the bright, dazzling quality of that beaming boy.

Expressionless, Chu Wanning walked down those stone steps. Mo Ran had grown used to his indifference and paid it no mind. He tactfully stood aside as usual and waited for Chu Wanning to pass.

Chu Wanning came down the steps, one after another, and glided past Mo Ran as he did every morning. But that day, he turned his head ever so slightly and glanced back at the youth. In a voice crisp as a spring and as calm as a lake, he said, "My thanks."

Mo Ran stared for a moment. Then his eyes lit up. He waved a frantic hand. "There's no need, no need, it's this disciple's duty."

Chu Wanning paused. "I don't plan to take you on as a disciple." But his voice and expression were no longer so stern as they had been. He turned and continued on his way. Yet for some inexplicable reason—perhaps a twinge of conscience—after a few steps, he found himself glancing back once more. That was how he wound up catching sight of the youth, still holding his broom, jumping for joy, wholly unbothered by his final words. Excitement was written all over his face, exuding an endless light and warmth.

This rascal hadn't listened at all to Chu Wanning's second sentence. Was a mere "thank you" enough to make him so happy?

Another few days passed just like this. One morning, it happened to rain. The downpour wasn't heavy, and Chu Wanning wasn't the type to bother with an umbrella or barrier. He reckoned it would take less than half an hour to get to the Platform of Sin and Virtue. Even if he got soaked, he could steam himself dry with a spell.

When he pushed the door open, Mo Ran was still there. But he wasn't sweeping today. He had put the broom aside and instead held an oilpaper umbrella as he crouched low to the ground with his back to Chu Wanning, shoulders shifting as he fiddled with something in complete concentration. His already small figure seemed even smaller when crouched. With the large, dark brown umbrella over his head, it made for a comical sight, as if he were a mushroom that'd popped out of the ground after spring rain.

Resisting the urge to smile, Chu Wanning walked up behind him and cleared his throat. "What are you doing?"

"Ah." Stunned, the youth turned and looked up at him. The first thing out of his mouth was, "Yuheng Elder." But before Chu Wanning could reply, his eyes widened, and the second thing out of his mouth was, "Why don't you have an umbrella?"

Mo Ran stood on his tiptoes and raised his umbrella as high as it would go. His third utterance was, "Take this one."

But he was too short, and stood one step below Chu Wanning. Even with great effort, his umbrella barely cleared the top of Chu Wanning's head. His grasp faltered; a gust of wind blew, and he fumbled it—the umbrella tilted, sending water streaming into Chu Wanning's collar and down his neck. Before Chu Wanning could speak, Mo Ran devolved into a flurry of apologies. "Sorry, sorry!"

Still Chu Wanning said nothing. He could have said *Mn* the first time Mo Ran spoke. He could have said *I don't need it* the second time Mo Ran spoke. And he could have said *Keep it for yourself* at the third. But Chu Wanning was left somewhat speechless by the fourth outburst, as Mo Ran cried out his apologies. Chu Wanning's gaze was downcast; his expression might've been one of apathy or sternness. In the end, he only sighed and took the umbrella from Mo Ran's hand. He held it up over the two of them, both his posture and grip precise. As he glanced at Mo Ran, he paused for a moment and returned to his first question. "What are you doing?"

"Saving the earthworms."

"What?" Chu Wanning frowned, thinking he'd misheard.

Mo Ran smiled, cheeks dimpling sweetly. He scratched his head, embarrassed, and stuttered, "S-saving the earthworms."

Chu Wanning looked down at Mo Ran's hand, which held a still-dripping branch he must've picked up from the ground. Past that, on the stone steps, there was indeed a helpless little earthworm lying in a puddle, wriggling away.

"The worms came out of the dirt, but once the rain stops, the sun'll bake them into worm cakes." Somewhat abashed, Mo Ran continued, "So I wanted to put them back in the grass."

"With a stick?" Chu Wanning asked coolly.

A pause. "Yeah."

Seeing the man's icy expression, Mo Ran must have worried the Yuheng Elder was judging him. "I-it's not that I'm scared to use my hands," he hastily explained. "It's just that my mom told me when I was little that you can't touch worms with your bare hands, or they'll rot..."

Chu Wanning shook his head. "That's not what I meant."

He reached out and tapped a spot in midair. A delicate golden willow vine emerged from the cracks between the limestone steps and wrapped itself around the worm lying in the puddle, gently conveying it back into the grass.

Eyes widening, Mo Ran asked in astonishment, "What was that?"

"Tianwen."

"What's Tianwen?"

Chu Wanning shot him a glance. "My weapon."

Mo Ran looked even more dumbstruck. "Elder, why...why is your weapon..."

"So small?" Chu Wanning finished on his behalf.

Mo Ran snickered.

With a sweep of his sleeves, Chu Wanning said blandly, "There are times when it's ferocious, of course."

"Really? Can I see that?"

"It's probably best you never do."

At the time, Mo Ran hadn't realized what Chu Wanning meant. He turned to watch as that willow vine shimmied into each crack of the stone steps, picking up those hapless worms soaking in the water and returning them to the mud. Slowly, his expression became one of admiration.

"Do you want to learn how to do this?" Chu Wanning asked.

Mo Ran froze for a moment, then his eyes flew wide. He was so delighted he didn't know what to say; eventually, he managed to nod over and over with his handsome little face flushed red.

"After morning practice tomorrow, come to the bamboo forest behind the Platform of Sin and Virtue. I'll wait for you there."

Pristine silk shoes trod over damp stone steps as Chu Wanning descended the mountain path, umbrella held aloft. Mo Ran stared dazedly at his elegant silhouette. After more than a moment, the meaning of Chu Wanning's words finally dawned on him—the red of his cheeks deepened, his eyes sparkling. Heedless of the wet ground, he fell to his knees and kowtowed, his youthful voice ringing with joyful enthusiasm. "Yes, Shizun!"

Chu Wanning said nothing; he didn't acknowledge Mo Ran's words, nor did he stop him. He merely paused briefly before continuing down the steps, the raindrops skipping across the surface of the umbrella like the strumming of a harp.

Only after Chu Wanning vanished into the distance did Mo Ran rise from the ground—at which point he discovered a barrier set up over his head. The translucent gold of it, flowing with patterns of five-petaled flowers, had kept the drizzle from soaking him.

Xue Zhengyong had been both surprised and relieved to learn of this development. "Yuheng, what made you change your mind?" he had asked Chu Wanning.

At the time, Chu Wanning had been sitting on the dais at the Platform of Sin and Virtue, the umbrella Mo Ran had lent him still in his hand. His slender fingers stroked imperceptibly over the antique wood of the handle. At last he said, "To help him save the earthworms."

Xue Zhengyong made a noise of surprise, his panther-like eyes widening like a cat's. "Save the *what?*"

Chu Wanning didn't reply; the suggestion of a smile hovered in his eyes, fixed on the umbrella's bamboo ribs.

Time had passed in the blink of an eye. The youth he took in as a disciple had started pure, then wandered astray, yet thankfully, he had still grown into a good and proper xianjun in the end. He hadn't let Chu Wanning down.

One pale fingertip poked through the gauze. Through that sliver of a gap, Chu Wanning stared at Mo Ran's sleeping face. The youth of his memories was now a strong and handsome man; his features had grown more defined, and his maturity was visible in the lines of his face. But as always, his brow furrowed as he slept. Ever since he was young, Mo Ran's lashes had scrunched low in slumber, as if weighed down by some load on his mind. Chu Wanning found it amusing. Mo Ran was so young—were his dreams so melancholy?

Immersed in thought, he suddenly saw Mo Ran's long lashes flutter as his eyes slowly opened.

Locked in place with finger outstretched, Chu Wanning's first thought was to pull his hand back and pretend to be asleep. But Mo Ran was a peculiar person. He didn't wake up with the drowsiness one might expect from a young man. Rather, he woke up practically instantly, like someone much older than his years. He seemed hypersensitive to any change in his surroundings while he slept—as if the threat of assassination was lurking always around the corner, his every step like treading on thin ice. Before Chu Wanning could pull back from the canopy, Mo Ran's eyes landed on his questing fingertip with unerring accuracy.

Chu Wanning froze. The Yuheng Elder's dignity and reputation hung in the balance; in that critical instant, he was struck by a bolt of inspiration. He turned, letting his outstretched hand fall carelessly over the edge of the bed. As if he hadn't been trying to peek through the veil at all, but had simply rolled over in his sleep and stretched, sticking his hand out of the canopy as he shifted.

Mo Ran, unable to imagine the stern and serious Chu Wanning enacting such a farce, was completely fooled. He worried he might wake Chu Wanning, so he got up quietly—but instead of quickly stealing from the room, he took Chu Wanning's exposed wrist and carefully tucked it back under the blanket.

A few moments later, Chu Wanning heard the creak of an opening door. Mo Ran had left.

Chu Wanning opened his eyes and gazed at the dawn light filtering into the room, losing himself in his thoughts. He had never thought he might be together with Mo Ran; he'd hardly even dared imagine it. After the events of the past night, he still felt as if everything had been a dream.

In his memories, Mo Ran's crush on Shi Mingjing was so obvious. He'd spent so many years watching them from the sidelines; he knew and understood this well. He'd seen Mo Ran flash a brilliant grin at Shi Mingjing; he'd seen Mo Ran make noodles for Shi Mingjing; he'd seen Mo Ran secretly help Shi Mingjing finish his missions, smug in the belief that nobody would know he'd interfered. But Chu Wanning knew it all. He had been envious, jealous, upset, and dissatisfied—and eventually, he thought he'd come to terms with it.

But how could acceptance come so easily? Even knowing a relationship with Mo Ran was impossible, he'd still stubbornly clung to his feelings and brazenly refused to turn away.

Over and over, Chu Wanning had asked himself whether this doomed course was worth it, whether such hopeless yearning was contemptible. But after countless rounds of self-examination, he had never found an answer. He himself had once looked indifferently upon those fools suffering in unrequited love, failing to comprehend why they'd persist despite the pain, holding on so tightly despite the scars left behind. He'd never understood it until the karmic flames of unanswered yearning scorched his own heart. Only then did he realize that most true and sincere passion in this world was very much the same. One could force themselves to let go, but rarely could they give up completely.

It was precisely because of this that Chu Wanning, who didn't know of Mo Ran's change of heart toward Shi Mei, felt confused and hesitant. He didn't understand why Mo Ran would choose to shift his attention from the beautiful Shi Mingjing to his own somewhat pathetic visage. Was it out of gratitude? Or guilt? Was Mo Ran trying to devote his body to him the way a seductive demoness or flower spirit would repay a favor?

For fuck's sake, surely it couldn't be because Mo Ran had confessed to Shi Mei and been rejected...

Chu Wanning stared blankly. His mind buzzed with wild imaginings, all sorts of stories of spurned beauties and fickle men surging madly through his head. The more he thought, the angrier he grew, until he finally sat up in bed. Unobserved inside the cottage, he got up and stomped on the pallet Mo Ran had slept on last night.

Shizun's Little Candle Dragon

EVEN IF HE HAD his conjectures, Chu Wanning refused to obsess over them in the absence of facts; he was stressed enough as it was. Still, he had his reservations about these feelings that had seemingly appeared out of nowhere. As the refugees waited for the apocalyptic fire to die out and made ready to leave, Chu Wanning made his own preparations—he had no intention of traveling on Mo Ran's sword again.

Of course, this Yuheng Elder, who could barely manage to fly twenty feet in the air, wasn't planning to soar across the sea on Huaisha either. While everyone else assembled on the craggy rocks near the water's edge to be helped onto Mo Ran's enlarged sword, one after another, Chu Wanning pulled out his Rising Dragon Talisman.

Chu Wanning dabbed a drop of blood onto its scale, and that chatty little paper dragon sprang to life from the painting and darted into the sky. After turning several somersaults, it dove back down to circle its owner as it hollered: "Aiya, Chu Wanning, long time no see. What favor are you asking of this venerable one now?"

"Give me a ride to the opposite shore."

"Puh! This venerable one is the first immortal lord since Pangu[2]

---

2   *The first being in Chinese mythology, who came out of the egg containing the universe, split yin from yang, and pushed apart the sky and the earth.*

broke through Chaos, the Dragon of the Candle—how could I debase myself to become a beast of burden? No rides, no rides!"

The paper dragon the length of a man's palm wagged its head and whipped its tail, grumbling as everyone looked on. It was small and weak, but its voice was sonorous. Upon hearing its words, a child in the crowd burst into laughter.

Chu Wanning's face was like rolling thunder. He lifted one hand and a golden flame erupted from his palm. "Then burn."

Infuriated, the little dragon threw itself on the sandy beach. Huffing and puffing, it brandished its claws and glared. "Why're you always like this? Rude and unreasonable, callous and shameless. No wonder you're alone every time I see you!"

Mo Ran turned his head as if to refute its words. But after a moment's thought, he realized there were too many eyes on them, and Chu Wanning was too prideful. In the end, he said nothing and only shook his head with a smile.

"Enough!" Chu Wanning snapped. With a wave of his hand, he sent the ball of flame hurtling straight down toward the dragon on the ground. Of course, Chu Wanning didn't actually intend to incinerate the little creature; though the fireball's blaze was fearsome, it merely landed on a stone next to the dragon's whiskers. The dragon wailed in terror, howling as it turned and patted its whiskies with chubby paws. "How's this venerable one's tail?! How's this venerable one's whiskies?! How's...how's this venerable one's noggin?! Is it still there? Is it still there?!"

"Not if you keep talking," said Chu Wanning through gritted teeth. A hissing golden flame rose in his hand once more. "Transform."

"Waaugghhh!" The little dragon threw itself into its melodramatic wailing, but just as it was about to pitifully flick away nonexistent tears, its beady little eyes met Chu Wanning's piercing cold gaze.

It shuddered, its sobs stopping short with a comical hiccup. The dragon feebly clambered up from the ground, now resembling a paper dragon in truth: weak and boneless, whiskers and horns drooping limply. It hiccupped again and mumbled, dejected, "Just this once, never again."

"As you wish." *Whatever. You said the same thing last time.*

The paper dragon extended its limbs as if stretching. With a sharp cry, a beam of golden light burst from its slim body, expanding to swallow the paper dragon. The paper dragon's shrill cry became a majestic roar; lightning crackled over that golden halo, and a wild wind rose. The waves crashed madly on the shore; everyone closed their eyes as they lowered their heads or covered their faces with sleeves.

Chu Wanning narrowed his eyes, his ponytail and robes whipping in the wind. When the golden light faded, the assembled villagers looked around, but the little dragon was nowhere to be found. The beach was quiet, wholly empty.

"Huh? It disappeared?" a brave child exclaimed.

At that moment, a colossal roar shook the heavens. Choppy waves cut through the water as dark clouds billowed on the biting wind. Everyone looked up in shock. In the lull, a majestic dragon soared from between the dense clouds. Its furious eyes were wide and round, its claws strong and sharp—even its whiskers were as thick around as centuries-old trees. It coiled amidst the clouds, magnificent, then reared its head and dove toward the ground wrapped in a fierce gale.

"Ahhh! Daddy!" Terrified, the orphaned boy called for his father out of habit. Mo Ran hastily scooped him up to console him.

Chu Wanning hadn't expected to scare this child yet again and froze for a moment. Watching the massive creature streak downward, he quickly commanded, "Slow down."

"Rrr?" The colossal dragon let out a dumb grunt, then landed with a *boom* on the rocky shore. Slowly, it lowered its body for Chu Wanning to climb up. It was so large that riding it was almost like sitting on the ground. No wonder Chu Wanning disliked sword-riding but was willing to fly on dragonback.

In an attempt to ease the atmosphere, Mo Ran cajoled the boy in his arms. "Do you want to ride the Dragon of the Candle with that gege?"

The boy didn't want any such thing. Burying his head in Mo Ran's shoulder, he whispered, "To tell you a secret...I don't like him..."

"To tell you a secret, I really do," Mo Ran answered.

"Huh?" The boy stared. Innocent as he was, his only response was another whisper. "Really?"

"Shh, don't tell anyone."

The boy broke into a smile, covering his mouth and nodding.

"What are you two whispering about? Are we leaving or not?"

Chu Wanning had no intention of riding with the rabble. Casting them a cool glance, he soared into the sky astride the dragon and swiftly disappeared amidst the clouds.

Loaded down with passengers, Mo Ran's sword was somewhat slower; by the time they arrived at Wuchang Town in Sichuan, it was dusk. By then, Chu Wanning had already landed and spoken with the major families of the town. This was the town that benefited most from Sisheng Peak's protection, so they scrambled to accommodate him.

The refugees from Linyi were quickly taken into the care of several prominent clans. The boy Mo Ran had been holding turned to wave at him wistfully as he left. "See you, Savior-gege."

"Mn, see you." Mo Ran smiled. He watched them walk away, standing in the last of the sun's glow.

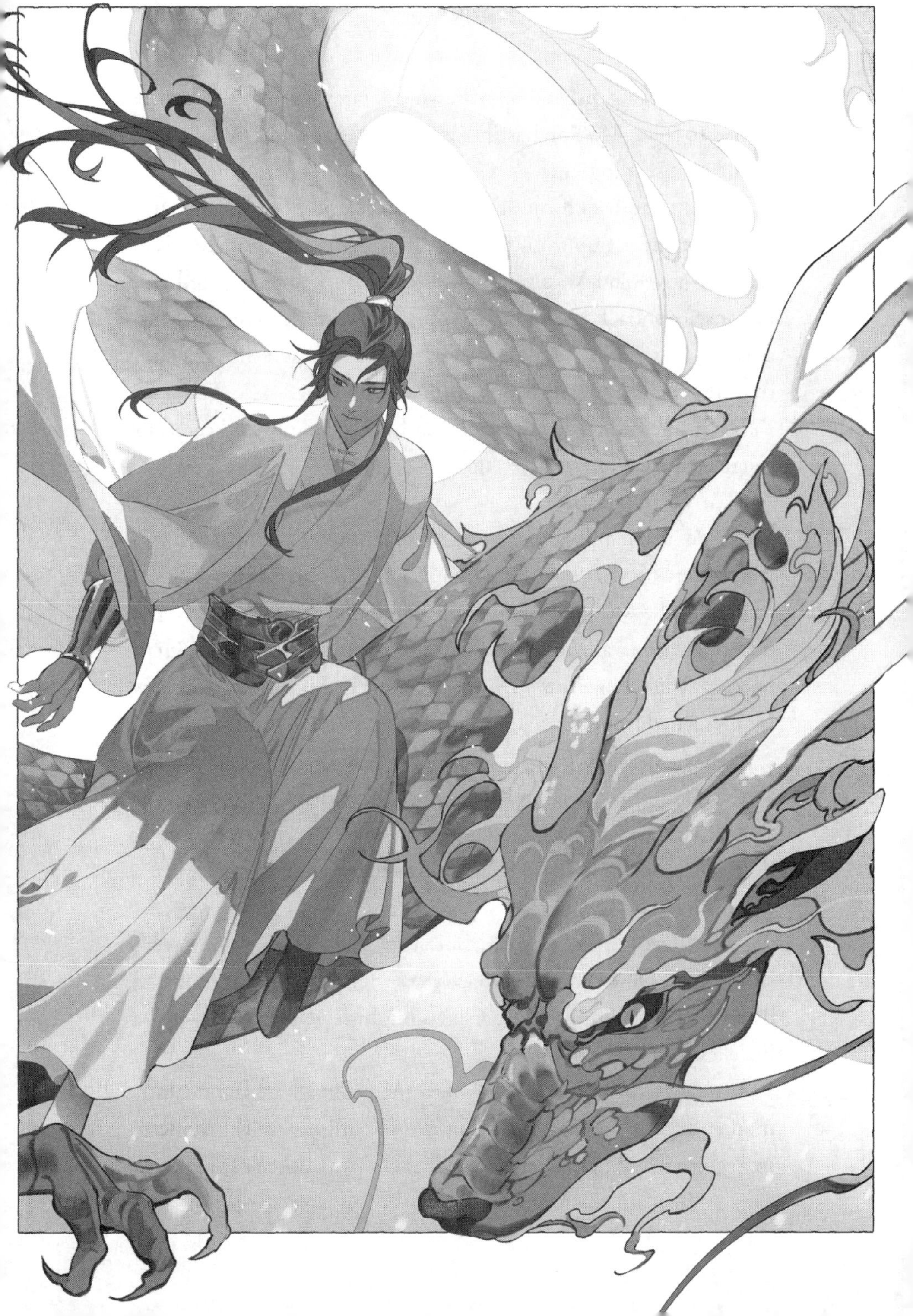

Chu Wanning disliked such drawn-out farewells. After a beat, he turned to leave. Mo Ran hastily rushed after him so they could walk back to the sect together.

Against the backdrop of swaying trees and rosy sunset, they walked in silence up the stone stairs, one step at a time. Mo Ran recalled how Chu Wanning had once dragged him, injured and unconscious, back to the peak despite his own depleted spiritual energy. To see Chu Wanning now, walking beside him as they returned together, made Mo Ran's heart tighten.

Swept up in that tide of emotions, he reached out and carefully caught Chu Wanning's fingertips.

Chu Wanning froze.

They'd held hands before, but Chu Wanning still seemed stiff and clumsy, terribly ill at ease. He strove to maintain his calm expression, to pretend he was unaffected and unbothered. Unfortunately, the man by his side was Mo Ran, Mo Weiyu—the one who knew him to his core; who knew how sensitive the mole by his ear was, and how his toes shied from the cold.

Neither spoke. Observing that Chu Wanning didn't pull away, Mo Ran finally clasped Chu Wanning's entire hand in his own.

The path ahead was long, but he wished the journey were longer. For the chance to hold Chu Wanning's hand a while longer, just a while longer.

Their destination was far, but he wished the journey were shorter. If it were shorter, perhaps the suffering Chu Wanning had borne to bring him home years ago might have been less—just a little less.

In this manner they walked onto the peak, where the majestic mountain gates rose before their eyes. Suddenly, a slender silhouette in a white fox-fur cloak appeared from between the rustling trees.

Before the two of them could get a clear look, they heard a man's voice. "Shizun?!"

Startled, Chu Wanning yanked his hand out of Mo Ran's and let his sleeve fall over it. He stopped in his tracks and raised his head.

Shi Mei came down the steps above them. In the setting sun, his face was as luminous as the fresh petals of a lotus, a splendid sight. Even the sprawling colors of the sunset paled in comparison; he was loveliness personified. Shi Mei appeared not to have noticed them holding hands; he only looked surprised and delighted to see them again. "Thank goodness, you're finally back!"

Mo Ran hadn't expected to run into him here. Embarrassed, he asked, "Shi Mei, are you heading down the mountain?"

"Mn, I'm on my way to pick up some things for the sect leader. I didn't expect to meet Shizun and A-Ran. The sect leader received Shizun's messenger haitang a few days back, but of course he couldn't rest easy until he saw you..."

"Mo Ran and I are unharmed. How are the others from the sect?"

"They're all fine," Shi Mei replied. "The young master was planted with a black chess piece, but not for long enough to do permanent damage, thankfully. Tanlang Elder has been overseeing his care, and today he was able to stand and walk around."

Chu Wanning sighed. "That's good."

Shi Mei smiled and looked at Mo Ran. His lashes lowered gently as he dipped in a bow. "I'd like to chat longer, but I'd hate to keep the Guyueye messenger with the medicinal ingredients waiting. If you'll excuse me, Shizun, A-Ran—I'll see you tonight."

"Mn, go on ahead," Chu Wanning said. "We'll talk soon."

Shi Mei left in a flutter of robes, disappearing into the distance. Chu Wanning looked back at Mo Ran. He knew Mo Ran hadn't been the one to let go—that he had pulled away first—yet he still felt the inexplicable burn of fury. He shot Mo Ran a cutting glare, then turned and left with a sweep of his sleeves.

Mo Ran could only stare in his wake.

The two arrived, one after the other, at the threshold of Loyalty Hall. When the doors opened, both were stunned speechless by the scene before them.

The main hall of Sisheng Peak was piled with precious metals and silks, gems and corals, magical implements and spiritual stones, spanning from the dais at the rear of the hall all the way to the entryway. Chu Wanning couldn't even fully open the door—a pile of sparkling spiritual stones for refining magical devices had entirely blocked the way.

The gifts were one thing, but for some reason, there were nearly three dozen beautiful women waiting anxiously inside as well. Xue Zhengyong stood in the middle of it all, desperately trying to reason with a Huohuang Pavilion disciple garbed in pink. "No thank you, absolutely not. We can accept the rest, but please take these song-stresses back to the pavilion master with you. We really have no need for song or dance here, thank you very much."

Mo Ran entered the hall behind Chu Wanning. As soon as he stepped in, a wave of strong perfume hit him in the face from the three dozen songstresses hovering beside the doorway. Always sensitive to such fragrances, he burst into a flurry of sneezes.

Xue Zhengyong's head whipped around, and his face instantly lit up in joy. "A-Ran, Yuheng! You're finally back! Quick, come help me persuade this...this envoy here."

Chu Wanning arched a brow. "Envoy?"

Before Xue Zhengyong could answer, the disciple turned with a toothy grin. "This one is the eldest disciple of Huohuang Pavilion, here on our pavilion master's orders to build an alliance with Sisheng Peak."

Chu Wanning was speechless. An alliance offer was not something they could brush off so easily. The three spent ages politely turning down the envoy's generosity until they finally managed to send him away.

As Xue Zhengyong watched his retreating silhouette, he heaved a gusty sigh and mopped his brow. "Do you know? All kinds of sects from the upper cultivation realm have been sending messengers these past few days, and they all want to make connections with Sisheng Peak. I haven't had many dealings with them—in the past, the only one willing to talk to us was Kunlun Taxue Palace. Now that they're suddenly coming in swarms, and with gifts too, I really don't know what to say."

Chu Wanning frowned. "What have we missed in the upper cultivation realm?"

"The times, they sure are changing," Xue Zhengyong sighed.

"How so?"

"It's a whole mess. That madman Xu Shuanglin exposed so many debts and grudges with that memory scroll. Everyone knows he did it for revenge, but what difference does that make? Jiangdong Hall has splintered, Guyueye and Taxue Palace have renounced their ties and become enemies, and of course I needn't remind you about Rufeng Sect. As for Wubei Temple..."

Recalling that Master Huaizui was Chu Wanning's shizun, Xue Zhengyong snapped his mouth shut. But Chu Wanning seemed unbothered. "Despite Wubei Temple being a place of purity, its previous leader involved himself in the power struggles of Rufeng Sect and even devised underhanded tricks to help Nangong Liu all those years ago. Of course its reputation is in shambles."

"Mn..."

Chu Wanning's callousness toward his own former sect bewildered both Xue Zhengyong and Mo Ran, who watched him quizzically. Chu Wanning pressed his lips together. After a beat of silence, he asked, "What about Nangong Si?"

"I don't know. We haven't heard anything from him and Ye-gong—I mean, Miss Ye, since the apocalyptic fire died down."

Mo Ran exclaimed softly in surprise, a look of worry on his face. Would these two kind and honorable souls be refused a gentle ending even in his second lifetime?

Noting Mo Ran's cryptic expression, Xue Zhengyong turned. "What's wrong, Ran-er?"

Mo Ran couldn't possibly speak the truth, so he said, "I was just thinking, Xu Shuanglin's gone missing as well, and they have deep ties with him. I'm worried they'll be implicated."

"Don't worry too much. The sects have sent scouts out to investigate every trace of unusual magic," Xue Zhengyong said. "Unless Nangong Xu buries himself forever, they'll definitely find him. Nangong-gongzi and Miss Ye might just be trapped where they are and unable to get word to us."

"Mn, I hope so," Mo Ran said.

The three exchanged what they knew about the events of the last few days. Though Xue Zhengyong had received the messenger haitang and knew Chu Wanning and the others made it to Flying Flower Isle, he didn't know much about what happened after they'd arrived. Chu Wanning answered his questions thoroughly, except when they touched upon Mo Ran. Then, he invariably paused and swiftly changed the subject.

Xue Zhengyong, for his part, would never in his wildest dreams have guessed what had passed between Chu Wanning and Mo Ran.

Aside from their equally good looks, the two of them were ill-matched in every way: age, status, and personality. Even their skin tone, taste in food, or sleeping posture—they weren't alike in the slightest.

Yuheng of the Night Sky, the Beidou Immortal, had always been the emblem of pristine purity, the symbol of cool distance. Chu-zongshi was unattached and ascetic, a man who prized his dignity above all. How could he possibly entertain a romance with his own disciple? Even the boldest and most absurd folktales wouldn't dare posit such a plot. If any storyteller had the temerity to tell such a tale, his audience would spit their melon seed shells and dump their tea on him, then beat him under his own beechwood table.

But inexplicably, this love had flourished. In a dim, inconspicuous corner, a delicate and mysterious flower slowly unfurled its petals. Although not yet in full bloom, its fragrance was hauntingly beautiful.

Since they had returned at last to Sisheng Peak, Chu Wanning intended to go to Mengpo Hall for dinner that night. But when he pushed open the doors of the Red Lotus Pavilion, he saw a figure standing on that bamboo-lined mountain path, atop the bluestone steps. At the creak of the door's hinge, this person turned, his back shaded black as ink by the shadows of dusk, the last glow of sunset gilding his handsome face.

"Shizun." Mo Ran grinned at him.

Chu Wanning's feet in his pristine white shoes froze. Memory folded over itself; he seemed to see Mo Ran the year he had arrived on Sisheng Peak, when he stood before Chu Wanning's door every day and watched him leave, then waited for him to return.

But time never flowed backward. The Yuheng Elder from the past had long since turned into the shizun this young man had called thousands of times. His reverence now contained a tightly restrained passion and an undisguised tenderness.

"What are you doing here?"

"Waiting to eat dinner with you."

Chu Wanning's gaze fell upon the food box in his hand. "It's been a while since we've been home. I want to eat at Mengpo Hall today; I wasn't planning to stay in the pavilion for dinner."

Mo Ran stared for a moment, then understood. "Shizun's mistaken," he said with a smile. "This box is empty; I just brought Xue Meng dinner. He doesn't have much of an appetite, so I borrowed a small stove and made him a bowl of noodles."

Chu Wanning looked back at him with some surprise. As long as he could remember, these two had never been close. Although they were cousins, they were at each other's throats the moment they were left alone together.

When had this changed? Perhaps he'd missed too much in his five years asleep, or perhaps Mo Ran and Xue Meng had merely grown up. Whatever it was, without their teacher realizing, the two had warmed to each other. They were still far from embodying perfect brotherhood, but Xue Meng would still make an ugly little clay figurine of Mo Ran when he was sculpting; and when Xue Meng was ill, Mo Ran would still make a bowl of noodles and bring it to his bedside.

Chu Wanning sighed. "How is he? When I went to look in on him earlier, he was still asleep."

"He's awake now. After he ate, he wanted to take a walk outside—I barely managed to get him to lie down again. The Zhenlong Chess Formation is unique. Anyone made into a black chess piece needs to rest no matter how little time they were controlled."

"Mn." Even as Chu Wanning agreed, he felt a small bubble of doubt rise to the surface. Mo Ran had spoken carelessly, but Chu Wanning had been listening. He sensed something faintly *off* about that straightforward statement—Mo Ran seemed to know a bit too much, and speak a bit too lightly, about the Zhenlong Chess Formation's strengths, weaknesses, and effects.

"Shizun?" Chu Wanning blinked, coming back to his senses. Mo Ran was smiling. "What were you thinking about?"

"Nothing much," Chu Wanning replied after a moment's hesitation. He was worrying unnecessarily. Mo Ran was a zongshi now. It wasn't strange that he should have some understanding of forbidden techniques. Changing the subject, he asked, "Where are we going? I don't want to go out."

"I don't either," Mo Ran said, rubbing his nose. He chuckled warmly. "As long as it's with you, anywhere's good."

Chu Wanning would never admit that his heartbeat quickened at those words, but he did gaze a fraction too long into those dark and shining eyes. They were bright and earnest, filled with the reflection of the setting sun and his own silhouette. Simple and clean.

He couldn't think of any excuse to refuse those eyes, so in the end, he went with Mo Ran to that bustling dinner hall. Mo Ran used to put food into Chu Wanning's bowl without hesitation and had even been known to reach out with a smile to wipe sauce from the corner of Chu Wanning's mouth. But now, after crossing the bridge of that final confession, they could no longer be so carefree. Under the watchful gazes of so many, even making eye contact was awkward.

At the end of a very courteous and respectful meal, Chu Wanning rose to clear their table. Mo Ran called him back. "Shizun, hold on."

"What is it?"

Mo Ran reached out, but his hand paused a hairsbreadth from Chu Wanning's cheek. He retracted it and pointed at the corner of his own grinning mouth. "You have some rice."

Chu Wanning froze in place. He set down his tray and wiped the rice away with every appearance of calm. Pursing his lips, he asked quietly, "Is it still there?"

Smiling, Mo Ran said, "Not anymore; very clean."

Chu Wanning picked his tray back up to leave. Annoyed and embarrassed, he also felt a faint sense of disappointment, one he wasn't ready to admit to. In the past, Mo Ran had always just reached out. This sudden imposition of cordial distance unnerved him.

The next few days passed in much the same way.

This man who had once been so uninhibited now acted like a blushing youth. He expended every effort to treat Chu Wanning as well as possible, but never put a toe over the line. It was as though Mo Ran feared startling him; every move he made was careful. At times, Chu Wanning thought he could clearly see the blazing lust in the depths of his eyes—but that man would somehow let his lashes fall in silence as he engulfed Chu Wanning's hands in his own broad palms. When Mo Ran looked up once more, the hunger in Mo Ran's eyes was always hidden beneath tenderness. Such gentle handling gave Chu Wanning the vague impression of being treated like a ceramic figurine that had been shattered and slowly pieced back together, as though Mo Ran was terrified a sudden move would crush Chu Wanning to pieces and grind him to dust.

Chu Wanning thought this state of affairs was fine, unhurried and calm. The sizzling inferno of his dreams was exciting, certainly, but he was satisfied with it remaining a dream. If it were real, he doubted he could handle it.

Yet regardless of how carefully and closely they trod the steps of love, this path must eventually come to an end. One day, Chu Wanning ate his dinner as usual and took a peach as he left. Before he could take more than a few bites, someone caught his hand. Stunned, Chu Wanning looked up to see Mo Ran. In a low voice laced with reproach, Chu Wanning asked, "What are you doing?"

Shizun, I've Quit Spicy Food

THERE WAS NO ONE ELSE around. Mo Ran pulled Chu Wanning into a tiny alleyway behind Mengpo Hall, so narrow hardly any space remained with him and Mo Ran squeezed into it.

Chu Wanning glared at him, peach in hand.

Perhaps Mo Ran's long repression had finally stirred this red-blooded man to action; his chest heaved as he stared, eyes shining, at Chu Wanning. Then he reached out and pulled him into his arms.

"My peach!"

Too late. That plump and juicy fruit fell from his fingers and rolled to a stop in a corner.

"Shizun." Mo Ran's blazing breath brushed Chu Wanning's ear. Despite the tortuous fervor of his words, his tone was clear. There was restraint within that scalding heat; his voice had been burnt to a crisp by the fires of lust, yet he kept himself from taking further liberties. He only held him, tight to his chest, voice a rasp. "It hurts."

Chu Wanning's eyes widened. "What's wrong? Where does it hurt?"

Mo Ran stared, then burst into laughter. Before Chu Wanning's hand could lift to his forehead and check his temperature, Mo Ran grabbed it and brought it to his lips for a kiss.

Frowning, Chu Wanning pressed him. "If you're sick, go see the Tanlang Elder."

"It's no use seeing wintertime pickles," Mo Ran said in exasperation. "Only a little napa cabbage will do."

Finally Chu Wanning realized what was going on. He snapped, "Who are you calling a cabbage?"

"Sorry, sorry." Mo Ran grinned. Pausing, he turned those bright black eyes back on Chu Wanning. "But Shizun, I've missed you so much."

Cradled like this, gazing into those eyes, the fury of being named a little napa cabbage had no ready outlet—it could only express itself as a flush at the tips of his ears. After a long beat, Chu Wanning pointed out, "We just ate dinner together."

"That doesn't count."

A pause.

"Shizun, I just want to spend more time with you. Every time you finish your meal, you walk away into the crowd; I can't even touch you..." There was a faint note of hurt in his voice. "Stay with me a little longer. Don't go."

Flustered, Chu Wanning's cheeks burned hotter the longer Mo Ran spoke. Mo Ran's scent was so distinct, so masculine, so overwhelming. In that tight embrace, Chu Wanning couldn't muster a single word.

"Shizun," Mo Ran murmured, "let me hold you a while longer..."

Their paths did not naturally cross often on Sisheng Peak. Visits from the other great sects grew ever more frequent, and Xue Zhengyong often pulled Chu Wanning aside to discuss strategy, further cutting into their time together. Even in the hard-won moments when they could sit close and eat, there was still the bustling crowd around them, the fear that a sharp-eyed disciple would notice something if they slipped. They had barely gotten a chance to hold hands since the confession. Mo Ran had endured this state of things for too long; it was little wonder he could bear it no longer.

As night descended, the crowds leaving Mengpo Hall became denser. A group of giggling female cultivators walked past the alleyway and ran across some of the Xuanji Elder's firelight mice. Those little mice with tiny dots of spiritual fire on their tails squeaked as they skittered every which way, sending the whole group into gales of laughter.

Chu Wanning grew uneasy amidst the noise and gave Mo Ran a push. "Let's go."

"Just a bit longer..."

"People will be coming soon. Go."

Despite everything, Chu Wanning was still an ascetic cultivator. Unless some great liberties were taken, he wouldn't succumb even if flustered. Mo Ran sighed and released him.

Chu Wanning stepped out of the dimness of the narrow alley, then turned back to look at him. "What are you still doing in there?"

Mo Ran cleared his throat, somewhat abashed. "Shizun, you go on ahead. I'll wait here for a minute."

This puzzled Chu Wanning—but his next words were forestalled by the flush on Mo Ran's handsome, golden face. His dark eyes were glittering, like stars twinkling nervously in the night sky. Understanding dawned, and Chu Wanning reflexively glanced downward. As his gaze landed upon a certain area, his ears rang, and his cheeks went scarlet as if stung by a scorpion. "You're... You're really..." He couldn't seem to finish the sentence. With a flick of his sleeves, he turned and left in a huff, metaphorical smoke pouring out of his ears.

A dozen days thus slipped by evasively. Even if this wolf named Mo Ran had been made gentle, the bloodthirstiness in his bones thickened with the passage of time, like the looming sense of an oncoming storm. Every day during the morning practice and the evening greeting, he stared up at where the Yuheng Elder stood on the high platform, eyes filled with an undisguised hunger that grew more rapacious by the day. When someone was so deeply infatuated, even if they concentrated every speck of their energy on hiding their love, it would prove impossible.

At such times, when Xue Meng inadvertently caught sight of Mo Ran's eyes, he jumped in surprise. He looked at Mo Ran, then at Chu Wanning. The naïve little phoenix couldn't begin to imagine the reality of what had happened, and so grew more and more confused. What the emotion flashing in Mo Ran's eyes was, he had no idea. He only knew that he felt discomfited, yet he couldn't say how or why.

One day while they were alone during morning practice, Xue Meng caught Mo Ran's attention. He lowered his voice and said, "Hey, I have a question."

"What is it?"

"Is Shizun sick?"

Mo Ran started. "Why do you ask? Is something wrong with Shizun? Why don't I know about it?"

"You don't?" Xue Meng rubbed his chin. "Weird. Why are you looking at him like that then? Always with that same concerned look on your face."

At Xue Meng's description, Mo Ran finally understood. Clearing his throat, he lowered his lashes and said, "What are you talking about? Don't jinx Shizun."

"I *wasn't*." After a pause, Xue Meng continued in a mumble, "Then why are you always staring at him?"

"I'm not."

"I'm not blind."

"Yes, you are."

"I'm blind? Then you're a dog!"

Hearing these two grown men break into squabbling, Chu Wanning cast his cool gaze down from the platform. Xue Meng and Mo Ran clamped their lips shut. Lowering their heads, they went back to transcribing the herbal medicine scrolls in their hands, still elbowing each other under the table.

After shoving back and forth, Mo Ran pulled his hand away without warning. Xue Meng had been exerting too much force; at the sudden loss of resistance, he fell right on top of Mo Ran with an audible *smack*.

Mo Ran burst into laughter, slapping his thigh. Heedless of their surroundings, Xue Meng roared, "Are you serious?! You tricked me!"

"Mo Weiyu, Xue Ziming." Vexed, Chu Wanning looked up, phoenix eyes narrow and brow furrowed, to see his disciples once again embarrassing him. "If you're going to fight, do it outside. Don't disrupt everyone else."

"Yes, Shizun." Mo Ran instantly sat up straight.

Xue Meng also reluctantly shut his mouth, but his feathers were ruffled. Humiliated by his earlier tumble, he pondered a moment, then tore off a small piece of paper, wrote a few large words on it, crumpled it into a ball, and threw it onto Mo Ran's desk.

Unfortunately, it flew too far. A fair and slender hand plucked the wad of paper from where it had landed on the open pages of his book. Perplexed, Shi Mei unfolded it and glanced at its contents:

You were staring! What are you planning? Are you trying to get Shizun to teach you his personal meditation techniques?!

Beneath that was a drawing of a dog, crossed out in heavy strokes of ink.

Shi Mei was left truly speechless.

When the disciples had dispersed after morning practice, Xue Zhengyong sought out Chu Wanning with the most recent news from Linyi. The apocalyptic fire had left the land uninhabitable for at least the next five years. The refugees they had brought from the upper cultivation realm couldn't return; they needed to be settled in villages within Sisheng Peak's jurisdiction.

"I've already started making arrangements for the people I brought back in Wuchang Town, Fenghe Town, and Baishui Village," said Xue Zhengyong. "For those who came with you and A-Ran...Wuchang Town doesn't have room for them all. Why don't we bring half to Yuliang Village? They need more young'uns, after all."

"Yuliang Village will be suitable," said Chu Wanning.

Xue Zhengyong nodded. "Yuliang isn't too far, but you guys should head over sooner rather than later—there are quite a few to settle. Meng-er isn't good with domestic affairs like these; I'll send Shi Mei with you. He'll be able to help."

After a moment's hesitation, Chu Wanning said, "Okay."

Chu Wanning and Mo Ran were more or less old friends to the inhabitants of Yuliang Village. The village head had received Xue Zhengyong's missive two days ago, and was up at the village entrance bright and early to await the three xianjun from Sisheng Peak. Miss Ling-er was there as well. It'd been a while since they'd last met, and she'd grown prettier in the interim. The instant she caught sight of Mo Ran, she hurried up to greet him.

Mo Ran smiled, somewhat surprised. "Miss, you didn't go to the upper cultivation realm?"

"No, and thank goodness I didn't. If I'd gone to Linyi, I might've lost my life as well." Ling-er laid a hand over her full bosom in apprehension. "I'll stay right here in the lower cultivation realm. The village's been getting better and better these days, anyway... All of us used to hope we could move to the upper cultivation realm someday—this is the first time they're coming *here*. I'm not going anymore, no way."

"That's right." Someone else chimed in to agree. "Times are always changing, after all. With Xue-zunzhu at Sisheng Peak, in a few decades, it's possible the people from the upper cultivation realm will all wish to come here instead."

"The lower cultivation realm has toiled for centuries," Shi Mei replied gently. "As they say, every lake has its shore. It can't be all suffering for us—we're due some good days."

He began to unpack the herbal salve Madam Wang had sent with him. Mo Ran grabbed one for a closer look. Noticing the snake emblem of Guyueye on top, he exclaimed, "This is...one of Hanlin the Sage's ointments?"

"Mn, Jiang-zhangmen had it delivered a few days back."

"Jiang Xi is a better gift-giver than Huohuang Pavilion," Chu Wanning commented. "Sichuan is rife with demons and monsters, and spiritual medicines are always in short supply. The sect leader was delighted to accept."

"Is that so?" Mo Ran mumbled. "They're all medicines crafted by Hanlin the Sage to boot. It's barely exaggerating to say his remedies could bring back the dead. Ah..." His voice trailed off as the second half of the sentence remained unsaid: *Ah, Jiang Xi is so rich.*

Years ago at Xuanyuan Pavilion, Chu Wanning had spent two million, five hundred thousand gold on but a few bottles of Tapir Fragrance Dew—only for Sect Leader Jiang to now send them an entire carriage's worth of medicine with a wave of his hand.

Mo Ran put the jar back in the bag without a word and sighed inwardly. Rufeng Sect had fallen, but Guyueye was next in line to fill their shoes. Sisheng Peak wasn't even under consideration. It would likely be a few more centuries before the lower cultivation realm could rise to such heights.

By dusk after a busy day, room and board for the Linyi refugees were finally in good order, and the rooms had been cleaned and tidied for their new occupants. The trio from Sisheng Peak prepared to depart. The village chief, however, insisted they stay for dinner, an invitation they couldn't possibly refuse under the circumstances. They followed him politely to the ancestral hall of Yuliang Village.

The hall was the site of all important events in the village—weddings and funerals, as well as New Year's Eve dinner and the performances during the Lantern Festival, were held here or in the large courtyard outside. Today, the villagers had set up more than thirty feast tables and made elaborate dinner preparations to welcome the villagers from the upper cultivation realm. The village chief even recalled Chu Wanning's sensitivity to spice and specifically arranged a table full of lighter dishes for the Yuheng Elder and any Linyi residents with similar tastes.

Mo Ran and Chu Wanning had saved the lives of everyone at the table. But although the Linyi commoners had become familiar with this ice-cold cultivator on Flying Flower Isle, that didn't mean they were comfortable sitting down to dinner with him. Etiquette demanded they stay in their assigned seats, making for a tremendously awkward meal. While laughter and wine flowed at the other tables, everyone at theirs kept their heads down, chopsticks moving in silence.

Mo Ran was a skilled cook and had gone to the kitchen to lend a hand. He didn't join the diners at the tables until the last dish was brought out, his honey-gold face gleaming with sweat from the cookfires. With his shining eyes and regally sloped nose, his handsomeness made him conspicuous amidst the crowd.

"Soup buns!" called the cook, hefting her platter stacked high with bamboo steamers. "One for every table, one for every table, twelve buns in each! Six with pork and shepherd's purse filling and six with pork and mushroom! Eat 'em while they're hot!"

Grinning, Mo Ran helped her pass out steamers to each table.

"Thank you, Mo-xianjun!"

"Thank you, Xianjun!"

The children more familiar with Mo Ran piped up with, "Thank you, Weiyu-gege!"

Ling-er's eyes followed his figure, unable to look away. Even if she knew he didn't like her and never would, she couldn't help watching him hungrily. *Hmph*. Looking was free of charge. "Thank you, Mo-xianjun," she cooed when the steamer arrived at her table, syllables soft between vermilion lips.

Mo Ran beamed at her without any hint of flirtation in his gaze. His frank regard conversely embarrassed the girl, and she swiftly cast her eyes downward.

Two tables remained: Chu Wanning's and Shi Mei's. Due to their differing tastes, they hadn't sat together. Mo Ran brought a steamer to Chu Wanning's table first. Chu Wanning frowned as he received it. "Stop running around—the food's getting cold."

When Mo Ran arrived at Shi Mei's table, Shi Mei smiled. "A-Ran is so skilled. Thank you."

"Ha ha, not at all. I was only helping the cook."

Duty done, Mo Ran turned from the table. Shi Mei thought he was going to get himself a bowl, so he made space for Mo Ran on the bench. "Why don't you sit here?" he called to Mo Ran. "I asked for an extra bowl earlier; you don't need to grab another."

Mo Ran stared at him for a moment, then smiled and scratched his head. "I'm going to sit with Shizun."

Shi Mei blinked. "When did you stop eating spicy food? That's the table for mild food only."

"I quit."

Shi Mei fell silent, pupils shadowed, then suddenly smiled. "I've heard of quitting alcohol or smoking, but never spice."

"To be honest, I can't really call it quitting. After not eating it for a while, I just don't have the taste for it anymore." Mo Ran hurried away toward the kitchen with a smile and a hasty wave. "I'm off to grab a bowl. You'd better stay there and eat—the soup buns are getting cold!"

184

Shizun, I Made You Wait So Long

MO RAN CAME BACK out of the kitchen in a trice. When he sat next to Chu Wanning, he brought with him not only a heaping bowl of rice for himself, but also a lidded box.

Surprised, Chu Wanning hesitantly asked, "Aren't you...going to sit over there with Shi Mei?"

Mo Ran stared. "Why would I?"

This response swiftly cheered Chu Wanning. Lashes lowered, he cleared his throat. "I thought the dishes over there would be more suited to your taste."

Spotting the pinkening tips of Chu Wanning's ears, a thought occurred to Mo Ran: Could Chu Wanning be jealous? His heart pounded, a smile spreading across his face. "My taste is to sit wherever you are," he whispered.

This time, Chu Wanning's ears went completely scarlet. His knee had been pressed to Mo Ran's, but now, suddenly skittish, he tried to inch it away. Mo Ran refused to let him—beneath the table, he put a hand on Chu Wanning's thigh.

"*You—!*"

One of the villagers at the table looked over. "Xianjun, what's wrong?"

Chu Wanning knew he'd misspoken. He schooled his face to calm and said, "Nothing."

Mo Ran hid his smile. Chu Wanning really was so amusing. It wasn't as if Mo Ran actually planned on doing anything scandalous; that would be a surefire way to bring calamity down on his own head. He simply didn't want any distance between Chu Wanning and himself. He grabbed Chu Wanning's leg and childishly yanked it back, so that his shizun's knee leaned against his. Chu Wanning jerked away again, so Mo Ran pulled him back once more.

In the end, Chu Wanning hit his limit and kicked him under the table, but he stopped trying to move. Mo Ran grinned from ear to ear.

"There's something wrong with you," Chu Wanning hissed.

They ate. Mo Ran glanced at Chu Wanning's bowl. As expected, there were a few vegetables and a piece of tofu, while those soup buns had long since been gobbled up by the unruly kids at the table. Mo Ran passed him the little food box of woven bamboo.

"What's this?"

"Soup dumplings," Mo Ran murmured. "I made them just for you—six with crab roe and six shrimp. *Shh*, eat up and don't say anything. I knew everyone would beat you to the punch."

Chu Wanning eyed him. It would make him stick out to be the only person eating them at the dinner table; Chu Wanning was almost too embarrassed to do it. But the sight of Mo Ran's dark eyes, so earnest, and the smudge of flour on his cheek, kept his refusals trapped inside his mouth. The words *I made them just for you* were indeed capable of melting hearts.

Chu Wanning said nothing. After a moment, he silently opened the box and propped the lid in front of him like a screen. With a deliberate furtiveness that only made his actions more obvious, he ate one piping-hot crab dumpling. Rich broth burst from the delicate skin and warmed his chest from the inside out.

"Good?" Mo Ran watched for a look of approval.

Chu Wanning bit his chopsticks. "Not bad. You try one."

"I've had plenty. These are all for you." Mo Ran smiled, his eyes overflowing with warm light. "As long as you like them. Why don't you try a shrimp one next?"

His attention was completely focused on Chu Wanning, the streak of pale flour setting off his dark and shining eyes, making him look all the more pathetically adorable. Why would Mo Ran forget Shi Mei and turn to him? This question still gnawed at Chu Wanning. But Mo Ran's eyes were so clear and certain they left no room for doubt. In that moment, his gaze had the power to soothe the worries of anyone he bent it upon.

After dinner, the village chief invited everyone outside the hall to watch a play the villagers had staged on a platform next to the river. With a clang of copper cymbals and the strum of a huqin fiddle, the actors of this humble opera took to the stage. The show was a rowdy one, full of trailing sleeves whirling and painted masks swapping. One actor grabbed the colorful lighter, held the pine-sap pipe in his mouth, and tipped his head up with a ferocious puff of breath. Flames exploded across the sky, glinting across the actors' headpieces and winning delighted shouts from the audience.

Chu Wanning had never enjoyed such theatrics. Firstly, the mortal realm's tricks were unsophisticated; he could identify their mechanisms at a glance, and thus much of the wonder and excitement was lost on him. Secondly, the audience crowded so closely and noisily that he was too uncomfortable to appreciate any of the remaining charms of the stage.

Neither he nor Shi Mei were interested in the show, and after a few moments, both turned to leave. Mo Ran said nothing as he followed in their wake. At the last moment, he glanced back once more at the stage.

"Let's go," Shi Mei suggested gently. "If we're late returning, the sect leader will worry."

"Mn."

Mo Ran lowered his head and walked after them. But they had gone only a few more steps when he heard Chu Wanning ask mildly, "Do you want to watch?"

"They're doing the battle of the bankrollers between Wang Kai and Shi Chong.[3] It's pretty interesting."

He didn't say he wanted to watch it, but neither did he say he didn't. Chu Wanning listened quietly and said, "Then let's watch the end before we go."

Shi Mei paused, slightly taken aback. "Shizun, we've already delayed our return to stay for dinner. If we stay even longer for the show..."

"Just this act, we'll go when it's over."

"Okay," Shi Mei agreed with an easygoing smile. "We'll do as Shizun says."

The three returned to the audience, squeezing back through the thronging crowd. Few of the Linyi refugees had ever traveled to Sichuan, and this style of opera was completely new to them—those swirling sleeves and flashing faces left them clicking their tongues in admiration. Some of the smaller children couldn't see the stage and were either hoisted onto the shoulders of adults, or, left to their own

---

3 A classic tale from the Song dynasty of two Jin dynasty historical figures, Wang Kai and Shi Chong, who competed to outdo one another in increasingly outrageous displays of squandered wealth.

devices, crawled over to the edge of the stage, craning their necks to look up.

"This coral-jade tree gifted by the emperor, magnificent in its beauty—"

The Wang Kai and Shi Chong up above were showing off their wealth with all their might, huffing and puffing in their determination to one-up each other.

"Fifteen miles of purple brocade to line the roads for my return— who can match that?"

"Great! Ha ha ha, do another!"

The eyes of the audience shone. Village children, having stuffed their sweets into their mouths, clapped delightedly along with the adults. This wasn't the upper cultivation realm, obsessed with outward appearances. Here, no one was dumb enough to watch shows from their seats, sipping a cup of jasmine tea as servants massaged their shoulders and handmaidens waved broad fans. The cool response from beneath those stages would dull even the actors' spark atop their platform, their voices so dry they made *The Tyrant Bidding Farewell to His Concubine* sound like a toad leaving his cricket. The people here were inelegant in their excitement, standing as they clapped. They stamped their feet and raised their voices, crude and noisy.

As Chu Wanning stood in the packed sea of people, he was left at something of a loss. Boring people like him would probably rather listen to *The Toad Leaves His Cricket* in the upper cultivation realm than stand in the throng watching Wang Kai versus Shi Chong.

He wasn't the only one who didn't enjoy this kind of overstimulating environment. Shi Mei stood for a spell, good-naturedly opting to stay despite the suona and cymbals making his head ache. But at the scene with the breaking of the coral tree, a broad-shouldered man nearby got so excited he leapt to his feet and started clapping, sending his neighbor's cup of hot tea splashing all over Shi Mei.

"Aiya! Sorry, sorry! Xianjun, my apologies, look at my clumsiness."

"Not to worry, it's fine," Shi Mei hastily replied. But his clothes were indeed soaked. He sighed and turned somewhat helplessly to Chu Wanning. "Shizun, why don't I head back first? I'll get changed and update the sect leader on our assignment."

"Very well," Chu Wanning said. "Take care on the road."

Smiling, Shi Mei bid farewell to Mo Ran and left on his own.

Chu Wanning thought his method of escape quite effective— perhaps he should bump into someone too and find an excuse to flee this exuberant crowd. He was deep in thought when he heard another burst of excited cheering. Onstage, the Wang Kai actor was in an apoplectic rage, mustache huffing with each breath. With the firebag in his mouth, he spat a long tongue of flame toward the river.

Boom! The water's surface roiled, its ripples dyed a blazing orange.

"Whoa!"

"Again! Do it again!"

Chu Wanning was silent. He didn't understand what everyone found so thrilling about this... If Xue Meng were here, he wouldn't need any firebag to throw hundreds or even thousands of flames.

As Chu Wanning's interest waned, he caught Mo Ran's smile out of the corner of his eye. Mo Ran was so tall he had no need to strain on tiptoe; he stood calmly where he was, and no one could block his view. His handsome face was illuminated by the light of the fire, his dimples deep and his gaze gentle yet shadowed, as if inscrutable thoughts moved in their depths.

Sensing Chu Wanning's eyes on him, he turned, beaming more brightly. His dark eyes seemed almost to glimmer—but perhaps Chu Wanning was mistaken.

"When I was little, I always tried to eavesdrop on this opera outside the theater. Every single time, the manager would chase me off before I got to the end." Mo Ran's voice was slow and measured. "This is the first time I've ever heard the whole thing... Shizun, do you like it?"

Chu Wanning couldn't answer. Gazing into Mo Ran's eyes, all he said was, "Mn, it's not bad."

Mo Ran's smile unfolded, and the very night seemed to brighten. Another song rang out from the stage as one act ended and the next began. Brows dark as smoke, the riotous headpiece quivering; *My king has met his end; How could this humble concubine think of life—*

"Oh, it's *Tyrant Bids Farewell.*" Mo Ran glanced over at the stage, then smiled. "Let's go. The battle of the bankrollers is over; I've had my fill. We can head back."

"Let's stay a little longer."

"Hm?"

"It's not boring. There's no harm in watching a little more."

Mo Ran's brows rose slightly in surprise. "Okay." he grinned.

Scenes from *Tyrant Bids Farewell, White Snake, The Nail Murders,* and *Water Margin* played before them one after another. Not a single person left the audience. Their excitement grew with each performance, every upturned face bright with interest. An old man recited the words along with Grandma Yan's actor onstage. "Kind words are warm for three winters long, cruel talk brings six months of cold—" And at the act's climax, when Song Jiang lashed out to kill, the entire hall whooped and hollered, the applause nearly drowning the voices of the singers onstage.

A drunken villager jostled Chu Wanning with a grin, clapping him enthusiastically on the back. Chu Wanning had nowhere to retreat to, and he couldn't berate a villager. As he fretted over this dilemma, warm hands clasped his shoulders. Chu Wanning turned to meet Mo Ran's eyes. Somehow, Mo Ran had come to stand behind him. He pulled Chu Wanning closer with a grin, shielding him from the press of the crowd.

For a moment, the din of the crowd and the crash of the cymbals seemed far away. Chu Wanning's ears burned. He held Mo Ran's gaze for a flash before averting his eyes, unwilling to look at him. But the body behind him was like a blazing flame, and the man's breaths were searing. That sturdy chest pressed against his back, those fine-boned hands encircling his shoulders. As the drumbeats quickened and the fire breathers did their work, the crowd's attention went to the stage. Cheering and whistling, the audience's applause was a sharp staccato.

In an effort to hide his embarrassment, Chu Wanning moved to half-heartedly clap along with the rest. Before he could raise his hands, Mo Ran had drawn him into a full-body embrace. Perhaps he thought no one would notice in the crush of the crowd, or perhaps the boisterous atmosphere intensified his desire to be close to his beloved—close enough to meld into one, flesh and blood mingling. Whatever the reason, Mo Ran lowered his lashes and held him close, wrapping sturdy arms around him. Chu Wanning thus caged in his embrace, he turned his head and—in the instant the flames from the stage lit up the night—kissed Chu Wanning's earlobe.

The fire licked up into the sky, illuminating the faces of the actors and igniting its watchers' hearts.

"Thank you for keeping me company," Mo Ran whispered into his ear. His voice was a low rasp, surpassingly gentle. "I know you don't actually like it."

"You're overthinking. I like it fine."

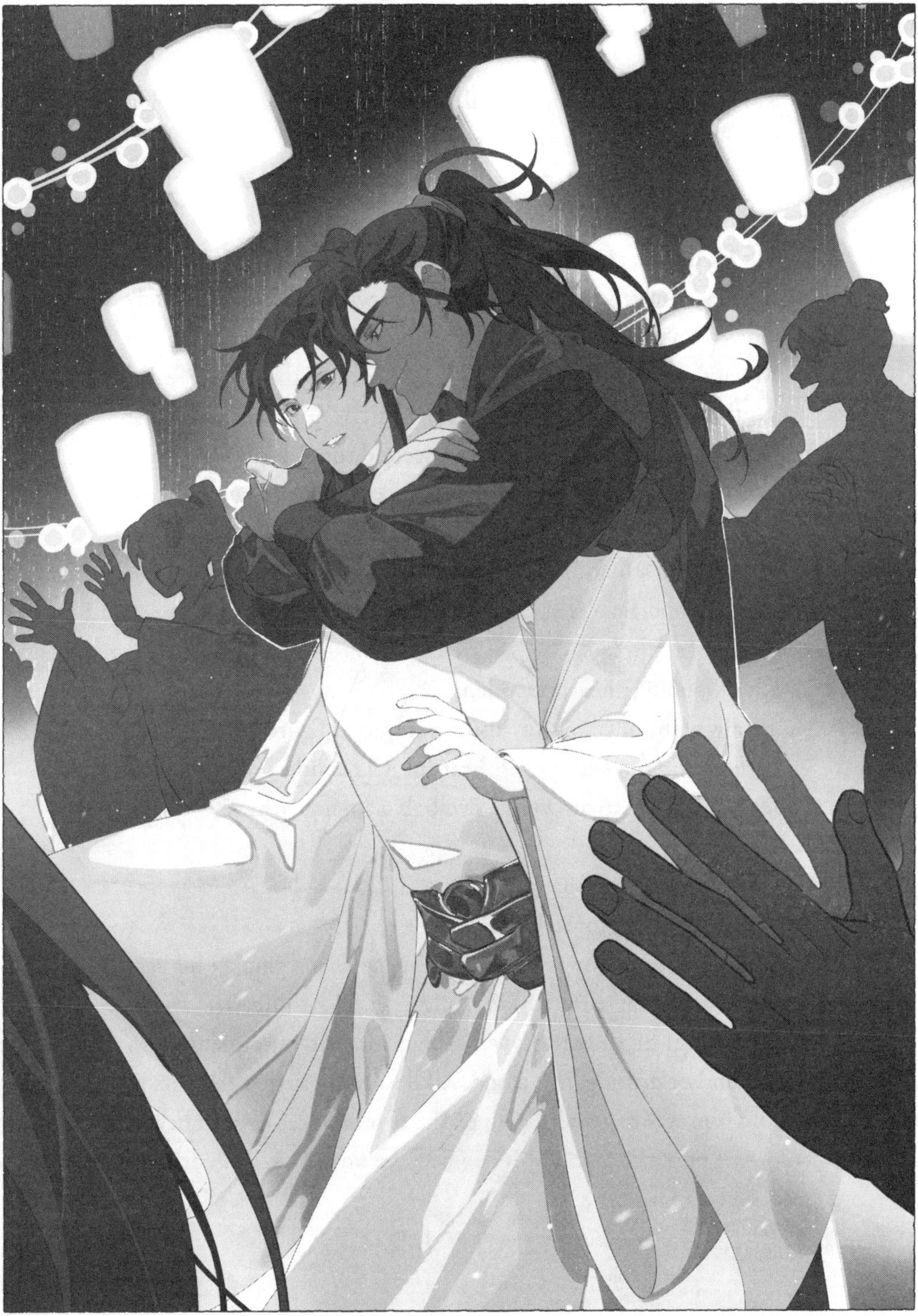

Mo Ran chuckled and fell silent. But he held Chu Wanning tighter, his chin coming to rest on his shoulder.

As the flames danced, the question rose again in Chu Wanning's heart. "Mo Ran, why did you..."

"Ha ha ha, amazing!" someone shouted from the crowd. Chu Wanning's voice had been soft, and his words were completely swallowed up by the cheering throng.

"What?" Mo Ran asked.

"Nothing." Chu Wanning covered his flush with a scowl of displeasure. He didn't want to ask a second time; asking once had already exhausted his resolve. He was too embarrassed, and refused to speak again.

Mo Ran was still for a moment. He really hadn't heard what Chu Wanning asked. But he suddenly said, "The one I like has always been you."

Chu Wanning's heart pounded.

"It's always been you. I was just too stupid to figure it out."

Badum, badum, badum. His heart beat a relentless rhythm, loud enough in his ears to drown the cymbals clanging onstage.

"I'm sorry."

Chu Wanning was silent.

"I made you wait for so long."

Chu Wanning's eyes were dazzled by flame and smoke; his ears rang with clashing echoes. He couldn't hear a thing. The world was spinning; he didn't know whether his feet were planted on the ground or drifting on a cloud. All he knew was that the person behind him was real and tangible. The breeze never used to have a color or a presence, but now it had become Mo Ran's scent, drifting past the tip of his nose.

He had never wanted any lengthy explanation. All he wanted was this simple acknowledgment from the one he loved. To so abruptly receive it turned everything around him into a whirling kaleidoscope of color, the oil-paint intensity leaving him unable to think or move, dazed beyond hope of recovery.

Shizun Gets Caught Red-Handed

WHEN HE RETURNED to his senses and could finally comprehend his surroundings, Chu Wanning fuzzily realized they were no longer in that thronging crowd. Secreted in the nearest copse of trees, they were kissing passionately, panting hotly as their mouths opened to one another with a searing thirst.

They had craved each other for so long. Their kisses were without care for technique—urgent, impatient, even frantic. Their throats bobbed as they swallowed, their mouths meeting with such bruising need that they drew blood, but neither of them noticed; neither of them could stop.

Mo Ran had Chu Wanning shoved against a tree, the rough bark digging into Chu Wanning's shaking back. There seemed to be string music in the distance, but it was unimportant. All other sounds, whether near or far, high or low, were broken and shattered—the only noises that came with clarity were those of their rough breathing. Their lips and tongues tangled, shamelessly entwined.

Shamelessly...

Chu Wanning stubbornly refused to let Mo Ran lead. But he'd ever been abstinent, and Mo Ran's unleashed desire was vivid and terrifying, like a ferocious beast baying for his blood, lunging to tear out his throat.

He didn't know how he'd become like this, or how they'd gotten this far. He didn't know whether this was right or wrong, or what would happen next. In the present moment, this rule-following, ascetic, restrained, and lonely man who always planned his next hundred steps in advance seemed to have been wholly ravaged. All that remained was his bone-deep obstinance, his supporting driftwood amidst the choppy seas of desire. He refused to show vulnerability or weakness. Even if his spine was prickling and his soul was dissolving, he'd still rather throw himself forward than be a limp plaything, ripe for the plucking.

Alas, though he had ambition enough, his skills left much to be desired. So much so that Mo Ran's mouth was soon scraped raw—Chu Wanning didn't mind his strength and bit the tip of Mo Ran's tongue, filling his mouth with the tang of blood. So much so that as his breaths came quicker and his face flushed redder, every inhalation became difficult.

In the end, Mo Ran had to laugh; he found Chu Wanning, who was doing his best but whose skills were awful, perfectly adorable. His cold, hard heart had melted, becoming a rippling pool of spring water, an endless expanse of lake that glimmered with golden waves, soft as flowing silk.

When they parted, a gossamer thread of spit connected their mouths. Their lips were red and wet, their eyes shining with tenderness and desire. Mo Ran's voice was thick with arousal. He stared down into Chu Wanning's eyes, the rough pads of his fingers caressing Chu Wanning's cheek.

Chu Wanning knew his technique was so poor it could make one's hair stand on end, but he refused to admit it. Narrowing his eyes, he asked, caustic, "What are you laughing at?" Mo Ran didn't answer, eyes sparkling with amusement. Chu Wanning's temper flared. "Was I...not good?"

Mo Ran's mirth finally showed at the corners of his mouth. He embraced Chu Wanning once more, this time face-to-face. With two equally angular men holding each other, it wasn't as seamless as an embrace between a man and a woman, but this friction created sparks that were brighter, cinders that burned even hotter. "Not at all. You were great." Mo Ran nuzzled the top of his head, then whispered into his ear, "Shizun is the best..."

"Then why are you laughing?"

But Mo Ran only chuckled again. His chest was blazing, hot and hard, but his heart was soft, gentling to a warm glow. "Laughter isn't the only reaction I'm having."

It took Chu Wanning a moment to grasp the implication. As Mo Ran pulled him closer, as they went from merely embracing from the waist up to having their whole bodies entwined, he sensed this man's threatening, ferocious desire hard against his skin, straining in time with their breaths. The sensation was so sharp, so intense, that his scalp prickled and his heart beat faster; he shivered despite the heat as his throat tightened and his mouth went dry. Chu Wanning abruptly remembered how domineering, how strong, and how ruthless the gentle-looking man before him actually was. He remembered that his blood and flesh were both life-threatening and soul-destroying.

Chu Wanning broke out in goosebumps. He suddenly wanted to push Mo Ran away, but before he could raise a hand, Mo Ran's hot mouth had captured his once more, catching his lips between his own and sucking. Every breath was an inferno; with every rise and fall of Mo Ran's chest, his body pressed against Chu Wanning's through their clothes. Chu Wanning could hardly think past the terrifying urgency of it. Mo Ran's tongue invaded his mouth, kissing him hungrily, drunkenly, grinding against him. In the end, there was nothing in Chu Wanning's head but a vast blank; even his legs were numb. He shivered at those sensations, at that unfamiliar weakness, at the heat and hardness, at that scalding tide of passion.

That night, Chu Wanning had no recollection of returning to Sisheng Peak. He felt wooden, mindless; the only thing he remembered was how they had embraced, panting, in the dark before parting at the Red Lotus Pavilion. They'd kissed for a long time, wanting nothing more than to swallow their beloved along with their lust. It wasn't enough... Nothing was enough...

In the haze, he remembered Mo Ran quietly calling out to him, asking Chu Wanning to let him spend the night in the Red Lotus Pavilion. Chu Wanning must have used the last of his lucidity to collect himself, gasping for air as he refused.

He wasn't sure why he said no. Perhaps out of an inexplicable sense of pride, or a discomfort born of having been alone so long. Or perhaps it was plain stubbornness, or that he found all of it absurd. This new development was tempting, but it had come on far too quickly.

Having found a reprieve from lust, a reprieve from Mo Ran, Chu Wanning pushed open the pavilion doors. As he walked inside, he understood for the first time what it meant to be afraid of even turning his head. He knew his bowstring had already been drawn to its limit. If he turned around now, he'd lose all control, desire spilling past the dam. Never again would he have the will to push away the man before him.

They would both be reduced to ash, leaving nothing behind.

When he went to bathe and get changed, Chu Wanning discovered his underclothes were damp. That musky scent made his face go scarlet. He didn't know what to do; even those sharp phoenix eyes were red at their tips, blushing the soft red of haitang flowers.

He stood there in a daze for a long interval, helplessly thinking: *How did this happen? How did it come to this?* All his life, he'd never lost control or been moved like this. Never.

Fuck. What was he supposed to do?

In the past, whenever Chu Wanning faced a difficult problem, his first recourse was to seek the answer in books. Thus he had always been widely read, his mind stuffed full of all sorts of texts. Now, for the first time, those countless scrolls were of no use to him. He was caught unprepared; he didn't know a thing about what he should do or how he should respond.

Thankfully, Mo Ran knew him all too well. After Chu Wanning's first refusal, he realized how lost and anxious Chu Wanning was, and he didn't press him for more. But the intimacy they shared was no longer limited to clasped hands. They kissed passionately in the alley behind Mengpo Hall, and nuzzled, whispering in each other's ears, in the dead of night in some deserted forest. Mo Ran wasn't one for sweet nothings, and sometimes he only spoke when Chu Wanning asked a question. But his eyes were eloquent, filled with every endearment and tender emotion. He was just too dumb to express them—or express them well, at least.

Mo Ran often chose action over speech. And for some reason, Chu Wanning felt Mo Ran had an uncanny knack for sensing his wants. They'd shared their feelings mere days ago, but sometimes, Chu Wanning had the impression that Mo Ran had already spent many, many years by his side.

As the weeks passed, they spent more and more time kissing, but it became less and less effective at dampening those flames of desire. They were insatiable, their blood running hot at each parting.

This posed little problem for Chu Wanning. He'd followed an ascetic cultivation path for many years and was possessed of exceptional strength of will. Mo Ran was a rather different story. He cultivated a method entirely different from Chu Wanning's, and he was young and red-blooded. He had to wait before standing after almost every one of their rendezvous. It was too obvious otherwise; his clothes couldn't hide it at all. Someone was bound to notice. He was enduring too much torment indeed.

One particular evening, the two had snuck off after dinner to tryst in a deserted area for most of an hour. All the elders were to meet later that night. Considering the time, Chu Wanning decided it was getting late, and told Mo Ran he had to go. But when Mo Ran considered the time, he felt they still had plenty, and refused to let Chu Wanning leave.

Mo Ran's method of refusal was rather crude: he said not a word but simply kissed Chu Wanning again.

Several large, abandoned garden stones were scattered throughout this part of the forest. Mo Ran was sitting on one, holding Chu Wanning on his lap so they were face-to-face. Most people in Mo Ran's position would find themselves looking up at their partner, but Mo Ran was so tall that he and Chu Wanning were the same height like this; he wasn't disadvantaged at all.

Their searing kisses continued as Mo Ran's mouth moved from Chu Wanning's lips to his neck. When he nipped at Chu Wanning's throat, the sound of Chu Wanning's low panting awakened new desperation, as if Mo Ran's heart had been set aflame.

Chu Wanning couldn't bear it either. He wanted to struggle free, to leave, but his limbs were soft, and his legs wouldn't obey his commands. Mo Ran had been very fond of this position recently because he could hold him so close. As dizzying tension stretched between them, Chu Wanning could imagine how thrilling this scene would be without their clothes in the way.

Perhaps they'd really reached the precipice; even the most fervent kisses weren't enough to sate their desire. Each one added fuel to the fire, stoking the flames higher and hotter.

When Mo Ran finally let Chu Wanning's lips part from his own, his eyes were wet and his breathing was rough, the jut of his throat bobbing sensually. He stared at Chu Wanning with a single-minded intensity, as if he wanted to say something—but he never did. He merely bit viciously back down. And it was indeed a bite, teeth and all. Chu Wanning found it both painful and stimulating, like the quivering ache of a needle inserted precisely into the acupoint.

Mo Ran was bound by his love. Broken noises issued from his throat as he embraced the man in his arms, caressing that fall of inky locks. His shizun was so good. He only wanted to show him the most tender, truehearted adoration. At the same time, his shizun was so enticing. He only wanted to viciously, forcefully bully him. In the still evening air, his primal breaths came heavier and heavier.

Closing trembling lashes, Chu Wanning tilted his face up. It felt awful— these embraces and kisses were not nearly enough. He was in distress, to say nothing of the young man holding him. The ends of Mo Ran's eyes were crimson and mist-dampened. "Shizun..." he said, voice low and hoarse, filled with an enduring hurt.

Chu Wanning said nothing.

"Please, I can't take it anymore..."

What would he do if he couldn't take it anymore? Chu Wanning thought of those fragmented dreams and a shiver ran up his spine. He made no sound, but his ears had gone scarlet. What would Mo Ran do...if he couldn't take it anymore...

Before Mo Ran captured his slick and swollen lips once more, Chu Wanning said softly, nearly inaudibly, "Then...not here."

Not here meant there could be more, as long as it was elsewhere. Mo Ran's head shot up, shock and delight mingling on his features. He pressed yet another ferocious kiss to Chu Wanning's lips, then stood, scooping Chu Wanning up in his arms.

The shame of it ran through Chu Wanning. "Put me down!" he snapped, furious.

Mo Ran set him down but didn't forget to kiss him. "Where does Shizun want to go?"

Before Chu Wanning could answer, a rustling came from the bushes nearby. Stunned, his mind cleared, and he shoved Mo Ran away.

In the moment they separated, they spied someone walking toward them from the depths of the bamboo forest. The lantern in the newcomer's hands swayed, and his robes fluttered in the breeze. After a long beat of silence, a voice rang out. Although he seemed to be trying to hide it, it was full of surprise and confusion: "What... are you two doing here?"

186
Shizun, Mengmeng Is So Gullible Ha Ha Ha

THE NEWCOMER'S FEATURES were exquisite and haughty, his limpid eyes wide with shock in the lanternlight.

Xue Meng.

Chu Wanning froze; he had no idea how much Xue Meng had seen or heard. Mo Ran was the first to break the silence. "I had something to discuss with Shizun."

Xue Meng narrowed his eyes. He had been passing by when he heard suggestive panting coming from this section of the forest and figured it was a pair of depraved and misguided disciples trysting in the backwoods.

Honestly, it wasn't any of Xue Meng's business. None of the ten great sects save Wubei Temple and Shangqing Pavilion explicitly forbade romantic relationships or dual cultivation. Sisheng Peak had a rule against debauchery, but that was meant to forbid frequenting brothels or partnerships that violated social norms. But Xue Meng was Chu Wanning's disciple, after all—his very first disciple. All these years Xue Meng had held up Chu Wanning's every word and action as a standard for himself. Since Chu Wanning disliked public displays of affection, Xue Meng mindlessly followed him in disdaining cultivator pairs and dual-cultivation couples.

The mountain's backwoods were a crucial area where the barrier to the ghost realm was thin. For two people to get cozy in such a place—

did they lack all sense of decorum? Indignant, Xue Meng had stomped over in a huff, lantern aloft.

He would never have imagined the couple caught in the halo of light would be these two. Xue Meng was thunderstruck. So much so that he failed to properly greet Chu Wanning before blurting, *What are you two doing here?*

The barrier here was solid; it wasn't in need of repair. There were no spiritual plants here, nor any scenery worth looking at. It was far out of the way, so an idle stroll couldn't possibly have brought them here.

Under normal circumstances, if one were to ask Xue Meng: "Suppose there were two people who, in the dead of night, refused to walk on the broad and bright main road, chose not to sit in the beautiful and scenic back garden, but instead *insisted* on talking somewhere impossibly secluded... Young master, what would you think?"

Xue Meng would certainly scoff, "What kind of talk are they having? Dirty talk?"

If one then continued: "Both are unwedded men who've known each other a long time, equal in looks and status. Young master, what kind of relationship do you think they share?"

Xue Meng would definitely roll his eyes. "What kind of relationship do *you* think they share? They're clearly a pair of cut-sleeves, snip-snipping away—disgusting."

And if one pressed on with: "Ha ha, Young master, you're incorrect. These two are actually master and disciple. Young master, please refrain from unseem—"

Odds were, Xue Meng wouldn't let them finish the sentence before slamming his hands on the table and bolting to his feet. "What nonsense! How could that be?! Where are these immoral beasts?

I'll kick them through the mountain gates and chase them off Sisheng Peak!"

But if he were told that said disciple was called Mo Weiyu and the master was Chu Wanning—then, beyond a shadow of a doubt, Xue Meng would pause, his complexion flickering through a rainbow of colors before he sat, palm pressed to his forehead. "Um, forget everything I just said. S-s-start over from the beginning. I'm sure there's another explanation here."

Which was all to say—

Xue Meng would never—*could* never—associate Chu Wanning with anything dirty, inappropriate, or immoral. He swiftly assumed he must have misheard. But he still felt bewildered, mumbling to himself, "What kind of conversation do you need to have here?"

Chu Wanning opened his mouth, but before he could say anything, Mo Ran squeezed his hand under his wide sleeve, cautioning him to silence. Chu Wanning's lies couldn't fool a three-year-old. It was better if Mo Ran did it.

Mo Ran said, "At dusk, I saw an osmanthus rice-cake spirit here."

Chu Wanning shut his mouth.

"What?" Xue Meng asked, baffled.

"An osmanthus rice cake that cultivated into a spirit," Mo Ran continued, all earnestness. "It was just about ten inches tall with a lotus leaf on its head. It even had a little tail, with a pale blue light shining at the tip."

"What kind of beast is that? I've never seen it in any books."

"Me neither," Mo Ran replied with a smile. "I wondered if it was some long-lost demon that escaped when Rufeng Sect's demon-suppressing tower fell, so I brought Shizun out here to take a look with me."

Xue Meng instantly let out a breath of relief. He didn't know why he felt so reassured by this explanation, but the tension in his face eased. Holding the lantern high, he stepped closer to them and looked around. "Did you guys find it?"

"No."

Xue Meng glared at Mo Ran. "I didn't ask you. I'm asking Shizun."

"...We did not," Chu Wanning said.

Mo Ran grinned. "That sweet rice cake probably saw Shizun and thought it would wind up as dessert, so it scampered away to hide."

After a beat, Chu Wanning snapped, "Mo Weiyu! Do you *want* to go copy books in the library again?"

At this sharp back-and-forth, Xue Meng's initial unease finally dissipated like mist. He sighed to himself. For a moment, he'd actually thought his shizun and that scoundrel Mo Ran shared some unspeakable secret... How absurd, how impossible! His shizun was a cupped handful of the purest sacred water in the world. *No one* could touch or pollute him.

"Enough about us—what about you?" Mo Ran asked. "What are you doing here?"

"I'm looking for Veggiebun," Xue Meng mumbled. "For Mom."

Mo Ran arched a brow. "That new fat cat?"

"Mn."

"The orange one with the striped forehead, who won't eat meat and only eats fish?"

"Yeah, have you seen him?" Xue Meng sighed, visibly exasperated. "I don't understand how such a fat cat can run so fast. I've looked everywhere a person can look on both sides of the mountain, but I've seen neither hide nor hair of him..." Struck by a thought, his eyes widened. "Ah! What if the rice-cake spirit ate him?" he exclaimed in alarm.

Neither Chu Wanning nor Mo Ran could muster a response.

Mo Ran badly wanted to laugh, but he managed to turn his guffaw into a cough. "Um, that rice cake looked pretty small. It's a demon, but I doubt it can do much. If Veggiebun ran into it, I think the rice cake should be the one to worry, not the tabby."

Xue Meng stroked his chin. He considered Veggiebun's physique and agreed, "Makes sense... That sounds about right..."

"The backwoods are dangerous," Chu Wanning said. "Don't go any farther. I'll help you search."

Xue Meng hastily waved his hand. "I wouldn't dream of inconveniencing Shizun."

"I have nothing urgent to attend to," insisted Chu Wanning. "I'll help with your search, then I have to go to Loyalty Hall for the elders' meeting. Mo Ran can join too—the search will go faster with three of us."

Mo Ran was speechless. Chu Wanning was impressively optimistic; did he seriously think Mo Ran's body was like a flame that could blaze up and go out with a snuff? He was being asked to stand up and look for a cat, *now*? He hadn't even gone soft yet.

Noting both the discomfort on Mo Ran's face and how he hadn't moved a muscle, Xue Meng asked, "What's wrong?"

"Oh, nothing," Mo Ran answered. "I'm just feeling a little strange. You two go on ahead, I'll join you in a few minutes."

Chu Wanning looked at him askance. Only then did he notice the difference between Mo Ran's clothes and his own. Mo Ran usually wore slim-fitting black and gold robes, which cut a striking silhouette. They were well-suited for combat, but their shortcomings were becoming clear: when worn without a cloak, any sign of arousal would be obvious.

In the dark, Chu Wanning stood in stunned silence. His usually cool face flushed as red as the last rays of sunset falling on the cloudy whiteness of ice. Bitter cold and warm light melded, setting the translucent surface aglow with rosy dusk.

After this incident, Chu Wanning refused to fool around with Mo Ran on Sisheng Peak under any circumstance. It was by pure coincidence that things started to get busy around this time. The sects throughout the cultivation realm were restless; every day Xu Shuanglin lived meant another sleepless night. They sought the help of Tianyin Pavilion, a judicial organization independent of the ten great sects, skilled at investigating thorny cases. But Xu Shuanglin had acted ruthlessly and left no evidence behind. Even the Tianyin Pavilion Master could do little.

Near the end of the month, Li Wuxin reached the limits of his patience. He sent out a heroes' invitation, summoning the leaders and key elders of sects large and small to Spiritual Mountain for a conference. Chu Wanning and Xue Zhengyong were naturally among those in attendance.

The last major congregation at Spiritual Mountain had been the competition in which Xue Meng and Nangong Si had distinguished themselves. In the blink of an eye, the entire cultivation realm had since been turned upside-down. The seats that should've belonged to Rufeng Sect were barren, and Huohuang Pavilion was a shadow of its former self. The newly named sect leader was a junior who couldn't speak without stammering, and sat cowed and silent amidst the crowd. The masters of Wubei Temple spoke every word with care, refusing to touch on the scandals of their previous leader. Remembering a time when all these sects had gathered here in high spirits, Xue Zhengyong felt those scenes were from another lifetime. He sighed.

On the dais, Jiang Xi had been selected leader of the ten great sects, responsible for overseeing the entire Nangong Xu investigation.

He was as night and day from the previous leader, Nangong Liu, who was never without a smile, courteous to everyone regardless of their status, and careful to never offend. But Jiang Xi? Practically the moment the assorted sect leaders revealed the results of the vote and asked Jiang Xi to take charge, he coolly made himself comfortable in what was once Nangong Liu's seat. Nangong Liu had hemmed and hawed before accepting the position, acting out the expected show of humble refusal. Even after he'd taken the seat, he spent a solid hour giving stately speeches, spittle flying as he waxed eloquent about how grateful he was for their confidence, how earnestly he'd seek guidance from all present, and how sincerely he asked for their patience.

Jiang Xi spoke four words. "As it should be."

He genuinely said this position *should've been* his. But that was Sect Leader Jiang—as unhinged as he was rich, and sorely lacking in both patience and tact.

Xue Zhengyong murmured to Chu Wanning: "He's skipped out on more than one gathering at Spiritual Mountain, hasn't he?"

Chu Wanning didn't pay much mind to these machinations of power. He frowned. "What do you mean?"

"Ever since Nangong Liu stepped into the position of leader and Rufeng was recognized as the foremost sect, Jiang Xi stopped attending sect leader gatherings..."

Eyeing Jiang Xi, Chu Wanning said, "That man is arrogant. He wouldn't submit to a wastrel."

Xue Zhengyong felt wronged. "I wouldn't submit to a wastrel either."

Chu Wanning smiled faintly. "Sect Leader, you were merely enduring it; you didn't submit."

As they spoke, a member of Guyueye Sect's retinue bustled over to their table. He bowed, holding out a brocade box.

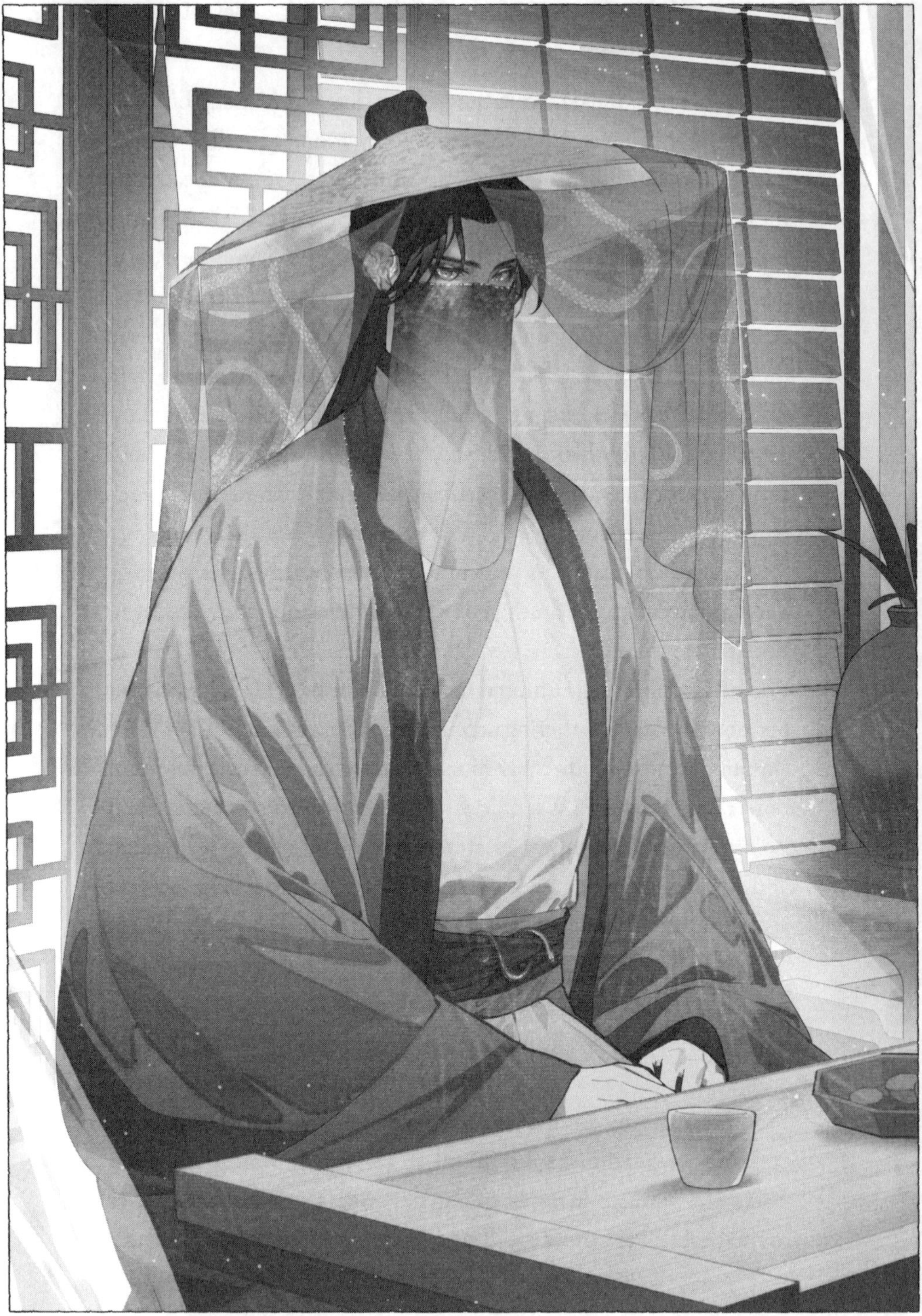

Xue Zhengyong turned. "What's this?"

The attendant shook his head, pointing at his ears, then mouth—he was a deaf and mute servant.

Studying him, Chu Wanning noticed this servant was different from the other Guyueye disciples—around his neck hung a silver snake pendant.

"Hanlin the Sage...?"

The servant noticed the direction of Chu Wanning's gaze and nodded several times. He bowed low, lifting the box over his head to present it. The brocade surface was adorned with an exquisitely detailed snake emblem. Xue Zhengyong guessed aloud, "He probably works directly under Hanlin the Sage."

He looked toward Guyueye's table. As expected, the world's foremost medicinal zongshi—Hanlin the Sage, Hua Binan—was quietly watching them, only his eyes visible in the slice of skin between his hat and veil.

187

Shizun, You're My Lantern

S CHU WANNING TURNED and met his gaze, a hint of
a smile curved Hua Binan's eyes. He extended a pale hand
from beneath jade-green silk robes and gently gestured
for Chu Wanning to take the brocade box.

Chu Wanning nodded and looked back toward the servant.
"Thank you." The servant performed a last low bow and returned to
his master.

"Yuheng, you know Hanlin the Sage?" Xue Zhengyong exclaimed.

"I don't," Chu Wanning replied, considering the box before
him. "If I did, I wouldn't have spent two million gold at Xuanyuan
Pavilion for his Tapir Fragrance Dew."

"Then what's this about?"

"I don't know either," Chu Wanning said. "Let's open it and take
a look."

When they lifted the lid, they found five multicolored bottles
of Tapir Fragrance Dew sweetly nestled within, along with a letter.
Chu Wanning opened it. Its contents were simple—Hanlin the
Sage wrote that he knew Chu-zongshi paid an exorbitant price at
Xuanyuan Pavilion for the dew, but because he felt it wasn't worth so
much, he'd always wanted to present him with another five bottles.
Unfortunately, their paths had never crossed, so now that he was so

lucky as to meet Chu-zongshi at the Spiritual Mountain gathering, he hoped the zongshi would accept.

"Looks like he wants to befriend you," Xue Zhengyong observed.

Chu Wanning thought a moment. To refuse such a gift would be a slap to the giver's face. He nodded his thanks at Hua Binan from a distance, then surreptitiously passed the brocade box to Xue Zhengyong.

Delighted, Xue Zhengyong asked, "For me?"

"For Tanlang Elder," Chu Wanning said. "I've always found this Hua Binan rather peculiar. Xuanyuan Pavilion auctions off so many of his medicines every year at prices they don't merit—does he plan to reimburse every buyer?"

"I don't think it's strange at all," Xue Zhengyong mumbled. "The prices *are* high, but they were never as ridiculously high as the bid *you* made."

Chu Wanning's face showed displeasure. "It was a means to an end. What's so ridiculous about it? Anyway, give these five bottles to Tanlang. I doubt there's poison in them, but if Tanlang can figure out the recipe for Tapir Fragrance Dew, it wouldn't be wasted."

"You don't need it anymore?"

"I…"

Strangely enough, those absurd, vivid dreams had subsided in recent months. Other than those few days after they'd left Rufeng Sect when he periodically dreamt of fragmented scenes, he always slept soundly. Drinking any more Tapir Fragrance Dew would be an unconscionable waste. Chu Wanning didn't think he needed any more of such fine medicine for himself.

The Spiritual Mountain gathering lasted several days. When they returned to Sisheng Peak, Mo Ran was gone.

"He's off exorcising demons," Xue Meng said.

A faint furrow appeared between Chu Wanning's brows. "Demons again? It's the nineteenth time this month."

"They're all escapees from Rufeng Sect's Golden Drum Tower." Xue Meng sighed. "He's already shoved all the ones he's caught into our Heaven-Piercing Tower, but ours isn't as strong as Golden Drum Tower. It's small, and the spiritual stones and talismans aren't as powerful as Rufeng Sect's. If this keeps up, the tower is going to fail before the demons stop coming."

"Next time Li Wuxin's here, ask him to take some to Bitan Manor," Xue Zhengyong suggested. "He can keep them suppressed in their Sacred Spirit Tower."

Xue Meng smiled. "That's a great idea."

"Guyueye can take some too, I heard their Star-Plucking Tower is twice the size of Rufeng Sect's Golden Drum Tower..."

This idea was much less pleasing. Xue Meng's brows drew together in anger, and he snapped, "No way!"

"Why not?"

"I don't like that Jiang asshole, he's super annoying. I'd fill Heaven-Piercing Tower to bursting before I'd give him any demons we caught!"

Chu Wanning shook his head. This father-son duo squabbled with no sign of stopping, so he turned to leave.

He returned to the pavilion to sleep off his travels. As usual, he slept soundly with no disturbance from those old dreams. When he awoke, the setting sun had turned the horizon crimson. Dusk had fallen over half the dome of the sky, leaving only a hint of bloody sunset at the edge of the world. He was hungry, but Mengpo Hall wouldn't be serving anything this late. Chu Wanning straightened his clothes and pushed the door open to head to Wuchang Town for some snacks. But as he descended the long stairs of the Red

Lotus Pavilion, he ran into Mo Ran returning from his exorcism mission.

Mo Ran smiled when he caught sight of Chu Wanning. "Shizun, Uncle said you were sleeping. I thought I'd stop by to wake you up."

"Is something the matter?"

"Not at all," Mo Ran said. "I just wanted to walk with you."

So it was a coincidence. This small stroke of luck somehow cheered Chu Wanning. When one was in love, the slightest quirk of shared fate was enough to brighten one's heart.

"Where to?" they asked at the same time.

Both froze. "You choose."

Once again, they had spoken simultaneously. Chu Wanning's hands clenched with embarrassment within his sleeves, clammy between his fingers, and his eyes were dark and warm. Yet his gaze was calm as he watched Mo Ran.

Mo Ran grinned. "Anywhere's fine."

Chu Wanning was privately delighted. He maintained his aloof demeanor out of habit, but his joy was rich and deep, like a branch of xifu haitang blossoms with their pale faces hiding vivid petal-backs. "Let's head to town then and get something to eat."

He didn't ask how Mo Ran's mission went, or if there were any troubles. Now that everything had fallen into place, he didn't have to. The moment he stood outside those bamboo doors and saw Mo Ran's black clothes billowing in the wind, scrollwork curling in dark gold at his hems and glimmering in the darkness, he understood that everything had gone well. There was no need for words.

They went to Wuchang Town together. In the past few years Wuchang Town had flourished, expanding from six streets to eleven, essentially doubling in size.

"When I first came to Sisheng Peak, the doors here would be tightly shut before nightfall. There'd be incense ash sprinkled in the courtyards, trigram mirrors hanging from the doors, and soul-suppressing bells hanging from the eaves." Chu Wanning watched the townspeople striding ahead of them in the glow of early-evening lanterns. "Aside from the name, this town is nearly unrecognizable."

Mo Ran smiled. "With Sisheng Peak here, it's only going to get better."

They walked along the re-paved cobblestone street, taking in the dizzying array of stalls: the sugar blowers, the shadow puppeteers, the barbecue and gudong soup joints all abustle. Row after row of lanterns swagged across the streets, shining down on the night market's noisy domesticity.

Catching sight of the gudong soup stall, Mo Ran thought of how he, Xue Meng, and Xia Sini once ate there. He smiled and tugged Chu Wanning to a halt. "Shizun, why don't we eat here? They have your favorite soymilk."

They sat on creaky bamboo chairs. The night was cold, but the cook's face ran with sweat. Mopping at his brow with a bare arm, he sidled up and asked, "Xianjun, what would you like?"

"Twin pot," Chu Wanning said.

"One pot of clear mushroom broth," Mo Ran said.

Chu Wanning eyed him. "Don't you want something spicy?"

Mo Ran grinned and lowered his lashes, voice warm and low. "I want to quit."

Chu Wanning blinked for a moment as it came to him why Mo Ran would suddenly choose to stop eating spicy food. It was as if a fish swam through the waters of his heart, bubbles rising to the surface and stirring up rippling waves. "You don't need to..."

"No, I'd just like to."

Chu Wanning said nothing.

"I'd like to quit—I want to quit." He watched Chu Wanning, thick lashes fluttering as his gaze fell on the man's reddening ears. Beaming, he left the rest unsaid—

I want to be just like you. When we eat hotpot, I want both our chopsticks to dip into the same bubbling pot; no longer one red and one white, sharply divided.

Mo Ran ordered a few other dishes. This stall had no fancy desserts, so he asked for three stout jars of soymilk and sat to wait for the food.

They were surrounded by diners from all walks of life, young and old, male and female. The steam from the pots curled in the air as the flames from the wok flared; shouts and drinking games echoed alongside jokes and whispers; amidst the bubbling steam and delicious aromas, the sounds of the night merged into an endless wash of tenderness.

How peaceful this mortal life; how colorful this world. Before Mo Ran turned fifteen, he'd spent his days starving. He'd never dreamed of such sumptuous food. And even after he'd become Emperor Taxian-jun and stood at the peak of the world, such serenity had never been his.

Now, he had both.

The cook tossed the wok, and the fire roared from beneath to cast a coppery gleam over the bare-armed man's torso. Another sprinkle of seasoning, and those burly arms shook the wok and poured out a plate of stir-fry. It arrived at their table steaming.

"Fried double crisp!" shouted the server.

Taxian-jun of the previous life had remained unfazed by the finest delicacies, but for some reason, this shout won a laugh from him. He folded his fine-boned hands under his strong jaw. As his thick lashes fluttered, countless bright dots seemed to merge beneath those two inky veils as if scattered from the waters of every sea, dyeing the darkness with light.

"Why are you laughing?" Chu Wanning asked.

"I don't know. I'm just really happy."

Chu Wanning didn't say any more. But for some reason, when faced with this man's mesmerizing smile, he felt the same brightness in his heart.

After dinner, they looked to the overcast sky, dark with the portent of rain. Those beneath it didn't appear to care; they strolled calmly through the brilliant night.

As they passed a lantern stall, Mo Ran stopped to look at its wares. Following the line of his gaze, Chu Wanning found the old craftsman carefully papering a pagoda lantern. A similar lantern, already complete, was sitting on its stand. They were river lanterns, meant to float on the water.

"Uncle, could I please have that pagoda lantern?" Chu Wanning didn't ask the price, or if Mo Ran wanted it. He stepped up and handed gold leaves to the elderly man engrossed in his craft, then passed the lantern to the disciple waiting behind him. "Here."

Mo Ran was surprised, pleased, and slightly bemused. "For me?"

Chu Wanning didn't respond. With half a jug of wine from dinner still in his hand, he looked around, his gaze falling on the babbling river in the distance, and walked toward the water.

The lantern flickered, then burned brighter. The embellishments glittered, festive accents to the solemn little pagoda. Holding the river lantern, Mo Ran mumbled, "Every year I've wanted to set one in the water, but I never had the money."

"True." Chu Wanning glanced at him. "You're always broke."

Mo Ran laughed.

The river flowed tranquilly at their feet. Chu Wanning didn't feel like making his way down the stone steps, so he crossed his arms and leaned back against the railing of the covered bridge. This white-clad daozhang stood with his back to the black bridge pillar, holding a jug of wine complete with scarlet tassel. He leaned back and took a sip, then turned. The red lanterns swinging from the eaves cast their warm light over a face delicate as jade. His features were serene, but his eyes were full of an unconcealed affection as he watched the man holding his lantern, slightly clumsy in his delight.

You little dummy, what's so fun about this?

Still he watched, unblinking, as Mo Ran walked down to the river and babbled under his breath to the pagoda lantern before lowering it into the water. Gold-red light glimmered on the rippling waves. Mo Ran dipped his hand in the water and pushed, sending the pagoda on its journey.

Mo Ran stood on the dark riverbank for a long time. There was no festival happening that day. Other than him, no one had put lanterns on the river. There was only that single small pagoda lantern, casting its weak, stubborn glow as it drifted in the cold waters of that endless night. Onward it went, dwindling to a dot of flickering ember until it disappeared, swallowed by the dark.

Mo Ran stood in silence, his thoughts his own. He watched the lantern until it was gone, until the wide river's surface was lightless once more.

The clouds suddenly opened. Rain beat down on the duckweed, and on the dark roofs and white walls of the town. The crowd dispersed, shouting, faces creased with laughter. Such rainstorms were rare in winter. The stall workers rushed to cover the tools of their livelihoods with brown oilpaper, pushing their carts as they fled in every direction from the driving rain.

Chu Wanning stared woodenly into the downpour. Spring wasn't far off, but it was still winter. This storm had descended with surprising speed. Under the shelter of the bridge, the rain only soaked the edges of Chu Wanning's hem. When Mo Ran hastily ran up from the riverside, however, he was thoroughly drenched. His clothes were wet and his face was dripping, and even his eyes were gleaming, dark as the night. He gazed at Chu Wanning, smiling warmly and with some embarrassment.

"Dry yourself with a spell," Chu Wanning said.

"Mn."

A deluge like this was no obstacle to cultivators, especially two zongshi like Mo Ran and Chu Wanning. A simple barrier would see them clean and dry to Sisheng Peak. But neither moved to put up such a barrier. They stood under the bridge's awning, side by side, waiting for the rain to stop.

But the storm showed no sign of weakening. The world entire was shrouded in mist and falling water, and the warmth and bustle of the night market had disappeared as if the freezing rain had diluted its colors and smeared its ink.

"It doesn't look like it'll stop," Mo Ran said.

"It's really raining cats and dogs," Chu Wanning coolly replied.

Mo Ran burst into laughter. He turned to Chu Wanning and said, "What do we do? We can't go back."

Chu Wanning knew he should answer with, *Aren't you a cultivator? Don't you know how to make a barrier? What do you mean we can't go back?*

But for some reason, he didn't argue, nor did he agree. He just looked, face upturned, into the vast night rain. His palms were hot, his curled fingers clammy. Just as he was thinking how to respond, Mo Ran reached over. Chu Wanning's trembling hands, with their warm palms and their slight sheen of sweat, fell undisguised into Mo Ran's own.

Mo Ran looked at him. After a beat, the jut of his throat bobbing, he said, "Shizun, I—I want to..."

The words came to the tip of his tongue; he couldn't quite voice them. But his heart pounded, prickling in his chest, so couldn't he swallow them either. In the end, eyes wet and warm, he spoke a few words, their fervency veiled in a suggestive ambiguity. "I mean...it's raining too hard," he said quietly. "Let's not go back tonight. It's so far, you'll catch a cold."

Chu Wanning didn't yet understand. Blinking, he said, "I'm not cold."

"Then are you hot?"

"I'm not hot either—"

Breath scalding, chest rising and falling, Mo Ran didn't let Chu Wanning finish his sentence. He took his hand and brought it to his own pounding heart. "I am," he whispered.

The rain beat down on the duckweed, but Chu Wanning saw flames in Mo Ran's eyes. He saw molten rock, and the blazing heat of summer. This young man was so frustrated he was almost pitiable, painfully adorable.

His voice was hoarse. "Let's go to the nearest inn, okay? Right now."

188

Shizun, I Really Love You So Much

C HU WANNING'S HEART juddered. There was nothing stopping them from returning to Sisheng Peak, yet here was Mo Ran using an excuse that even he found patently ridiculous to bring Chu Wanning to an inn. No matter how oblivious Chu Wanning might be, he couldn't miss Mo Ran's meaning.

Mo Ran was testing the waters, tentatively probing. If Chu Wanning were to shake his head *no,* Mo Ran wouldn't press him. But if he were to agree, then it would be a tacit admission that he was willing to...

...To do what exactly?

Chu Wanning didn't know, and even if he did, he couldn't bear to think about it. He felt his cheeks burn with a heat the rain couldn't allay. He lifted the wine jug by its slender neck, thinking to take another sip, but only dregs remained. The last drop of cool, heady pear-blossom white slipped down his throat. He looked at his feet, fingers pale against the jar's scarlet tassel.

Mo Ran wasn't fond of wine, but he unexpectedly asked, "Is there any left?"

"No."

"A shame," said Mo Ran. Dipping his head, he softly kissed Chu Wanning on the mouth. "Guess I'll only be able to get a taste like this, then."

Pear-blossom white wine was pungent and sweet, with a fragrant note of osmanthus. In the year Mo Ran turned thirty, he'd drunk it all night long on the rooftop after Chu Wanning's death. By the end, the wine was bitter in his mouth.

From then on, even after his rebirth, Mo Ran had little urge to drink again. The flavors had turned to bitterness.

He kissed Chu Wanning's cool lips, tentative at first. They touched and separated cautiously.

The rain crashed down, the world a blur.

There was no one else beneath the covered bridge, and the storm was like a curtain falling from the sky. Before they knew it their arms were around each other as they kissed eagerly, their lips and tongues tangling. The mortifying sounds of their hungry kisses were drowned by the pounding of the rain on the beams above; Chu Wanning's ears were filled with it. The roar of the storm battered his heart like the clamoring drums and blaring horns of war.

Where the rain was cold, Mo Ran's breaths were blazing hot. His kisses wandered from Chu Wanning's lips up to his nose, his eyes, the space between his brows. They reached Chu Wanning's temples, and a wet, rough tongue licked his ear.

This kind of stimulation was more than Chu Wanning could bear. He clenched his fists, every muscle tense, but he wasn't willing to let out a single sound.

Pressing closer, Mo Ran captured his earlobe and nuzzled the tiny mole behind it, earning a shiver from the man in his arms. In response, Mo Ran tightened his hold as though to crush him, as if he wanted to pulverize Chu Wanning into his body, to meld him into his very soul. "Shizun..." His voice was low and hoarse in Chu Wanning's ear.

His address was respectful, but his hands around Chu Wanning's waist were anything but. This young man had kept a lid on his passion for so long, but now it finally burst, the scalding water roiling. The pot had nearly boiled dry, yet the cookfire was burning hotter and hotter. That agonizing heat tormented him—it tormented both of them.

"Come with me, all right?"

At some point, Chu Wanning let Mo Ran grab his hand. They ran frantically through the pouring rain.

The rain was freezing, but it seemed warm as it landed on them. Neither opened a barrier nor stopped to buy an umbrella. They let themselves be lashed by the rain and wind like two ordinary commoners with not a shred of spiritual energy between them. Chasing a trail of red lanterns swaying in the storm, they ducked into an inn.

The receptionist behind the desk stifled a yawn. Given the hard rain and the late hour, he'd likely expected no more travelers to come for the night. When two drenched men charged through the door, he jumped in fright.

Mo Ran was gripping Chu Wanning's wrist, his palm hot enough to turn all the rain to steam. He swiped at the rivulets running down his handsome face, and said impatiently, "We'll stay the night."

"Ah, yes, yes, here are keys for two rooms. That'll be..."

"What?" At *two rooms*, Mo Ran grew more impatient. Throat bobbing, he rapped his strong, slender knuckles against the counter. "No, just one room."

The receptionist stared, his eyes flitting back and forth between Mo Ran and Chu Wanning.

Chu Wanning jerked his face aside. Cheeks burning, he wrenched his wrist out of Mo Ran's grip. "We need two rooms," he said.

The receptionist hesitated. "If it's too much money," he said placatingly, "one is fine."

"Two," Chu Wanning repeated with an air of finality, glaring daggers at the receptionist. The poor man took a step back, unsure how he had managed to anger this white-robed cultivator standing in the shadow of the first. He fearfully handed over both keys and accepted the money.

Chu Wanning slowed his breathing, feigning his usual calmness. Unfortunately, he was soaked from head to toe. At that precise moment, a droplet rolled off the end of his dark brow straight into his eye. He blinked furiously through wet lashes. "I'm going to sleep. Get some ginger tea and dry towels before you come up."

His words were solemn and dignified. He made sure to take only one of the brass keys from Mo Ran as the receptionist looked on, then made his way up the stairs unaccompanied.

He was the picture of sodden virtue. Mo Ran said nothing, but inwardly, he stifled a laugh. Chu Wanning was so thin-skinned; no matter what, he was compelled to go through the motions in front of others.

Chu Wanning stepped through the door into a single room with a narrow bed. A glance at that bed and his throat went dry, while his face seemed to blaze with heat. He didn't dare look at it twice. He stood in the middle of the room with the candle unlit, at something of a loss. His mind was a murky haze. This was so absurd, reckless, unexpected. How did it end up like this... How did he end up standing here *like this*, dripping rain, about to engage in such folly? How did he...

The door opened behind him. Mo Ran.

Chu Wanning froze, fingers curling into fists in his sleeves. No matter how he tried to stop the trembling that wracked his body, he couldn't. Never in his life had he felt so lost and helpless, like a kite whose spool had been handed off to another. His palms were slick; whether with rain or sweat he didn't know.

The bar over the door fell into place. All the hairs on his body stood on end at that crisp *click*, like an executioner's blade pressed to his throat, reeking of iron. Like a predator sinking its fangs into prey, stinking of blood.

Chu Wanning was seized by the sudden urge to flee. Yet somehow, his face didn't show a thing.

"Why didn't you light the candle?" Mo Ran's voice was gentle and restrained—not overly urgent, though somewhat husky.

"...I forgot."

Mo Ran set the wooden tray down on the table and handed him a small bowl, warm to the touch. "The ginger tea you wanted. Drink it while it's hot."

He crossed to the window to light the candle. The rain hadn't let up outside, but for some reason, the grapevine-carved window was open. From the dark interior of their room, they could see the flames of candles in nearby buildings as pinpoints of shuddering light.

Mo Ran stood before the open window, next to the delicate, crane-shaped candle holder. Against the backdrop of misty rain, his tall figure was refined and upright, a clean-lined silhouette. As he fiddled with the flint lighter, the sweep of his long lashes stood out starkly, like two black butterflies.

He was a cultivator; he could light a fire with a flick of his fingers, yet he insisted on using the most commonplace method, as any ordinary person might. Calm and steady, he reached for the candle. In the next instant, the wick would catch, and the wax would shed a melting scarlet tear.

The flint sparked. As he raised it to the wick, Chu Wanning called out, "Don't light it."

Mo Ran turned to him, hands hovering in midair. "What?"

Chu Wanning didn't know how to explain himself. All he could do was repeat stiffly: "Don't light the candle."

Bewildered, Mo Ran stopped. As he watched Chu Wanning standing woodenly in the dark, it slowly occurred to him: even Yuheng of the Night Sky would have moments of fear, objects of terror, domains of which he knew nothing.

Everyone Mo Ran had slept with in the past life, men and women alike, wanted Emperor Taxian-jun to look upon their faces. No one had ever asked him to put out the light. They would rather dispel the darkness with crimson candles, using every trick in the book, every manner of flirtation, to lure him onto the hook. But Mo Ran was never snared. Strangely enough, it had all been the same, whether with Rong Jiu in the beginning or Song Qiutong at the end. He had pampered them and kept them around because they looked like Shi Mei, making such a show of his obsession it was as if he was putting on an act for someone else. But he never liked to look at their faces in bed. He always made them turn away, never kissing or caressing them. Amidst the tedious cadence of bodies colliding, his mind felt clear, as though he might suddenly wake up and realize it was meaningless.

He couldn't remember any of those smiling, fawning, climaxing, flushing faces beneath the candlelight. When he thought back on those love affairs, those romantic liaisons, they seemed to have nothing to do with love or romance. It was rather like he had fallen into a mire of chaos, covering himself in filth as he sank, giving himself up to the darkness, wishing for even the gaps between his bones to be stained black. So black he would no longer yearn for the light or dream of impossible salvation; so black it would kill his fantasy of embracing the very last flame he had in this world.

That would have been for the best. But despite everything, he couldn't restrain himself. No matter how much he told himself to stop thinking about him, to stop pining after him; no matter how he told himself that life was without hope and the world was nothing but darkness—even so, in the storm-lashed Wushan Palace, amid those tormentuous entanglements, he still extended shaking fingers and closed them around Chu Wanning's neck. He pinned him down, against the cold tiles, on the somber bluestone steps in the courtyard, between the sweat-tangled sheets. On the snow, in the hot spring, even on the great throne and in the ancestral temple. In the most dignified and solemn places, those places most worthy of respect, he took him while studying his face; mouthing his neck, his cheeks, his lips; chanting his name. He took him apart.

Back then, Chu Wanning had surely also wanted darkness, had wanted the candles to be extinguished. He surely hadn't wanted any light. But back then, Chu Wanning hadn't said so; he wouldn't say so. He wouldn't ask for anything at all.

Now that he thought of it, during his eight long years of imprisonment, Chu Wanning had only asked Mo Ran for something twice—once at the very beginning and once at the very end. The first, when Mo Ran had stepped across the threshold of Wushan Palace, was for Mo Ran to spare Xue Meng. The second, before he left the world for good, was for Mo Ran to spare himself.

Why else, unless Chu Wanning had lost all hope...

Mo Ran put down the flint and steel. He didn't speak for a long time—so long that enough tension bled out of Chu Wanning's body to ask, voice soft, "What's wrong?"

"...Nothing," Mo Ran responded. His voice was warm, throaty, and soaked with bitterness.

He stepped over to Chu Wanning and put his arms around him, gathering up that solitary figure in the darkness. The damp of the rain lingered on both of them. Holding him, Mo Ran spoke at last: "Wanning."

In the moment of silence that followed, Mo Ran had a sudden, destructive urge to tell him everything. But his throat was choked, like a fishbone was stuck in it; he couldn't say the words. He genuinely couldn't make a sound. This warmth right now was far too precious, to both him and Chu Wanning. His sins and regrets were innumerable, but he didn't want to speak of them—he *couldn't* speak of them. He didn't want to wake up. He wanted to keep dreaming until daybreak came to slit his throat.

In the absence of light or flame, Mo Ran held Chu Wanning in the darkness, kissing him carefully, slowly drawing him in. The room was quiet, cloaked in a stillness the rainfall couldn't disturb. They could hear each other's breaths and heartbeats, the sounds of their lips meeting and parting, the soft, slick noises when they shifted.

Chu Wanning strove to keep his breathing even, but the heaving of his chest grew urgent under Mo Ran's mouth and hands. Chu Wanning himself was a tall, well-built man, but Mo Ran, towering over him, could so easily cage him in his arms. His figure was a broad and imposing mountain as he pressed Chu Wanning to his searing chest.

Those soft, tentative kisses grew deeper, more searching. Guiding Chu Wanning's lips open, Mo Ran's rough tongue licked into his mouth, insistent as a parched man taking a first drink of sweet dew, or a man on fire begging for water to douse the flames. But to Mo Ran, Chu Wanning's breath was not fresh water but pine oil. A splash sent the flames roaring toward the sky.

It was unclear who started taking off the other's clothes. Their sighs filled the night, mixed with the soft sounds of kiss after kiss swallowed between lips and teeth. Whether because they yanked open their sashes so hard it hurt, or because the thrum of anticipation was simply too intense, faint moans escaped between the minutes.

More frequent were the rough pants of men consumed by desire. Chu Wanning's inner robe had been pulled open, and he was still getting used to the cool air on his skin when he felt Mo Ran lean down to kiss his neck, then his collarbone, his lips closing around a nipple, wet and warm...

Chu Wanning gasped for air, throwing his head back in humiliated arousal. He was blushing furiously, but they were fortunately surrounded by darkness. Although he knew Mo Ran couldn't see his flaming cheeks, he said softly, "The window..."

"What?"

Mo Ran raised his head hazily, meeting Chu Wanning's downcast, dewy eyes. He *had* intended to let Chu Wanning finish his thought, but this glance was enough to make his scalp go numb. Blood pounded in his ears, and an irrepressible lust washed over him as he leaned in to take Chu Wanning's lips once more. He plundered that mouth again thoroughly before finally letting it part from his own. Catching his breath, he snuck in a final peck before asking hoarsely for the second time, "What?"

"The window..." Chu Wanning's heart was racing. He hadn't found the knack of breathing during these passionate encounters; he felt a little lightheaded. "You haven't closed the window."

Mo Ran stepped over to the window and shut it, cutting them off from the last glimmers of light outside. The room was plunged into darkness, so the flames of desire could burn all the more brightly.

Every drop of Mo Ran's blood was on fire. Bodies colliding once more, the pair tumbled onto the bed, drawing a low groan from its aged frame.

Giving Chu Wanning no time to react, Mo Ran pinned him under his body to pull off that last snow-white layer, already askew. He felt Chu Wanning shaking beneath him, not unlike the first time they had slept together in the past life. Tremors wracked his body, no matter how he tried to suppress them. Heartsore, Mo Ran cupped Chu Wanning's face in his palm, dropping kisses on his eyelids, his lips, his jaw. He murmured hoarsely into Chu Wanning's ear, "Don't be scared."

"I'm not... I'm not scared..."

Mo Ran took his trembling hand, lacing their fingers together. His warm breath puffed against Chu Wanning's earlobe as he soothed, "I've got you... Good, that's it. You're doing great..."

Chu Wanning wanted to reply, to fire back a fierce retort. Even if he could only manage a few words, that would be sufficient. But he couldn't speak at all, as though his brain was made of wood. All he felt was Mo Ran's weight on top of him, Mo Ran's callused hands wandering across his waist, his back. The feeling was unbearable; he arched his spine against it, inadvertently pressing into Mo Ran's chest. Mo Ran's inner robe had long been stripped away, leaving his sturdy torso bare. It radiated such terrifying, powerful heat that Chu Wanning felt he might melt away entirely.

Their sweat-slick bodies twined together, each brush of skin on skin sending sparks flying. Their breaths echoed in the room, heavier and deeper, encumbered by desire. However they kissed, it wasn't enough to quench this incurable thirst.

Hazy images flashed through Chu Wanning's mind—writhing bodies, boneless legs, scarlet canopies and crimson sheets. The scenes from those dreams came suddenly into focus. Mo Ran was gripping him by the waist, hips ramming against him as he fucked him deep and hard. Whether due to pleasure or something else, Mo Ran's handsome face looked sinister in this dream, a feral glint in his eyes. Chu Wanning was ignorant of sex or romance, and he'd never second-guessed the origins of these visions. He imagined it was human nature that the awakening of desire should provoke such realistic dreams.

But Mo Ran knew nothing of those visions; he thought Chu Wanning wholly oblivious of congress between men and women, to say nothing of the ways in which two men made love. He worried he might startle or hurt Chu Wanning, so he caressed him tenderly, moving slow. He didn't want Chu Wanning to suffer in this lifetime.

Lust's hold on them tightened as they kissed, hands roaming. Chu Wanning finally couldn't take it; he gripped Mo Ran's fingers with one hand and the bedding with the other. Cheeks aflame, he longed to reach down and take himself in hand, but how could he do something so shameful in front of the person he loved? He was so hard, the evidence of his arousal straining against his underclothes. Chu Wanning felt mortified; the ache was nearly unbearable. He wanted so badly to touch himself, yet he refused to give in. His narrowed phoenix eyes misted, everything blurring within...

Gradually, his awareness faded until he knew nothing at all. Somehow, in his bones, he seemed to understand what he was supposed to do, how two men were supposed to be together. Love and desire filled his breast, and he loved this man on top of him very much. He wanted to dive into the ocean of desires with him, to sink into the abyss of want and never surface.

Scattered visions flitted across his eyes once more, a swirl of dancing colors. How strange... Why did it look like they were on Sisheng Peak...in Loyalty Hall...

A spark of realization flickered to life in his mind, only to fade a breath later. He saw Mo Ran sitting on the throne in Loyalty Hall, where the sect leader received guests. This was a dignified place, yet somehow, he was straddling Mo Ran on that seat as Mo Ran's arms supported him. He was stark naked, every inch of him shamefully bare, while Mo Ran was dressed neatly save for the front of his pants, pulled down just enough. Even so, whatever he exposed was hidden beneath Chu Wanning's open legs.

Kissing him, Mo Ran canted his hips upward as he stared unblinkingly into Chu Wanning's face. "Does it feel good?" he asked.

Chu Wanning watched himself shake his head in anguished silence.

Mo Ran's fingers slipped into his mouth and pried open his jaw as though to pull the moans from his throat. "That's it, I want to hear you scream."

But Chu Wanning wouldn't. Only a broken whimper escaped.

Mo Ran remained fully seated inside Chu Wanning. He gripped Chu Wanning's waist, then slid his hand down to his ass and pinched it hard. "Go on then," he demanded, voice a harsh rasp.

"No..."

Mo Ran grabbed his ass and lifted him up and down, a slow torture. That maddening friction drove Chu Wanning insane; he felt he was about to be run through. "I can't... I don't want to..."

"Who cares what you want?" The man on the throne laughed coldly. "Aren't you enjoying this? Look, you're hard."

In the inn, Chu Wanning lay on the bed, dazed and shivering, painfully hard. These sights and sounds came to him as through a murky glass, hallucinations born of his overwhelming arousal. What was going on... What to do...

The images smeared, but he could still see Mo Ran viciously thrusting into him from atop the throne, pulling out nigh completely before burying himself again. It was too much. In the end, Chu Wanning couldn't take it; sprawled upon Mo Ran's lap, he gasped and moaned, "Ah... *Ahhh*..."

Mo Ran, too, was panting as he fucked him. Everything was so blurry... He couldn't see...

It was an illusion, a hallucination. It couldn't be real, so it *had* to be fake. It was an overlapping dreamscape, an unending nightmare. Yet that overpowering, irrepressible feeling of invasion was so vivid. Was it...supposed to be like this?

Chu Wanning's phoenix eyes were half-lidded, glassy and unfocused. "In me..." he muttered.

Mo Ran jumped. Chu Wanning knew how sex worked?! But how? Here was a man who had never so much as looked at erotic pictures, untouched as a sheet of white paper—how would he know?

"Is that...what we're supposed to do?" Chu Wanning haltingly asked the man on top of him, his face so red it could drip blood.

"Where...where did you learn that?"

Chu Wanning couldn't possibly say he had dreamt it—how indecent, how depraved would that make him sound? "I accidentally saw it in the library..." he mumbled. "Someone shelved a book in the wrong place," he added quickly.

Naturally, Mo Ran had no reason to doubt him. Feeling both relief and an overwhelming fondness, he kissed the corner of Chu Wanning's mouth, then the tip of his nose. "Don't be hasty."

Chu Wanning's eyes flew open. Hasty? Who said he was hasty?! His head throbbed with fury and embarrassment, but Mo Ran was still holding him, chest pressed against his own. He stroked Chu Wanning's temples and said softly, "It'll hurt."

"Never mind then," Chu Wanning replied without hesitation, eager to save face.

Mo Ran chuckled, low and mellifluous. "Don't worry about me," he said. "Tonight..." His voice faded.

Chu Wanning blinked. What about tonight? He watched Mo Ran prop himself up on sturdy arms, pulling back to gaze at him from above. Mo Ran slowly sat up and shifted down on the bed. Nothing like this had ever happened in Chu Wanning's dreams. What was Mo Ran going to do?

"Tonight, I just want to make you feel good."

Before Chu Wanning realized what was happening, Mo Ran had loosened the ties of Chu Wanning's underclothes to reveal his straining erection. His gaze sparked with ardent affection as he leaned forward and took Chu Wanning into his mouth.

"Ahh—!" A shudder raced down Chu Wanning's spine as he cried out in surprise, breath running out of him. What was this sensation? How... How could this be possible... It was so *dirty*...

But it felt so good to have his beloved's warm mouth around him. Mo Ran kept his teeth carefully out of the way as he gently licked and sucked.

At Chu Wanning's hitched breaths and low pants, Mo Ran raised his eyes to gaze at him indulgently. Taxian-jun had never done anything like this; he had never even considered that someday, he might *want* to do something like this. But now, he was fully willing, smitten—delighted to do so.

"Don't... How could you... Quick, spit it out." Face crimson, Chu Wanning bit his lip and shook his head back and forth. His phoenix eyes, usually so sharp, showed intoxication and panic.

How cute.

Mo Ran took him deeper in, past his throat. Chu Wanning couldn't bear it. Arching his back, he tossed his head back, panting for dear life, eyes losing focus. At length, Mo Ran pulled away, drool dripping from the corner of his mouth. Eyes dancing, he asked, "Babe, do you like it?"

Chu Wanning felt like a skyful of fireworks was going off in his head. Hearing Mo Ran address him like this felt both mortifying and sweet, a combination that made his already sluggish limbs go weak. How could he... He was Mo Ran's shizun, he was so much older than him, he was the Beidou Immortal, he...

"Ah..." Another low gasp shattered the room's darkness.

Mo Ran's rough, clever tongue lapped at the plump head of Chu Wanning's cock, running along those places Chu Wanning himself had scarcely touched. The sensation was enough to make Chu Wanning weep. He wanted to control himself, but he wasn't guarded or defiant, as he had been in the past life. This time, he entangled with Mo Ran of his own volition, and therefore didn't resist. His throat bobbed, hoarse cries leaking from parted lips.

He closed his mist-filled eyes. When Mo Ran put his mouth around him again, this time moving rhythmically up and down, Chu Wanning reached out and buried his slender fingers in Mo Ran's dark hair, weakly trying to push him away.

"Don't... Don't do that... That's dirty... Ahh..."

But Mo Ran only raised his glistening eyes, desire heavy in his gaze. "I like you, and I want to do this for you—I want you to feel good... How could it be dirty?" He laid a gentle kiss on that achingly hard shaft, lips ghosting over where the vein on the underside stood out. "Every inch of you is perfect."

Mo Ran dipped his head back down to continue sucking Chu Wanning off. Chu Wanning had no experience; he was powerless against this onslaught of pleasure. After all, it was his first time. It wasn't long before he reached his climax, unable to stop himself from bucking up into Mo Ran's throat as he came.

Surely this was very uncomfortable for Mo Ran?

Chu Wanning's world was a snow-white haze, all unfocused save for the sharp ecstasy of that moment. He had never conceived of such intense pleasure, to say nothing of experiencing it himself.

As bliss threatened to drown him, his mind came vaguely back to what he had done at the very end. He wanted to sit up and wipe Mo Ran's mouth, to smooth his hand over his cheek and kiss him, to express his gratitude. But he was sapped of strength, legs numb and tingling. He couldn't get up.

By the time he looked up through trembling lashes, Mo Ran had swallowed. Chu Wanning's thoughts stalled completely, the back of his neck prickling and his blood pulsing a steady beat.

Mo Ran pulled himself up and draped his warm bulk over Chu Wanning's still-heaving chest, his hand coming up to stroke Chu Wanning's face. His hot, rock-hard erection pressed into Chu Wanning's abdomen, and his eyes were stained red, almost bestial. But, as always, his gaze on Chu Wanning was tender.

"I love you."

I really, really, really love you so much. With reckless ambition, with boundless contrition; bearing the weight of my guilt and sins, yet unwilling to give up; selfishly, desperately, ardently, hungrily—I love you.

189

Shizun,
You're the Best

IT WAS QUIET in the room, rendering the sound of their breaths and the pounding of their hearts louder in their ears. The air was redolent with some scent—musky but sweet.

Mo Ran shifted on the bed, drawing Chu Wanning into his arms from behind and planting gentle kisses on his eyelids and the nape of his neck. Both were covered in sweat, their bodies feverish as they lay pressed together, damp skin sticking to damp skin, limbs entwined in a clinging embrace. Chu Wanning felt faint; he didn't dare dwell on what they'd just done. The very thought was absurd.

But his heart was warm and glowing. Gentle waters surged beneath his ribcage, about to spill over.

Mo Ran heard the man in his arms murmur, "What about you?"

"Huh?" Mo Ran went still, taken aback.

Chu Wanning cleared his throat. "You…" He began. He turned in the darkness, lifting those bright eyes to meet Mo Ran's.

Even in the gloom, Mo Ran imagined he could see the flush on Chu Wanning's cheeks.

"You're still…" Chu Wanning hesitated for a long beat, incapable of voicing his thoughts. In the end, he lowered his lashes. "I'll help you."

Realization broke over Mo Ran, and his heart ached. Embracing Chu Wanning, he said, "Why are you so silly? It doesn't matter. That can wait."

"I'm not silly," Chu Wanning said stiffly. He rejected the word. "Aren't you the one being silly? Aren't you...uncomfortable like this?"

Mo Ran coughed awkwardly. "Once you're asleep, I'll go take a bath and..."

But Chu Wanning would not be dissuaded. "I'll help you."

"It's all right." Mo Ran hastily stopped him.

Chu Wanning fell silent. His clumsiness in bed was shameful; how could he give Mo Ran any pleasure? Mo Ran's excuse of taking a bath later was probably merely thrown out to placate him—what Mo Ran really meant was that using his own hand would be better than relying on Chu Wanning's skills, or lack thereof. At this thought, his eyes slowly dulled. "Forget it then, if you don't want it."

Mo Ran paused. In the afterglow of his own pleasure, Chu Wanning's voice wasn't controlled, as it usually was. His usual cool detachment had fled, leaving his dissatisfaction and indignance sharp and vivid. How silly could this man be? How could Mo Ran *not* want it? He wanted it more than anything; he wanted this night to be eternal, for the torrential downpour outside to fall forever. He wanted to drown in pleasure with Chu Wanning in this inn for the rest of time, to devour the man in his arms until their flesh and souls were one. He wanted to see Chu Wanning tormented to the point of sobbing; he wanted to leave his unmistakable mark inside this man's body.

But it would hurt him.

He remembered the high fever Chu Wanning had run after the first time Mo Ran had taken him the past life. Even now, Mo Ran couldn't forget his face in the aftermath, skin pale and lips cracked. He wanted to take it slowly. It didn't matter how much effort he had to put in to resist his desires; he wanted Chu Wanning's first time to be good. And he wanted him to feel pleasure and enjoyment in every subsequent dalliance; he wanted him to savor the sensation and sink into its depths with him.

But Chu Wanning had clearly misunderstood.

Mo Ran kissed his brow. "How could I not want it?" he said huskily. "What are you thinking?"

Chu Wanning said nothing.

"Can't you see the state I'm in?" Mo Ran's fiery, labored breaths fanned his ear. "I'm *this* hard, and you somehow think I don't want you... Dummy."

Chu Wanning's temper flared. "Call me dumb again and I'll cut your head off! You—*mngh*..."

Mo Ran had caught his hand and tugged it downward. The instant it met Mo Ran's body, Chu Wanning was too startled to manage a harsh word. Steam seemed to rise from his ears.

"Look what you've done to me."

Wrapped in soft darkness, Mo Ran kissed Chu Wanning's eyelids again, then ducked to capture his mouth. He suckled and licked at Chu Wanning's lips, intoxicated by infatuation.

After several more kisses like these, neither of them could take any more. The desire in the room thickened; as their mouths entwined, so did their legs. They ground against each other, the blaze of lust almost enough to light up the dark. In the haze, Mo Ran heard Chu Wanning mumble, dissatisfied and embarrassed, with all his habitual stubbornness: "I also...want to make you feel good..."

The last syllables came out shaking, as though shame threatened to engulf them. Mo Ran's heart was close to melting, and his neglected cock was an angry red. Chu Wanning's hand was still pressed against him, the ready heat emanating from his palm to the small of his back.

Chu Wanning could feel just how formidable that weapon described in the cultivation rankings was in its state of arousal; it was so thick, so hard, and so heated, even through the fabric it strained against. That ferocious thing would never fit in his mouth...

Making love with a man like this would be life-threatening.

Chu Wanning finally realized Mo Ran's insistence that it would hurt wasn't a baseless worry. *Hurt* was the least of it—he'd be torn to pieces, rent asunder, his whole body split apart. But thinking how Mo Ran had taken care of him, Chu Wanning mustered up courage from who knew where—or perhaps he'd always been able to steel himself so ruthlessly—and bent down to try.

Mo Ran panicked. It was hard enough for him to maintain control as it was. If Chu Wanning really took him into his mouth, he feared the last of his gentleness would be reduced to ash by the flames of lust. A man entirely at the mercy of his desire was a beast devoid of reason. He knew himself—he'd crave the heights of pleasure; he'd madly take and take. He stopped Chu Wanning, voice ragged, "Don't, Wanning. You... You..."

"It's fine, I'm only doing the same as you."

"You can't." Mo Ran's voice was like water on the verge of boiling. He swallowed. "I won't be able to stop myself."

Chu Wanning didn't understand. "Stop yourself from what?" he asked, confused.

Mo Ran cursed under his breath. He couldn't take it anymore. Chu Wanning's scent, his voice, his body were slowly prizing apart his self-imposed chains, burning him to the ground.

After catching his breath, Mo Ran abruptly stood. He turned Chu Wanning over and pinned him face down in the bedding. Before Chu Wanning could react, he felt himself shoved into the sheets with force. Mo Ran's fervid body pressed down on him, engulfing his own.

In that instant, he felt something of terrifying proportions thrust up against his ass through the layer of thin fabric. Chu Wanning cried out, a whimper softer and more lewd than he'd anticipated. His face flushed, hands wringing at the bedding as he bit his lip, refusing to make another sound.

What was it that Mo Ran couldn't stop himself from doing? Chu Wanning was beginning to understand. Mo Ran ground against him through his underclothes, the rest of his words a growl. "Stop myself from wanting to put it in, from wanting to fuck you—how have you not realized..."

Those scalding breaths fell upon the shell of Chu Wanning's ear. Mo Ran braced one strong arm on the bed and wrapped his other around Chu Wanning's hips, thrusting forward and panting roughly. After a moment of ineffectual grinding, Mo Ran patted Chu Wanning's rump and said, "Press your legs together."

Mind a haze, Chu Wanning did as he was told, but he didn't feel Mo Ran move. As he made to turn around, he felt something hot, hard, and thick thrust between his thighs. The sensation ripped a gasp from him, eyes losing focus as his scalp prickled.

Mo Ran pulled his underclothes away to reveal his fully erect cock, flushed dark from arousal and leaking clear fluid at its tip. It pressed between Chu Wanning's thighs, surrounded by the slick, soft heat of the flesh there. Mo Ran groaned in pleasure. Gripping Chu Wanning's waist, he drove his hips forward, fucking into Chu Wanning's thighs.

"Ah..."

Chu Wanning had never even imagined such a thing was possible. That thickness rubbed obscenely against him, pulsing as it ground between his legs. Chu Wanning was going limp, his straight spine melting as his eyes went glassy. He was delirious; he couldn't sense a thing beyond the sharp thrill of the man he loved thrusting against him. He gasped for breath in silent pants, turning his face and burying it in the bedding, his hair falling loose...

Mo Ran's cock rubbed several times against his entrance. If he lined it up and pressed in, he could wholly take his shizun, he could have this unyielding man beneath him. Inflamed by the threat of being overpowered, being run through, Chu Wanning's spent cock hardened once more alongside Mo Ran's quickening pace. Mo Ran's hips snapped against his, his movements fierce and fervent, unbridled and insatiable. The slap of flesh on flesh echoed in the room; with each thrust, coarse hair rubbed against the tender skin of Chu Wanning's thighs, the abrasion driving him further and further into rapture.

"Shizun, tighten up... Ah..."

The pleading voice of the man behind him was so low, so thick with desire—what could he do but obey?

"Yes...just like that... Even tighter... *Fuck*..."

Mo Ran's reason was drowned beneath the rising tide of lust. In the heat of the moment, carnal instinct gradually swallowed him; he arched his neck, swallowing with difficulty.

"Shizun...baby...you're so hot inside... Ah... Mn..."

He was referring to the space between his legs, but those words still sounded unbearably vulgar. Those low, absorbed mumblings, that crass and crude language—yet somehow, none of it seemed dirty. Chu Wanning thought perhaps he'd lost his mind. As he listened to Mo Ran's panting, he felt feverish, his thoughts spinning out of his control. "Is it good?" he asked softly.

"Yeah..." When Mo Ran opened his eyes, they were bright and wild. He bent, broad shoulders enfolding Chu Wanning as he held him steady. He pressed him into the bed, their bodies inseparable, his hips still thrusting, frantic heat washing over them both.

He sought Chu Wanning's mouth, seizing him by the jaw to kiss him with a desperate hunger. Their tongues entwined, sliding wetly.

Mo Ran's cock pushed between Chu Wanning's legs, thrusting with such force that it sent the bed swaying. It strove to press deeper, Mo Ran's toes going white with the exertion in the bedsheets.

Under this brutal onslaught, Chu Wanning felt as if he really were being taken. Cloaked in the night's darkness, he let himself fall prey to his basest urges without shame, tilting his head to return Mo Ran's passionate kisses, saturated with adoration.

In this position—on all fours, with his head wrenched back—he looked debauched beyond measure, a wanton and tempting sight. Between the pounding of his heart and the fervor of the kiss, he couldn't catch his breath. Dizzy, Chu Wanning glimpsed another fragmented scene—

Where it was, he didn't know. But he was also on a bed, a very wide one, spread with bloodred sheets. Their legs were tangled, their breaths coming fast. Sweat steamed from their skin, heady with desire.

They were in the same position: Mo Ran was fucking him from behind, grabbing his jaw to kiss him. But in this scene, his body had been stretched open, that massive cock pushing fiercely into him. Chu Wanning didn't know how long Mo Ran had been fucking him like this—there seemed to be some salve, so it didn't hurt as much. All was hot and wet as Mo Ran drove hard against a bundle of nerves deep inside him.

"Ah... *Ah...*"

Someone was moaning, panting, whining, their voice weakened to a whisper. Who was it? Was it *him*?

Mo Ran pounded into him with no sign of stopping; instead, he slowly increased his pace. Chu Wanning's body was filled to bursting and flooded with pleasure; he felt he was being speared through, yet somehow it felt so good. He was addicted to this feeling, like he'd been trained for it, legs going limp as Mo Ran fucked into him while still instinctively pushing back, grinding against Mo Ran and taking him deeper yet.

The discomfort he felt was indescribable—it was as though there was an insatiable flower pistil inside him that only sex could gratify; it was like the strongest aphrodisiac in the world, capable of destroying the mightiest men. He was falling into pleasure, reciprocating it; gripped by ecstasy, a low whine escaped his throat.

Who was it... What a strange scene... Such a bizarre dream... illusion...reality...

What was this, really?

"Chu Wanning, does it feel good when I fuck you?"

"You look like such a slut when you're taking me like this."

"Relax, you're squeezing me too tight..."

"I'll come inside you, come for you... Ah..."

Everything was disjointed, unintelligible, surreal; yet it seemed to have happened just this way.

What was going on...

That man's voice sounded like Mo Ran's, but not the Mo Ran he knew. Mo Ran had never spoken in such a twisted way, never... Chu Wanning couldn't hear clearly... It probably wasn't real...

His head was swimming, his thoughts a mess.

As the night wore on, the snapping of Mo Ran's hips grew rougher, more fevered. He braced his feet against the bed, heaving for breath, the pillows and blankets a disheveled snarl. Finally, Mo Ran pulled Chu Wanning into a bruising embrace. They were like rutting beasts, the one on top craving an ardent kiss, the one beneath yearning to entwine with sloppy urgency.

"Wanning... Shizun..." Mo Ran's voice was hoarse and low, mad with love and desire. "Baby..."

Hands kneading Chu Wanning's waist, Mo Ran's full buttocks tensed ferociously as he bucked forward. He was close to climax, his gaze almost vicious. After burying himself between Chu Wanning's thighs with such intensity it seemed like he might shatter him completely, he grabbed the man in his arms, biting and sucking at his earlobe, his nape.

Mo Ran pressed his heaving chest to Chu Wanning's sweat-soaked back, his lucidity hanging by a thread. With a low grunt, nearly undone by the pleasure, he reached down to guide his thick cock, throbbing with need, to Chu Wanning's entrance.

Now having experienced the full ferocity of Mo Ran's arousal, Chu Wanning finally began to panic. Spine tingling, he cried in protest, "Didn't you say you wouldn't put it in? Hold—hold on—"

Breaths heavy, Mo Ran kissed his neck. He swallowed, then turned to whisper against his cheek. "Don't worry, I won't. But..." This was all the control Mo Ran had left. "I want to come, right... here." He pressed the smooth head of his cock against Chu Wanning's clenching hole.

Mo Ran swore under his breath, then pushed himself between Chu Wanning's legs with renewed violence, that sense-shattering pleasure building to its peak. Stroking himself, he pressed his cock flush against Chu Wanning's hole and released everything with a growl. Spurt after spurt covered that tight furl, dripping down Chu Wanning's thighs and smearing onto the sheets. The sight was unspeakably obscene as the musky smell of sex filled the room.

Chu Wanning shook minutely, shivering under Mo Ran's climax. Reaching down, Mo Ran wrapped his fingers around Chu Wanning's stiff cock. He stroked him off, his touch tender but insistent.

Shame overwhelmed Chu Wanning. "No more..." he mumbled, face flaming. "Stop touching me... I've already..."

Eyes sparkling, Mo Ran whispered in a voice soft with infatuation, "Mn, I know you already came."

Chu Wanning was more stubborn than anyone. He snapped, teary-eyed, "Don't... Don't say that word."

"What word?"

Chu Wanning pressed his lips together.

"Oh." Mo Ran gave him a broad smile. "Okay." He kissed him, his hand never stopping for a moment. "Shizun, I want to see you climax again."

"Mngh..."

Chu Wanning was at the mercy of this young man's skills, swiftly brought to a second orgasm. This kind of drawn-out pleasure was more than he could endure, to say nothing of how his mind had felt fogged this whole time, fragmented scenes swimming across his vision as voices echoed in his ears. He felt so drained, so sleepy...

"Wanning."

He heard Mo Ran calling out to him from behind, so gentle, tender, adoring.

Their most primal urges sated, the two gradually caught their breath. Mo Ran caressed him, kissed him, thanked him, drawing him into his arms as if protecting a great treasure.

Chu Wanning, delirious and naked, stared blankly into the night, resting his cheek on Mo Ran's broad chest. At last, he slowly closed his eyes and fell into sleep.

When Chu Wanning awoke the next morning, the early light had snuck into the room through a crack in the window. He could hear rain drumming down on the roof tiles; the downpour hadn't let up.

His head ached dully. Scattered images from the night before flashed through his mind like the glint of fish scales in a dike, glimmering as they rose and fell in the water. He cast his mind after them, but those scales sank deeper and deeper, swallowed by the darkness.

Suddenly he stiffened, cheeks blazing. He recalled what he and Mo Ran had done last night. His first thought was to get up, but Mo Ran was still holding him, sturdy arms wrapped around him, and chest pressed to Chu Wanning's spine as it rose and fell evenly. He was still asleep.

So Chu Wanning waited, just like that, for who knew how long. Time felt unclear in that darkened room. It must have been a long time—long enough that his arms seemed to go numb, and his pounding heart gradually slowed. Long enough that it no longer felt so embarrassing.

He finally turned to gaze at Mo Ran's sleeping face.

Mo Ran was undeniably handsome. Such arresting looks were rare in this world: his brows, nose, and lips were all as beautiful as they could be. But just now, his brows were knit tight, as if something weighed heavy on his mind. Chu Wanning watched him silently for a long time. At last he couldn't resist. Very gently, he kissed Mo Ran on the cheek—the first time he'd taken the initiative to do so.

He nudged Mo Ran's arms aside and swung his legs over the edge of the bed, pulling on his underclothes, then reaching for his pristine white robes. They were covered in suggestive wrinkles—Chu Wanning tried to smooth them out to no avail. He had no choice but to put them back on and pray no one from Sisheng Peak would notice. He fixed his lapels, lost in thought.

Warm arms came around him from behind. Chu Wanning jolted, though it only translated to a brief pause in his movements.

Mo Ran had woken some time ago. He sat up to hug Chu Wanning and kissed his earlobe. "Shizun…"

He didn't know what to say. This was their first true morning-after in this life—even Mo Ran was struggling with the awkwardness of a newlywed, to say nothing of Chu Wanning. He let the silence stretch for a long moment before he softly said, "G'morning..."

"Morning? It's late." Chu Wanning put on his clothes without turning.

Mo Ran smiled. He reached out, helping Chu Wanning straighten the pendant around his neck. "This is for expelling cold; it has to be worn against the skin or it's no use." His voice was slightly hoarse.

Struck by a late recollection, Chu Wanning whirled to face him. Last night as they'd made love, he'd felt something fastened around Mo Ran's neck, but he'd been too dizzy to get a good look. Now, he saw it was a dragonblood crystal pendant, the exact twin of his own.

"Didn't..." Chu Wanning's jaw dropped. "Didn't you say at Rufeng Sect that this was the last one? Then how—"

He fell silent as Mo Ran smiled back at him, dimples tucked softly into his cheeks, his eyes gentle. In a flash, he understood Mo Ran's little act of selfishness back then. Chu Wanning turned without another word, flustered, and bowed his head as he fiddled with his clothes. "We should go back soon." He didn't look at Mo Ran. "Any later and someone will notice."

Docile, Mo Ran replied, "Of course—whatever you say, Shizun."

But in the next moment, a devious heat flared in his chest once more. Grabbing Chu Wanning, who'd already pulled on his boots and was ready to stand, he nuzzled close and pressed a sweet kiss to his lips.

"Don't be mad. I'll have to hold back once we return; I just want something to remember this by." Mo Ran grinned, forestalling whatever Chu Wanning was about to say with a finger to his lips. "Shizun, you're the best."

That sentence left Chu Wanning wandering in distraction until they passed back through the mountain gates. He didn't think those words applied to him. It was Mo Ran who was the best. This young man was handsome, gentle, and loved him with an all-consuming focus. Sometimes, even Chu Wanning felt it couldn't be real. Mo Ran was too perfect—how could he belong to someone as boring as himself? A man who couldn't even muster a single soft endearment.

But when Mo Ran looked at him, his expression was earnest, without the slightest hint of falsehood. When Mo Ran kissed him, he was so passionate, as if he'd handed control of his every breath to Chu Wanning, along with everything else. Last night, though Chu Wanning's actions had been clumsy and his words dry, and his mind had sometimes wandered... Mo Ran hadn't been put off by any of it. When he woke in the morning, he still wanted to kiss Chu Wanning's lips and say, *You're the best*.

"Shizun."

"Mn?"

Returning to his senses, Chu Wanning saw Mo Ran waving at him from beneath a red haitang-patterned barrier. "Where are you going? Let's go this way—the Red Lotus Pavilion's over there, but let's eat at Mengpo Hall before you go back."

In the dining hall, Mo Ran sat across from him as usual. But with a constant stream of passersby chatting around them, they became self-conscious. They kept their heads down and applied themselves to their meal in silence.

Those disciples who liked betting on Chu Wanning whispered among themselves. "Why isn't the Yuheng Elder talking to Mo-shixiong today?"

"Never mind talking, he's not even looking at him."

"That's weird. Mo-shixiong isn't putting food in the Yuheng Elder's bowl either. Isn't he normally really clingy...? What happened, did they fight?"

"Would you still sit at the same table as your shizun after a fight?"

"Ha ha, fair enough."

They saw Chu Wanning stand up to fetch another helping of congee. When that white-clad figure swept past them, those busy-bodies fell silent, keeping their heads down and their mouths busy with their steamed buns. Only once Chu Wanning sat back down did they start chittering like rats once again.

"Have you noticed? There's something off about the Yuheng Elder today."

Someone nodded. "There is! I just can't tell what—his clothes maybe?"

Six pairs of eyes snuck curious glances at Chu Wanning. Finally, one of the disciples clicked his tongue. "They're all wrinkled—they aren't as perfect as usual."

The observers all realized this was indeed the case, but no one's thoughts drifted in any untoward direction. After some back and forth, they concluded that the Yuheng Elder must have dealt with some demons in the forbidden area of the backwoods last night, or patched up a small Heavenly Rift.

These disciples admired and revered him. At most, they might find him a source of occasional entertainment. But no one had ever treated him as a man of flesh and blood, a man with his own desires. Although Mo Ran and Chu Wanning hadn't been as painstakingly careful as they might have been, although they had left behind many obvious clues, none of those disciples noticed or paid attention.

When a man was placed on a holy altar and elevated by the masses, he must be silent and unmoving, cold and aloof. The slightest blunder and everything he did would be considered wrong. That was why, much later, when Mo Weiyu and Chu Wanning's relationship was made known to the world, many felt their deity had crumbled. They were furious and disgusted, finding it unbelievable—*unacceptable.*

No one remembered that to raise someone to the heights of worship—demanding he take every step along the path the masses dictated, demanding he live only according to the whims of the people, refusing to let him show the slightest hint of selfish desire—was, at its core, an act of cruelest coercion.

118 THE HUSKY & HIS WHITE CAT SHIZUN

190

Shizun's in Seclusion Again

AFTER THAT DAY, Chu Wanning and Mo Ran had no more opportunities to meet in private. The rain that had started that night continued to plague Sichuan, uncanny in its perpetuity. Dead fish and shrimp floated on the surging rivers outside Baidi City, and aquatic beasts dragged themselves up the riverbanks and roamed the city streets. The elders and disciples of Sisheng Peak were dispatched on endless exorcism missions that sent them rushing from village to village. Both Chu Wanning and Mo Ran were powerful cultivators, and Xue Zhengyong didn't waste their abilities by doubling them up. One was sent off to Three Gorges, while the other went to Yizhou.

Countless beasts had been trapped within the Golden Drum Tower over the centuries of Rufeng's existence. In a single day, all had been unleashed upon the world again, creating chaos everywhere. Outside of Sichuan, grisly cases of demon beasts killing and eating civilians cropped up even in the once-peaceful lands under protection of the upper cultivation realm: Yangzhou, Leizhou, Xuzhou. The sects sent so many members that the investigation into Xu Shuanglin's whereabouts slowed to a crawl.

Mo Ran was possessed of astonishing spiritual energy and had plenty of experience exorcising demons. He settled the case in Yizhou in just four days and hurried back to Sisheng Peak. Upon hearing that Chu Wanning had returned as well, he was naturally delighted. He rushed to the Red Lotus Pavilion without stopping to rest.

He found its doors were shut tight against him. On inquiry, Xue Zhengyong replied in confusion, "Yuheng's cultivating in seclusion—didn't he tell you?"

"Again?" Mo Ran was shocked. "Was Shizun injured?"

"What do you mean? It's because of his cultivation method—he has to go into seclusion every seven years. You helped take care of him last time. Have you already forgotten?"

Mo Ran had. At that time, he had only been Chu Wanning's disciple for around six months. Chu Wanning had explained he'd been reckless when cultivating in his youth and injured himself. Though it wasn't a serious ailment, it required him to cultivate in seclusion for ten days once every seven years. During those ten days, Chu-zongshi's cultivation withered, leaving him powerless, a mere mortal. He had to meditate in silence for his body to recover, and only left that state for two hours each day, during which he could drink some water and eat a little. Other than that, he absolutely mustn't be disturbed or, heaven forbid, injured. To that end, Chu Wanning surrounded the Red Lotus Pavilion with the most powerful barriers he possessed before beginning this ritual, allowing only Xue Zhengyong, Xue Meng, Shi Mei, and Mo Ran to enter and see him safely through this challenging period.

The last time Chu Wanning had gone into seclusion, tensions between teacher and student were high from the flower-plucking incident. Mo Ran had just been punished and felt horribly disillusioned, so he hadn't cared for Chu Wanning during his seclusion at all. He had instead run off to help his uncle tidy the library. As he thought back on it, unease rose in Mo Ran's heart. "I'll go see him," he hastily said.

SHIZUN'S IN SECLUSION AGAIN ●—○ 121

"There's no need," said Xue Zhengyong. "Before he went in, he said we would do the same thing as the last time. Xue Meng will stand guard for the first three days, Shi Mei the next three, and you'll only need to do the last four."

"I just want to see him..."

"What for?" Xue Zhengyong smiled. "Didn't Meng-er and Shi Mei handle it perfectly well the last time? What're you so concerned about? Besides, if you go while Meng-er's there, you know he'll end up talking to you. We can't disturb Yuheng with the racket."

Mo Ran agreed and promised to wait. But he couldn't sleep that night. The thought of Xue Meng and Chu Wanning alone together in the Red Lotus Pavilion made his heart twinge with an unbearable jealousy. Of course he knew Xue Meng was an innocent soul with no interest in men, but he was bothered and uncomfortable—he just *was*. After tossing and turning half the night, he only managed to sleep for a handful of hours before daybreak.

Upon waking, Mo Ran felt he couldn't go on like this. He desperately wanted to see Chu Wanning, even if only a peek from a distance.

The Red Lotus Pavilion was closed and sealed with barriers, but Mo Ran was Chu Wanning's disciple—the barriers couldn't stop him. The door of green bamboo was basically decorative. Using his qinggong, Mo Ran pushed off his toes in a leap that landed him nimbly within the courtyard.

It was always Chu Wanning's way to meditate in one of the green bamboo pavilions built over the lotus pond. Mo Ran reasoned this time would be no different. He sought out that elegant pavilion rising over the rippling waters and the lotus leaves, its gauze hangings fluttering in the wind. As expected, Chu Wanning sat in the center, white robes a pool around him.

Xue Meng stood at his side. The sun was shining brightly, and he had tied up one of the snowy gauze panels so the sunlight could warm his shizun as well. The wintry morning light spilled into the pavilion, shining down on Chu Wanning's pallid face. A flush slowly appeared on his cheeks as he sensed the warmth even in his trance.

After a while, the repeated rounds of internal energy circulation left sweat beading on Chu Wanning's brow. Xue Meng wiped it for him with a snowy handkerchief kept nearby. Once done, he felt compelled to look up. "That's weird," he mumbled, glancing left and right. "Why does it feel like someone's glaring at me?"

Mo Ran wasn't glaring. He was staring. He looked calm, but his heart was thundering. Hadn't Xue Meng spent a fraction too long wiping Chu Wanning's brow with the handkerchief? Hadn't he been a little too close, his gaze a little too intimate? He silently heaped all sorts of baseless accusations upon Xue Meng's head. He *was* frustrated, he *was* annoyed.

Mo Ran couldn't bear another minute of it. Why should he make himself suffer like this? He turned to leave. But in his preoccupation, he failed to muffle his footsteps.

Xue Meng instantly hurled a cold-glinting throwing star filled with spiritual energy toward the sound. "Who's there?!" he cried.

The throwing star was nothing; Mo Ran could catch it bare-handed. But Xue Meng's shout made his heart jump up into his throat. He hastily leapt from the bamboo forest and over the lotus pond, landing softly within the pavilion.

Xue Meng's eyes widened in shock. "What are you—"

"Shh." Mo Ran slapped a hand over his mouth, keeping his voice at a whisper. "Why are you so loud?"

"*Mmmph!*" Xue Meng struggled before finally tearing himself from Mo Ran's grip. Face flushed, he swiped at his tousled hair in a huff and snapped, "You've got some nerve asking me that! What were you looking at, skulking around like a thief in the forest?"

"I didn't want you to start shouting—like you are right now."

"It's not like Shizun can hear!" Xue Meng exclaimed. "There's a silencing spell at work! Can't you see Shizun's already cast it on himself? Unless you undo it, he won't hear you even if you scream into his ear..."

Xue Meng kept babbling as Mo Ran blinked in astonishment. "Silencing spell? Then why did Uncle say he didn't want me to disturb you two?"

"Dad probably thought you were too tired after returning from Yizhou and wanted you to rest," Xue Meng said in exasperation. "And you believed him? Why didn't you take a moment to *think*— when has Shizun ever not cast the silencing spell on himself so we'd feel more relaxed around him? You're seriously so stupid."

Mo Ran was speechless.

Seeing that Mo Ran was about to sit down, Xue Meng stopped him. "Oi, what d'you think you're doing?"

"In that case, I'll stay here too."

"Who wants *you* to stay? It's *my* turn for the first three days—are you trying to be a shizun's pet again? Go away, don't try to take my job."

"Can you even take care of him by yourself?"

"Of course I can. It's not my first time watching over Shizun when he's in seclusion."

Faced with Xue Meng's indignation, there wasn't much more Mo Ran could say. He turned to leave, then stopped as he glimpsed a cup of tea on the table. The leaves were wide and dark, the scent delicate and pleasing. "Frost fragrance tea from Kunlun?"

"Huh? How could you tell?"

Of course he could tell. This was Xue Meng's favorite tea. Xue Meng loved to bring Shizun all his favorite things without bothering to consider if those things suited his shizun, or if Chu Wanning liked them.

"Frost fragrance tea is chilling by nature, and Shizun is sensitive to the cold. Won't he feel ill if you bring him such tea?"

Xue Meng froze, face pink. He explained helplessly, "I didn't think that far, I just know frost fragrance is a fine tea, I..."

"Switch it out for Bengal rose tea and add two spoonfuls of honey. Wait until he wakes up to steep it. I'll go make some desserts now—I'll bring them over once they're ready."

Eager to salvage his dignity, Xue Meng hastily retorted, "He can't have sweets. He needs to fast for all ten days."

"I know, but Uncle said he can eat a little." Mo Ran waved his hand and left the pavilion. "See ya."

Xue Meng stared at his retreating figure, lost in thought. Once Mo Ran was out of sight, he lowered his head and snuck a look at the nape of Shizun's neck. He had noticed a faint bruise there yesterday. In the afternoon sunlight, it was clearer still. It didn't look like a mosquito bite, and neither was it a wound.

He wasn't a teenager anymore. Perhaps he lacked certain experiences, but that didn't mean he hadn't heard of them. This mark on Chu Wanning's neck made him deeply uneasy. He picked through all sorts of clues, returning to the sounds he'd heard that day in the backwoods. He'd always told himself it was the sound of the wind—nothing but the wind. Yet a vague foreboding rose in his heart once more. Beneath the winding tendrils of fog, a very colorful idea gradually took shape. In the warm sunlight, Xue Meng suddenly felt chilled for some reason. He shuddered, frowning.

Xue Meng couldn't shake his unease. On the sixth day of Chu Wanning's seclusion, he made up his mind: he was going to spy on Mo Ran.

It was the last day Shi Mei was watching over Chu Wanning. Mo Ran was due to swap with him at midnight, but he had eaten dinner at Mengpo Hall early, then gone up to the Red Lotus Pavilion with a box of sweets.

Xue Meng hadn't expected him to change places with Shi Mei before the agreed time. Leaving his food unfinished, he snuck out behind Mo Ran, tailing him all the way to the doors of the Red Lotus Pavilion. Xue Meng hesitated a moment, then copied Mo Ran's move from a few days ago and hopped over the wall.

The sun had set, and the crescent moon was climbing the horizon. The sky had washed away its brilliant makeup, leaving a last smear of red at the corners of its eyes. The glory of that dazzling dusk had retreated almost fully, its paints and powders swallowed by the dark of night, the starry sky clear as water.

Mo Ran, holding the food box, spotted Shi Mei in the distance. His back was to Mo Ran; oblivious to his approach, Shi Mei walked into the pavilion and stopped before Chu Wanning.

Mo Ran smiled. But as he made to wave and call out, he saw a cold gleam in Shi Mei's hand, pointing directly at Chu Wanning, still in his trance. Something flickered in Mo Ran's head. "Shi Mei!" he shouted. A chill crawled up his spine, setting his hair on end. He'd said too many final farewells in both lifetimes; to this day, the slightest rustle would put him on high alert. As the saying went, a burned child would dread even painted flames.

The Red Lotus Pavilion had once held Chu Wanning's corpse for two full years, until the day Mo Ran died. He didn't care for this place. When he came here, he always saw flashes of those last few months of his past life, when Chu Wanning had lain amongst the lotuses with his eyes closed, chest unmoving. Subconsciously, Mo Ran thought of the Red Lotus Pavilion as a cursed place, a bottomless maw that might devour the last spark of flame in the world.

Shi Mei turned, lowering his hand and tucking that silver light within his sleeve. "A-Ran? Why are you here early?"

"I—" Mo Ran's heart pounded. He couldn't breathe or think, brows sharply drawn together as he asked, "You're holding..."

"Holding what?" Confused, Shi Mei raised his hand. In his palm lay a silver comb, inlaid with crushed spiritual stones with the power to smooth meridians.

Mo Ran was speechless. After a long pause he managed, "You're... combing Shizun's hair?"

"Mn. Is something the matter?" Shi Mei scanned him from head to toe, then knit his slender brows. "You're so pale, did something happen?"

"No, I just..." He trailed off, his face going from white to red. Thankfully it was dark, so his flush wasn't obvious. After a moment, Mo Ran turned aside and cleared his throat. "It's nothing."

Shi Mei watched him silently. Then, something seemed to click— he looked stunned. "Did you think..." he began hesitantly.

"I didn't," Mo Ran hastened to say. Shi Mei was so good to him, someone he saw as family. Mo Ran was dismayed at his own momentary suspicion. He blurted his response out of guilt.

Shi Mei paused. At last, he said, "A-Ran."

"Mn?"

"I hadn't even finished my sentence." Shi Mei gently cleared his throat. "You didn't have to deny it so quickly."

So Shi Mei had realized that, for a moment, Mo Ran had taken the silver comb he held for a weapon. It was the lingering terror of seeing Chu Wanning die in two lifetimes. No matter who might have been standing there with their back to Mo Ran, even if it had been Xue Meng or Xue Zhengyong, Mo Ran would have no doubt felt the same shock of fear.

But as Mo Ran faced Shi Mei, he steadied himself, though his heart still twisted in his chest. "Sorry," he said, lowering his lashes.

The Shi Mei he knew had always been gentle and kind to everything and everyone. He was rarely indifferent or harsh. But that night, by the lotus pond, Shi Mei watched Mo Ran in silence for a very long time.

The night wind rose. The lotus leaves curled on the water, their blossoms swaying.

"I won't even bring friendship into it but—A-Ran, we've known each other almost ten years. How can you think so little of me." His voice was soft, devoid of hostile fury or woeful hurt. Mo Ran looked into his eyes, twin pools of clear spring water that seemed to have seen everything, yet refused to bicker or complain.

Shi Mei passed Mo Ran that gleaming silver comb and said mildly, "Before Shizun entered the trance, he asked me to tie up his hair. Since you're here, you can do it."

"Shi Mei..."

But that tall and beautiful man had already strode past him. His steps were unhurried, but he didn't once look back as his solitary figure left the rustling leaves of the Red Lotus Pavilion behind.

Shizun, Xue Meng and I...

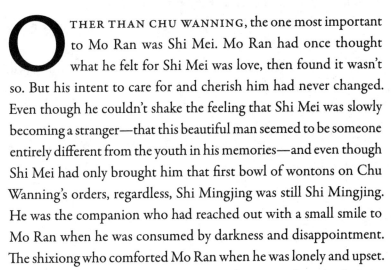

OTHER THAN CHU WANNING, the one most important to Mo Ran was Shi Mei. Mo Ran had once thought what he felt for Shi Mei was love, then found it wasn't so. But his intent to care for and cherish him had never changed. Even though he couldn't shake the feeling that Shi Mei was slowly becoming a stranger—that this beautiful man seemed to be someone entirely different from the youth in his memories—and even though Shi Mei had only brought him that first bowl of wontons on Chu Wanning's orders, regardless, Shi Mingjing was still Shi Mingjing. He was the companion who had reached out with a small smile to Mo Ran when he was consumed by darkness and disappointment. The shixiong who comforted Mo Ran when he was lonely and upset.

Come to think of it, Shi Mei was also an orphan; he had no family in the world. Though Xue Meng was friendly with Shi Mei, he was proud and arrogant; in all these years, Shi Mei had never called him by name, only respectfully using the title *Young master.* The only one who could really claim to be a friend to Shi Mei was Mo Ran himself.

And yet he'd hurt him.

Hiding in the bamboo forest, Xue Meng watched for a long time with his arms crossed. Mo Ran stood unmoving, fiddling with the silver comb as if there was much on his mind.

After waiting the better part of an hour with nothing to show for it, Xue Meng started to wonder if he was the idiot. What the hell was he thinking? How could he suspect Shizun and Mo Ran were close in *that* way? Was his brain broken...? The longer he stood, the more awkward he felt and the less he could justify his actions.

At last, Xue Meng turned to leave—but these two martial siblings were cut from the same cloth. Xue Meng made the exact same mistake as Mo Ran: he relaxed and forgot to step with care.

Mo Ran leapt to his feet, voice ringing through the gauze hangings. "Who's there?"

Under the moonlight, Xue Meng reluctantly showed himself, eyes evasive. He cleared his throat.

Mo Ran stared. "What are you doing here?"

"Double standards much?" Xue Meng couldn't make himself meet Mo Ran's eyes. He spoke with such conviction, but he looked left and right, his cheeks reddening. "I just wanted to see Shizun, too."

Mo Ran abruptly realized that Xue Meng must have followed him; he froze for a moment, then adjusted his expression before Xue Meng could notice. "Since you're here, why don't you take a seat?"

Xue Meng did not refuse. He joined Mo Ran in the bamboo pavilion.

"Tea or wine?" Mo Ran asked.

"Tea," Xue Meng replied. "Wine will get me drunk."

There was both tea and wine on the table. Mo Ran set a little pot of red clay over the fire. In the darkness, its light flickered over his chiseled features. He put the eight treasures tea in the pot, then placed it on the stove. The two cousins—one sitting on the bench, one leaning against the pillar—waited for the water to boil.

"Why did you come so early?" Xue Meng asked. "Shi Mei should've stayed till midnight."

"I didn't have anything else to do, so why not." Mo Ran smiled. "Didn't you do the same?"

Thinking about it, Xue Meng had to agree. Like him, Mo Ran was probably worried about Shizun. This cousin of his had changed after the battle at the Heavenly Rift. After all these years, he was nothing like that churlish youth of the past. The disciple Chu Wanning saved at the cost of his own life had finally grown into a proper young man.

Xue Meng lowered his lashes and fell silent a moment, then smiled.

"What's up?" Mo Ran asked.

"Nothing. I was just thinking about the last time Shizun was in seclusion. You were so angry at Shizun back then. During those ten days, you only took a single glance at him before saying you weren't skilled enough to care for him and running off to help Dad in the library. I held a grudge against you for that. I never thought you'd change so much in seven years."

Mo Ran was quiet. Eventually he said, "Everyone changes."

"If you could do it over, would you still run off?"

"What do you think?"

Xue Meng thought seriously. "You'd probably try to stay with Shizun all ten days."

Eyes downcast, Mo Ran laughed.

"*Hmph,* what do you think you're laughing at?" Xue Meng shifted, placing a foot on the bench and an elbow on his knee. He let his head fall back, glancing sidelong at his cousin. "Now both of us feel the same about Shizun. Your thoughts wouldn't differ too much from mine."

Mo Ran lowered his eyes. "Mn."

Xue Meng squinted at him, then raised his eyes to the bells hanging from the corners of the eaves. "That's good. Back when Shizun passed,

I resented so much that your life was saved at the cost of his. But now that I look at it, you're not without a conscience."

Mo Ran didn't know how to respond, so he again went "Mn."

The bells tinkled in the breeze.

After some silence, Xue Meng found himself turning to Mo Ran. His eyes sparkled and his brows drew low as he said, "*Ahem*, um. I actually have a question for you."

"Go ahead."

"Tell me the truth. That day, in the backwoods, were you..."

Mo Ran knew Xue Meng had been wanting to ask this question for a long time. He'd danced around it, but couldn't escape it in the end. Mo Ran waited for Xue Meng to continue. But after hemming and hawing for half an age, his face pinking and paling in turns, Xue Meng still couldn't get the words out. He watched Mo Ran carefully as he said, "Were you two...really looking for an osmanthus rice-cake spirit?"

The water in the teapot came to a boil, sending wisps of steam spiraling into the cold night air. They locked gazes. Xue Meng's pupils were blazing, spitting fire, whereas Mo Ran's black eyes were as still as an old well, deep and unfathomable.

"Tea's ready."

Xue Meng grabbed his arm, staring into his eyes. "Were you two really looking for an osmanthus rice-cake spirit?!"

Mo Ran extricated himself from Xue Meng's hold and picked up the pot on the table. He poured two cups, then looked up. "If we weren't looking for a rice-cake spirit, what could we be doing?"

"You—"

"Shizun wouldn't lie to you. Even if you don't believe me, you should at least believe him."

Xue Meng was like a little snake caught by the throat; the hand resting on his knee tightened and he ducked his head. "I do believe him."

"Then have some tea." Mo Ran sighed. "Why are you always overthinking?" He lowered his eyes to blow at the piping-hot cup. Wreathed in the steam, his face was like a mirage—handsome yet hazy, impossible to bring into focus.

The eight treasures tea was warm and rich. Xue Meng savored it, letting its comforting heat soothe the pounding of his heart. When he finished, the cup was still warm; steam rose from its center. Head down, Xue Meng murmured half to Mo Ran and half to himself, "I overthink because I care about him so much. Really. The slightest rustle and I'm..."

"I know," Mo Ran said. "I'm the same way."

Xue Meng turned to look at him. Leaning back against the pillar with his unfinished tea, Mo Ran took another sip. "Earlier, I had a misunderstanding with Shi Mei for the same reason. At least you're better off than me. Not so impulsive."

Xue Meng's curiosity was piqued. "No wonder Shi Mei didn't say much before he left. What happened?"

"It doesn't matter." Mo Ran grimaced. "I'm even more of an overthinker than you."

Xue Meng wrinkled his nose. "He hasn't had it easy. People will eat children during a famine if they get desperate enough—if Dad hadn't rescued him, he'd've probably ended up as meat in a stew... Shi Mei's always been good to you, so you'd better not bully him."

"Mn," Mo Ran said. "I know, something just set me off earlier. It won't happen again."

The two sat in the pavilion, watching over Chu Wanning as they chatted. It was a strange experience. Mo Ran gazed at Xue Meng's handsome, arrogant face in the moonlight. This was the same man who'd carved a hole in his chest in the past life, then met him with tears and blood in every subsequent encounter. He had never expected they could talk like this, so calmly.

The moonbeams streamed down on the lotus pond as they steeped tea and warmed wine. Yes, wine. They'd finished the tea, but Xue Meng wasn't ready to leave. Mo Ran heated a pot and poured out a few cups. Just a small accompaniment to their conversation. There was no harm as long as they didn't get drunk.

Yet he seemed to have overestimated Xue Meng's tolerance. Between Chu Wanning and his three disciples, Chu Wanning could down a thousand cups, Mo Ran could acquit himself respectably, and Shi Mei was a lightweight. But Xue Meng was utterly hopeless. Two scant cups of pear-blossom white saw him dizzy and incoherent.

Wary of causing a disaster, Mo Ran hastily removed the wine from the table. Xue Meng was a little tipsy, but he wasn't that far gone. "Good, put it away," he chuckled, cheeks ruddy. "I... I've had enough."

"Mn," Mo Ran agreed. "You should hurry back to rest. Can you walk? If not, I'll send a voice message to tell Uncle to come pick you up."

"Ohh, he doesn't have to, he doesn't have to." Xue Meng waved him off with a grin. "I can walk back by myself; I haven't forgotten the way."

Skeptical, Mo Ran extended a finger in front of Xue Meng's eyes. "What number is this?"

"One."

He pointed at Chu Wanning. "Who's this?"

Xue Meng smiled. "Immortal-gege."

"...Be serious."

"Ha ha, it's Shizun! I can tell." Clutching the pillar, Xue Meng laughed.

Mo Ran frowned. This rascal's alcohol tolerance was getting worse every year. Still unconvinced, he pointed at himself. "What about me? Take a good look, don't try to be funny. Who am I?"

As Xue Meng stared at him, the years seemed to fold over themselves; Mo Ran saw that New Year's Eve at Mengpo Hall. Xue Meng had been drunk then, too. He had recognized Shi Mei, called Chu Wanning *Immortal-gege*, then burst into laughter when he looked at Mo Ran and called him a dog.

Mo Ran stared placidly back at him. If Xue Meng called him a dog again, he was prepared to pin him down and beat him up before calling Xue Zhengyong to drag the little drunkard home.

But Xue Meng only considered him for a long time, expression unreadable. In the end, his lips parted almost in a pout, as if shaping the syllable for "dog" once again.

Mo Ran raised a hand, ready to slap it over his mouth.

"Ge..."

He froze. Xue Meng gazed at him through misty eyes. Quietly, slowly, he said again: "Ge."

Mo Ran was stunned. The word was like the sting of a wasp: a stabbing pain morphing into agony, soon numb from its venom. Something was caught in his throat—he couldn't say anything as he stared at Xue Meng's face, at those young, prideful, headstrong features. Mo Ran had seen hatred, fury, and disdain on this face, but never an emotion like this.

Xue Meng touched Longcheng at his waist, inlaid with the lunar crystal Mo Ran had sent him after risking his life taking down a great spirit beast. Without this blade, he mightn't have taken first place at the Spiritual Mountain Competition. Without this blade, he might've ended up a nameless cultivator lost to the annals of time, the bearer of an eternal regret.

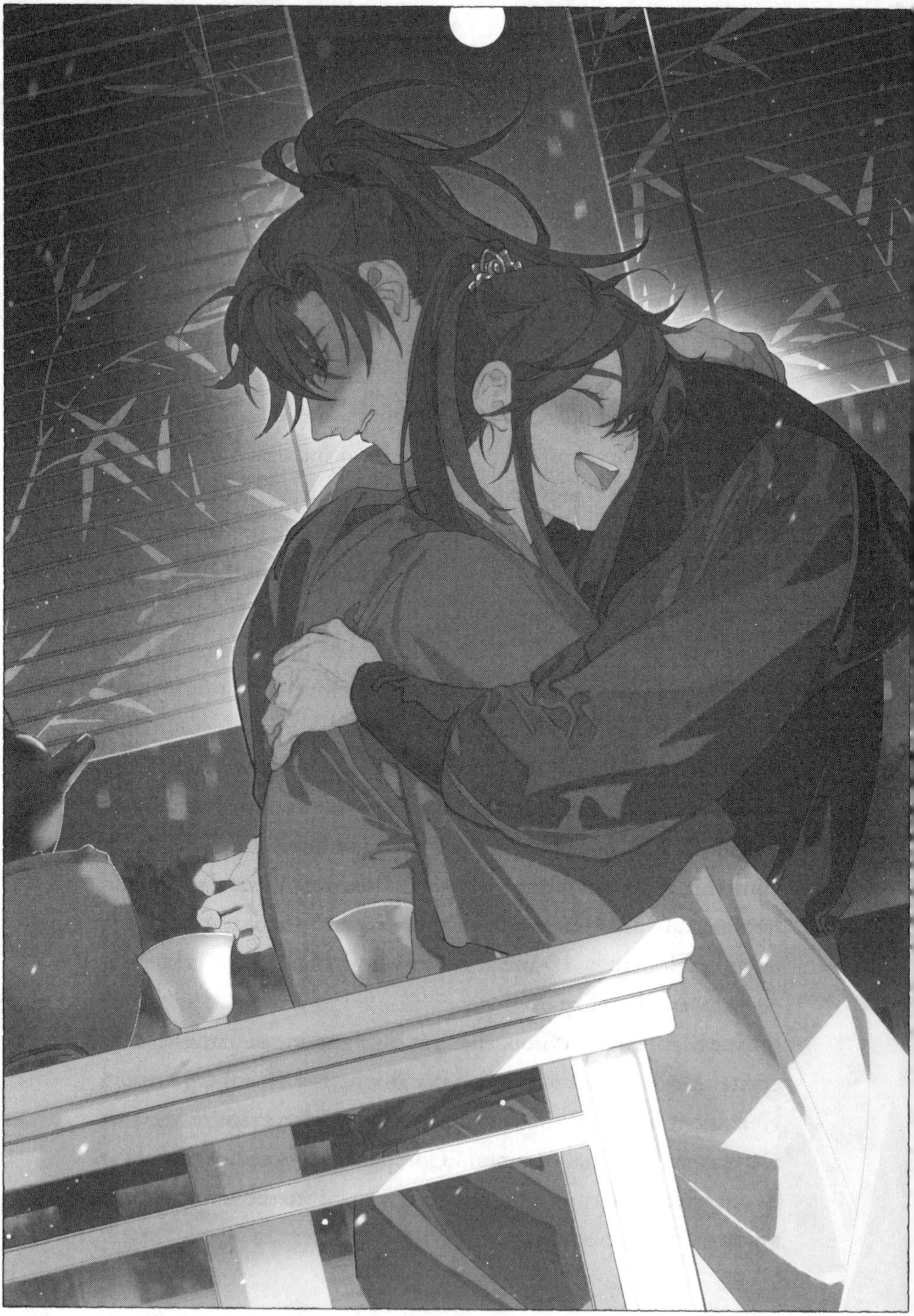

He had never properly thanked Mo Ran for the gift, for various reasons—because of his pride and because of his sense of dignity. Yet it always ate at him. Whenever he cleaned Longcheng, it weighed on his heart and mind.

After they had returned from Rufeng Sect and Xue Meng learned it was Mo Ran who saved him from Xu Shuanglin, he felt only more tormented. When he woke and heard Mo Ran and Chu Wanning were missing, he'd sobbed himself hoarse. Everyone had thought he was crying for his shizun. Only Xue Meng knew that when he lay in his sickbed that night, clutching Longcheng and gazing into the darkness, he'd rasped: "Ge, I'm sorry."

Where are you... Are you and Shizun...okay?

Mo Ran couldn't say a thing or move a muscle. He seemed to have been rooted to the spot, stock-still. Scenes from the past rushed through his mind.

Sisheng Peak in the past life, Xue Meng storming up the mountain alone to stand in the chill air of Wushan Hall. Asking, eyes red-rimmed, what he'd done with Chu Wanning.

"Mo Weiyu," Xue Meng had said. "Look back properly."

When he became Emperor Taxian-jun and Xue Meng joined hands with Mei Hanxue to attack him. In broad daylight, Mei Hanxue cut off his escape while Xue Meng roared, features twisting, driving that scimitar into his chest. Blood spraying.

"Mo Weiyu," Xue Meng had said. "You're beyond salvation; this world has had its fill of you!"

Those hateful grudges, blazing furiously as they swirled around him.

The day Chu Wanning died in this lifetime, and Xue Meng leaping up with a roar and pinning him to the wall. Pulse beating in his neck as he shouted like a trapped beast: "How could you say he didn't save you? *How could you say he didn't save you?!*"

Another flash of memory, appearing as a faint glow before him. Perhaps Mo Ran had stood stiffly for too long, long enough for those oldest, blurriest memories to creep up on him.

He saw two youths. One was skin and bones, trembling like an abandoned dog awaiting his next beating. He hunched anxiously at one of the tables in the disciples' quarters, sitting on a little stool with his hands tightly fisted over his knees, unmoving. He recognized himself.

The other youth had a complexion pure as jade or snow, precious and proud as a peachick coming into his dazzling plumage. He stood, a finely wrought scimitar at his waist and a foot propped on a nearby chair. Clear black eyes stared unblinkingly down at Mo Ran. "Mom told me to come visit you," the young Xue Meng muttered. "You're my new cousin?" He paused. "Kind of pathetic, aren't you?"

Mo Ran said nothing. He kept his head down, unaccustomed to such intense scrutiny.

"Hey, what's your name?" Xue Meng asked. "Mo...um... Mo something? Tell me, I forgot."

Mo Ran didn't answer.

"I'm asking you a question; aren't you going to say something?"

Still no answer.

"Are you mute?!"

After three attempts, the young Xue Meng burst into exasperated laughter. "They say you're my cousin, but look how timid you are. You're so frail the wind could blow you over. There's no way I have such an embarrassing gege—what a joke."

Mo Ran hung his head lower still, silent. A blur of crimson appeared before him. It took Mo Ran a moment to realize it was a stick of tanghulu. The hand that offered the sugar-coated hawthorn did it so roughly the stick nearly poked him in the nose.

"Here," Xue Meng said. "I can't eat it anyway." He had brought a box of sweets with him as well, and now tossed it carelessly on the table like a coin to a beggar.

Mo Ran could only watch in dazed shock. He thought Xue Meng too generous, impossibly generous—no one had ever offered him so much to eat at once, even if he begged on his knees. "I... This..."

"What?" Xue Meng frowned. "What do you mean—what are you trying to say?"

"Can I have the whole stick?"

"Huh?"

"Just one berry is enough...or if you can't finish it, maybe I could..."

"What's wrong with you? Are you a dog? You want to eat *leftovers*?" Xue Meng's eyes widened, his tone one of disbelief. "Of course it's all yours! This entire stick and that entire box are yours!"

The lacquered box was beautifully crafted, golden linework depicting a scene of cranes amidst clouds. Mo Ran had never seen an item of such luxury before. He didn't dare reach out, but his eyes fixed on the box with a look so intent Xue Meng's skin prickled with goosebumps. He thought he might as well open it for Mo Ran.

The rich scents of cream and fruit and bean paste wafted out with the lift of the lid, mingling under his nose. The sweets were arrayed in a neat grid of three by three, for a total of nine. Some were golden-brown and crisp, some were soft and delicate, while others were gleaming and fragile, wrapped in a beautiful translucent skin that offered a faint glimpse of the soft red bean paste within.

Xue Meng spared them scarcely a glance. He pushed the box in front of Mo Ran and said, impatient, "Go on and eat. If that's not enough, I have more. I can't finish all this, so giving it to you is perfect." The little gongzi had a bad attitude and unkind tone, constantly rolling his clear eyes in pompous disdain. But the desserts he offered were sweet and soft.

Through the bitterness and blood of another lifetime, that distant sweetness seemed to return to Mo Ran's tongue. Mo Ran gazed at Xue Meng's wine-flushed face beneath the moonlight, and Xue Meng squinted back.

After a moment, Xue Meng laughed, so tipsy even he didn't know what he was laughing at. He let go of the pillar as if to clap Mo Ran amiably on the shoulder, but his legs were unsteady. Stumbling, he fell into Mo Ran's arms. "Mmph... Ge..."

Still staring, Mo Ran slowly lowered his lashes and patted Xue Meng gingerly on the back. The evening breeze tousled his bangs, obscuring his handsome face. What expression Mo Ran wore, only heaven knew.

A long time later, when the pathetic lightweight Xue Meng had fallen asleep snoring in his arms, Mo Ran finally spoke, voice rough: "Xue Meng, I'm sorry. I'm not worthy to be your gege..."

192

Shizun Gave Me My Life

O N THE LAST DAY of Chu Wanning's seclusion, an uninvited guest arrived at Sisheng Peak.

While Mo Ran was helping Chu Wanning dress, bright and early, a quick rapping came on the doors of Red Lotus Pavilion. After ten days of cultivating in a deep trance, Chu Wanning was still muzzy and disoriented. He rather indifferently said, "Please come in."

Mo Ran snorted.

"What are you laughing at?"

"Shizun set barriers at the door. Other than myself, Xue Meng, and the others, who else could come in?"

Only then did Chu Wanning remember the spells and lift a hand to release them. A panicked messenger disciple hurtled in like a headless chicken, smelling strongly of wine. "Bad news, Yuheng Elder! A powerful demon's making a mess at Loyalty Hall!"

Mo Ran and Chu Wanning exchanged a quick look and rushed out without delay.

They were still some distance away when Mo Ran caught sight of a massive gourd spinning in circles in the courtyard. A crowd of elders and disciples watched in helpless exasperation.

"...A powerful demon?" Mo Ran asked.

The fat gourd gurgled.

At the sight of Chu Wanning and Mo Ran, Xue Zhengyong's eyes brightened. He slapped his thigh. "Ah! Yuheng! You woke up in the nick of time! Thank goodness, thank goodness!"

Chu Wanning was baffled, but his features were so accustomed to indifference that even bewilderment made him look wise. "Mn?"

"Another demon that escaped the Golden Drum Tower." Xue Zhengyong grimaced, both amused and disgruntled. "It won't *leave*—the Gourd of Debauchery!"

Chu Wanning looked up at the gargantuan gourd rampaging through the courtyard. It was as tall as two men and gleamed with a pearly glow; pink fog and gouts of wine spewed from its mouth. Indeed, this was the legendary Demon Gourd of Debauchery.

"It's harmless," Chu Wanning said.

"But it forces you to drink!"

This was true. The gourd was presently chasing a group of disciples, emitting a series of incomprehensible gurgles. Whenever it caught one, a hole would appear in its side, from which it sprayed wine into its victim's mouth.

Chu Wanning was speechless.

"Apparently it only concedes to people with a better tolerance than itself," Xue Zhengyong added pitiably. "Yuheng, could you..."

Chu Wanning raised a hand to his temple as if his head ached already. Leaping down to the courtyard, he summoned Tianwen and held the willow vine out in front of the gourd.

"Stop," he said. "I'll drink with you."

The fat gourd wobbled in delight. An opening immediately appeared and shot a stream of wine at Chu Wanning's elegant face. Chu Wanning dodged it; a flare of golden light, and Tianwen had the fat gourd tightly bound.

"Why don't we try it another way? Do you have cups?"

Glug glug! It spat a small gourd ladle out of the opening, filled with clear wine.

Under the watchful eyes of the crowd, Chu Wanning sat down and started drinking with the Gourd of Debauchery.

Glug glug splat!

"Not bad. Give me another."

Splash!

"Do you have any pear-blossom white?"

Splish splash!

"Yuheng," Xue Zhengyong cried out in wonder. "Can you tell what it's saying?"

"Mn," Chu Wanning replied. "I understand something of the speech of this type of demon."

Splash! said the gourd.

Mo Ran smiled. "Shizun, what did it say?"

"It's just chatting—it said it hasn't seen the sun for a long time."

The gourd seemed ecstatic; and for whatever reason, it seemed to also understand Chu Wanning. It sidled over to pour him another brimming ladleful, all solicitousness.

"Is it pear-blossom white this time?"

Splash!

"I don't like nü'erhong."

Sploosh... The gourd dumped it out and poured another.

Everyone looked on in stunned silence. The human-demon duo drank until noon, the human sober and the demon in high spirits. As the day wore on, the crowd before Loyalty Hall swelled. Even Xue Meng and Shi Mei came to see.

As soon as Mo Ran saw Shi Mei, he recalled their earlier misunderstanding. Guilt weighed on him, and he immediately thought to apologize. But the second Shi Mei caught sight of him, he turned and left.

Xue Meng noticed too and elbowed Mo Ran. "I think he's still upset."

"Then what do I do?" Mo Ran said morosely.

"Go talk to him. You two are at odds, and I'm caught in the middle. I can't do anything," Xue Meng said. "Go on, it's not like you're helping here anyway."

Mo Ran glanced at Chu Wanning, still exchanging toasts with the wine gourd. Nothing serious was going to happen without him. "Then I'll go after Shi Mei. Stay here and watch over Shizun. If anything happens, you have to tell me right away."

It didn't take long for Mo Ran to catch up. Upon reaching the Dancing Sword Platform, Mo Ran called out: "Shi Mei!"

There was no response.

"Shi Mei!"

Finally Shi Mei came to a stop and turned, looking at him consideringly. "A-Ran, what is it?"

"Nothing..." Mo Ran waved his hands, frowning. "I just wanted to say—what happened last time. It was all my fault."

"Which time are you referring to?"

Mo Ran froze, eyes widening. "What?"

Shi Mei's expression remained blandly gentle. As the wind picked up, he tucked a lock of hair behind his ear. "Do you mean the time you thought I was going to hurt Shizun at the Red Lotus Pavilion, or the time you two wouldn't sit with me during that dinner in Yuliang Village? Or even earlier, when Shizun first woke up and I met you in Wuchang Town to bring you wine, and you barely spoke to me the whole meal. Which one do you mean?"

Mo Ran hadn't expected him to dredge up events that had happened so long ago. For a moment, he was too dazed to reply. "You... You've been angry with me all this time?"

Shi Mei shook his head. "I wouldn't say angry, but yes, it's bothered me."

Mo Ran said nothing.

"A-Ran, you've been pushing me away since Shizun came back to life."

At this, Mo Ran didn't know what to say. He *was* pushing Shi Mei away. They'd once been so close even Chu Wanning could see it clear as day. But it had always felt like something was missing. The vague understanding they'd shared when they were young had never been explicitly addressed. Later, when Mo Ran recognized his true feelings, he didn't know how to handle his relationship with Shi Mei.

He'd contemplated telling Shi Mei outright but discarded the idea. He had never confessed to Shi Mei. Nor was he entirely sure of the nature of Shi Mei's feelings for him; if he rashly ran up and said he wanted to cut any romantic ties, would it not be too abrupt, too presumptuous? In the end, he had decided to let time fade whatever it was they'd shared.

Shi Mei watched him quietly for a while before continuing. "When you first came to Sisheng Peak, I told you that I, too, was an orphan who didn't have many friends, and that from then on we'd be family."

"...Mn."

"So why have you changed?"

Mo Ran was devastated. He suddenly felt lost; why had he alienated Shi Mei so? Had he and Shi Mei exchanged more than a hundred words since his return from the ghost realm? They'd once been inseparable, but now they were drifting apart. Perhaps he'd really overdone it.

"I'm sorry," he said.

"There's nothing to be sorry for." Shi Mei looked away. "Forget it, it's fine."

"Don't be angry. If you're angry, I'll... I'll feel awful too. You've always been good to me."

Shi Mei finally showed him a faint smile. "I'm good to you, but how does that compare to Shizun?"

"That's different."

Shi Mei gazed out toward the dusky mountains in the distance. "You once told me I was good to you, that I'd brought you a lot of warmth. What about Shizun?"

"He gave me my life," Mo Ran said.

It was a long time before Shi Mei spoke. "I understand."

Mo Ran's heart ached terribly at the sight of him like this. "There's nothing to compare anyway. Everyone is different, you—"

Shi Mei didn't let him finish. He turned, the wind at his back, and patted Mo Ran's chest. "It's okay, you don't need to explain. I know what you mean. To be honest, I'm not that petty. But I really was hurt that you could think that of me."

"Mn..."

"Let's start afresh. It's water under the bridge."

Mo Ran's eyes were dark and gleaming. After a beat, he nodded and said gratefully, "Okay."

Leaning against the jade railings of the Dancing Sword Platform, Shi Mei looked especially tall and slender. He gazed out at the leaves fluttering below. The silence stretched until Mo Ran said—

"Let's head back."

"What did you want to say back then?"

They spoke at the same time. Mo Ran was confused. "Back when?"

"Before the Heavenly Rift," Shi Mei said.

Only then did Mo Ran recall the confession he'd left half-made at Butterfly Town.

"You never finished. I don't know what you wanted to say. May I ask you what it was now?"

As Mo Ran opened his mouth to answer, they heard a massive crash from the direction of Loyalty Hall. Both their faces paled. "Shizun's over there!" Mo Ran exclaimed.

Shi Mei had also lost his appetite for idle chatter. "Let's hurry back."

They turned and raced back toward the main compound, where they found yet another fat gourd in the wide courtyard of Loyalty Hall.

"What the hell is this?" Mo Ran blurted.

Xue Zhengyong covered his face. "Another Gourd of Debauchery."

"How many are there?"

"Two—one for wine and one for lust. They grow in pairs from the same stem." Xue Zhengyong looked like his head was about to explode. "The one testing Yuheng's tolerance is just the younger brother. Now the older one's here too."

Mo Ran's face was inscrutable as he worked through this new information. "If the wine gourd likes to drink, then the lust gourd..." He turned, face ashen, toward that spinning pink gourd.

"The lust gourd knows every trick of seduction on earth," Xue Zhengyong said in deep embarrassment. "It only obeys the orders of the purest people."

Mo Ran turned and shouted, "Xue Meng!"

"Why isn't Xue Meng here?" Shi Mei asked in confusion. "Where is he?"

Xue Zhengyong pointed at the lust gourd. "He's already inside undergoing the trial. He said he wanted to help Yuheng."

Mo Ran breathed a sigh of relief. "That takes care of that then. If Xue Meng doesn't count as pure, no one on earth does."

He'd hardly spoken when there was a great *boom*. They watched as Xue Meng was unceremoniously ejected from the mouth of the lust gourd and landed sprawling in the crowd. Chu Wanning, still drinking with the wine gourd, glanced over at the commotion.

"What happened?" blurted Shi Mei.

"Don't tell me that even the young master..." someone else exclaimed.

Xue Meng stumbled to his feet, coughing up a storm with his face flushed red. His eyes showed furious embarrassment as he howled at the gourd. "You—you stupid demon, y-y-you're so freakin' shameless!"

Looking back and forth between them, Mo Ran realized Xue Meng was somehow in wedding robes of red and gold. He couldn't keep the amusement out of his voice as he asked, "What happened?"

Xue Zhengyong put a hand over his face, unable to utter a single word.

"I've heard of this," Shi Mei said. "The lust gourd isn't actually lustful—it's a hopeless romantic. It wants to marry the person with the cleanest and most adoring heart in the world, someone who has no one else in their heart. Apparently, those sucked into the gourd find themselves in a wedding chamber."

"Then what?"

"The gourd's primordial spirit transforms into the image of a veiled bride or groom. Their victim needs to remove the veil with their own hands."

"Will they be blessed with the sight of the lust gourd's true face?" Mo Ran asked.

"Of course not. What they see depends on each individual. If there's someone they love, they see that person's face. If they don't, but are lustful, I heard they'll see..." Shi Mei cleared his throat. "A stunning man or woman without a stitch of clothing. Only the truly purehearted will see the lust gourd's original form."

Mo Ran glanced in some disbelief at Xue Meng, so angry smoke was practically rising from his ears. "Then what did Xue Meng see?"

There was no way Xue Meng was in love with someone, but Mo Ran refused to believe Xue Meng would've seen some nude man or woman either. Yet Xue Meng had indeed been thrown out by the lust gourd, and it was clear from the way the gourd was bouncing and rolling around that Xue Meng had been an object of *immense* entertainment.

Shi Mei couldn't bear to watch. In an attempt to spare Xue Meng some embarrassment, he began, "The lust gourd might've made a mistake—"

He never finished. Xue Meng had unsheathed Longcheng and pointed it at the gourd. "You fucking turned into *me* to seduce me!" he hollered. "You dressed an illusion of me in women's clothes! You—you garbage gourd! How dare you slander me?!"

The watching disciples of Sisheng Peak, Mo Ran included, all fell silent, trying to hold back their laughter. But it couldn't last; guffaws burst from the crowd.

The narcissistic Xue Ziming, the peacock in love with his own tail, had become the bride the lust gourd created—when Xue Meng lifted the veil, he had seen his own made-up face.

"Makes sense when you think about it." Mo Ran was trying his best not to laugh too loudly. He nodded. "I'm sure Xue Meng would be very pretty as a girl."

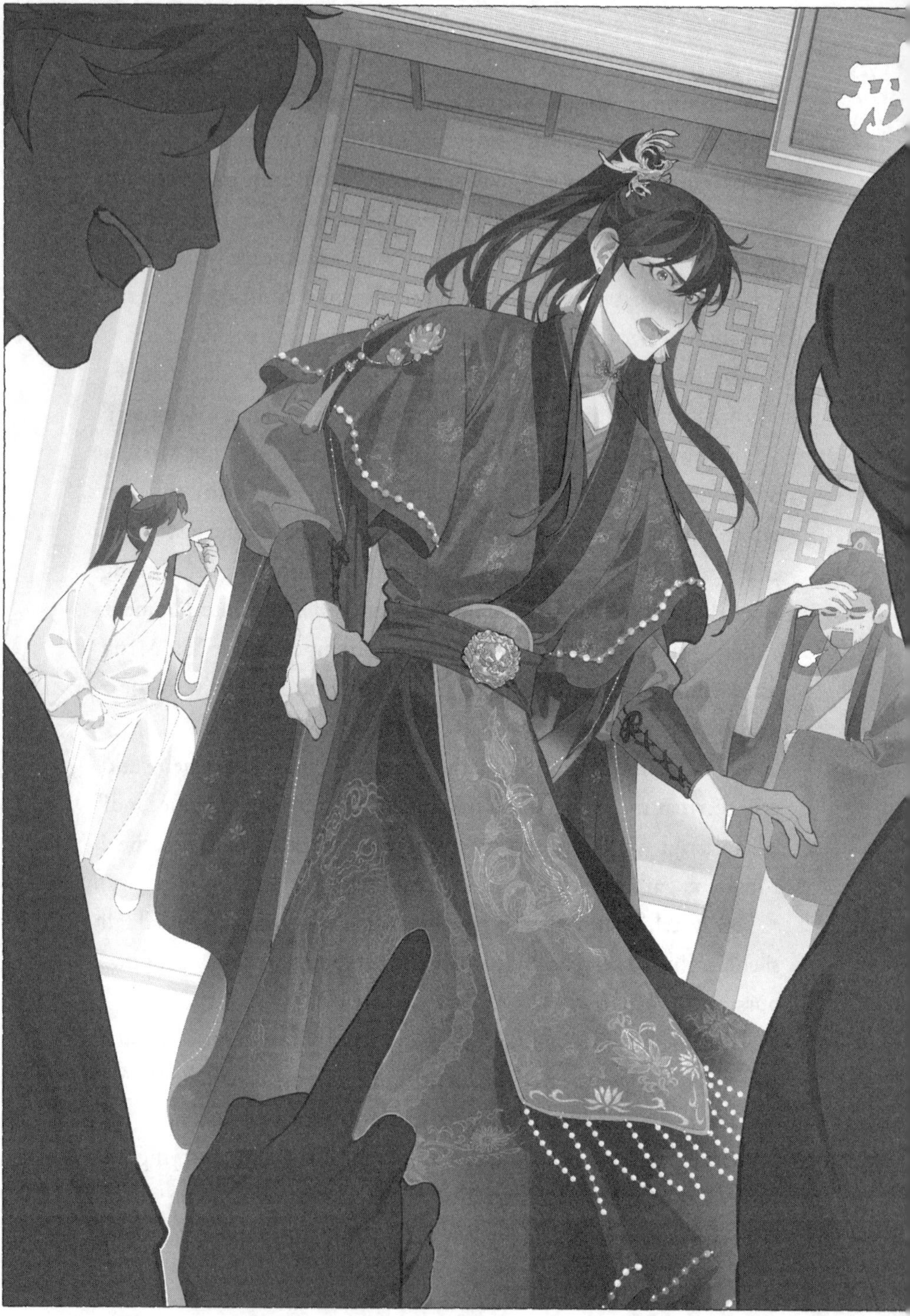

Before Mo Ran doubled over with laughter, he heard Xue Zhengyong shout once more, exasperated. "Yuheng, once you've dealt with the wine gourd, why don't you handle this one?"

193

Shizun, Did You Make Me Your Wife?

THE THREE PUREST and most arrogant people on Sisheng Peak were Xue Meng, the Tanlang Elder, and Chu Wanning. Xue Meng had already been tossed out by the lust gourd, and the Tanlang Elder hadn't always been celibate. He'd once had a wife, but her health had been poor, and she'd passed not long after the wedding. It was said the Tanlang Elder learned the healing arts so he'd never again lose those he cherished to illness.

Which only left Chu Wanning.

"The Yuheng Elder has this in the bag."

"Definitely. If the young master can't handle it, we'll have to rely on the young master's shizun."

These words needled Mo Ran, but he couldn't do a thing. He scrambled for a random solution and turned to Xue Zhengyong. "Wh-why don't I give it a try?"

Xue Zhengyong looked him up and down before tactfully replying, "Ran-er, the first condition to subdue the lust gourd is virginity."

Mo Ran didn't offer again.

Across the courtyard, Chu Wanning had successfully drunk the wine gourd under the table. It toppled over with a *thunk;* when the smoke cleared, only a small jade-green gourd remained, quiescent on the ground. Xue Zhengyong scooped up the little wine gourd and stowed it in his qiankun pouch, delighted. "Ha ha, there's really no one like the Yuheng Elder. Here, have a go at the lust gourd next."

Chu Wanning's expression was unchanged, but he lowered his lashes, refusing to meet Xue Zhengyong's eyes. "No thanks."

Xue Zhengyong gaped at him. It wasn't just him—the whole assembly of disciples and elders stood stunned. "Wh-why?"

"I've had too much to drink. I'm tired."

Xue Zhengyong wasn't stupid; it was no exaggeration to call Chu Wanning a man who could down a thousand cups. He stared long and hard at that aloof man in white, until Chu Wanning lost patience and turned away with a flick of his sleeves. Suddenly it dawned on Xue Zhengyong; he blurted, "Yuheng, don't tell me you've—"

Chu Wanning's ears flushed crimson. He turned back in a fury, phoenix eyes spitting sparks. "What nonsense are you speaking?"

Xue Zhengyong's lips couldn't even shape the words "had sex." *Impossible*, he thought. Who was Chu Wanning? Yuheng of the Night Sky, the Beidou Immortal; if *he* had any salacious encounters... No, who would believe it? Xue Zhengyong slapped his own thigh. "Then—then give it a try? Otherwise the gourd will keep wandering about here. It'll annoy us to death even if it doesn't attack anyone. The Gourds of Debauchery have thick skin. You couldn't cut through it even if you hacked at them for years at a time."

Chu Wanning scanned the crowd. The disciples all looked back at him eagerly—save for Mo Ran, who watched him with hot guilt he couldn't quite hide. Chu Wanning swore inwardly, but he was indeed stuck. If he left now with a sweep of his sleeves, there'd be talk tomorrow. After some thought, he said, "I'll give it a try, then."

In the next moment, the lust gourd sucked Chu Wanning into its hollow middle, spinning in place. The disciples of Sisheng Peak were certain the lust gourd would submit to Chu Wanning; Mo Ran alone knew the truth. On a rainy night not long ago, in the dark little room of a Wuchang Town inn, on that bed where mouths met and skin brushed, he had despoiled the purest cultivator in the world with his own hands.

Chu Wanning opened his eyes.

Contained within the gourd was a dreamlike world. Just as the legends described, a wedding chamber lay inside, red candles shining bright and bed canopies hanging low. As he stepped to the center of the chamber, he saw a rosewood bed covered with thick blankets, strewn with dates and peanuts. Every detail was rendered, from the coverlets to the hangings.

An old woman stood at the doorway, obviously an avatar of the gourd. Her hair was jade-green, and her grin revealed teeth the same hue. Chu Wanning knew he had no hope of defeating the lust gourd and preferred not to waste his breath. Taking a few steps toward the old lady, he said, "Grandmother, you can send me out now. I've no need to lift the veil."

The old woman smiled. "Mhm mhm," she mumbled.

Chu Wanning blinked. He hadn't expected the old woman wouldn't understand human speech; she wasn't as intelligent as the wine gourd and couldn't understand Chu Wanning's intentions. He had no choice—he took a breath and braced himself, then turned to the bed.

A person sat at its foot, dressed like a bride in black upper robes patterned with dragons and crimson skirts embroidered with phoenix feathers. His feet were bare, and his head was veiled, hiding his face.

The old lady tottered closer. There was a small pop as smoke rose from her hand and transformed into a jade ruyi scepter. She handed it to Chu Wanning and gestured for him to approach the bed.

The idea of Mo Ran dressed in a bridal gown hardly bore thinking about; the thought repelled him. But when he remembered how he himself had been made a ghost bride at Butterfly Town, he realized he would be missing a unique opportunity to see Mo Ran looking silly if he didn't take a peek. More than distaste was at stake—he would never forgive himself for missing such a chance.

Face green-tinged, Chu Wanning took a deep breath. He stepped forward.

The old woman seemed to be getting impatient. "Mhm mhm."

"I know, don't worry." He lifted the scepter and let the veil fall back. Chu Wanning's eyes widened slightly. "You're..."

In the crimson light of the canopy, a man in a beaded crown looked up. The candlelight played over his pale yet handsome face, his dark eyes filled with a mocking ridicule. He tilted his chin to smile up at Chu Wanning.

Chu Wanning froze.

It was indeed Mo Ran, but his face was unnaturally pallid, his complexion sickly. On the whole he appeared bizarre.

"Ah, it looks like Wanning truly can't forget this venerable one." Chu Wanning's face must have shown his shock. The man reached out and grabbed his wrist. His touch was ice-cold, and the look he pinned Chu Wanning with was a vulture's cruel glare.

Mo Ran grinned, but his smile was eerie; it held no warmth. "This venerable one is glad."

...What was this nonsense?

Chu Wanning thought with exasperation that this lust gourd

might've been locked inside Golden Drum Tower so long it had lost its mind. Its creations were incomprehensible. "Let go."

Mo Ran did not.

Chu Wanning turned to the green-haired old woman. "Make him let go."

He was still speaking when the "bride" Mo Ran shot to his feet. Chu Wanning saw the beads of his crown sway and felt a sudden grip around his waist; the world spun, and when he returned to his senses, he'd been pushed down on the red and gold bed. Mo Ran was bent over him, pinning him beneath his body as he reached down to grab his jaw.

"Looks like you really enjoyed what this venerable one offered you." The man's hot breath scalded the crook of his neck. "You *still* can't forget me..."

Chu Wanning shoved him away, brows knitting in a frown. The dialogue this lust gourd had devised was too outrageous. Mo Ran had always been gentle, courteous, and respectful toward him. Why would he ever speak like this? Awkward and amused, embarrassed yet helpless, Chu Wanning evaded his touch, making a wrinkled mess of the bedding.

Suddenly Chu Wanning narrowed his eyes, looking again at the crimson embroidery on the bed. Realization struck like lightning.

The dream.

He froze, scarlet rising in his cheeks.

This—this was the dream he'd had. Mo Ran had been just like this in those visions, his mouth full of filth and his hands rough and brutal. This wasn't an illusion the lust gourd had created whole-cloth, but something drawn from his own unspeakable imaginings. The shameful realization left him mortified. Even the tips of his ears were burning.

"Baby…"

He felt a scalding wetness. In his moment of distraction, Mo Ran had started sucking on his earlobe. He stuck his tongue greedily into Chu Wanning's ear.

"Ah…" The sensation drew an involuntary gasp from Chu Wanning. His voice was hoarse in his ears, thick with humiliated tears. Hearing it made him feel beyond disgraced.

For some reason, the scene before him felt real, as if he'd been with Mo Ran like this a very long time ago. As if they had tangled together just like this, Mo Ran pinning Chu Wanning to the bed, kissing his neck, his cheek, his ear, his movements rough and urgent.

Panicked and furious, even the ends of Chu Wanning's eyes had gone red. He struggled uselessly to break free, until Mo Ran's mouth nearly landed on his own—

Boom!

The illusory Mo Ran froze, staring disbelievingly at Chu Wanning.

Seizing his chance, Chu Wanning pushed him aside. Golden light shone in his hands; Tianwen crackled to life and slammed down on Mo Ran in the illusion.

The sight of the golden willow vine left Mo Ran stupefied. "You're…" he blurted. "You're…"

Tianwen lashed down again, showering sparks. Mo Ran took the blow without fighting back. He stared, eyes wide in abject shock.

A faint haze of smoke rose. The green old woman disappeared, as did the illusory Mo Ran. Within the wedding chamber knelt a green-haired and pointy-eared young man with exquisite features, whom Chu Wanning didn't recognize.

Still incandescent with rage, Chu Wanning rose from the bed, clutching at his gaping lapels. He glared at the little demon with eyes both sensual and furious, his voice like an angered panther, low and dangerous. "Beast," he pushed through gritted teeth.

This was the lust gourd's true form. It stared at Chu Wanning, face colorless in shock and fear. "It's you..."

Chu Wanning whipped around in rage. "What do you mean, *it's me?*"

The lust gourd had been reduced to a trembling mess. It fell to its knees, kowtowing again and again. "This junior didn't know it was..." It couldn't seem to say Chu Wanning's name. Flinching, it slammed its head against the ground. "Xianjun, please forgive me. Xianjun, please forgive me."

Chu Wanning eyed the creature. Many years ago, Chu Wanning had defeated countless demons and spirits on exorcism missions. Tianwen was infamous among their number, and several lesser spirits were known to go shocked stiff at the mere sight of him. He hadn't expected the lust gourd to be the same.

Chu Wanning recalled Tianwen and rose from the bed, staring down at the young man kowtowing on the floor. "Let me out."

"Yes, yes!"

The lust gourd didn't dare delay. It recited the incantation, and mist exploded from the ground, forcing Chu Wanning to close his eyes. When the fog cleared and he could see again, he'd returned to the courtyard before Loyalty Hall.

The crowd rushed forward and surrounded him.

"Shizun, are you alright?"

"Nobody does it like you, Yuheng!"

"Shizun, Shizun, were you injured?"

The mist smelled of rotting gourds. Chu Wanning felt dizzy, and it took him a moment to realize the giant lust demon had disappeared. In its place, on the stone slabs before him, lay a little pink gourd.

Still caught in the shame of the illusion, Chu Wanning wasn't in the mood to elaborate. He turned to Xue Zhengyong. "Take both gourds and keep them in the demon-suppressing tower."

"Okay. Um..." Xue Zhengyong's gaze fixed upon Chu Wanning. He opened his mouth and let it hang, as if hesitant to speak.

Chu Wanning had a bad feeling. "What is it?"

"Nothing."

Xue Zhengyong's expression certainly said otherwise. Chu Wanning swiftly realized everyone else was eyeing him with a barely concealed curiosity and amusement. When he turned, he found even Mo Ran watching him with an awkward look, his tanned skin flushing.

"What..." Finally, Chu Wanning realized what was happening. He looked down at his clothes.

At some point—perhaps the second he'd entered the lust gourd's bowels—his customary white had been swapped for a set of auspiciously embroidered robes like Xue Meng's. Precisely the sort of clothes worn when performing wedding bows.

Chu Wanning was left speechless.

The story of the Yuheng Elder defeating demons in wedding garb swiftly made the rounds through all of Sisheng Peak. The question most debated by the disciples was: whom had the Yuheng Elder married inside the gourd?

Someone who had their fill of living cheerfully answered, "I'm sure it was a gorgeous woman."

Someone wholly ready to die waggled their brows and added, "Who knows, it might've been a beautiful man."

Someone who cherished their life replied in all seriousness, "When he lifted its veil, the elder likely saw the lust gourd's true form.

If he saw anything else, the lust gourd would've been angered, and he wouldn't have been able to defeat the demon."

The group cast disdainful looks at this spiritless coward who cared so much about his continued existence. Shaking their heads, they left it at that.

There was one brave warrior on Sisheng Peak, however, who feared not death. One gloomy morning when morning practice was canceled, Mo Ran snuck into Red Lotus Pavilion with breakfast to canoodle with Chu Wanning.

After they ate, the man upon whom the masses had bestowed such titles as "gorgeous woman" and "beautiful man" took Chu Wanning's hand with a grin and asked, "Shizun, inside the lust gourd, did you make me your wife?"

194

Shizun, Am I Not the Ran-Mei You Love Anymore?

CHU WANNING was too full to deal with such silliness. "What's this about a wife? You're a *man,* how can you say these things without blushing..."

Mo Ran smiled more brightly. "Then, if you didn't make me your wife, did I make you mine?"

This infuriated Chu Wanning. And he wasn't just furious; he was ashamed. He couldn't tell this Mo Ran that the shape the lust gourd had taken was *that* Mo Ran, the pale-skinned phantom who appeared in Chu Wanning's dreams. Nor could he tell him about the intense, obscene entanglements they'd shared in those visions.

As the saying went, humans needed face like trees needed bark. The Yuheng Elder's dignity was of the greatest importance. Chu Wanning swept his sleeves aside and said, "If you're going to keep babbling, you can show yourself out. You're banned."

As expected, Mo Ran came to heel. Pursing his lips, he gazed woefully at Chu Wanning with dark and shining eyes, then nuzzled his cheek, voice a soft pout. "Okay, okay, I won't ask any more questions. Dear Shizun, don't chase me off."

"Stick with *Shizun,* don't call me *dear.*" Mo Ran's tender address melted Chu Wanning's heart; he couldn't bear it. Still, he pushed Mo Ran away, expressionless. "Stop with the random names."

"But just saying *Shizun* isn't affectionate at all."

"Is that so?"

Mo Ran tried to persuade him. "Look, it's boring if I call you Shizun in front of others but also call you Shizun when we're alone. Wouldn't you agree?"

Chu Wanning wasn't falling for it. "Nope."

Mo Ran tried a different tack, pulling at Chu Wanning's sleeves as he said, "Shizun, Shizun, Shizun." His tone was honey-sweet, raising the hairs along Chu Wanning's spine.

At the end of his patience, Chu Wanning smacked a book against Mo Ran's face. "Shut up."

It was a thick tome, but it struck him so lightly it didn't hurt a bit. Mo Ran lowered the book with a smile, revealing that peerlessly handsome face. "I worry if I get too used to addressing you this way, I'll do it in front of others by accident. So it's better to use a different term."

Chu Wanning frowned. "Don't you think you'll get accustomed to using a different term and use it in front of other people as well?"

Mo Ran sighed. "Why do you never take the bait?"

Chu Wanning's hackles rose at that. Displeased, he wholly turned his attention to his own book, refusing to acknowledge the disciple sprawled on the desk, idly blowing at his own bangs. After a few moments of mutual peace, Mo Ran spoke, the picture of dejection. "I just wanted some special treatment from Shizun."

"Hm?"

"Both Shi Mei and Xue Meng call you Shizun. If I also call you Shizun, there's no difference at all. I... I'm not really asking for much... I just want a different name, something only *I* can call you."

Chu Wanning set down his brush and turned to him, straightening his spine.

"It's not like I'll use it very often." Mo Ran's thick lashes were lowered, leaving a smudge of shadow on the bridge of his nose. "Only sometimes... Is that still not okay?"

Chu Wanning eyed him silently.

"It's fine." Mo Ran looked crestfallen. "I won't. It doesn't matter."

In the end, Chu Wanning relented. Not even a decade of seniority gave him the strength to endure this young man's incessant cajoling and pouting pleas.

As he studied this handsome man who grinned so brightly at his nod of assent, Chu Wanning suddenly felt he'd been tricked. It seemed he was always the fierce and intimidating one brandishing his claws, yet he always wound up conceding, indulging Mo Ran in every particular. He was like a fish swimming in circles, only to end up taking this bait named Mo Ran in the end.

"What should I call you?" asked the bait.

"Whatever you want," Chu Wanning wearily replied.

"No way! This is very important."

Mo Ran racked his brain, but his brain was lacking and rather crude besides. After thinking for some time, he ventured, "Baby?"

Chu Wanning recalled that dream and couldn't bear it. "No."

"Chu-lang?"

He couldn't abide this either. Face stormy, he asked, "Then should I call you Ran-mei?"[4]

"Ha ha, you're right." Mo Ran scratched his head with a smile, then furrowed his brow in thought once more. Unfortunately, he had overtaxed what scant inspiration he had and produced something even worse. "Chu-lang baby?"

Even Mo Ran couldn't take that one seriously. He clapped his hand to his forehead in despair.

---

4 Both -lang and -mei are terms of endearment for one's lover, primarily used for men and women respectively.

Chu Wanning smiled against his will. "You can stop trying. What's the point of thinking so hard about it? These things have to come naturally."

Mo Ran privately agreed, yet he didn't want to give up. In the end, he grinned. "Then I'll think properly about it in the future and come up with a name that suits you best."

He grabbed Chu Wanning from where he'd been tidying the books and pulled him into his lap, his hand on the back of Chu Wanning's neck. He stared at him for a long time.

Uneasy, Chu Wanning asked, "What are you doing..."

Mo Ran sighed. "I can't stop myself," he mumbled, "no matter how many times I look."

"Ridiculous... Mngh..."

Chu Wanning's lips were captured before he could say more. Mo Ran's mouth moved against his, lips deliciously sweet over the wet heat below. He wrapped the man in his lap in his arms as they kissed with consuming adoration.

Rain fell in sheets outside, drowning the shameful noises of their lips and tongues. When they parted, Chu Wanning blinked open teary eyes. He both wanted to look at Mo Ran and didn't dare.

Mo Ran smiled. He knew Chu Wanning was thin-skinned; he couldn't help pulling him close to caress him, their heartbeats pounding an interweaving duet. "It doesn't matter what I call you."

"Hm?"

"Nothing," Mo Ran said, smiling. "*Shizun* is the best."

Chu Wanning pillowed his head on Mo Ran's shoulder. There was a sweetness in the sensation, but also a certain precarity. Sitting as he was on Mo Ran's lap, he could vividly feel something hot and hard beneath. He thought smoke must be coming from his ears.

After a long pause, he whispered, "Are you really..."

Mo Ran cleared his throat. "It's nothing."

"I'll help you..." Chu Wanning's cheeks burned as he said it.

"You don't need to," Mo Ran hastily cut in. "Shizun has to go to the elder's meeting soon."

Chu Wanning glanced at the water clock. "Not for fifteen minutes, it should be..."

"It's not enough," Mo Ran said, awkward.

"Huh?"

"I can't come that quickly."

Chu Wanning stared at him. When he understood, he flushed to the roots of his hair. He quickly got up from Mo Ran's lap and took a step back. Then he felt angry with himself, thinking such behavior too cowardly. He stepped forward again.

Mo Ran found him adorable. He sat on the chair, hiding nothing; even with clothes in the way, the bulge in his pants was still shockingly ferocious, capable of taking a man's life.

"I'll stop teasing." Mo Ran caught Chu Wanning's wrist. He wanted to pull him close and kiss his mouth again, but Chu Wanning's taste was so tempting he was afraid a single indulgence would destroy his restraint. So he only held Chu Wanning's hand. He brought it to his lips, eyes fixed on Chu Wanning until the moment he lowered his lashes and kissed it sincerely.

Mo Ran licked the back of Chu Wanning's hand. "Shizun, you're so sweet."

The rain fell on Sichuan for another two weeks before the clouds broke apart for a clear, sunny day.

Mo Ran picked through the puddles in the bamboo forest, some shallow and some deep. Morning practice was back on today, but Chu Wanning hadn't appeared. A quick inquiry located him in the backwoods, where'd he apparently gone to teach a few of Xuanji's thicker disciples how to toss throwing stars.

Mo Ran heard Chu Wanning's stern voice before he saw the practice grounds. "You need to relax your hands. Hold the star between your index and ring fingers. Concentrate your spiritual energy in your fingertips. When the light glows gold, release it at your target."

Shrrrk.

The sound alone told Mo Ran the disciples had failed. They sighed piteously.

"Man, this is so hard."

"Elder, could you show us again?"

"When the light turns gold, the throwing star will grow hot to the touch," Chu Wanning said. "Feel for it, don't try to look."

"Can you hit your target without looking?"

A cheerful voice answered from behind him. "Of course you can."

Chu Wanning turned. "What are you doing here?"

"Mo-shixiong," the new disciples chorused.

Among them was an exceptionally pretty female disciple. She flushed when she caught sight of Mo Ran, hastily making her bows along with the rest.

Mo Ran scarcely acknowledged Xuanji's disciples as he walked straight up to Chu Wanning. "Shizun, why don't you put on a blindfold and show them how it's done?"

Chu Wanning hesitated. "Okay."

Permission granted, Mo Ran took down his own pale purple hair ribbon, three fingers wide, and laid it across Chu Wanning's eyes. He tied it tightly, but not painfully so, the silk of the ribbon like flowing water. Its ends danced in the breeze.

"Throwing star," Chu Wanning said.

One of the Xuanji Elder's disciples came up and handed their throwing star to Chu Wanning.

"Three," Chu Wanning continued.

"Huh?" Confused, the disciple retrieved an additional two stars from their weapons pouch and handed them to Chu Wanning.

Chu Wanning stroked pale, slender fingers over the cold metal surface, pursing his lips. Without word or pause, the stars shot from between his fingers with a flick of his wrist and a momentary flash.

Cling! Clang! Their collisions rang out.

"Aiya, right on target! Right on the bullseye! But...only one of them."

Chu Wanning said nothing, but Mo Ran blandly replied: "The other two are on the targets behind you."

The new disciples turned to look in disbelief. The remaining two stars, one on either side, were stuck deep in the exact center of targets in completely opposite directions. Morning sunlight spilled down through the rustling bamboo forest. Xuanji's disciples were stunned speechless.

Chu Wanning raised his hand to remove the blindfold, revealing half-lidded phoenix eyes and fluttering lashes. He handed the ribbon back to Mo Ran. "The first sound you heard was the three throwing stars colliding in midair. Control your spiritual energy properly, and you can make two of them ricochet and fly in opposite directions. In battle, you can use this to catch your opponent off guard and take first-strike advantage."

The disciples exchanged glances. One youth, face shining with anticipation, cried, "Elder, h-how do we learn this? Is there a trick to it?"

"Mo Ran," Chu Wanning said. "Show them your hands."

Mo Ran held them out with a smile. The disciples crowded around him, shoving at each other in an attempt to figure out what trick would be revealed to them.

After staring for a long while, they hadn't figured out a thing. But that female cultivator's heart was pounding, her eyes bright. She and her friends were all new to the sect. They hadn't yet reached a focused state of mind and often went down the mountain to buy books for pleasure reading. They too had perused that *God-Knows-What Rankings* Chu Wanning had once read. When the girls had seen the size ranking, they'd been scandalized, giggling as they nudged and goaded one another. But their bashfulness didn't stop them from discussing the contents in whispers back in the disciples' quarters.

"I heard the longer a man's fingers are, the larger *that* thing is," said one feisty shijie with an ample chest and the courage to match. "When I get the chance, I'll sneak behind Mo-shixiong at Mengpo Hall. I want to see how big his hands are."

Later, that shijie really did carry out her plan. In order to line up behind Mo Ran, she'd run so fast she accidentally knocked over a bowl of hot soup and spilled half of it on her quarry. Her lips parted in shock and embarrassment.

As she stood, shaken, a large, fine-boned hand picked up her spilled bowl and placed it back on the counter before handing her a new one.

"Careful. It's a shame to waste good food."

His low and husky voice left her unable to so much as lift her head. Her cheeks flamed red, both her face and the bowl steaming. Throughout the entire episode, she'd only dared peeks at Mo Ran: at his waist, well-muscled and trim, at his lapels, which framed his broad chest, and of course she snuck the most glances at his hands...

"Exquisite." She returned unable to describe those hands even with a dictionary's worth of praise. This was the only worthy descriptor. All the shimei in the room had fallen silent, pursing their lips. Their hearts were ablaze, kindled with wild and suggestive imaginings.

In the present, a chilling voice broke through the female disciple's reverie. "What have you noticed?"

"Elder, please forgive me," another disciple said. "This disciple is stupid and has not noticed anything."

"Mo-shixiong's hand looks particularly powerful?"

Everyone made their guess, but when it was her turn, her mind went blank. She blurted, cheeks crimson, "His fingers are very long."

Mo Ran was stunned. What on earth were these youths looking at? He pulled his hands back and scratched his head, turning to Chu Wanning.

Chu Wanning might not know what was meant by the comment about Mo Ran's fingers, but he wasn't stupid—one glance at the female disciple's blushing face told him it was nothing good. His face darkened and he swept his sleeves back. "What the hell are you looking at."

His visible displeasure frightened the disciples into bowing their heads. Mo Ran didn't want Chu Wanning to be called harsh; sensing the building tension, he smiled and volunteered the answer. "It's calluses."

He shot a look at Chu Wanning and continued. "Scraping your fingertips bloody, letting the calluses form, then scraping them bloody again—after about a hundred times, you'll be able to accurately control your spiritual energy. There's no shortcut."

Chu Wanning taught them until noon, by which time most of the disciples had more or less grasped the basics. Then it was time for him to take his leave. These were someone else's disciples, after all. Some pointers were fine, but teaching them in too much detail might offend the Xuanji Elder. Chu Wanning was no longer a fifteen-year-old teenager who'd just come down from the mountains; he'd finally grasped the intricacies of such social rules.

He and Mo Ran left the bamboo forest and arrived at Naihe Bridge. They crossed it together, shoulder to shoulder. Beneath their trailing sleeves, the backs of their hands brushed lightly with every step. It was a fleeting touch, but it made their hearts soften and melt, revealing the tender sprouts of spring.

There was no one around. Mo Ran finally reached out and interlaced his fingers with Chu Wanning's. Though they'd have to let go very soon, both of their ears flushed pink, their throats dry and hot. Ever since that rainy night in Wuchang Town, they'd had hardly any time alone together at all. Even during their infrequent trysts at the Red Lotus Pavilion, they worried constantly about Xue Zhengyong suddenly popping in unannounced. At this point, a momentary touch of the hands was enough to stir the flames in Mo Ran's chest. "Shizun," he murmured, "Tonight, can we go..."

He was still speaking when he saw someone running toward them. Mo Ran swiftly straightened to his full height, pressed his lips together, and fell silent, stepping to one side.

The newcomer hadn't noticed anything amiss. When they reached them, they bowed their way forward and said, "Yuheng Elder, there's an urgent matter. The sect leader requests your presence in Loyalty Hall at once."

"What is it?" Chu Wanning asked.

"Guests have come, bringing important information relating to Xu Shuanglin. Xue-zhangmen can't make the final decision on his own, so he called all the elders over in the morning for a discussion. You're the last one."

The name *Xu Shuanglin* drove all thoughts of affection from Chu Wanning's mind. He rushed straight for Loyalty Hall.

Mo Ran followed a step behind. "Wait for me. I've fought Xu Shuanglin before. Maybe I can help."

The two leapt swiftly with qinggong and soon arrived at Loyalty Hall. When they pushed open the door, they were met with silence. Aside from Xue Zhengyong and the elders, two others stood within the hall, covered in blood. Mo Ran's gaze fell upon a familiar scabbard on one of their backs. After a moment, his eyes widened in shock and his face instantly paled. "Ye Wangxi?!"

195
Shizun Knows Best, Duh

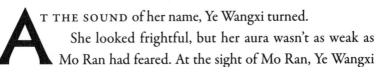

AT THE SOUND of her name, Ye Wangxi turned.

She looked frightful, but her aura wasn't as weak as Mo Ran had feared. At the sight of Mo Ran, Ye Wangxi lowered her lashes and bowed, still in masculine dress—she couldn't shake the habit. "Mo-gongzi," she said.

Mo Ran looked at her, then to Nangong Si at her side. "Where... Where did you two come from? All this blood..."

"We ran into many ghosts and demons on our way out of Linyi," Ye Wangxi said. "We haven't had a chance to change. My apologies."

Mo Ran had more questions, but Xue Zhengyong cut in: "Ran-er's here too? Good, let's all come in."

Chu Wanning entered the room without looking at Mo Ran. He went directly to his place and sat down, fixing his clothes before turning to Nangong Si. Even if he and Nangong Si weren't truly master and disciple, Chu Wanning had been one of Nangong Si's first teachers. His heart ached when he looked at Nangong Si, but what left his mouth was the simple question: "Are you two all right?"

This was the first time since the fall of Rufeng Sect that anyone had asked such a thing. The rims of Nangong Si's eyes reddened; he bent his head, fingers tightening into fists. He closed his eyes, managing after some moments to control the urge to cry in Chu Wanning's presence. "W-we're fine," he squeezed out. "It's been bearable."

But Chu Wanning sighed softly; he lowered his lashes and said no more. Of course he didn't believe Nangong Si. Linyi was a great distance away; it was impossible that they hadn't suffered over the course of their turbulent journey.

Xue Zhengyong was in obvious distress. "Yuheng, since you weren't here earlier—Nangong-gongzi and Miss Ye discovered a clue and specifically came here to tell us about it," he explained.

"So I was told. Something to do with Xu Shuanglin?"

"Mn."

"Sit down and let's hear it, then."

Mo Ran fetched some chairs, but Nangong Si and Ye Wangxi knew they were filthy and stinking and declined to sit. Chu Wanning didn't insist. He took a breath and began: "After we parted at Linyi, where did you two go?"

"The apocalyptic fire forced Ye Wangxi and me past the river to Wei Mountain," Nangong Si said. He paused. "Wei Mountain is deserted, so there was no way to send a message, and Ye Wangxi was injured. After the fire died down, we gathered our strength there before returning to…returning to Rufeng Sect."

The sect where Chu Wanning himself had found refuge when he'd first set out in the world. Nangong Si's words reminded him how much things had changed; he couldn't identify what he felt. After a long silence, he sighed. "It must be completely barren now."

"Zongshi is correct. It is barren, but these things have crawled out from the ruins."

Chu Wanning looked up. "What have?"

"Insects."

Nangong Si untied a bloody pouch placed in front of him. Through its half-open mouth, they could see a mass of buzzing and crawling insects, their green backs spotted with black. Three large spots and two small marked each carapace, and the faint stench of blood emanated from their long abdomens. Most stayed quietly in the bag as if they feared the light, but a few flew out to crawl across the walls and pillars of Loyalty Hall, leaving streaks of blood in their wake.

Mo Ran recognized these bugs: soul-eaters. They could only be found in the blood pool near Rufeng Sect, a type of undead insect that relied on human flesh and souls for sustenance.

The assembled elders found them unspeakably vile; the Lucun Elder even pulled a handkerchief over his face to block the stink.

"We found these soul-eaters in the wreckage," Nangong Si said. "At first I thought they'd been drawn over from the blood pool, but soon realized that couldn't be right."

"Why not?"

"There were too many of them. Ye Wangxi and I walked through all seventy-two cities of Rufeng Sect, and these soul-eaters were everywhere—in the cracks between bricks, in the mud and filth, in the ashes. We found it too strange. After digging a little deeper, we discovered there were larvae as well as adults." He hesitated. "Zongshi, I'm sure you see the problem."

Chu Wanning wasn't familiar with gu witchcraft, but it only took him a few moments to follow Nangong Si's line of thought. The blood pool was near Mount Wei, separated from Linyi by a wide river. Soul-eaters couldn't fly great distances, and it hadn't been long since the fire; perhaps adult insects might have gone fluttering over upon scenting death, but larvae? How could larvae sprout legs to ford the river and the creeks? How could they get to the scorched earth of Rufeng Sect by themselves?

Frowning, Chu Wanning asked, "Someone planted them there ahead of time?"

"Mn, that's what I think as well."

At this, the Tanlang Elder immediately understood. "Soul-eaters can store spiritual energy. After the fire, resentful spirits would be everywhere. There were so many cultivators in Linyi. If the insects placed there fed on their spirits, they would've effectively become seeds containing every type of spiritual energy they consumed. Once possessed of such a multitude of seeds, anyone could draw on their spiritual energy to construct many types of arrays."

Then the question was, who planted the insects there? Someone who knew of the disaster that befell Linyi ahead of time, who needed spiritual energy from outside sources...

No one spoke, but the answer was plain. It could only be the perpetrator himself, Xu Shuanglin. Or to call him by his true name: Nangong Xu.

"So the upper cultivation realm has spent all this time hunting for traces of Xu Shuanglin's spiritual energy, while he's not been using his own power at all, but that of the bugs?" Xue Zhengyong asked.

"Mn, exactly so." Nangong Si said.

"Ah..." Xue Zhengyong murmured. "The tracking spell seeks human spiritual energy but not that of beasts or demons. If Xu Shuanglin has been using this strategy, he could indeed hide his tracks for a very long time." He turned to the Tanlang Elder. "Could we find Xu Shuanglin by following the bugs?"

"Impossible," the Tanlang Elder replied. "Soul-eaters move through the underworld; after eating their fill of scraps of soul, they burrow into the earth. There's no trail to follow."

At this point, Xue Zhengyong had another thought. "If they go to the underworld, why don't we ask Great Master Huaizui? He knows much about the ghost realm."

Chu Wanning swiftly cut in. "There's no need to ask him."

"Why?"

"It would be pointless," Chu Wanning said. "He's unwilling to involve himself with the mortal world; he won't say a thing."

Chu Wanning had been Huaizui's direct disciple. Even if the listeners didn't understand, his resolute words brooked no argument. The hall lapsed into silence.

At length, Xue Zhengyong mumbled, "Then what do we do? If Xu Shuanglin can use the gu insects to evade detection, our efforts are useless. Do we do nothing?"

"What if we try another method?" Chu Wanning suggested.

"Such as?"

"Sect Leader, when Xu Shuanglin left, he took three things with him. Do you remember what they were?"

Xue Zhengyong named them one by one: "Luo Fenghua's spiritual core, Nangong..." He glanced at Nangong Si and softened his voice, "...Nangong-zhangmen, and a holy weapon."

"Right," Chu Wanning said. "No one does anything without purpose. Even in his rush to escape, he still took these with him. It wasn't because he had nothing better to do. Sect Leader, from your perspective, why would Xu Shuanglin take his elder brother?"

"Mn... For revenge?"

"Then why take the holy weapon?"

Xue Zhengyong considered it. "To use as one of five sources of pure spiritual energy to reopen the Heavenly Rift."

"He tore open the Heavenly Rift to retrieve Luo Fenghua's spiritual core." Chu Wanning said. "There's no incentive for him to open it again."

"So what was the reason?"

"I believe it's possible he wishes to use the Rebirth technique," Chu Wanning said.

Xue Zhengyong stared. "But you don't need five types of pure spiritual energy to use Rebirth. Didn't Great Master Huaizui do it before?"

Chu Wanning shook his head. "Huaizui once said Rebirth techniques aren't all the same. Sect Leader, we can't take his method as the model."

The Tanlang Elder scoffed. "The Yuheng Elder speaks with no evidence. How are you so sure Xu Shuanglin means to use the forbidden Rebirth technique?"

"Because of the last thing he took. Luo Fenghua's spiritual core."

In the great hall, Chu Wanning's voice was steady and methodical. "Many years ago, I interrogated a girl in Butterfly Town who died in tragic circumstances. This girl had once met a madman covered in blood, who force-fed her tangerines and said her eyes resembled those of an old friend. That madman left her with a certain phrase—*There was a man from Linyi whose heart died at twenty.*"

Twenty... The age Nangong Xu had been when he was framed and vilified by the masses. At that year's Spiritual Mountain Competition, he'd gone in with high spirits, secure in the assumption that all his talent and years of hard work would receive fair reward. That he would get everything he was due.

But his hard work only earned him a lifetime of infamy. The blade in his hands and the ambition in his heart fell to nothing before his brother's silver-tongued flattery.

He was consumed by hatred. There was no one he could turn to; the whole world mocked him, blamed him, spurned him. In the end, a living man became a corpse, and the corpse became a vengeful ghost. That ghost crawled out from his jagged hate, intent on regaining all he deserved from all the righteous gentlemen of the cultivation realm.

"There's no question that this madman was Xu Shuanglin. But who was the old friend he spoke of? Who did he see in Luo Xianxian's eyes?"

"Similar in looks, surnamed Luo..." Xue Zhengyong exclaimed, "It couldn't have been Luo Fenghua?!"

"I think it was," Chu Wanning said. "At the bottom of Jincheng Lake, Xu Shuanglin tried to use the Zhenlong Chess Formation as well as Rebirth. He used the Zhenlong Chess Formation to control others, but why practice Rebirth? He took Sect Leader Nangong and Luo Fenghua with him. The Rebirth technique couldn't possibly be for Sect Leader Nangong."

"But why revive Luo Fenghua?" Xue Zhengyong murmured. "Didn't Luo Fenghua plot against him?"

"Human hearts are unfathomable. We can't know for sure," Chu Wanning replied. "But I can't think of another reason for him to take Luo Fenghua's core other than for Rebirth."

The hall was stunned. Upon careful thought, they found Chu Wanning's analysis reasonable, but it still lacked evidence. These were merely guesses; the truth was perhaps known only to the elusive Xu Shuanglin himself.

After the meeting was adjourned, Mo Ran, too, thought it over. When night fell, he went in search of Xue Zhengyong. The sect leader was in a side room poring over books for information on the soul-eaters, searching for some clue they could use to find Xu Shuanglin.

"Uncle."

"Ran-er? It's so late, why haven't you gone to bed?"

"I can't sleep. I wanted to ask Uncle about something."

Xue Zhengyong nodded toward a chair, inviting him to sit. Mo Ran wasted no time getting to the point. "Uncle, what was Luo Fenghua...Xu Shuanglin's shifu...like?"

"Ah, Luo Fenghua." Xue Zhengyong frowned, racking his brain. He shook his head. "I never knew him well. In general he was... righteous, stalwart, and fair. He was a man of few words, but he had a good temper and was careful and competent. He was never sloppy in his work. During his stint as head of Rufeng Sect, he even sent his disciples to the lower cultivation realm to help exorcise demons."

"In short, other than planning to usurp the position of sect leader of the Nangong clan, he had no other scandals. Right?"

Xue Zhengyong sighed. "That's right. Far from being scandal-ridden, he was a good man. I don't understand how someone like him could cast such a hateful spell on his own disciple."

Mo Ran thought it over. "Uncle, don't you feel your description of Luo Fenghua is quite similar to someone else?"

Xue Zhengyong stared for a moment. "Do you mean Yuheng? No way, Yuheng's temper is terrible."

"Not him."

"Who?"

"Ye Wangxi," Mo Ran said.

"Ah..." Slowly, Xue Zhengyong's tiger-like eyes widened, his mouth working around those three syllables before slowly giving them voice. "Ye Wangxi..."

Ye Wangxi was kind yet resolute, steadfast yet not unbending. Indeed, she was quite similar to the Luo Fenghua in Xue Zhengyong's memories, the man who'd led Rufeng for one short year.

"Isn't that right?" Mo Ran asked.

"Yes." Shock grew in Xue Zhengyong. Ye Wangxi and Luo Fenghua were of different genders and far apart in age, and their status within Rufeng Sect was nothing alike. He'd never thought to compare them. But now that Mo Ran mentioned it, he saw that they had basically been cast from the same mold.

The same exact one.

The longer Xue Zhengyong thought, the greater his astonishment grew. Discarded memories surfaced one after another; even the style of clothes Luo Fenghua favored when he was a guest of Rufeng Sect was similar to those Ye Wangxi usually wore. Then there was their comportment and manner of speech. Even the way they drew their bows—

In Xue Zhengyong's younger days, he'd once seen Luo Fenghua shoot at a celebration for Nangong Liu's birthday. Rufeng Sect had extended an invitation to both Xue brothers. In his mind's eye, Xue Zhengyong saw Luo Fenghua in the snow, drawing his bow with only three fingers, his pinky taut. The arrow whistling through the air, cutting through the fluttering snowflakes and taking down a snow rabbit demon at nearly a hundred paces. The onlookers applauded his archery skills, but Luo Fenghua had merely smiled and flipped the bow around so it leaned on his left arm, his fingertips brushing the string. It was a natural gesture, without thought. Even his finishing movements differed from the majestic posturing of others. The sight had left a deep impression on Xue Zhengyong, watching nearby.

But now that he thought back, during the battle of the Heavenly Rift when Ye Wangxi and Nangong Si had been firing their bows back-to-back, Nangong Si's arrows had flown straight and true, yet Xue Zhengyong hadn't taken much note. Rather, it was Ye Wangxi who, upon depleting a quiver, habitually looped the bow around her left arm with a flick of her wrist and unwittingly caressed the string with her fingertips. At that time, he'd only watched, eyes drawn to that gesture, so smooth, so carefree and yet self-assured—a gesture that reminded him of a certain someone.

Xue Zhengyong smacked his head. "Aiya, you're right... You're really right! They're basically identical!"

Mo Ran arched a brow. "What do you mean, identical?"

"The way they shoot. Luo Fenghua is far too much like Ye Wangxi, they're not similar, they're exactly the same!"

Mo Ran smiled against his will at Xue Zhengyong's shocked exclamations. "Uncle, you're wrong."

"Ah? How so?"

"Cause and effect."

"Effect?"

"Mn, it's not that Luo Fenghua is like Ye Wangxi," Mo Ran sighed. "But that Ye Wangxi is like Luo Fenghua." His eyes were bright. He was finally sure that his guess was correct: Xu Shuanglin's pursuit of Rebirth was an attempt to bring Luo Fenghua back from the dead.

Mo Ran couldn't speak to the secrets that still lay hidden in Rufeng Sect's past, but he'd been through two lifetimes. In the last life, Xu Shuanglin had died for Ye Wangxi; in this one, he'd devasted Rufeng Sect yet spared her alone. Why?

It couldn't be simply because Xu Shuanglin didn't have the heart to hurt his adoptive daughter. There was a certain carelessness to Xu Shuanglin's actions—speaking words like "There was a man from Linyi whose heart died at twenty," giving his residence a name like Farewell to Three Lifetimes—in some ways, it seemed as if he wanted nothing more than to forget his past. Even the name he'd given his adoptive daughter was so clear and undisguised: *Wangxi*, to forget the past.

To forget his past self, to forget all the bygone grudge and gratitude.

But, perhaps unknowingly, Xu Shuanglin had raised Ye Wangxi to be like the shadow he couldn't forget; he'd molded this abandoned orphan into another's form. This man who wished so fervently to forget his past was forever mired in the mud of memory.

At this point, a faint suspicion unfurled in Mo Ran's mind. Mo Ran knew what it was to wander insane in the darkness; he felt his guesses regarding Xu Shuanglin's actions were more accurate than most. Yet by the same token, he couldn't share his hypotheses; he could only draw his own conclusions and quietly observe events.

The next day, Xue Zhengyong summoned everyone once more; his search through the library had yielded nothing of use. "Poisonous insects and strange beasts are the forte of Guyueye. Why don't we tell Jiang Xi we've found soul-eaters in Rufeng Sect's ruins?"

The Xuanji Elder agreed. "Hanlin the Sage, the finest healer in the world, is a member of Jiang Xi's camp. His expertise would be a great help to our investigation."

But Chu Wanning frowned. "Miss Ye, did you ever see your yifu raise any poisonous insects or beasts?"

"Never."

"What about the healing arts or beast-taming techniques? Did he use any of those?"

"He...looked after a parrot. Other than that, he wouldn't spare the effort to adopt a dog, much less any fantastical beasts. The healing arts had even less appeal to him."

Chu Wanning turned to Xue Zhengyong. "Let's not tell Guyueye about the soul-eaters just yet."

"Why not?"

"Xu Shuanglin wasn't learned in the healing arts or beast-taming techniques. It might not be him feeding and controlling the gu insects. There's still the hand that reached out of the Rift at the very end."

"You suspect Guyueye."

"I won't jump to rash conclusions," Chu Wanning said. "But it always pays to be cautious."

Shizun, Shall We Take a Bath?

ND SO IT SEEMED they couldn't depend on Guyueye. As the meeting adjourned, Xue Zhengyong asked the Tanlang Elder to come with him to the greenhouse to discuss tracking spells with Madam Wang. Every type of spiritual technique had its specialists. This one was outside the realm of Chu Wanning's expertise, so he wasn't much help. Thus, for a while, he would be less busy.

Some days later, as Chu Wanning was watching the fish from the pontoon bridge, there came a knock on the gate of the Red Lotus Pavilion. "Come in," he called.

Nangong Si stepped over the threshold, his face bright beneath the rising moon. "Zongshi wanted to see me?"

"I heard you and Ye Wangxi intend to leave Sisheng Peak the day after tomorrow," said Chu Wanning. "Where do you plan to go?"

Nangong Si lowered his lashes. "Mount Jiao."

Mount Jiao was one of Rufeng Sect's strongholds outside Linyi and a place of sacred importance. Legend had it that, centuries ago, Rufeng Sect's founder had formed a pact with a legendary jiao dragon. When this jiao died, its bones became the mountain, and the heroes of Rufeng Sect were henceforth laid to rest on its slopes. Any outsider who trespassed upon this peak that guarded generations of valiant Rufeng souls would be instantly slaughtered, their corpse mutilated beyond recognition. It was among the duties of the Rufeng Sect leader to offer sacrifices to the mountain at the Qingming festival[5] and the winter solstice each year.

In effect, Mount Jiao was Rufeng Sect's great ancestral hall.

"My dad…" Nangong Si's eyes seemed to darken. "My dad told me previous generations of sect leaders left relics in the shrine on Mount Jiao, in the event their descendants should someday require them. I think that day has come."

Nangong Si was unguarded with Chu Wanning; he revealed the location of those treasures without a second thought. Although he wasn't as close with Chu Wanning as Xue Meng and the rest, their connection was undeniable. It was only because fate had other plans that Nangong Si never became Chu Wanning's disciple in truth. Over these past weeks, Nangong Si had wondered—if his mother's life hadn't been ruthlessly cut short for a weapon from Jincheng Lake, would he now be calling Chu Wanning *shizun?*

"It's a long journey to Mount Jiao," Chu Wanning said. "And I've heard travelers must show their respect to the mountain by fasting for ten days before crossing its borders or the jiao's spirit will expel them. If you intend to go, you should complete the fast at Sisheng Peak before setting out."

Nangong Si shook his head. "Too many people from the upper cultivation realm have it out for me and Ye Wangxi. If they had their way, we'd be dead already. They're sure to find us if we stay here too long, and that'll be a headache for Xue-zhangmen. It's time for us to be on our way."

"Don't be stupid."

Nangong Si blinked.

---

5 清明 Qingming, the *"Pure Brightness Festival"* or *"tomb-sweeping day,"* is a celebration to honor the dead in early April.

"Fasting for ten days is a dangerous venture. What if your enemies catch you on the road?" Chu Wanning asked. "Besides, Xue-zhangmen is too kind to let you leave now. Take my advice—don't go yet."

After days of exhaustion, Nangong Si was worn thin. His heart throbbed painfully at these words, and tears filled his eyes. He quickly looked at his feet. "I will not forget Zongshi's benevolence."

"It's not benevolence—you're just staying a few more days," Chu Wanning replied. "Anyway, I called you up here to tell you something else."

"Please go on, Zongshi."

"Xu Shuanglin mentioned your spiritual core is difficult to control and prone to qi deviation. You should ask Madam Wang to take a look."

Nangong Si was taken aback; he smiled wryly. "This affliction has plagued the Nangong family for generations. My dad once asked Hanlin the Sage from Guyueye to examine me—even he deemed it impossible to suppress and said I can only let it run its course. If the best doctor in the world couldn't cure me, how could Madam Wang?"

"It may not be that Hanlin the Sage couldn't cure you—maybe he didn't want to," said Chu Wanning. "There are always grudges between sects; it's not out of the question that he might have some reservations. But Madam Wang has devoted extensive study to restraining an unmanageable spiritual core. She might be able to help."

Nangong Si was perplexed. "Why would she study that?"

"A happy coincidence. Don't ask too many questions—go on now."

After thanking Chu Wanning profusely, Nangong Si took his leave from the Red Lotus Pavilion. Chu Wanning watched him go, sighing. He remembered Nangong Si as such a spirited youth, haughty and bold. When he smiled, his eyes were bright as the dawning sun. Chu Wanning didn't know when he'd see such a smile again.

As he turned back inside, Chu Wanning heard another knock from the gate. Thinking Nangong Si had backtracked, he again said, "Come in."

The door opened, but the young man outside was not Nangong Si. Mo Ran held a wooden bucket in his arms and wore a tentative expression. He cleared his throat before speaking, as if wary of seeming overeager. "Shizun."

Chu Wanning was caught off guard. "What is it?"

"Not much—I just came to ask if you wanted to bathe together."

Something seemed to be stuck in Chu Wanning's throat; he coughed softly. "Where?"

Mo Ran hesitated. "Melodic Springs."

Chu Wanning didn't know what to say. Melodic Springs was a winding maze of pools, the mist so thick one could scarcely see their hand in front of their face. In a suitably covert spot, no one would notice a thing. But Chu Wanning hadn't imagined Mo Ran would invite him to bathe in Melodic Springs together. He began to panic slightly—could Mo Ran be *this* brazen?

That brazen man continued, "Xue Meng just returned from his bath and said it was pretty empty..." His face reddened. This seemed too direct, so he tried a different approach. "It's chilly out. I was worried Shizun might catch a cold if you bathe here at the pavilion..."

Of course Chu Wanning wouldn't catch any cold—he could set up a warming barrier with no more than a thought. Mo Ran knew this as well as anyone, yet here he was inviting Chu Wanning to Melodic Springs. His intentions were beyond transparent. He even dared say he was worried about Chu Wanning in the cold—the man had no shame.

Mo Ran ever-so-shamelessly fixed his eyes, dark as pitch, on Chu Wanning. "Shizun, shall we?"

Chu Wanning said nothing. If he nodded, it was as good as telling Mo Ran that he understood his impure intentions, yet was still swallowing his sorry excuse.

Swallowing...

He suddenly recalled their frenzied night at the inn. Mo Ran had gone down without hesitation, drowning him in an entirely new kind of pleasure. The eyes Mo Ran had turned on him then had been gentle yet fiery, misted by desire. Chu Wanning's heart had melted beneath that gaze.

"Come with me, pretty please?"

"What are you, five?"

The troublemaker flashed a good-natured grin. "Uh-huh. It's almost nighttime, and I'm sooo scared of ghosts," he said softly. "I can't walk in the dark unless Wanning-gege goes with me."

Pfft. This man was truly a lost cause. But Chu Wanning still went with him in the end.

Most of Sisheng Peak's disciples bathed after their evening cultivation training. At this hour, only a handful remained in Melodic Springs. Mo Ran lifted the gauze curtain, his bare, slender feet stepping onto the agate pathway. Wreathed in steam, he turned to grin at Chu Wanning. He pointed out a direction, then walked away.

Inwardly, Chu Wanning snorted. *Pretty eager for someone scared of ghosts, aren't you?*

Lotus Pool and Plum Pool were the two largest areas of Melodic Springs. Medicinal plants grew along their banks, and the waters teemed with spiritual energy. Most disciples preferred these two pools. Though there were smaller, unnamed ponds as well, those remote corners had no special properties, so most wouldn't bathe there unless it was very crowded indeed.

The Yuheng Elder trod the narrow path alone, a vision of ascetic purity. From the corner of his eye, he spotted shadows in the larger pools, but it was impossible to make out faces through the steam. Clearer were the snatches of conversation that reached him as those disciples chatted idly.

As he neared Plum Pool, the mist thickened until he could barely see his own fingers. A large hand suddenly grabbed him from behind and Mo Ran's warm, firm chest pressed up against Chu Wanning's back.

They were so close, with only the flimsiest layer of clothes between them. He could distinctly feel Mo Ran's burgeoning erection.

Chu Wanning jumped. "What are you doing? Stop messing around."

Mo Ran chuckled, mouth to Chu Wanning's ear. "Wanning-gege, don't go over there. There are ghosts up ahead."

Chu Wanning hesitated, torn between blurting *Ghost, my ass* and *Ge, my ass.* What came out in a low voice was, "Let go."

Mo Ran did no such thing. He laughed softly. "It's so hard to let go. I can't."

"What is *wrong* with you?"

"Mn, there really is something wrong with me," Mo Ran murmured. "If you don't believe me, take a look."

Chu Wanning's ears were turning red, but he snapped caustically, "I won't."

Mo Ran's reply was another chuckle. When he spoke again, his voice had roughened. "All right, whatever you say."

His words were dutiful, but his actions were quite the opposite. His fingers trailed over Chu Wanning's throat before tracing its line upward and closing around his jaw.

"Stop...messing around!"

Chu Wanning could hardly see in the mist, and his other senses seemed to sharpen in compensation. He felt Mo Ran bury his face in the crook of his neck. Chu Wanning trembled as his hot breaths skimmed over his skin.

"Wanning-gege's shaking. Are you scared of ghosts too?"

"Don't call me that!"

Mo Ran chortled and looped an arm around his waist from behind. Kissing down the side of Chu Wanning's neck, he said deferentially, "Okay, okay, I'll be good. Then...Shizun, would you please permit this disciple to help you undress and bathe?"

Somehow, this was even worse. Chu Wanning was at the limit of his tolerance, and the steam was scalding him inside and out. He blurted, eyes red with humiliation, "I'm not taking a bath. I'm leaving."

Mo Ran knew he was thin-skinned, but he still found Chu Wanning's attempt to turn tail and flee adorably hilarious. "But Shizun, can you make it out of here in your current state? What if someone sees?"

"Who cares," Chu Wanning shot back with a scowl. "I'd rather be bitten by a dog than mess around with you."

"Bitten by a dog?"

"You heard me."

Mo Ran laughed. His gaze was dark with desire, with an edge not usually present. Baring his teeth, he bent and ghosted his lips across the back of Chu Wanning's ear.

Chu Wanning thought he was going to say something outrageous again. He was about to lose his temper when he heard Mo Ran rumble softly and dangerously into his ear, "Rrrruff."

"...I beg your pardon?"

"Hey, I thought that was pretty good." Mo Ran sounded genuinely disappointed. "I used to have a little puppy with blue eyes and a flame-shaped mark on his forehead. He barked just like that."

"Don't be absurd," replied Chu Wanning, exasperated. "Why are you barking?"

"What do you think?" Mo Ran chuckled. He kissed Chu Wanning's ear, then licked up the side of his neck. "I've barked and everything—Shizun, you said it yourself, you'd rather be bitten by a dog."

Chu Wanning went rigid; all the blood in his body seemed to boil.

Of course Mo Ran had to add, "Can I bite you now, Shizun?" Without waiting for a reply, he pulled Chu Wanning into a deep kiss. They tangled together, losing themselves in each other. Mo Ran had wanted to take his time, but it was a hopeless endeavor. Chu Wanning was a poison that corrupted his mind and fanned the flames of his desire. Far from slow, he found himself careering forward, his willpower evaporating with each labored breath.

By the time they broke apart, Chu Wanning's phoenix eyes were glassy. Yet he hadn't forgotten his mission. "I came here to take a bath, so let's bathe first..."

Mo Ran made a soft noise of agreement, between an *mn* and a *hmph*. Chu Wanning braced himself against the drag of that low-pitched hum, even as a jolt of electricity raced down his spine and flames kindled in his eyes.

He led Chu Wanning down the steps into the warm pool by the wrist. The rushing waterfall covered the sound of their quickened breathing.

Chu Wanning was still uneasy. Just as Mo Ran was about to draw him into another kiss, Chu Wanning raised a hand to forestall him. "There's no one here?" he asked quietly.

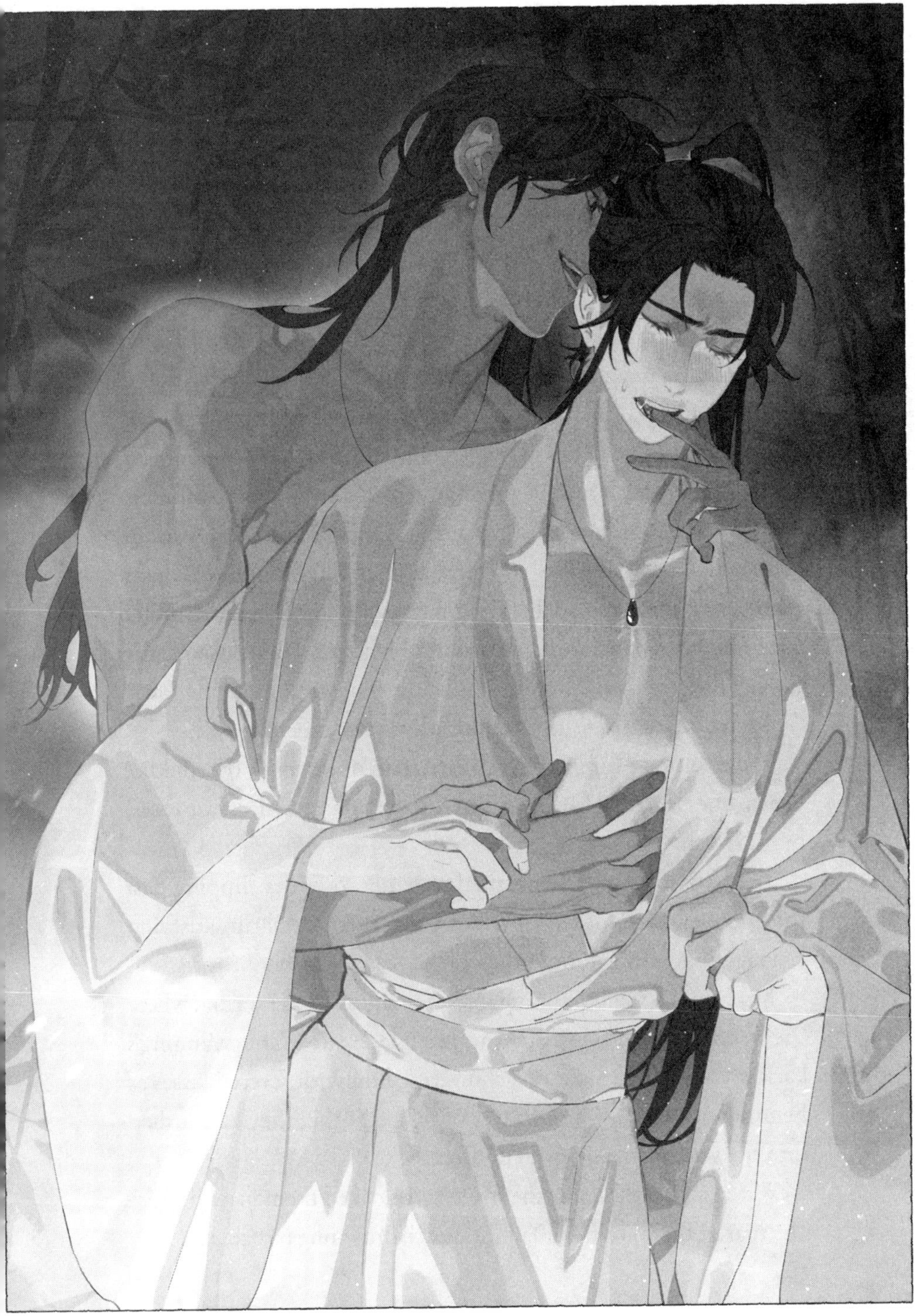

"No, I've checked everywhere." Mo Ran's voice was low and heated, more fervid than the water lapping at his legs. "Shizun, feel this—I think there's really something wrong with me. Why is it so hot...and so...hard?"

Chu Wanning's cheeks flamed red with shame, but he couldn't pry his hand from Mo Ran's grip. His palm pressed against something so fearsome his ears seemed to ring, and his entire body prickled with pins and needles. He wanted to pull away, but Mo Ran's hold was unrelenting. Chu Wanning's hand began to ache; he felt as if Mo Ran wanted to crush his fingers into his palm.

Mo Ran's breath came so quickly, so ardently—almost adorably impatient. Amidst the swirling steam, only those dark eyes in his handsome face were close enough for Chu Wanning to see, misty yet burning with desire. Chu Wanning watched him swallow, throat bobbing. He gazed into Chu Wanning's face and beseeched softly, "Shizun, help me..."

Then he captured Chu Wanning's lips once more.

The inferno of his lust was doused with oil; even water couldn't drown the flames. Waves of heat crested and crashed, a vast forest burnt to ash.

They kissed, their lips crushed together, tongues slipping past for a taste of one another. It was torturously, fruitlessly unsatisfying, leaving them aching for more.

Mo Ran led Chu Wanning into the depths of the spring, where the water was just below their waists. He pressed Chu Wanning's back to a slippery stone wall, showering him with fevered kisses as he tore open the last flimsy layer of his bathrobe; they had rushed into the water too quickly to undress.

Water splashed against the stone and cloaked them in a fine mist. The roar of the waterfall filled their ears, drowning out all else.

Chu Wanning's robe was wide open as Mo Ran kissed him against the wall. His lapels, pulled down to his elbows, pinned his arms in place.

"D-don't..."

But the mortification and thrill of this restraint only increased Chu Wanning's sensitivity as he panted under Mo Ran. As a rough tongue lapped over the pale blush on his chest, Chu Wanning furrowed his brow. He was disoriented by want; bewilderment blurred the lines of his solemn features. As desire and reason clashed within him, the sparks flying in his gaze were enough to drive Mo Ran mad.

"Not... Not so hard..." Chu Wanning rasped. He threw his head back, phoenix eyes narrowed as he heaved for breath.

Mist billowed around them, shrouding the world from sight. Mo Ran spun Chu Wanning around so he faced the wall. He felt Mo Ran's leg braced solidly against his beneath the water. Compared to the cool stone against his cheek, the heat of this contact was startling.

His eyes were half-lidded. Never had he imagined fooling around like *this* with his own disciple, engaging in such acts in the pools of Melodic Springs, where anyone could come across them at any moment. Shame, confusion, lust, and exhilaration fogged his gaze. He felt something huge and blazing-hot press between his legs, rubbing against the cleft of his ass. Caught off guard, he let out a soft cry of surprise. "Ahh..."

Behind him, Mo Ran stilled. Then, as though inflamed by that bitten-off gasp, Mo Ran's hand closed around Chu Wanning's waist as he thrust forward harshly below the water. Although he was only caught between Chu Wanning's legs and not actually inside him, Mo Ran was unbelievably turned on. The man beneath him was Chu Wanning—this alone was the most potent aphrodisiac in the world. The water's surface betrayed but a few ripples, yet in the depths of the hot spring, his thick length rubbed hotly between Chu Wanning's thighs, brushing past that hidden entrance. So muddled was his awareness that he almost wanted to heedlessly lift Chu Wanning's leg and press into him, to bury himself as deeply as he had so many times in the past life. He almost wanted to take Chu Wanning into his arms and claim him completely, to hook Chu Wanning's legs around his waist and fuck him to tears, to release.

"Wanning..." Mo Ran's voice was low, scattered with glowing embers, his eyes dark. The soft splash of water sounded so much like the rhythm of their joining from another lifetime. Wrapped in the warmth of the spring and the silky skin between Chu Wanning's legs, Mo Ran saw his rationality slipping away.

Before he could cross the line, he drew in a breath and pulled Chu Wanning around to face him. He pressed that chest to his own as the spray clouded their vision, scalding droplets falling over their enraptured faces. Mo Ran kissed him frantically, trailing his way down to his chin, only to fiercely take his lips again, consumed by yearning. His other hand felt its way down, closing around Chu Wanning's painfully hard arousal and pressing it to his own.

Chu Wanning had never dreamt such a thing was possible. His lashes fluttered shut with pleasure as Mo Ran stroked them together. "Mo...Mo Ran," he whined, letting his head fall back.

He only had time to utter that name once before Mo Ran stoppered every other sound with a kiss. He lined up Chu Wanning's cock with his own, his hand moving feverishly as he wrapped his other arm around his shizun. He could feel Chu Wanning shivering in his embrace, rousing his tender adoration, his manic obsession.

Their lips were slick when they came up for air. Swept up in this outpouring of primal desire, Chu Wanning opened his eyes and unconsciously looked down at where the two of them were pressed together in Mo Ran's hand. His scalp went numb with that glance. For the first time, he got a clear look at Mo Ran's cock. It was a weapon of flesh and blood, thick and hard with an alarming heft, veins bulging in its current state of arousal. It rubbed against Chu Wanning's abdomen, its gleaming tip gliding over skin.

Chu Wanning squeezed his eyes shut. A tremor ran through him, his mind crumbling. How was it so big... How would it possibly fit? He was sure he couldn't fit it in his mouth without gagging. *How...*

The corners of his eyes burned with mortification. If that thing went inside him, wouldn't he die? Those dreams must have been figments of his imagination after all. Chu Wanning's cheeks were flushed crimson. How could he possibly... How could he possibly kneel on the bed and be invaded like that? How could he possibly take in something like that while panting and moaning so wantonly, begging to be fucked harder and faster like an animal in heat? How could that possibly feel good? How could he possibly come from that...

How.

The more he thought on it, the more preposterous it seemed. Shame, indignation, and self-loathing threatened to drown him. Fortunately, Mo Ran gave him no time to ruminate. His broad hand was wrapped around both their shafts, deftly stroking them off. The tendons in their necks strained as heat built between them. Soft cries slipped from between Chu Wanning's lips.

"*Shh.* You can't see through the fog here, but you can still hear noises," Mo Ran cautioned, reaching up to cover Chu Wanning's mouth and nose.

The sweltering mist eddied around them. He felt like he was suffocating under Mo Ran's tight grip. With his arms pinned by his robe and his voice stifled, that feeling of being held against his will was both agony and thrill.

"Ngh..." He couldn't stop the tears that leaked from his eyes. He was like a sacred crane drawing his final breaths, delicate neck arched to reveal his vulnerable throat, shaking his head repeatedly—*I can't, I can't...*

But Mo Ran didn't stop; he bent his head to nip at the jut of that throat. Slowly, he raised his eyes, taking in Chu Wanning's harrowed expression—his furrowed brow, his helpless despair. "Shizun..." he murmured.

He couldn't hold back a moment longer; he released Chu Wanning's mouth and pulled him into a bruising kiss. Water surged around them, and the falls thundered down from above. Chu Wanning could scarcely breathe through Mo Ran's kiss. His lips were swollen, his gaze unfocused as he gasped for air.

Mo Ran held him close, burying his face in his neck. In the hidden depths of the spring, their ardent breaths mingled. They were near to drowning, drenched in sweat and torrid water. They tangled like mating beasts, as though no closeness was too much; they wished to meld together, flesh into flesh, bone into bone.

"Enough... Really, that's enough..." Chu Wanning struggled to free himself, shuddering against that prickling onslaught of pleasure. "Stop, I'm done..."

At Chu Wanning's low mumbling, Mo Ran's eyes only darkened. He kissed him on the cheek. "Just a little longer, babe," he panted. "Wait for me..." His hand moved faster, his hips instinctively bucking forward. Eventually there was nothing left in their minds save for the man before each of them, save for love and desire.

"Ah... *Ahhh*..."

Whether it was the physical ecstasy or the rush of adrenaline from sneaking around in Melodic Springs, their climax was over-powering. As Chu Wanning came, he couldn't help the hoarse moan that escaped him, completely forgetting to keep his voice down. The two of them gasped as one, rough yet adoring, filthy yet pure, their eyes filled only with one another's faces as they came...

They kissed again, lingering and tender, the afterglow spreading through them like ripples on the water.

"You came so much..." Mo Ran murmured indistinctly. His hand was covered in it. He reached over with a distant look in his eyes, smearing his fingers over Chu Wanning's stomach, along his toned abs, all the way up to his chest. Chu Wanning shivered in his arms, shaking uncontrollably with pleasure and overstimulation. Mo Ran gathered him close, whispering into his ear, "That felt good, didn't it?"

Chu Wanning couldn't speak.

"Next time...if you're ready..." Pressing his damp torso to Chu Wanning's, Mo Ran kissed him. "We'll do it for real, okay?"

In some sense, Chu Wanning had long known this was coming. But upon hearing these words spoken aloud, added to the fact that he had just seen that monstrosity with his own eyes, Chu Wanning's spine tingled, and all his muscles tensed.

Mo Ran could feel Chu Wanning flinch in his embrace; he kissed him ever so gently. "I won't hurt you; I'll make sure it's good for you..."

They entwined in the depths of the waterfall, lingering pleasure coursing through them. Mo Ran's voice was husky with adoration and desire. "I'll make sure you like it, really... It might hurt just a little when I first go in, but I'll go as slow as you want..."

Shame blazed through Chu Wanning. He wanted to throw Mo Ran off and leave in a huff, but his legs were unsteady. "Stop talking..."

Perhaps Mo Ran knew Chu Wanning wasn't actually opposed to the idea; he forged ahead with uncharacteristic willfulness. He pressed wet lips to Chu Wanning's earlobe, his voice mesmerizing. "I'll make sure everything will go right... Shizun, if you're scared, I'll get some medicine... Trust me, once you get used to it, it'll feel amazing."

In the past life, I saw you get fucked senseless. But back then it was all hatred and punishment. In this life, I want you to hold me, to become one with me, to never part from me. I want you to want it, to enjoy it, to never forget me.

He kissed Chu Wanning, his eyes glowing as though embers smoldered within. His next words were devious yet tender, lascivious yet earnest, doting yet ferocious. The first half of the sentence was respectful, but the second was entirely out of line. "My dear shizun, next time, could I make you come on my cock?"

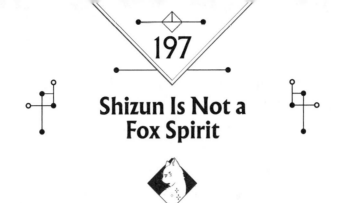

197

Shizun Is Not a Fox Spirit

HOW COULD CHU WANNING tolerate such an unspeakably mortifying question? The moment they left Melodic Springs, he stalked off without a backward glance at Mo Ran.

A man needed face like a tree needed bark. How did Mo Ran have the nerve to ask him such an appalling question... Did Mo Ran imagine he would nod in agreement? What was the point of *asking* him something like that? It would be far better to just go ahead and do it!

The next day, the elder in charge of teaching classics fell ill, and Xue Zhengyong asked Chu Wanning to supervise the students as they memorized their texts. Classics was one of the largest courses; Chu Wanning couldn't possibly keep an eye on all the disciples by himself. Thus, he brought Mo Ran, Xue Meng, and Shi Mei to assist.

Shi Mei and Mo Ran soon became the busiest among the four. The reason was simple: Shi Mei was gentle and beautiful, and Mo Ran was gallant and kind. The younger disciples took a natural shine to them. Shi Mei, with his long legs, narrow waist, and face out of a painting, was especially popular. The softness of youth had long gone, and he had grown into a stunningly attractive man, with a mild temper and a voice that was music to the ears. He left a favorable impression on just about everyone, men and women alike.

As for Mo Ran, he had been entrapped in a crowd of female disciples.

"Mo-shixiong, Mo-shixiong, I don't understand this sentence. Can you take a look at it for me?"

"Mo-shixiong, what's the difference between these two spells— I don't get it. Shixiong, could you explain it to me?"

"Mo-shixiong—"

By the time Mo Ran explained to the ninth smiling little shimei why the Sigil of the Returning Billows must be drawn exactly as its inventor specified, Chu Wanning's patience was spent. Frowning, he shot Mo Ran a cool glance over the rows of disciples dividing them.

Mo Ran had endured the cold shoulder from Chu Wanning since the evening before and was feeling rather low. He'd been accustomed to taking by force in the past life; this time around, he moved with painstaking care. Every time they tried something new, he checked to see if Chu Wanning was enjoying himself. He didn't know where he'd gone wrong—should he not have asked? Maybe he had called him the wrong thing. Instead of "My dear shizun, next time, could I make you come on my cock?" should he have said "Babygirl, next time, could I make you come on my cock?"

Thus, after being ignored for an entire day, he was quick to notice Chu Wanning's eyes on him. Though Chu Wanning was pinning him with a ferocious glare, Mo Ran reacted like a wilting cabbage that had been watered; his eyes lit up, and he flashed Chu Wanning a brilliant smile.

Chu Wanning was speechless. Clearly this idiot had no clue why this gaggle of girls had so many questions. Were they genuinely confused? In that case, the inventor of the Sigil of the Returning

Billows was standing right here. Why didn't they come over to ask Chu Wanning? Why would they take the circuitous route of asking Mo-shixiong instead?

Chu Wanning was immensely displeased. But he said nothing, merely staring flintily at Mo Ran.

After feeling Chu Wanning's gaze on him for some seconds, Mo Ran eventually realized something was amiss. At that moment, the tenth little shimei eagerly tried to flag him down. "Mo-shigeee!"

"Sorry, gotta go." Mo Ran grinned and pointed at Xue Meng. "Why don't you ask Xue-shixiong?"

The little shimei, her hair in a neat bun, looked on crestfallen as Mo Ran walked toward Chu Wanning. Chewing on the end of her brush, she heaved a gusty sigh.

"Shizun, what's wrong? You don't look happy."

Chu Wanning pressed his lips into a tight line. It wouldn't do to speak his mind now. "I'm a little tired. Let Xue Meng take care of those students and help me keep an eye on things over here."

Mo Ran didn't suspect a thing. Nodding, he diligently fell into step behind Chu Wanning as he made his rounds. Walking with his shizun, Mo Ran noticed something—far fewer people were asking questions on this side. *How odd,* he thought. Were these disciples smarter than the others?

Having escaped those vexing cries of *Mo-shixiong* and the doubly infuriating *Mo-shige*, Chu Wanning's mood lightened considerably, though his face betrayed none of it. Just as before, he walked impassively among the junior disciples as they studied their texts. It was in this way that he overheard a particular conversation between two students.

"Shixiong, shixiong, I'm telling you, there's a fox spirit in Melodic Springs."

"Huh? What do you mean?"

"Last night, I was taking a bath in Plum Pool. I was about to leave when I heard...uh...you know...some *noises*..."

The shixiong's mouth fell open in astonishment. "Maybe it was a couple of reckless disciples?"

"Who would be *that* reckless? No way. Disciples would sneak around in private and call it a day. If the Yuheng Elder or Tanlang Elder caught anyone messing around in public in Melodic Springs, they'd break their legs! It couldn't be any of the disciples."

"Fair enough."

"I'm telling you, it must have been a fox spirit absorbing yang essence to replenish her yin! A bunch of us are going back tonight to see if we can catch the little vixen. We'd be doing everyone a favor if we succeed, right? We can't just let her go around seducing our sectmates!"

"Sure, sure. Did you see who she was fooling around with yesterday though?"

"It's so hazy in Melodic Springs; I would've had to walk right up to them. You won't see *me* going over there—I'm just a kid. What if that fox spirit took a liking to me and made me dual cultivate with her?"

As the little disciple rambled on, a strange look came over his shixiong's face. He reached out and waved a hand. "What's wrong? What's with you?" His shixiong said nothing, but the little disciple felt a prickle on the back of his neck. He slowly turned to find the Yuheng Elder standing right behind him with an inscrutable expression on his face, emanating an arctic chill.

"Aiya!" the disciple yelped. "Elder, begging your pardon!"

"Class is for memorizing texts, not discussing evil spirits or *essences*, or even dual cultivation." Chu Wanning glowered. "Quite the imagination you've got. Now get back to studying. If I hear another peep of such nonsense, there'll be consequences." With a flick of his sleeves, he strode away.

Mo Ran, too, happened to overhear this conversation. As much as he wanted to, he didn't dare laugh. His gaze lingered on Chu Wanning's retreating figure. How had such a proper person ever fallen in love with him? Why would he want to be with someone like Mo Ran...

He felt a warm ache in his chest, his mood bittersweet.

After class ended, he couldn't resist clinging to Chu Wanning as he tidied the texts in the reading room. He wrapped his arms around him, kissing him tenderly.

Furious, Chu Wanning rapped Mo Ran on the head with a scroll. "Brilliant idea, Melodic Springs... What have I become now?"

Mo Ran held back a laugh. Rubbing his nose against Chu Wanning's ear, he crooned as though he didn't already know the answer, "What *has* Shizun become now?"

How could this man be so shameless? Chu Wanning's eyes flew wide in rage. "You—!"

Mo Ran grinned, dimples deep and sweet, overflowing with honey. He kissed Chu Wanning again. "Those shidi were really full of it—a fox spirit? Absorbing... What was it... Ha ha, absorbing yang essence to replenish yin?"

"One more word and I'll kill you." Chu Wanning brandished the scroll as if to stuff it down Mo Ran's throat.

"Oof..." Mo Ran chuckled. "Then, can I at least choose how I'll die? I want the fox spirit in Melodic Springs to suck all the yang essence out of me, what a way to go..."

"Mo Weiyu!"

From that day forward, no amount of persuasion could convince Chu Wanning to visit Melodic Springs with Mo Ran ever again.

One morning a few days later, Madam Wang requested Mo Ran come and see her. Taking his hand, she asked, "Ran-er, during your travels, did you ever come across a strange girl in Snow Valley?"

"What kind of girl? Strange in what way?"

"Very pale, with a bloodless complexion. She favors red robes, and always carries a basket in her arms as she chats with travelers passing through Snow Valley..."

Mo Ran smiled. "Oh—Auntie, do you mean the Maiden of the Snow?"

Madam Wang blinked in astonishment. "You know of the Maiden of the Snow?" she exclaimed in delight. "I didn't think you'd have heard of such a rare spirit, so I thought I'd describe her... Who would've thought..."

"Shizun mentioned her in his journals, so I happened to read about her," said Mo Ran. "Auntie, why do you ask?"

"Nangong-gongzi came to see me a few days ago. After examining his pulse, I do think his turbulent yang spiritual flow could be brought under control, but the ingredients for the treatment are hard to come by. The rarest is the icicle fish the Maiden of the Snow carries in her basket." Madam Wang sighed. "Young Nangong-gongzi and Meng-er are about the same age. It's terrible what he's been through; I want to help however I can. But the Maiden of the Snow is famously elusive. Twenty years back, she was spotted in Snow Valley. Before that, the last recorded sighting was in Kunlun Taxue Palace's records a century ago. I thought I'd try my luck if you'd seen her."

Mo Ran was torn between elation and sorrow. If Nangong Si's ailment could be cured, he could lead an ordinary life. Perhaps he and Ye Wangxi could be together at last, given their feelings for one another. But despite spending a year in Snow Valley, he'd never come across the legendary Maiden of the Snow; he couldn't help Madam Wang. "After we settle Xu Shuanglin's case, I'll make a trip to Snow Valley and scour it for any trace of her. Who knows, I might find some leads."

Cheered by the prospect, Mo Ran took his leave to share the news with Nangong Si. Madam Wang called after him: "Ran-er, don't walk so fast—I've already told Nangong-gongzi, you don't need to..."

But Mo Ran was already too far away to hear.

After searching everywhere, he finally caught sight of Nangong Si standing at one end of Naihe Bridge. He was striding forward when he noticed someone had appeared on the other end. Peering over, Mo Ran saw that the newcomer was none other than Ye Wangxi. Mo Ran's pulse quickened. He stilled, hanging back in the bamboo grove to watch instead of calling out to Nangong Si.

Ye Wangxi was as gallant as ever, her features betraying not a hint of feminine softness. Her cultivation and training had shaped her into a form nearly indistinguishable from a man. If not for her feelings for Nangong Si that she hid within her heart, she might have long forgotten she was actually a woman.

Upon seeing her, Nangong Si cleared his throat, looking down at the distant river.

"Gongzi summoned me?"

"Ah..." Nangong Si looked rather embarrassed. He folded his hands over one of the bridge's stone lions, then hummed in assent.

"Is something the matter?"

"Not—not really," said Nangong Si. He didn't so much as glance at Ye Wangxi as he traced the curls of the lion's mane. "I just... I just wanted to give you something."

"What?" Ye Wangxi asked, bewildered.

Head bowed, Nangong Si turned away from Ye Wangxi and untied a pendant from around his waist, fumbling with the knot for several seconds before he finally managed to loosen it. He coughed softly and handed the pendant to Ye Wangxi. "Thank you for always... Never mind, I don't know how to say it. These days I have nothing worth much, so I can only give you this. I've had it for a long time; it's not the most valuable jade, but..."

He didn't continue; his cheeks had turned pink. Throughout all this, he had kept his eyes downcast, too nervous to look at Ye Wangxi. Realizing Ye Wangxi still hadn't said anything, he was overcome by dejection and embarrassment at his impulsivity. He reached out tentatively, as though to take back the phoenix-shaped ornament. "I-I know it isn't pretty," he muttered. "If you don't like it, just...just give it back, it's fine, I don't mind... After we rebuild Rufeng Sect, I'll get you the most beautiful pendant, I—"

Ye Wangxi, who had been staring at him in silence all this while, suddenly broke into a smile. Girlish sweetness bloomed upon her handsome features, a newfound blush coloring the edges of her eyes. Her fingers—her calloused, scarred, unladylike fingers—closed around the jade pendant. As the wind picked up, rustling through the bamboo, she said, "This is enough. Thank you, Gongzi."

Nangong Si's face was beet red. "A-as long as you like it..." he said stiffly. "I just...uh...I don't know what to say."

From the depths of the grove, Mo Ran stared at him, incredulous. He had an almighty urge to bash Nangong Si's head into the stone lion. Was this guy good for anything besides raising wolf pups? After all that hemming and hawing, *I don't know what to say* was seriously the best he could do?

"Madam Wang said my unmanageable spiritual core can be suppressed," Nangong Si blurted. "I might not have to dual-cultivate to treat it."

Ye Wangxi froze for a moment, then murmured a quiet "Mn." She lowered her lashes and didn't say more.

It seemed she had misunderstood. If Nangong Si's condition could be treated without dual cultivation, then he could be with anyone he wanted. She would no longer have an excuse to so selfishly remain by his side. Ye Wangxi had her pride too; she wouldn't beg for Nangong Si's love or pity. So Nangong Si was giving her this jade pendant as something to remember him by...

"Do you...um...do you get what I mean?"

"...Mn."

Nangong Si was clearly delighted. "Th-then, if you want..." he stammered clumsily, "you can...uh, you can address me the way you used to, when we were little, I...I think that would be great... Um, sorry... I really don't know what to say... Err..." He heaved a sigh of despair. At last, as though even he couldn't stand it any longer, he clapped a hand over his eyes. "Heavens above, *what* am I saying?"

Now it was Ye Wangxi's turn to be taken aback. She jerked her head up in surprise; eyes wide, a faint flush crept over her face. Bamboo leaves swirled over Naihe Bridge. Her robes rippled in the wind as she held the jade pendant warm in her hand, its scarlet tassel fluttering between her fingers. Finally—tentative, wary, and whisper-soft—she ventured, "A-Si?"

Perhaps it was his imagination. In that moment, her voice, irrevocably distorted by the voice-changing spell, seemed to carry a note of its old tenderness as it floated over the breeze. Nangong Si looked up and caught Ye Wangxi's face in the resplendent glow of dawn. A smile unfolded upon her handsome, elegant features, but within her half-closed eyes was a wet glimmer. In the end, she couldn't stop the tear that rolled down past her brilliant smile.

As Nangong Si gazed at her face, so familiar, a hazy childhood memory rose before his eyes.

He saw a young girl with rosy cheeks and long lashes, her face gentle and sweet. Back then, Nangong Liu hadn't yet sent Ye Wangxi to train and cultivate in the shadow city. Xu Shuanglin had recently brought her home, and she followed Nangong Si everywhere to learn some basic spiritual techniques.

On this day in particular, Nangong Liu had sent the pair into one of Rufeng Sect's simplest illusions as a training exercise. Although the illusion wasn't a difficult one to break, it was frightening. Vengeful ghosts roamed within, hair draped over their faces as they wailed and groaned.

At first, Nangong Si didn't pay Ye Wangxi much mind; he was focused on dispatching the ghosts. But as he walked deeper into the illusion, he realized Ye Wangxi had fallen behind. Her tiny figure was curled up in the abandoned temple, too scared to move an inch.

He shot her a backward glance and snorted. But as he was about stride off, he saw a hanged ghost drift over, its long, scarlet tongue reaching toward her neck—

"Aaaaaaahh!"

By the time Ye Wangxi noticed, she was too terrified to do any-thing but scream. Clutching her sword to her chest, she turned her face away.

But somehow, nothing happened.

When she summoned the courage to open her eyes, she saw Nangong Si standing in front of her. He had run the hanged ghost through and stuck it with a lightning talisman. Sparks danced around him as he looked down at her. He'd meant to scold her, but her expression was too pitiable. She looked like an affrighted kitten, tears spilling from eyes wide and round as saucers.

Nangong Si froze. Finally he managed to stammer, "Wh-why are you so useless? How can you be scared of ghosts..."

"They're *ghosts*!" Ye Wangxi sobbed. "If you're not scared of ghosts, what *are* you scared of?"

"Why are girls so useless?"

"But I don't want to be useless!" the pretty girl wailed, so overcome with indignation her nose began to run. "Who would want to be a burden? I want to help, but you were walking too fast, you didn't even wait for me... I... I *am* scared of ghosts..."

"Huh..."

In the end, Nangong Si squatted beside her. He didn't know how to cheer her up, so he watched blankly as she cried.

Before she started training in the shadow city, Ye Wangxi's tears had rolled down her cheeks just like any other girl's. Between sobs, she choked out, "What are you looking at?"

"I'm waiting to see when you'll be done crying."

Ye Wangxi stared at him.

"Once you're done, we can go together. Why are you so weak anyway?" Nangong Si sighed. He lifted a hand and flicked Ye Wangxi's pale forehead. "Stay with me. I'll protect you."

As Nangong Si stood lost in reminiscence beneath the golden sun and blushing clouds, he realized that, before today, the only time he'd seen Ye Wangxi cry was within that illusion so many years ago. That was the first and last time she wept in terror, as any girl might. In the years that followed, she had been forged into steel, frozen into ice. She sealed her hopes and fears beneath a stoic facade so complete even she had forgotten the girl she used to be. She only knew she was to follow this scion of Rufeng Sect from childhood

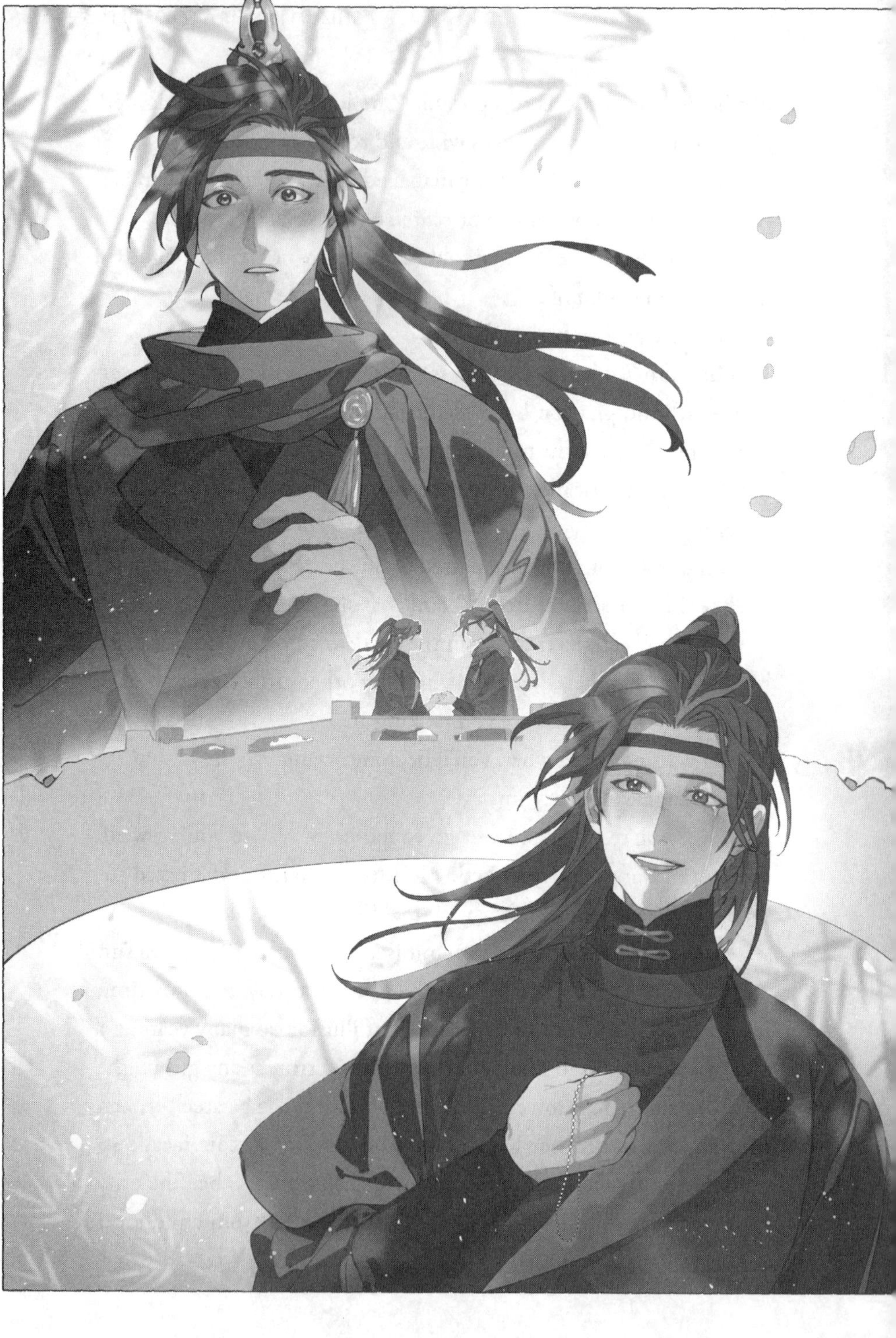

into youth, until he had become a gongzi, and she had forsaken her beauty.

And just like that—without shedding a tear, without burdening him—she had quietly followed him for two decades.

Shizun Sets Out for Mount Huang

W HEN THEIR TEN-DAY fast had ended, Nangong Si and Ye Wangxi set out for Mount Jiao. Naobaijin had been heavily wounded and couldn't carry his master on this long journey. The massive faewolf had transformed himself into a tiny puppy no larger than a man's palm and curled up in Nangong Si's quiver, fuzzy head hanging out.

Mo Ran saw them off at the sect's main gate. Stroking the mane of the horse he led, he grinned. "Mount Jiao is a long journey, and riding swords is too taxing. Take these horses. They were raised on spiritual grass and can cover hundreds of miles in a day. They're no match for Naobaijin, but they'll see you safely to the mountain."

The pair swung up astride their horses. From his seat, Nangong Si cupped his hands and respectfully lowered his gaze. "Thank you, Mo-xiong. No need to accompany us any farther. I hope our paths will soon cross again."

"Mn, take care. Be safe."

Mo Ran stood at the gate and watched as Nangong Si and Ye Wangxi's figures receded into the distance. As he turned to leave, he heard a creak from the forest to his left, as if a branch had snapped and fallen to the ground.

"Meow..."

Mo Ran narrowed his eyes. "A cat?" he muttered.

Ye Wangxi and Nangong Si rode down the mountain side by side, guiding the horses onto the winding, narrow road toward Wuchang Town. Sunlight streamed through the dense canopy overhead, turning the dust kicked up by their hooves into flecks of dancing brilliance.

Nangong Si turned to Ye Wangxi. As he parted his lips to speak, Naobaijin's fuzzy head popped out of the quiver, followed by two snow-white, golden-clawed paws. The little wolf pup threw its head back in two plaintive howls.

Pulling hard on the reins, Nangong Si jumped. "Watch out!"

Darts whistled at them from all directions as the horses whinnied in fright. Nangong Si and Ye Wangxi drew their swords in the same instant, falling into the old habits of their youth. They leapt up without a word, Nangong Si's blade flying left, Ye Wangxi's sword dancing right. A series of clangs, and the poison-tipped pear-blossom needles fell to the ground. Ye Wangxi tossed out a talisman and brought down a barrier around them.

"Who's there?!" Nangong Si bellowed.

A shadow flickered over them, though there was nary a cloud in sight. They raised their eyes to see a man at the tip of a tree branch, his wide sleeves flapping and long beard flying. Backlit by the bright sky, he peered down at them, his eyes filled with hateful scorn.

Nangong Si placed him as Huang Xiaoyue, the cousin of the former sect leader of Jiangdong Hall.

He stared daggers of ice at Ye Wangxi, lofty and silent up above. Around them came the ominous rustling of leaves as a hundred Jiangdong Hall disciples stepped out of the forest. Each wore a scarlet circlet at their brow, signifying their status as foremost disciples of the sect.

Huang Xiaoyue twirled his beard around a finger. "It seems you two enjoyed your stay at Sisheng Peak. You've been holed up in there for ten long days—it's really very inconsiderate of you."

"Huang Xiaoyue, why must it be you again?" Nangong Si fumed.

"So what if it is?" Huang Xiaoyue replied evenly. "Don't tell me you're unaware of the grievances between Jiangdong Hall and Rufeng Sect."

"We fended off four of your sect's attacks between Linyi and Sichuan, yet you still insist on hounding us?" Nangong Si ground out. "What grievance do you speak of—haven't you had your fill? Your sister-in-law murdered your brother, and the one who revealed it was Xu Shuanglin, yet you insist on picking a fight with *us*—haven't you any shame?"

"Shame? I think the shameless one is *you*, little gongzi," Huang Xiaoyue growled. "It's your Rufeng Sect that brought my Jiangdong Hall to ruin. Do you deny it?"

"If you insist on avenging yourself on Rufeng Sect, then let justice be determined out in the open," said Ye Wangxi. "Instead you waylay us on the road and attempt an assassination."

"Shut up. Girls shouldn't chime in when men are talking." Huang Xiaoyue flicked his sleeves. "Don't get ideas just because your shitty old man raised you like a boy. You'll never be anything but a stupid wench. A woman's place is in the kitchen—who do you think you are, talking back to me?"

"Huang Xiaoyue, you watch your mouth!" Nangong Si snarled.

"Heh, watch my mouth? Let's lay out the facts, shall we?" Huang Xiaoyue pointed at Nangong Si and continued, menacing, "Your father seduced a married woman and convinced that bitch to poison my brother and seize his position. As for *her*"—he jabbed a vicious finger at Ye Wangxi—"her bastard yifu aired Jiangdong Hall's dirty laundry to the world and smeared our reputation. I've led our sect's best fighters here today to get justice for Jiangdong Hall and the rest of the world!"

He leapt down with a flourish as the crowd of leering disciples rushed toward Nangong Si and Ye Wangxi.

Before they reached their targets, a great swath of flames roared up to block their path. Gale winds tore through the trees, throwing the disciples several yards backward.

"Mo-xiong?" Nangong Si exclaimed.

It was indeed none other than Mo Ran. Willow whip in hand, he alighted on a tree facing Huang Xiaoyue and fixed him with a cold stare.

Huang Xiaoyue hadn't expected this encounter. His expression grew ugly as he cast about for a retort. "Mo-zongshi, what brings you down the mountain today? Seeing the sights?"

"Zongshi, why don't you ask your disciple why he's hiding in a tree pretending to be a cat."

Huang Xiaoyue's brow was twisted, his complexion as sallow as the yellow of his namesake. "What does Zongshi mean by this?" he said between gritted teeth.

"Huang-qianbei, I should be the one to ask you," Mo Ran replied. "You've attacked Sisheng Peak's guests in our own territory. Did you find my sect so pristine you were inspired to sprinkle blood onto our dirt?"

"We're no longer on the mountain; your sect has no right to meddle. I'm avenging my dead brother—Mo-zongshi, no one asked your opinion!"

"Huang-qianbei is quite correct," said Mo Ran. "We've come down from the mountain. Sisheng Peak has no business meddling in the grievances of private citizens."

Huang Xiaoyue snorted. "Well, step aside!"

Mo Ran didn't budge, but Jiangui glowed brighter, its scarlet leaves glittering like beads of blood. "But what if I myself want to meddle?"

"You!"

He had no illusions about Mo Ran's abilities, but he couldn't back down with blood vengeance on the line. He rumbled threateningly, "Mo-zongshi, do you intend to make an enemy of Jiangdong Hall?"

"Oh, not at all. I simply want to ensure my guests make it out of Sichuan in one piece," Mo Ran replied. "Jiangdong Hall or Jiangdong Wall—it doesn't matter who's standing in my way."

Huang Xiaoyue narrowed his eyes. The hatred in them was tangible, as if they might burst into flames and burn Mo Ran and the cypress he stood on to ash. "You insist on protecting these two Rufeng Sect vermin?"

"Vermin?" Mo Ran asked coldly. "Qianbei, please enlighten me: what do Miss Ye and Nangong-gongzi have to do with Jiangdong Hall's misadventures?"

Huang Xiaoyue didn't respond.

"Did they instigate Jiangdong Hall's power struggles? Expose Jiangdong Hall's scandals?" Mo Ran stared at Huang Xiaoyue. "Did they kill the previous sect leader? Did they sabotage your brother?"

"Who cares?!" Huang Xiaoyue shouted furiously. "The son shoulders the father's debts! That's the way of the world!"

"Is that so?" Mo Ran asked carelessly. "No need for more words between us, Huang-qianbei. Let's let our weapons do the talking."

"Mo Weiyu!" Huang Xiaoyue sputtered in rage. "You're being completely unreasonable!"

"How interesting—who's the unreasonable one here?" A new voice, sharp and haughty, rang out from the mountain path. Brandishing Longcheng before him, Xue Meng strolled out of the forest, his frigid silver blade blinding in the sun. "Screaming bloody murder right on my doorstep, as if you could just kill as you please—does Jiangdong Hall think everyone in Sisheng Peak is dead? Aren't you asking for trouble?"

Huang Xiaoyue knew he couldn't defeat Mo Ran in a head-to-head battle, but he might have conceivably found an opportunity to kill Nangong Si and Ye Wangxi while Mo Ran was occupied fighting the others. Yet now Xue Meng had stepped in as well—the darling of the heavens who had taken the top prize at the Spiritual Mountain Competition. Who didn't know the fearsome might of the blade Longcheng in his hand?

These two cousins both stood outside the sect to defend Nangong Si and Ye Wangxi. No matter what tricks Huang Xiaoyue had up his sleeve, there was no way he could catch both of them off guard.

Yet at Xue Meng's arrival, Mo Ran's expression grew somber. "Go back," he said to Xue Meng.

"I'm here to help—"

"I'm acting of my own accord; this has nothing to do with Sisheng Peak. Don't interfere."

Mo Ran frowned. What was this kid thinking? Even if Jiangdong Hall's power had waned, it was still one of the nine great sects of the upper cultivation realm. It shouldn't be underestimated. In addition, the niece of Jiangdong Hall's former leader was wedded to one of Huohuang Pavilion's senior disciples. If Xue Meng came to Mo Ran's aid now, Sisheng Peak would effectively make enemies with not just one but two of the upper cultivation realm's sects. This wouldn't do.

"Go back," said Mo Ran.

But Xue Meng was too naïve to tease out these subtleties; he was merely galled that Mo Ran didn't want his help. As they stared each other down, a cloud of dust rose in the distance. A white steed arrowed toward them, its lovely rider clad in snow-bright robes with a pipa on her back—a cultivator from Kunlun Taxue Palace.

"Urgent! An urgent message!" she called out, brows knitted, urging her horse to greater speed.

She rounded the corner at full gallop, only to come across an apparent standoff. Pulling her horse up, she blinked at them in confusion from her saddle. "Urgent—uh... What... What are you all doing?"

The sudden arrival of the messenger put an end to Mo Ran and Huang Xiaoyue's fight before it had even begun. At Xue Zhengyong's invitation, Huang Xiaoyue went up to Sisheng Peak, and Nangong Si and Ye Wangxi followed behind.

Once in Loyalty Hall, Taxue Palace's messenger bowed respectfully. Vermilion lips parted as she announced, "I bring an urgent message—we have news of Xu Shuanglin's whereabouts."

The color drained from Ye Wangxi's face.

"Our sect dispatched ten thousand of our jade butterflies to follow Xu Shuanglin's trail," the messenger continued. "This morning, two finally returned. They discovered traces of a spiritual disturbance near Mount Huang. The palace leader believes Xu Shuanglin may have taken refuge there. She gave immediate orders to deliver this news to each of the major sects so you may convene and discuss."

Xue Zhengyong was overjoyed. "You found him?"

"We cannot be sure yet," replied the messenger. "But the jade butterflies reported a persistent stench of blood lingering around Mount Huang in recent days. There's a good chance Xu Shuanglin is hiding on the mountain."

Xue Zhengyong clapped once and jumped to his feet. "Outstanding! Now that we have something to go on, there's no time to lose. What is the palace leader thinking?"

"The palace leader is of the same mind as you, Sect Leader. She feels that time is of the essence, and we ought to investigate at once."

"Excellent!" Xue Zhengyong turned to Huang Xiaoyue. "Huangdaozhang, why don't we go together? Xu Shuanglin is the one to blame for your troubles—if we catch him, you can avenge your brother."

Huang Xiaoyue's heart thudded in his chest. He knew it would be nigh impossible for him to kill Xu Shuanglin on his own. Besides, all this talk of avenging his brother was nothing more than flimsy pretense. After all, it wasn't as if the young Nangong Si and Ye Wangxi really had anything to do with his brother's death. Huang Xiaoyue blustered about justice for his brother, but privately, he had other motives. The recent crisis had severely diminished Jiangdong Hall's strength, and Huang Xiaoyue had long heard rumors that Rufeng Sect possessed a secret trove of treasure. If he could capture Nangong Si and Ye Wangxi and force them to release the ancestral seal, those valuables would fall into his hands.

He clenched his fists within his sleeves. After a moment's consideration, he forced himself to smile, face creasing like a desiccated tangerine. "It's too early to say whether Xu Shuanglin is truly on Mount Huang. The bridges between Jiangdong Hall and Rufeng Sect have already been burned. It's not only my personal grievance that hangs in the balance, but the reputations of all sects. This will require a careful reckoning."

"Fair enough," said Xue Zhengyong. "How about we find Xu Shuanglin for your personal grievance first, and you can settle your debts with Rufeng Sect later?"

"An interesting proposition, Xue-zhangmen. But Rufeng Sect is scorched earth these days. Where do you suppose I ought to go to settle my debts?"

"I'm afraid I don't know—Huang-daozhang, you'll have to answer that question yourself," Xue Zhengyong chuckled. "Since Rufeng Sect has been reduced to a pile of rubble, why are you in such a hurry to eliminate these two youngsters?"

"*You!*" Huang Xiaoyue snarled, waving his sleeves with a scowl. "That's none of your business."

"You were talking about the reputations of all the sects just a moment ago, but now it's none of our business?" Xue Meng asked with a smile. "Jiangdong Hall is one of the nine great sects of the upper cultivation realm—shouldn't you be a bit more consistent?"

Huang Xiaoyue knew he was in the wrong, but he could think of no riposte and thus resorted to glaring viciously at Xue Zhengyong in silence. At last he shook out his sleeves and stalked to the gate with Jiangdong Hall's disciples trailing after him. Leaping onto his sword, he led the crowd out of Sisheng Peak toward Mount Huang.

Ye Wangxi was weighed down with remorse. "Xue-zhangmen, I'm so sorry for the trouble. We—"

"A hunter wouldn't kill a baby bird that fell into his net," said Xue Zhengyong. As he watched Jiangdong Hall's contingent dwindle into the distance, his smile faded, and his eyes grew cold. "Jiangdong Hall is beyond vicious." He gazed into the sunlight outside the hall, a faint frown creasing his brow. Finally, he sighed. "Come, let's go to Mount Huang."

The party from Sisheng Peak set out on the long journey to Mount Huang via sword. By the time they reached the mountain, a large group of cultivators from each of the other nine major sects had already convened at its base. Indistinct faces darted to and fro like a school of carp, the reason for their urgency unclear.

Chu Wanning was first to dismount from his sword. His first steps on the ground wobbled slightly, his face stark white. Fortunately his complexion was pale to begin with, and no one noticed aught amiss—no one but Mo Ran. He sidled up to Chu Wanning and lightly rubbed the back of his hand while nobody was looking. "Shizun, you flew very well."

"Hm?"

"Really." Mo Ran smiled.

Chu Wanning cleared his throat and looked away. Raising his eyes to the top of Mount Huang, he found it shrouded in a visible haze of malevolent qi. At the moment, the leaders of the other eight sects were heading the group at the foot of the mountain. Hands raised, they funneled spiritual energy into a towering barrier before them. Xue Zhengyong touched down and rushed over to help.

The rest of Sisheng Peak's cultivators arrived one after another. Xue Meng landed nimbly next to Mo Ran and Chu Wanning, frowning at the scene before them. "What are they doing? Why aren't we going up the mountain?"

"It's not that we aren't—it's that we can't," Mo Ran replied.

"Why not?" Xue Meng asked, perplexed.

"Mount Huang is one of the cultivation realm's four great evil mountains," said Chu Wanning. "It's a strange place, and one not easily breached."

Xue Meng was taken aback. "I've heard of the four great holy mountains, but not four great evil ones. What mountains are these?"

"Mount Jiao, Mount Shell—"

"Mount *Hell*?" Xue Meng asked incredulously.

"...Shell, referring to the Xuanwu—the Ebon Tortoise."

"Ohhh." A flush crept up Xue Meng's cheeks. "Uh-huh."

"Mount Liao, and this right here—Mount Huang." Chu Wanning paused. "They're relics of the cultivation realm's bloody past. People seldom speak of them these days. I only know of them because I came across some obscure records."

"But why would evil mountains exist in the first place?"

Chu Wanning responded with a question of his own. "Do you remember how the founder of Rufeng Sect prevailed over the evil jiao dragon?"

"I do," said Xue Meng. "The jiao haunted the East Sea. Rufeng Sect's founder defeated the monster and sealed it within the Golden Drum Tower and formed a blood contract to use it for his own ends. After the founder's death, the jiao transformed into a mountain. Its sinews turned to earth, its blood to rivers, its bones to boulders, and its scales to the woods on its slopes. The peak protects the graves of generations of Rufeng disciples, so they call Mount Jiao the heroes' tomb."

Chu Wanning nodded. "Precisely. Mount Jiao was formed from the evil spirit of the Azure Dragon. You're familiar with the constellations of the four auspicious beasts—the Azure Dragon, the Vermilion Bird, the White Tiger, and the Ebon Tortoise. These beasts are legendary guardians of the four cardinal directions, but some of their descendants are evil beings that wreak havoc upon the earth."

Comprehension dawned on Xue Meng. "So the other evil mountains are also formed from the spirits of evil beasts, like Mount Jiao?"

"Mn."

"Then Mount Huang...was the descendant of the Vermilion Bird?" Xue Meng whipped around to look up at the mountain crouching within that malignant haze like a colossal beast. Its central peak was

228 o—• THE HUSKY & HIS WHITE CAT SHIZUN

precipitous, but the slopes at its shoulders were gentle—not unlike a phoenix crowing with its neck outstretched.

"Indeed," answered Chu Wanning. "The four evil mountains each have their own dangers. For example, no one can scale Mount Jiao unless escorted by a descendant of Rufeng Sect's founding bloodline. Dragon sinew vines will drag any trespassers into the mud and bury them alive. Mount Huang is similar."

"Weird." Xue Meng turned to look at the sect leaders lined up in front of the barrier, his father among them. "Everyone knows Mount Jiao belongs to Rufeng Sect. Then what about Mount Huang? Don't we just need to find a descendant of whoever subdued the Vermilion Bird and drag them over?"

Mo Ran at last broke his silence. "If the descendant were still alive, sure. But she just recently passed away in an accident."

Xue Meng blinked. "You know her?"

"I do," Mo Ran said indifferently. "We all knew her."

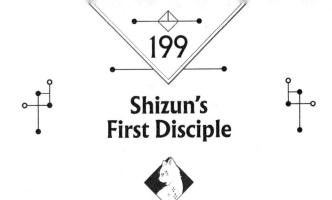

199

Shizun's First Disciple

"**H**UH? WHO WAS IT? Was she the only one Mount Huang would answer to? No other descendants?" Xue Meng demanded.

Mo Ran didn't answer him directly. "The Vermilion Bird was subdued a thousand years ago by one Song Qiao, courtesy name Xingyi."

Xue Meng paled. "The Jade-Hearted Lord, Song Xingyi?" he blurted.

"Mn."

"B-but he was the last zongshi from the tribe of the Butterfly-Boned Beauty Feast in the history of the cultivation realm!"

"That's right," said Mo Ran, his face devoid of expression. "The last person who could've opened the gates to Mount Huang perished in Rufeng Sect's inferno. It was Song Qiutong."

Xue Meng's jaw dropped. Before he could reply, there was a commotion in the distance. A crowd of cultivators in the jade-green robes of Bitan Manor had rushed over to the barrier.

"Li-zhuangzhu!" Several of them cried out in alarm.

A shift came over Chu Wanning's expression, and he gravely made his way through the crowd. Li Wuxin had collapsed and was propped up in a disciple's arms. His face was paper-white as he spat out a mouthful of blood, his salt-and-pepper beard stained a pungent scarlet. His lips were blue, and only the whites of his eyes were visible as they rolled up into his head. Insensible, he murmured tremulously, "I'm first... I...I came in first..."

With the absence of Li Wuxin's spiritual energy, the barrier sapped the strength of the remaining sect leaders more rapidly. Huang Xiaoyue had just come into power within Jiangdong Hall; his ability was a cut below the others. He was at his limit and could hardly even turn his head.

Jiang Xi had also paled, but he willed himself to look over at Li Wuxin. "He's been afflicted with the Phoenix's Nightmare."

The legendary phoenix had imbued Mount Huang's barrier with its own spells. Any who sought to break through and charge up the mountain risked succumbing to this horrifying vision. The Phoenix's Nightmare was similar to the Heart-Pluck Willow's illusion from Jincheng Lake yet more difficult to escape; those afflicted often never reawakened.

All the Bitan Manor disciples had fallen to their knees. Someone wailed tearfully, "Manor Leader! Please wake up, Manor Leader—"

The dreaming Li Wuxin giggled and muttered to himself. Suddenly he squirmed out of the arms of the disciple—Zhen Congming—who was supporting him. Lying on his back, his hands scrabbled in midair as he burst into laughter. "I came in first! First place! First place!"

A disciple from another sect murmured from within the crowd, "What does he mean, first place?"

Li Wuxin couldn't answer. Trapped in that joyous dreamscape, he bared his blood-stained teeth in an intoxicated grin. Yet after a while, the dream seemed to take a turn. His wizened features froze, settling into a furious scowl. "No—you can't do that! You can't! You said you were going to return Bitan Manor's sword technique scrolls to me! How could you go back on your word?" His expression turned sorrowful again.

This was a truly alarming sight—Li Wuxin had ever been mindful of his reputation. In his time as leader of Bitan Manor, no one had seen him betray such anger or grief. As he lay on the ground now, he didn't look like a sect leader nor like a Daoist. He scarcely looked like a man. Drool pooled at the corners of his mouth, and his wrinkled features distorted with despair, as if he could preserve his dignity by hiding it in the folds of skin that lined his aged face. "Eight billion gold is asking far too much. Those scrolls were Bitan Manor's to begin with, they belonged to the shifu of my shifu. Back then, the sect fell on hard times; we sold them to you out of desperation... Sect Leader...I'm begging, please lower the price..."

At this, a murmur rippled through the crowd. Eight billion gold? A sword manual?

A few still remembered the previous head of Bitan Manor: a blunt and fiery-tempered man who had alienated himself from his fellow sect leaders in the upper cultivation realm. When Bitan Manor came upon hard times, none were willing to lend a hand. After that, Bitan Manor's fortunes had gone from bad to worse. For three years straight, they hadn't even funds to support their own disciples.

Somehow, they came into money again. But for some mysterious reason, Bitan Manor's awe-inspiring Water-Parting Sword technique, previously renowned throughout the land, had been lost. Subsequent generations of disciples could never master the crux of this technique. Some denizens of the jianghu mocked Li Wuxin as an incompetent teacher; under his leadership, Bitan Manor, which had once produced legendary swordsmen of unparalleled ability, was reduced to the laughingstock of the upper cultivation realm.

But witnessing this now, the crowd realized the situation wasn't so simple. Could it be that Bitan Manor had managed to survive all those years ago by selling its founding sword manual? Faced with this act of shameless profiteering, many minds went immediately to one particular sect. Numerous surreptitious gazes swept over Jiang Xi.

"Could it have been Guyueye..."

"It was probably Jiang-zhangmen's shizu..."

Li Wuxin was still writhing on the ground in agony as Zhen Congming struggled to hold him in place. The old man sobbed and railed, then struggled up from the ground to kowtow every which way, blood and mucus streaming down his face. "Please give it back to me—I've spent half my life saving. I have five billion, one hundred million gold," Li Wuxin wailed. "Five billion, one hundred million is all I've got... I've done all I can; we have no more than this. I won't kill or steal or resort to evil for money! Gold flows into your esteemed sect like water, but Bitan Manor really doesn't have any more than this... Please, I'm begging you..."

Upon hearing *gold flows into your esteemed sect like water*, even those who hadn't eyed Jiang Xi before turned to look at him. Jiang Xi controlled Xuanyuan Pavilion, the biggest black market auction house in the entire cultivation realm. Who else could it be?

One of Bitan Manor's younger disciples shouted at Jiang Xi, eyes scarlet with fury, "Jiang-zhangmen! Your Guyueye has possession of the three most important scrolls of my Bitan Manor's Water-Parting Sword? To think you asked for eight billion gold... Have...have you no shame?!"

Before Jiang Xi could reply, a hoarse voice called out from the left. "There's no evidence—how dare you accuse Jiang-zhangmen so rashly?"

Surprisingly, the speaker was Huang Xiaoyue, barely able to gasp for breath at this point. The geezer couldn't stop his hand from shaking on the barrier, yet he jumped to defend Jiang Xi. His intentions were unmistakable.

An incensed Bitan Manor disciple lunged toward Huang Xiaoyue, ready to curse him out, as one of his sectmates bodily restrained him. "Zhen Fu, don't provoke them!"

Mo Ran froze. *Zhen Fu*—"*very wealthy*"? It would normally have prompted a laugh, like Zhen Congming's "very smart." But as he watched the bedraggled Li Wuxin kowtowing over and over in the dirt, all he felt was bitterness and pity.

"Five billion isn't enough...? Then...how about five billion, five hundred million?" Li Wuxin wiped his tears with his sleeves. "Five billion, five hundred million. I'll do some business with the Chang family of Yizhou and sell off some magical devices and spiritual stones. I can put it together. Five billion, five hundred million... Sect Leader, please show some compassion, some mercy... Please, just give the sword manual back to me."

Back bent, he knocked his forehead on the ground again and again, until the skin was raw and blood trickled down his face. "The Water-Parting Sword manual is the soul of Bitan Manor..." Li Wuxin sobbed. "Before my master ascended, his last wish was for me to reclaim the manual. I've done everything in my power, I've dedicated my life... My hair has gone from black to white; I begged your father first, then you... I even begged Luo Fenghua..."

"Ah!" There was a collective intake of breath. Luo Fenghua?! Li Wuxin had begged Luo Fenghua. So it wasn't Guyueye... It was...

Countless heads turned. Without anyone taking so much as a single step forward or back, a path somehow cleared through the sea of people. Every member of every sect craned their necks to look at Nangong Si and Ye Wangxi where they stood at the edge of the crowd.

"It's Rufeng Sect!"

There was no more need to whisper. Shouts rose from the throng.
"How could they!"

"No wonder Rufeng Sect's sword techniques improved by leaps
and bounds over the past few decades. People were saying they'd
started to resemble those of the old legendary masters! What
brutes!"

"Nangong Si came in third at the Spiritual Mountain Competition! Because of *stolen* sword techniques! He's a fraud!"

"Sickening!"

Nangong Si was rooted to the spot, his expression wooden. He
had no idea what crimes his father and the other Rufeng Sect elders
before him had committed. Those burdens ought to have fallen on
all of Rufeng Sect's seventy-two cities, but now, they were his alone
to bear. He didn't flee, but neither did he speak up. He stood in
silence, his face ashen.

Ye Wangxi reached for his hand, but Nangong Si shifted away
without batting an eye. He stepped in front of Ye Wangxi.

"He has the nerve to show himself here..."

"With a rank bastard like that for a father, how could the son be
any better?"

Bitan Manor was angriest of all. "Get lost!" someone bellowed at
Nangong Si and Ye Wangxi. "Get the fuck out of here!"

"There's no place for Rufeng among the ten great sects anymore!
Why are you still standing there? Fuck off!"

"You rotten bastards! Where do you get off?!"

Impassioned curses and rebukes assailed them from all sides;
hatred was etched into every face. Someone pelted out of the crowd,
Bitan Manor's green robes flying, and grabbed Nangong Si by the
lapels.

"A-Si!" Ye Wangxi cried.

In the chaos, Nangong Si shoved her out of the way. The Bitan Manor disciple pinned Nangong Si to the ground, raining blows down on his face, his chest, his stomach. There was no spiritual energy behind the punches, but each landed with ferocious violence.

A low, stern voice suddenly rang out. "Stop."

Nangong Si had taken a punch squarely on his handsome face. He coughed up a mouthful of blood, his hair in disarray, covered in mud as he lay on the ground. The enraged Bitan disciple had just drawn back for another blow when someone grabbed his arm.

"Piss off!" the disciple howled, whipping around. "I don't need you to—"

He choked on the rest. The man before him was none other than the world's foremost zongshi, Chu Wanning.

"Stop." Chu Wanning looked down at him, his eyes like a frigid mountain stream. His expression was impossible to describe, containing too many emotions yet none at all. Gripping the young man's arm, he pressed his lips into a thin line. "Stop fighting," he said after a beat.

Nangong Si spit blood into the dirt. Ye Wangxi rushed forward to help him up, but he stopped her with a wave. "Don't waste your energy. These are Rufeng Sect's debts; I'm answerable for them in my father's stead."

If anything, the disciple grew more incensed upon hearing this. He struggled to pull free of Chu Wanning's grip and throw himself at Nangong Si once more.

"Stop fighting!" Chu Wanning commanded, brows drawn low.

"It's none of your business! You're from Sisheng Peak; this has nothing to do with you," the disciple snarled, mad with fury. "How can you treat my shifu like this? How? How can you treat Bitan

Manor like this? We've groveled at Rufeng Sect's feet for so many years! Why do you... *Why!*" he howled piteously.

Behind him, Li Wuxin moaned and begged. He was trapped in his own consciousness, pleading with the Nangong Liu in his vision. "Luo Fenghua said he would return the manual to me... But he didn't know where it was... Sect Leader... You promised me... I'm seventy-nine—how many more years do I have? My cultivation's not strong enough for me to ascend; I probably won't be able to see my shizun again... But I must complete the one task he left to me. I must."

Each word was like a clot of blood squeezed from Li Wuxin's throat. "I can't fail, Sect Leader..." he wailed. "Please, give it back... Return Bitan Manor's rightful property to me... I beg you..."

The Bitan Manor disciple shuddered. Chu Wanning's hand, too, trembled where he gripped the young man. Tears of hatred and incredulity stood out in the disciple's eyes, but he couldn't win free. At last, he reared back and spit on Chu Wanning, the gob of saliva landing on his cheek. "Zongshi? No—all of you are *bastards*."

"Shizun!"

"Mo Ran, stay where you are. Don't come over."

Chu Wanning released the disciple, who made an immediate rush toward the bruised and battered Nangong Si. There was a flash of golden light—a haitang barrier descended around Nangong Si and Ye Wangxi, protecting them within. Chu Wanning had come down onto one knee; now, he slowly straightened and gazed at the indistinct faces of the watching crowd. Chu Wanning stood at one end; Li Wuxin, covered in blood and tears, kneeled at the other. Li Wuxin's aged voice was like a creaking tree branch in the winter, piercing the heavens with every word. "Isn't five billion, five hundred million enough..."

Caught within the dreamscape, the old man was still haggling with Nangong Liu. There was nothing of his dignity left, his wizened features crumbling like silt. "Five billion, eight hundred million?" His voice quavered.

Chu Wanning closed his eyes. Beneath wide sleeves, his clenched fingers were shaking. Still he said, deliberately enunciating each word, "On account of my deep regard for Rong Yan, mother of Nangong Si—"

In the great shadow of Mount Huang, before a crowd of thousands, the only sounds were Li Wuxin's wailing and Chu Wanning's low and austere voice.

On one side, Li Wuxin muttered, "Five billion, eight hundred million, surely that's enough? They're just three volumes of sword techniques after all..."

On the other, Chu Wanning intoned, "When I came down from the mountain, I had no money, nor did I know how to ask for aid from others. It was Madam Rong's kindness of a meal that allowed me to remain at Rufeng Sect for a time." When he paused, only Li Wuxin's sobs could be heard. "Madam Rong once asked me to take her son Nangong Si as my disciple. I was young and unqualified; I did not accept. But back then..."

Chu Wanning turned his head a fraction to glance at Nangong Si where he lay on the ground. He spoke for the watching crowd, slowly and clearly recounting this event even Nangong Si might not remember.

"Back then, Madam Rong brought her young son before the ancestral temple and bade him bow to me thrice. She said since Nangong Si had performed the rites to take me as his teacher, should I be willing to remain at Rufeng Sect, Nangong Si would honor this pledge." Chu Wanning looked up. "Nangong Si is my disciple."

The instant he heard this, Xue Meng's face drained of color. Mo Ran and Shi Mei's faces also fell, yet none said a word as they stared at Chu Wanning.

"If sons must shoulder their fathers' debts, so too must one who has served but a single day as a teacher afford his pupil a lifetime of protection. Nangong Si has bowed to me thrice; he can call me his shifu," Chu Wanning said. "His shifu is present. If you have grievances to avenge or beatings to dole out... I am here, and I will not resist."

"Shizun!"

"*Shizun!*"

Mo Ran, Shi Mei, and Xue Meng fell to their knees one after another while Nangong Si tried to struggle up from the ground. Blood leaked from his lips as he mumbled, "No... I didn't... I never bowed... I don't have a shifu... I don't have a shifu..."

On the other side, Li Wuxin let out a keening cry. Face upturned to the sky, mustache fluttering like windblown snow, he opened his eyes wide, blood streaming down his cheeks. He howled and screamed, sobbing and stammering. "Five billion, nine hundred million...surely that's enough? Nangong-zhangmen... Five billion, nine hundred million... Please, take pity on this old man and write off whatever remains. Leave me something to take to the grave... Please, won't you, please?" Like a lamb baring its neck for the slaughter, he cried with a final piercing sob, veins bulging, *"Please?!"*

With this third desperate entreaty, Li Wuxin coughed up a great gout of blood that splattered across the ground. Only silence remained.

Li Wuxin collapsed with a soft thud.

He was the leader of the bottom-ranked sect of the upper cultivation realm. In life, he had been an old man who ran about like a clown, sparing no effort to kiss up to any sect that might lend him a hand. He had spent most of his life trying to reclaim three measly sword technique scrolls, only to come away empty-handed, reduced to a laughingstock. He was a useless mediocrity who had crumbled wide-eyed into the dust and died.

The wind whistled past. All sorts of expressions passed over the faces of the crowd, but no one spoke a word.

Mo Ran suddenly remembered—there was a treasure trove hidden on Mount Jiao with enough riches to revitalize any sect. Even Jiangdong Hall knew of this. Bitan Manor had many dealings with Rufeng Sect; they would naturally know of it as well. After Nangong Liu's demise, sects large and small sought to capture Nangong Si and Ye Wangxi. Perhaps they claimed it was for vengeance; in truth, every one of them had designs on that mountaintop fortune.

And yet, Bitan Manor was never among them. Bitan Manor had spent its time clumsily trying to get into Sisheng Peak and Guyueye's good graces, hoping they might aid and support each other in the future. Li Wuxin's thoughts had never turned to Rufeng Sect's treasure, despite being bullied and humiliated by Rufeng Sect all his life. Perhaps it was because of this that the old man knew all too well: as desirable as wealth might be, the injustice that came with it was too much to bear.

From a distance, Mo Ran gazed at Li Wuxin's pathetically filthy face crushed into the dirt. It dawned on him then—on the night of Rufeng Sect's calamity, when everyone else had fled in all directions, Li Wuxin had remained behind despite his terror. His abilities were unexceptional, yet he'd steeled himself to brave the inferno. His sword had rescued dozens of complete strangers.

It was said the founder of Bitan Manor had a technique called the Water-Parting Sword, capable of cleaving water and splitting the skies. History venerated him as a legendary swordsman. But Li Wuxin had lost three volumes of the sword manual. He couldn't learn this miraculous technique or become a swordsman sage like his forebears. He could only expand his sword while the fire roared. He knew none of the people he rescued, among them many of Rufeng Sect's own disciples. Nevertheless, he had used his blade to bring every last one of them out of that sea of flames and return them to the world of the living.

Shizun, Mount Huang Has Opened Its Gates

NONE OF BITAN MANOR'S disciples imagined their leader would succumb before the battle even began. Li Wuxin was getting on in years; he had begun to show his age in his carriage. Yet he would never have met such a sudden end if not for the barrier's illusion spell throwing his spiritual energy flow into fatal disorder.

There was a long silence. Then the green robes of Bitan Manor rippled as its disciples fell to their knees. Their mournful cries rent the heavens as the rest of the crowd looked on. Even the disciple who'd attacked Nangong Si could no longer bring himself to fight. Weeping, he crawled over to his sect leader, swiping sleeves across his face as his tears flowed without cease.

The towering barrier before Mount Huang let out an ear-splitting shriek. Jiang Xi blanched. "Someone come take Li Wuxin's place!" he barked. "Or we'll all die here today!"

Xue Zhengyong turned. "Yuheng!" he shouted. "Come quick and lend a hand!"

Chu Wanning didn't need to be told twice. His expertise, after all, was in barriers. The screech they'd heard was from the curse left behind by the evil spirit of the phoenix. If this curse had reared its head, the sect leaders and elders weren't far from breaking through the barrier altogether. Should they succeed, all would be well. But should they fail, this curse would backfire with an earth-shattering strength, potentially more dire than the apocalyptic inferno that had laid waste to Rufeng Sect.

Chu Wanning leapt forward at once, his gaze sharp as the honed edge of a blade. He landed in the spot vacated by Li Wuxin and reached up with a sweep of his sleeves.

The moment his fingers touched the barrier, Chu Wanning flinched in surprise. His head whipped around to look at Huang Xiaoyue, standing silently beside him. Huang Xiaoyue was shaking from head to toe, dripping with sweat, his face flushed with exertion. He looked as though he was giving all he had to the effort, and the other sect leaders certainly seemed to think this was the case.

Perhaps he could fool the others, but how could he fool the barrier zongshi Chu Wanning? As soon as Chu Wanning stepped into Li Wuxin's place, he could feel that the barrier's retaliatory energy was overly concentrated there. Compared to the other sect leaders, Li Wuxin had likely been inundated with double the amount of demonic energy as he stood in this spot.

Seldom did such imbalances arise in cooperative arrays. When they did, there was only one possibility: the next cultivator over wasn't pulling their weight. Huang Xiaoyue was putting on an act!

Chu Wanning's fury was instantaneous. His dark brows drew together as he thundered, "You... The nerve of you to play games like this!"

"Wh-what..." Between gasps, Huang Xiaoyue's voice was faint as a mosquito's buzz; he looked as though he might perish in the next moment. All the nearby sect leaders with any energy to spare looked over at the commotion.

"Zongshi, what do you mean... What games..." Huang Xiaoyue mumbled.

"As if you don't know! Get the hell out of my sight!"

Xue Zhengyong couldn't stay silent. "Yuheng, why are you yelling at Huang-daozhang?" he called. "Look at him, he can hardly speak! If there's a problem, let's talk it out after we open the barrier!"

Huang Xiaoyue snuck a glance at Chu Wanning. The eyes that met his were like a frost-rimed dagger; a chill washed over his heart. He never had the ability to open the phoenix's barrier in the first place. He had only rushed to the front of the crowd and pretended to help with the aim of burnishing his own reputation. The upper cultivation realm needed to know that Jiangdong Hall was still formidable, and Huang Xiaoyue was a man to be reckoned with. He never expected that wimp Li Wuxin would buckle under the doubled demonic energy, ending up a target of the barrier's backlash and snuffing it right next to him. And his death would have been no big deal, if the person who took his place *hadn't* been Chu Wanning—this damned Chu-zongshi who deserved to be hacked into mincemeat!

Cold sweat ran down Huang Xiaoyue's greasy face. This wasn't part of his act anymore. *What do I do?* he wondered.

Faced with imminent danger, Huang Xiaoyue bit down fiercely on his own tongue. As warm blood filled his mouth, he let the bloody spittle drip from the corners of his lips. "Zongshi... I swear, there's been a misunderstanding... When Li-zhuangzhu collapsed I—I really...can't... I can't..." He coughed violently, flecks of blood flying. "I really can't take much more..."

As if Chu Wanning would fall for this. Between Li Wuxin and Huang Xiaoyue, it was patently clear who was more capable. If both truly gave their all, the first to founder would never have been Li Wuxin. With a furious snap of his sleeves, Chu Wanning summoned Tianwen. One lash sent Huang Xiaoyue flying through the air to crumple a dozen feet away. "Out!"

"Aiyo!" Jiangdong Hall's horrified disciples rushed forward and clustered around their fallen leader. More than a few others turned glares upon Chu Wanning.

"Chu-zongshi, why must you be so unreasonable?"

"Huang-daozhang was doing his best. Was there need to wave your whip around and throw a fit?"

"You think you should abuse people just because you can?"

Chu Wanning barely heard these indignant quips. Rage seethed in his chest, and his phoenix eyes glinted like ice. In the light from the barrier, his eyes seemed to flash scarlet.

"Get the hell *out*." His voice wasn't loud, but it was threatening in the extreme. Those who knew Chu Wanning understood that they might succeed in reasoning with him were he merely berating or reprimanding someone. But once he got this look in his eye, resolute and unbending, none could stand in his way. If anyone was foolish enough to try, one furious strike from Tianwen might mark their end.

"Yuheng... What's going on..." Xue Zhengyong asked weakly.

"Huang Xiaoyue, did you expend even a scrap of energy to open the phoenix's barrier?" Chu Wanning was so incensed veins protruded from the hand he braced against the barrier. "When Li Wuxin reached his limit next to you, did you shoulder even an ounce of his burden?"

"What are you talking about?!" cried a female disciple from Jiangdong Hall. "Our Huang-daozhang is spitting blood, yet you're accusing him of not giving enough? Will you only be satisfied if he keels over and dies like Li-zhuangzhu?"

Chu Wanning's dark brows drew together in a scowl. But as he made to reply, the colossal barrier before him shuddered. A bloodred glow enveloped the sect leaders' palms pressed to its surface.

"Focus!" Jiang Xi called. "This is the last layer—we're about to break through!"

Chu Wanning had no wish to argue with these lunatics. Turning back to the work at hand, he threaded his fingers together and placed both hands on the barrier. As spiritual energy laced with fury poured through his palms, a rift appeared in the red wall.

There was a resounding crash as a tremor rumbled through the earth. A huge rip had split Mount Huang's great barrier, more than eight feet tall and wide enough for five people to walk through abreast.

"It's open! It's open!" Xue Zhengyong whooped. "The barrier's open!" He stepped forward, craning his neck for a better look, and was hit in the face by a plume of deep red miasma. "Aiyo!" he cried. "What's that awful smell?"

The rest of the cultivators rushed up to take a look, immediately forgetting Bitan Manor and Jiangdong Hall.

Abbot Xuanjing of Wubei Temple was well-versed in such matters. Twirling his prayer beads in his hands, he said solemnly, "This mountain is a burial ground. The number of bodies on Mount Huang, and the resentful energy they have accumulated, likely far exceeds our expectations."

"Looks like that rat-bastard Xu Shuanglin made this mountain his hideout after all," said Jiang Xi, his expression gloomy. He glanced over his shoulder. "Listen up. Anyone who's injured, scared, useless, or pretending…" At this point, his chilly eyes swept over Huang Xiaoyue, still lying on the ground. He let out a soft snort. "All of you remain at the bottom of the mountain. The rest will come up with me."

Xue Meng watched Chu Wanning step through the rift in the barrier and rushed to catch up, only to realize Mo Ran wasn't beside him. He surveyed his surroundings and saw a commotion around Nangong Si. Bitan Manor's grieving disciples still hoped to avenge themselves; despite the protective barrier Chu Wanning had put down, a crowd of hateful faces still surrounded Nangong Si, hurling curses and insults.

"Mo Ran, what are you doing?" Xue Meng called out, urgent. "Everyone's going up the mountain! Let's go!"

"You go on ahead—keep an eye on Shizun and Shi Mei," Mo Ran replied. "If you run into trouble, send a messenger flower right away."

Xue Meng had no choice but to leave them.

By now, only those from Bitan Manor and Jiangdong Hall remained at the bottom of the mountain. Mo Ran tore his gaze away from Xue Meng's departing figure. "I understand how you all must feel, but Nangong-gongzi has nothing to do with the sword manual," he said. "If you must settle your debts, at least wait till we've captured Xu Shuanglin."

"These are two different matters entirely! Xu Shuanglin and Nangong Si both have to pay!"

"That's right! Neither of them can escape!"

Zhen Congming was one of the more reasonable in the group. He stared at Mo Ran through red-rimmed eyes. "Mo-zongshi, both you and your shifu have the title of zongshi. Yet you choose to protect criminals and put your own interests first?"

"I'm just trying to remind you that there's a right way to do this," Mo Ran said. "If you really want to redress your grievances with Rufeng Sect, wait for things to calm down. Then you can send Xu Shuanglin and his associates to Tianyin Pavilion for questioning according to the rules. The ten great sects will discuss his case and determine fair punishment. Right now, you're ambushing someone who doesn't intend to fight back. You want to tear him to pieces—but what good will that do?"

Zhen Congming had no ready answer.

"Ten great sects?" someone cried. "There are only nine! How can you still count Rufeng Sect?"

"No, there are eight," Zhen Congming said. His cheeks were streaked with blood from where he'd wiped his tears after cleaning his shizun's face. Under those bloodstains, he looked miserably forlorn. "There are only eight sects... Bitan Manor no longer has a leader."

"Shixiong..."

Zhen Congming ignored his weeping shidi, slowly turning to pin Mo Ran with his gaze. "After the Heavenly Rift, my shizun said Sisheng Peak was an honorable sect. But I see now that he misjudged you."

Mo Ran stared at him.

"Mo-zongshi, do you insist on protecting these two Rufeng vermin?" asked Zhen Congming.

Before Mo Ran could reply, Nangong Si rasped, "Mo Ran, go."

Ye Wangxi had knelt beside Nangong Si; now she helped him to his feet with difficulty. She didn't cry or wring her hands. She merely said, voice hoarse, "Mo-gongzi, you should go up the mountain. This doesn't involve you."

Mo Ran cast a sidelong glance at Nangong Si. "You think your allegiance to my shizun counts for nothing? We're two disciples under the same master; how could it not involve me?"

"You—" Nangong Si started.

But Mo Ran turned to look back at Zhen Congming. By now, Jiangdong Hall's disciples had joined forces with Bitan Manor to glare at them from all sides. Huang Xiaoyue had made his way over with the support of two female disciples, careful to be seen lurching this way and that. Chest heaving, he widened his eyes to lour at Mo Ran, then waved off the two disciples and jabbed a gnarled finger in Mo Ran's face. "I've lived by the righteous teachings of the upper cultivation realm all my life. I won't stand by and condone such behavior!"

"Huang-daozhang is indeed a great exemplar of the upper culti-vation realm's principles," Mo Ran replied coolly. "A moment ago you were at death's door, yet less than fifteen minutes later you're prancing around demanding justice. Your integrity is to be admired."

"You—!" Huang Xiaoyue burst into a violent coughing fit, clutching his chest as if overwhelmed by his anger. Mo Ran spared him hardly a glance.

The green of Bitan Manor and the purple of Jiangdong Hall swirled around the trio. The mob pressed closer, step by step, yet no one dared make the first move—any strike now would be impossible to take back.

"Mo-zongshi," Zhen Congming said in a low voice. "I'll ask you one more time. Do you refuse to step aside?"

Mo Ran had no chance to reply. A female cultivator's sharp cry rang out from up ahead as a pile of misshapen gray rocks tumbled out of the rift.

"What's going on?" Huang Xiaoyue exclaimed. "A landslide?"

Mo Ran narrowed his eyes. This was no landslide. Soon enough, the crowd realized it as well and gasps rose up from the assembly.

What had come careening out of the rift were charred human bodies. Their limbs and flesh were fused together and oozing, their faces barely recognizable as human.

Some of the watching cultivators immediately doubled over and vomited.

"That's so fucking gross…"

"*These* things are on the mountain?"

"How many bodies do you think there are..."

Mo Ran, too, was stricken by this sight.

A low rumble came from the slope above. The rift the elders had just torn into the barrier rippled; slowly, its borders began to shrink. This barrier could repair itself. Before long, it would close up and trap them on the outside.

"Let's go!" Mo Ran said anxiously. "Grudges can wait. Xu Shuanglin is at the top of the mountain—are you really not interested in hunting down the ringleader behind this whole mess?"

The group from Bitan Manor hesitated, but Huang Xiaoyue snorted and tugged at his mustache. "The best cultivators in the world are all at the top of the mountain. They can take care of Xu Shuanglin. But these two youngsters from Rufeng Sect have been as slippery as eels. If we let them go now, I'm afraid we won't get another chance."

"Huang Xiaoyue." Mo Ran's eyes blazed; there was a flash of scarlet as Jiangui materialized in his grip. "Are you about done?"

At the appearance of the holy weapon, all the hundred-odd cultivators drew their blades. They eyed him warily.

In his heart, Mo Ran knew this wouldn't end without a fight. He was happy to trade blows with any of them, but these people would undoubtedly view Sisheng Peak as the aggressor...

A low voice from behind disrupted Mo Ran's thoughts. "Everyone, please head up the mountain. I, Nangong Si, will wait for you here. I'm not going anywhere."

"Easy for you to say, kid, but who's going to buy it?" asked Huang Xiaoyue. "You don't expect me to believe you'll stay here just because you said so, do you?"

Nangong Si shot him a cold glance and rose to his feet. Without warning, he shoved Ye Wangxi out of the barrier Chu Wanning had cast.

"A-Si!"

Those within the barrier could leave, but those without couldn't go back in. Nangong Si stood alone inside the barrier and slowly drew his sword. Inch by inch, its snow-bright glare lit his face—his chin, his lips, his nose, his eyes.

Ye Wangxi guessed at once what he was about to do. Pounding her fist against the barrier, she yelled, "Stop messing around!"

"When my ancestor founded the sect, he left behind a teaching: As a gentleman of Rufeng Sect, I mustn't indulge in greed, resentment, deception, slaughter, obscenity, plunder, or conquest," said Nangong Si. "My father failed to live up to this teaching. But in my twenty-six years, though I may have been headstrong, I have never forsaken this maxim nor transgressed its commandments. Regarding these seven taboos, my conscience is clear."

The blade whizzed through the air like flowing water.

"No!" cried Ye Wangxi.

Mo Ran also saw what Nangong Si intended. He tried to break down Chu Wanning's barrier, but it could not be so easily undone. "Nangong..." he muttered.

Nangong Si paid heed to neither Ye Wangxi nor Mo Ran. "None of you trust me, so I have no other choice," he said. "Fortunately, I know some confinement techniques. I will secure myself here; please don't implicate anyone else. I, Nangong Si, will not move an inch from this spot. I will wait for your return."

"Nangong—!" Blood flew before Mo Ran had finished shouting his name. Nangong Si's sword plunged into the ground, half its length disappearing beneath the dirt. Between the blade and the earth was Nangong Si's left hand.

Using his own sword, Nangong Si had nailed his hand to the ground. Sparks flew from the blade as the confinement curse took hold.

Ye Wangxi crashed to her knees in front of the barrier. Nangong Si's blood flowed along the blade's surface, dyeing the ground red. Her face was lowered, her expression hidden from view. The watchers could only see her clenched hands on the flashing barrier, knuckles white and trembling.

This curse was used to confine evil creatures, vengeful ghosts, and beasts of burden. Any accomplished cultivator of the upper cultivation realm would recognize it, could use it. Nangong Si had used it to pin himself in place. His lips were bloodless with pain. Shudders wracked him, yet he didn't cry. At last, he raised bloodshot eyes. "Go," he said, voice firm.

Mo Ran rarely found himself shocked speechless. In the past life, only Ye Wangxi had ever managed this feat. In this life, it was accomplished by the man Ye Wangxi loved.

Truth be told, Mo Ran had never understood what Ye Wangxi saw in Nangong Si. He was a superficial, empty-headed rich brat who chased pretty girls. Why was Ye Wangxi so set on him? But at that moment, Mo Ran saw someone who resembled Ye Wangxi. He was doubled over, writhing in pain, losing blood—yet his resolve was absolute.

He saw Nangong Si.

"Go!" Nangong Si howled. "What are you still standing here for? Do I need to nail my legs to the ground too? Go already!"

Zhen Congming was first to turn away. He strode over to Li Wuxin's body. Leaning down, he smoothed his sect leader's robes, then picked him up and turned his back to the barrier.

"Shixiong!"

"Shixiong, you aren't staying?"

"Shixiong? Are we going to just leave like this? We're just going to let them go—"

"What's the point of staying?" said Zhen Congming. "Who knows how long they'll be fighting on the mountaintop? Should we wait around with the sect leader lying here on the dirt, without even a makeshift coffin?!"

Bitan Manor's disciples looked at one another. One by one, they bowed their heads in silence.

Zhen Congming walked away from the mountain, past Mo Ran. In the moment their shoulders drew level, he spoke: "Mo-zongshi, remember what you said. When this battle's over, I'll see you at Tianyin Pavilion."

"At least we have Tianyin Pavilion to uphold justice in this world," another interjected. It was the disciple who spat at Chu Wanning. He fell into step behind his shixiong, red-eyed with anger and bitterness. "The pavilion master is an impartial judge; they'll see our shizun passes on with no regrets. Mo Ran, Nangong Si... Karma's a bitch, you lowlifes. Just you wait—your days are numbered!"

201

Shizun, How Am I Supposed to Humiliate You?

WITH THE EXIT of Bitan Manor, Huang Xiaoyue had no more excuses to dawdle; he could do nothing but head up the mountain.

Mo Ran was in no mood for time-wasting and swiftly stepped through the rift, the disciples of Jiangdong Hall at his heels. Within moments of crossing the barrier, shrieks rose from the group behind him.

The dead were everywhere. Lying on the ground, hanging from trees, covering the slope like swarming ants. They moved and crawled, twitched and convulsed, sluggishly making their way toward the living.

They had entered a mountain of corpses.

In the face of such a sight, Huang Xiaoyue stepped forward alone. He struck out with his horsetail whisk, hitting several revenants on their heads. Where had this old man found so much courage? Before Mo Ran could wrap his head around it, Huang Xiaoyue let out a high-pitched scream. He collapsed to the ground, his limbs comically sprawled and eyes rolling back in his skull, coughing up bloody spittle.

Mo Ran stared, dumbfounded.

Jiangdong Hall's disciples rushed forward. "Huang-qianbei—"

"Qianbei..."

"Not to worry. I've been gravely injured, but I can fight on." Huang Xiaoyue made to clamber upright, but his knees gave out. He crumpled back to the ground, panting laboriously.

"Qianbei, you should rest at the bottom," a disciple said anxiously. "There's too much demonic energy here. It's no good for your heart."

"That's right!" another voice crowed in agreement.

Huang Xiaoyue made a great show of demurring as he coughed up a revolting mixture of blood and phlegm. After carrying on with this charade until he was satisfied, he donned an expression of deep regret. At last, and with a great swishing of robes, he led most of Jiangdong Hall's disciples out of the barrier once more like a school of carp making its way downstream. The barrier prevented people from entering but not exiting. Soon, only a handful of Jiangdong Hall's people remained on the mountain.

Before them appeared a young man making his way down the gentle slope. His hair was long and pale-gold, his eyes jade-green, and his expression somber. When he spied Mo Ran, both blinked in surprise.

Mo Ran was first to react. "Mei-xiong?"

Mei Hanxue nodded coolly.

"Have you seen my shizun and the others?" Mo Ran asked urgently.

"They're all up ahead." As he spoke, a corpse lurched up behind Mei Hanxue. Mo Ran opened his mouth with a warning when he saw the cold flash of a sword. Mei Hanxue drew his weapon without turning and carved a gaping hole into the corpse's chest. He pulled the sword out with a wet noise, its blade stained with dark blood. Features chilly, Mei Hanxue wiped the sword clean, then said to Mo Ran, "Straight up this path and take a left at the first fork. There are too many revenants. Everyone is trying to clear the way."

Mo Ran thanked him. As he stepped forward to leave, Mei Hanxue called out to him again. "Wait a moment."

"Does Mei-xiong have a request?"

"Mn. The palace leader was a friend of Madam Rong's. She's worried—she sent me to check on the two from Rufeng Sect. How are they? Are they still outside?"

Relief flooded through Mo Ran. "Yes, they're waiting outside the barrier. Nangong Si placed a confinement curse on himself. Huang Xiaoyue went down too; I'm afraid he'll make trouble for them again. If you could look after them, I'd be grateful."

Mei Hanxue pursed his lips and said no more. A graceful leap, and he disappeared through the barrier.

Mo Ran made his way up the mountain with all haste. So many undead lurked here; it would have been no surprise to stumble across at least a few bodies of fallen cultivators along the way. Yet curiously, all he encountered were dismembered and decaying corpses. They were disgusting, certainly, but not a single cultivator's remains stood out among them. Was it because the sect leaders had only brought their most accomplished subordinates?

He had no time to consider this; he threw himself into the fray to clear away the revenants. He had previously been passing by corpses others had already defeated; feeble and twitching the ground. But as Mo Ran met more of the fresh undead, the situation grew more curious still. Fighting them was too easy, nothing like what he would have expected from the reanimated bodies of warriors. He felt like he was cutting down ordinary people who barely had the strength to truss a chicken.

Mo Ran's unease redoubled. A terrifying notion was taking shape in his mind.

"Aaaargh!"

A corpse hanging from a tree, hair covering its face, lunged for Mo Ran's neck. Mo Ran jumped back, and the corpse turned its head to follow. Nostrils flaring, it sunk its bony fingers into Mo Ran's shoulder and thrust its decaying face toward his.

Unspeakably revolted, Mo Ran still thought strategically. One powerful kick sent the corpse flying into the thronging undead, knocking over several revenants that were closing in.

"Mo Ran!"

Xue Meng fought his way over and caught his breath; his cheeks were splashed with dark blood, eyes fiery. "What's going on?" he said in a low voice. "What's with these corpses? Are they trying to wear us down via sheer numbers? Why are they all so weak?"

Mo Ran's gaze was icy and distant. As the erstwhile Emperor Taxian-jun, he had read of many evil spells, and had a faint suspicion as to what was going on. He just didn't have sufficient evidence.

"These revenants aren't cultivators," Mo Ran said through gritted teeth. "They're commoners."

"What?!" Xue Meng turned to him in shock. "They're practically ashes, how the hell do you know they're not cultivators? I can't even fucking tell if they're men or women!"

In lieu of an answer, Mo Ran asked, "If we were fighting and you grabbed my shoulder because I didn't dodge quickly enough, what would you do?"

"How would you expose your shoulder to me in the first place? That's a rookie move. Even twelve-year-old disciples wouldn't make a mistake like that."

"Why is it a rookie move?"

"Because it's close to the spiritual core! If I grab your shoulder, it's as good as grabbing half of your spiritual core! I'd just need to use my other hand to pierce your chest and you'd be done for!"

"Right," replied Mo Ran. "One of the corpses grabbed my shoulder just now."

"How could you be so careless?" Xue Meng cried in alarm. "Do you want to die?"

"It didn't do anything."

"Huh?"

"It was so close, but it didn't occur to the corpse to go for my core with its other hand. Any cultivator should have a bone-deep instinct to protect their own core and attack their opponent's. Like you said—even a twelve-year-old would know that, and their bodies should retain those reflexes after death. But the corpse didn't do that." When Mo Ran continued, his voice was grim. "Why not? There are two possibilities: it either couldn't, or it didn't think of it."

Xue Meng stared at him.

"Its limbs were uninjured, and I was wide open, so that rules out the former," said Mo Ran. "It can only be that it failed to recognize the opportunity... These bodies probably all belonged to commoners. After death, they would be no match for top cultivators. Look, no one's gotten even a scratch in all the fighting."

"How could this be?" Xue Meng asked, astonished. "Why would Xu Shuanglin pile so many dead commoners onto Mount Huang? If he can control corpses, why not control the corpses of cultivators?"

"It's the same again: either he couldn't, or he didn't think of it."

"How could he possibly fail to think of it?"

"So that leaves only the first option. He couldn't." Mo Ran's gaze was dark. Jiangui's scarlet sparks danced in his eyes like molten iron falling into the vast sea of night. "Xu Shuanglin's spiritual power isn't enough to control so many cultivators using the Zhenlong Chess Formation."

"But what use is it to control these weaklings?" Xue Meng kicked down a row of undead, unsure whether to laugh or cry. "What's the *point* of this? Who would this possibly stop?"

Mo Ran said nothing. His conjecture was gaining form, sharpening at the edges. He surveyed the crowd of cultivators battling the corpses and noticed something bizarre: when the cultivators hacked off the revenants' limbs or heads, they collapsed to the ground. As he watched, a tiny vine sprouted from the earth and plunged into each of their chests. The vine wrapped around their heart and, with a soft *pop*, pulled it into the ground, vanishing from sight.

This seemed like it would be hard to miss, but the scene was incredibly chaotic, and everyone had their hands full with fighting. The vines were so small that unless someone stood to the side in observation, they were practically invisible.

"Mo Ran?"

Xue Meng called his name a few times, but it was like Mo Ran couldn't hear him at all.

Suddenly Mo Ran leapt into the air and grabbed a corpse by the neck, slashing open its chest with the dagger concealed in his palm. Black blood sprayed onto his face.

Xue Meng's mouth fell open. He took a few quick steps back, unable to speak. Had Mo Ran lost his mind...?

Turning his chiseled features aside, Mo Ran wrenched the corpse's shriveled gray heart from its chest and crushed it in his fingers.

Within was a black chess piece. This was no surprise. The corpses on Mount Huang would only fight like this under the control of

Zhenlong Chess. Mo Ran hadn't been looking for this black piece at all. Enduring the awful stench, he prodded through the gore.

Xue Meng couldn't take it any longer; he doubled over and retched. "You! Are you nuts? That's...so gross... Ugh..."

Mo Ran ignored him. He dragged his fingers through the congealed blood until they closed around the object he was looking for. A tiny scarlet insect was curled up on the reverse side of the chess piece. A soul-eater.

Without warning, a dozen vines burst from the ground and shot toward Mo Ran's bloody hands. He ducked out of the way, but the vines flew after him with increasing speed. They seemed to be hell-bent on bringing that chess piece, and the insect on it, into the earth.

By now, Mo Ran's guesses about Xu Shuanglin's plans and methods had been fully realized. Every hair on his body stood on end, and his blood ran cold. No one in the world could have devised this sort of dark forbidden technique—no one save the past life's Taxian-jun!

Just as the Sigil of the Returning Billows was Chu Wanning's creation, everything that stood before him—this chess piece, this soul-eater, this horde of corpses, this strategy—pointed toward a spell that Mo Ran couldn't be more familiar with: the Shared-Heart Array.

In the past lifetime, he himself had invented this spell.

If Mo Ran had merely suspected before, the appearance of this technique hit him over the head with the proof. It confirmed two things. Firstly, there was another reborn person in this world. Secondly, that person was intimately familiar with Taxian-jun's methods.

Mo Ran's hands were shaking. Dark blood dripped between his fingers as he clutched that black chess piece and the scarlet insect.

260 °—• THE HUSKY & HIS WHITE CAT SHIZUN

As he dodged the flailing vines, his mind was in chaos. Lost in confusion and shock, scattered memories from the past life swam into his consciousness.

In the beginning, he was only nineteen.

The Heavenly Rift had been recently repaired, and the pain of Shi Mei's death was fresh. Unbeknownst to all, Mo Ran had been teaching himself the Zhenlong Chess Formation in secret for almost half a year. But he had never succeeded—until today.

The nineteen-year-old Mo Weiyu sat cross-legged on the floor. Slowly, his eyes fluttered open. When he uncurled his fingers, two night-dark chess pieces nestled in his pale palm—the first Zhenlong chess pieces he had ever managed to refine.

He had tried thousands of different methods and met with failure after failure. He couldn't decipher the cryptic instructions in the forbidden technique scrolls, but he also couldn't ask Chu Wanning what they meant. By then, he was reluctant to speak to Chu Wanning about anything; Shi Mei's death had opened a chasm between them that could never be filled. They were master and disciple in name only, no more. In the few months before he revealed his fiendish plans to the world, he sometimes crossed paths with that man in white. But each time Mo Ran would pretend he hadn't seen him and walk away without a word.

Truthfully, there were several instances, as they'd walked past one another on Naihe Bridge, when Mo Ran had noticed Chu Wanning looking as though he wished to speak. But Chu Wanning's pride prevented him from calling out to his disciple, and Mo Ran didn't give him time to deliberate. He walked in the opposite direction, never turning back. In the end, they passed each other by.

Mo Ran toiled for months over those fragmented scrolls. At last, though no one would lend him aid, he teased out enough meaning to grasp the crux of the Zhenlong Chess Formation.

Every chess piece, whether black or the more powerful white that could share a spellcaster's will, must be refined from the caster's spiritual energy. The amount of spiritual energy needed to form each piece was terrifying. A black piece demanded the same amount of energy as making a hundred moves in a fight. The price for a white piece would be tantamount to draining all the spiritual energy of a great zongshi like Chu Wanning in a flashing instant. It mattered not how brilliant one was, or how well-versed in the subtleties of Zhenlong Chess. If one lacked the spiritual energy, they could never put it to practice.

Mo Ran was supremely gifted and blessed with copious spiritual energy, but he was still a young man, not yet twenty. Even after expending all his effort and failing countless times, he could refine no more than two black chess pieces.

And at that very moment, they lay in his palm.

He stared at those two black pieces, an uncanny glint in his eye. The only light in the room came from a guttering candle, flickering unsteadily over his face.

He'd done it.

Back then, he hadn't yet thought about the number of pawns he would need. Euphoria at this simple success washed over him. He'd done it!

Despite the handsomeness of his features, his face twisted with beastly malice. He walked, lightheaded, out of the dark cultivation room, half from joy, and half because these scant two chess pieces had sapped nearly all his spiritual energy. He was hollowed out and empty as he stepped outside. The brilliant sunlight dazzled him, making the world spin, taking his breath away.

His face flushed then paled; the scenery seemed to wobble before his eyes. He saw two Sisheng Peak disciples approaching from a distance. With his last scrap of consciousness, he stuffed those two black chess pieces into his qiankun pouch. Then his knees buckled— he crumpled to the ground and knew no more.

Some time later, as he walked between dreams and waking, he realized someone had brought him back to the disciple quarters. He was lying in his narrow bed. When he peered from between his eyelids, he saw a hazy figure sitting at his side.

Mo Ran was delirious with fever; he couldn't make out that person's features. Yet he sensed that the gaze on him held so much concern, attentiveness, and warmth; even some sharp slivers of self-reproach.

"Shi..."

Mo Ran's lips parted and shut, but his voice was so hoarse he couldn't get out more than a syllable. His tears, however, spilled freely.

The figure in white seemed to hesitate. Then Mo Ran felt a warm palm against his face, wiping the tears from his cheeks. That person sighed softly. "Why are you crying again?"

Mo Ran couldn't respond.

Shi Mei, you came back. Please, don't go... Don't die... Don't leave me alone... Since my mom left this world, there's been no one as kind to me as you were... There's no one else who doesn't look down on me, who's willing to remain by my side...

Shi Mei, don't go...

He couldn't hold back the hot tears that rolled down his face. It felt so childish, but he cried in his sleep as he dreamed on and on.

The person at his bedside didn't move. After a time, he took Mo Ran's hand in his own. He never spoke, but he kept him company, never leaving for a moment.

Mo Ran thought of the two Zhenlong chess pieces in his qiankun pouch. They were the fonts of sin, the seeds of evil. But they were also the hard-won bargaining chips with which he would take on heaven and earth. Refining chess pieces required more than spiritual energy—for this, he sacrificed his unblemished souls.

Beneath wet lashes, Mo Ran's gaze was murky. Staring at the vision of Shi Mei, he mumbled, "I'm sorry... If you were still here, I wouldn't..."

I wouldn't want to take this path either.

But he hadn't the strength to finish the sentence. He fell into unconsciousness once more.

When he next awoke, that white-robed man had gone. Mo Ran became convinced he was a figment of his half-dreaming imagination. But he remembered an incense burner had been lit in his room earlier. Xue Zhengyong had placed it there to soothe his nerves. It was good incense, but Mo Ran didn't like it. Now, that incense had been put out. It was a long coil, left unfinished—someone must have come and extinguished it.

Who had come here?

Mo Ran sat up, looking at the censer in a daze, but he couldn't figure it out. After a while, he decided to forget about it. He saw that his clothes, accessories, and holy weapon had been neatly laid out on his table. Among them was his qiankun pouch.

With a jolt of panic, he jumped barefoot from the bed and grabbed the qiankun pouch. Before he passed out, he had carefully triple-knotted the cord. Luck was with him—all three knots were still there, untouched. Mo Ran loosened them and let out a breath of relief. Rummaging through the pouch, he spotted those two Zhenlong chess pieces, dark as a lightless night, lying in wait in a corner like two ghoulish eyes. They looked as though they might swallow him whole.

He stared at those two pieces for a very long time.

Here, perhaps was the hand of fate—if Chu Wanning had looked through Mo Ran's qiankun pouch, everything after would have been different. But Chu Wanning was never the type to go through the belongings of others without reason. Even if their pockets were gaping open, he wouldn't take a second look.

Mo Ran picked out the chess pieces. His throat bobbed, and his heart pounded like a drum. What now? How should he use these two pieces? They were the very first fruits of his labor, and he was eager to test them. But on whom?

Inspiration struck like a bolt of lightning. A diabolical, deranged idea burst to life in his head.

Chu Wanning.

He wanted to put a chess piece in Chu Wanning.

Once it was in him, would this callous, hypocritical man obey his every whim? Would he kneel on command, and never dare to resist? Could Mo Ran make Chu Wanning fall to his knees before him and apologize? Make Chu Wanning cower at his feet? He could make Chu Wanning call him his master; he could wound him, stab him, tear him to pieces!

Ecstasy warped the light in Mo Ran's eyes. Yes, he could torment him. But how could he inflict the utmost pain, the utmost humiliation, upon this imperious cultivator?

Humiliation...

Mo Ran gripped those two chess pieces. His mouth was dry, and grew drier by the minute. Exhilaration and apprehension washed over him in turns. He licked chapped lips. He wanted this so badly; he wanted to see Chu Wanning lower his pale neck before him. He wanted to reach out and lay a hand upon it, to feel him trembling under his touch, and then...

Break his neck? Snap his bones?

Mo Ran felt displeased. For some reason, that seemed pointless, unsatisfactory. Letting Chu Wanning die would be a bore. Even the thought annoyed Mo Ran. He wanted to see him weep and grovel; he wanted to see him live a life worse than death, to be crushed by fury and shame.

There had to be a more gratifying way for him to vent his anger.

He touched a chess piece to his lips. Mouth pressed to its ice-cold surface, he murmured, "You can't stop me anymore, Chu Wanning. Soon, the day will come when I'll make you..."

Make you what?

At nineteen, he hadn't understood that the desire surging through him was in large part lust and a primal urge to conquer. But even then, he already possessed a terrifyingly strong masculine instinct to take the very first seed of evil he had nurtured and sow it within Chu Wanning's body.

He wanted to *defile* him.

Mo Ran stood up. He pushed open the door and stepped out of the room.

Shizun's First Brush with Evil

A FTER PACING around the Red Lotus Pavilion a few times, Mo Ran forced himself to calm. In the end, he did nothing so crazy—it was too dangerous. These were the very first Zhenlong chess pieces he had made, and he had no idea how effective they would be. If he rashly used them on the world's top zongshi, it would be the same as declaring he was tired of living.

So, at the end of several back-and-forths, Mo Ran suppressed his impulses and left the Red Lotus Pavilion. After some deliberation, he elected to plant the chess pieces into two little shidi. He needed to experiment, and the safest option was to use them on disciples who hadn't yet attained a stable spiritual foundation.

The evening was cool, the mountain's peak wreathed in darkness. Mo Ran moved like dark lightning. He watched as those two young disciples, who had moments ago been skipping stones on the river, froze in place. He was so anxious his hands were trembling, his pupils contracted to pinpricks. Face ashen in the moonlight, he pursed his lips, fingertips twitching, and strode forward. He had used a terrible forbidden technique for the very first time; he was enthralled by the power of it, yet sick with trepidation.

Robes rustled as the two disciples fell to their knees. Mo Ran startled like a bird at the twang of a bow, like an assassin who had just made the kill. The soft sigh of the wind through the grass was enough to scare him out of his wits. He dropped into a crouch in the copse of trees nearby, his heart ready to leap out of his throat.

Badum. Badum. Badum.

He waited for an age, but those two figures didn't budge; they knelt woodenly in place. Mo Ran's frantic heartbeat finally settled. His inner robe was drenched in sweat, his scalp completely numb.

He stepped out of the trees. Once more, he stood beneath the moonlight on the pebbled riverbank. Although much calmer than before, he hardly dared to breathe, careful as a snake slithering through the darkness. He looked down and scrutinized those two little shidi. Both had been giggling and yelling, but now, not a hint of vitality remained in their faces. They were still as a stagnant pond, kneeling motionlessly. Even under the full weight of Mo Ran's stare, they moved not a muscle.

With a silent twitch of his fingers, Mo Ran cast a spell.

The two shidi immediately prostrated, pressing their foreheads to the mud. Then they rose and turned to look at Mo Ran. In those two pairs of pitch-dark eyes, Mo Ran glimpsed his own reflection. The image wavered, unfocused—yet for some reason, Mo Ran felt as though he had seen the figure of a devil with perfect clarity, standing with the moon behind him, his face deathly white, his eyes gleaming scarlet.

He heard himself speak, his voice trembling, hoarse, and uncertain. "What is your name?"

The voices that answered were passive and tuneless. "My name is not mine to say."

Mo Ran's heart rabbited frantically as his blood pounded in his ears. He swallowed, throat bobbing, and asked again, "Where are you?"

"My location is not mine to say."

"How old are you?"

"My age is not mine to say."

Low-level pawns under control of the Zhenlong Chess Formation were incapable of divulging three things: their names, their locations, and their ages. These were all for their master to decide. It was just as the ancient scrolls described.

Mo Ran shuddered. It was strange: facing these two pawns he had created himself, what he felt most intensely was not elation at his success, but a naked fear.

Fear of what? He was unsure; his thoughts were a hopeless tangle. He felt himself standing at the edge of a cliff—no, he had already fallen from the ledge. Below him was darkness, an endless abyss. He couldn't see the bottom, couldn't see anything—neither death nor fire, neither the limits of this power nor his own end. One of his souls seemed to be howling and screaming inside him, a final cry before it shattered into dust, into ruins.

He reached out and touched one of the pawns on the cheek with a shaking hand. When he swallowed, his mouth was parched, his lips cracking. His handsome features contorted as he watched that little shidi.

"What do you want?" He asked at last.

"To serve as your pawn, sparing no effort, on pain of death."

All at once, Mo Ran's shaking stopped. The world became impossibly clear, sharp and still as ice. In making these pawns, he had taken these shidi, whose names he didn't even know, and transformed them into his puppets. If he told them to jump, they would ask how high. If he told them to kill, they would show no mercy, even to each other.

He was their master.

At its weakest, the Zhenlong Chess Formation could control dead bodies. At its strongest, it could control the living. Mo Ran's innate spiritual power was terrifyingly potent; he had a natural talent for the technique. His very first attempt had yielded chess pieces with the ability to control two living cultivators, young and untutored as they were.

Once his initial fear passed, an intoxicating flush of anticipation took hold of Mo Ran. A grand scroll seemed to unfurl before his eyes, upon which were spangled scenes of opulence and indulgence. Everything was within his reach; everything was *his*. He could seize all he loved, and he could ravage all he hated.

Spellbound, his heart raced faster, but no longer out of fear. Now, it was with heady thrill—the Zhenlong Chess Formation. The three great forbidden techniques. All his hard work, his toiling in secret, all the countless failures he'd suffered... Despite all of it, he'd succeeded. More than that—he'd *excelled*. Everything under the sun was his to claim. These two black chess pieces opened up endless possibilities. He could strew his pawns throughout the land, from the farthest reaches of the northern desert to the fertile southern river plains.

The world seemed to glitter before his eyes. He could do anything, anything at all...

"Mo Ran."

A familiar low voice doused his fantasies like a bucket of cold water. Those lofty towers and splendid spires crumbled to dust; he hurtled from the clouds and crashed to the cold, hard earth, finding himself in stifling reality once more. Mo Ran slowly turned his head, moonlight spilling into his scarlet, savage eyes. An austere man in white stood upon the gravel. Never had he wanted to see Chu Wanning less than at this very moment.

"What are you doing here?"

Mo Ran's hands silently curled into fists. He pressed his lips together and didn't reply. Those two imperfect pawns were still standing behind him. If Chu Wanning took a closer look, he would realize something was wrong—everything would fall apart. Knowing Chu Wanning, he would rip out Mo Ran's tendons, break his legs, destroy his spiritual core, then take those precious ancient texts he'd copied so painstakingly from the forbidden area of the library and toss them into a roaring fire.

When Mo Ran still didn't answer, Chu Wanning frowned slightly. He stepped forward on the pebbles with his spotless white shoes. But after a single step, he stopped and glanced at the two disciples standing, uncannily still, behind Mo Ran.

Mo Ran had been backed into a corner. Summoning all his willpower, he crooked a pinkie and internally hollered a command at those two disciples: *Move!*

One of them laughed out loud. "That rock hardly went anywhere. The one I threw went way farther than yours."

"Sure, sure, whatever. You're still... Ahh, Yuheng Elder!"

They chattered and gestured as cheerfully as before. But once they caught sight of Chu Wanning, both disciples froze. One after another, they bowed respectfully. Chu Wanning's gaze hovered on them, as though he felt a wrongness but couldn't quite tell why.

"Hope all is well, Elder."

"Good evening, Yuheng Elder."

The disciples adopted solemn expressions and made their greetings to Chu Wanning very properly before politely taking their leave.

Chu Wanning's frown didn't ease. His gaze followed the two disciples as they walked up from the riverbank and past him, heading into the bamboo forest... He stared after them for a long moment before finally turning away and fixing his gaze on Mo Ran. Just as Mo Ran was about to let out a silent breath of relief, Chu Wanning said: "Wait."

Mo Ran grew a touch paler. His fingernails had dug red crescents in his palms, but he said nothing. He stood calmly, taking in every detail of Chu Wanning's expression, every movement.

"Come back," Chu Wanning called to those two frozen silhouettes.

Mo Ran had no choice but to instruct those two disciples to slowly make their way back from the bamboo forest and stop before Chu Wanning. Wispy clouds drifted aside to unveil the full moon. In its cold and pristine light, Chu Wanning scrutinized the faces of those two disciples, then lifted his fingertips to one of their necks.

Chu Wanning's eyes flick back and forth as Mo Ran watched. His face betrayed nothing, but his heart was racing. If Chu Wanning was checking this disciple's pulse it was because he had sensed something amiss. Most people, when learning the Zhenlong Chess Formation, first learned to control corpses; it was far more difficult to control the living. These two disciples had been very much alive at the start, but Mo Ran couldn't be sure he'd done everything correctly. It was possible he'd killed them the moment he slipped those black chess pieces into their hearts.

He didn't know how long he'd been holding his breath when Chu Wanning finally lowered his hand. He swept his sleeves back and intoned, "You may go."

Mo Ran felt like the blade pressed to his throat had been withdrawn. Chu Wanning couldn't tell. The merciful heavens had allowed him to escape unscathed from right under Chu Wanning's nose.

When the two disciples had gone, Chu Wanning swung his gaze back to Mo Ran. "It's late. What are you doing here?"

"Just passing by," Mo Ran replied. He kept his voice under careful control; even as he dissembled, his attitude toward Chu Wanning remained as frosty as ever.

Perhaps it was because of Mo Ran's tone, so chilly and challenging, that Chu Wanning only silently pressed his lips together. Despite his misgivings, he said nothing.

Mo Ran didn't wish to spend a second longer than necessary in Chu Wanning's presence. He tore his gaze away and strode up the bank.

In the moment their shoulders drew even, Chu Wanning spoke: "Someone recently snuck into the forbidden area of the library."

Mo Ran tensed, silent and wary. He didn't turn, but his eyes flickered.

"That area contains ancient scrolls on forbidden techniques that the ten great sects have split up for security. You should know this."

"I know," said Mo Ran, falling still.

"Someone has clearly gone through one of the most important scrolls."

Mo Ran snorted. "And what does that have to do with me?"

He was bluffing. As soon as Tianwen lit up, as soon as it bound him, all crimes and schemes would be laid bare before Chu Wanning. All dreams and ambitions would be cut short.

Chu Wanning was quiet a moment. "Mo Ran, how long are you going to keep this up?" There was an indignant edge to his voice.

Mo Ran said nothing. He could almost see what would happen next. Tianwen's golden flash, Chu Wanning's oh-so-virtuous face as he interrogated him, asked him why he would do something so beastly. No matter what, in Chu Wanning's eyes, he would always be beyond—

"Don't you know how dangerous it is right now?"

—saving.

Mo Ran stiffly finished his thought. He turned, disoriented, and saw Chu Wanning's face beneath the moonlight. He was white as a sheet, those sword-straight brows furrowed with faint unease.

The eyes fastened upon Mo Ran were as penetrating as ever, but they hadn't glimpsed the truth tonight.

"If someone really attempts those forbidden techniques, they'll use them to kill. And yet here you are running around this godforsaken place in the dead of night instead of sleeping—have you no thought for your own safety?"

Chu Wanning's voice was low, as though he was speaking through gritted teeth. "So many died in the battle of the Heavenly Rift. Did that not impress upon you the value of life? If you know someone's been reading the ancient scrolls in secret, how could you be so careless?!"

Mo Ran stared at him in silence. His brow was sheened in sweat that had turned cold as ice in the breeze. Bit by bit, the tension bled out of his body and some strange emotion filled his heart, a feeling he couldn't identify. At last, his features creased in a smile. "Shizun..."

Chu Wanning's phoenix eyes flickered. Since Shi Mei's death, Mo Ran had never once smiled at him, and scarcely ever called him shizun.

That smile still playing over his lips, Mo Ran asked, "Are you worried about me?" At Chu Wanning's silence, Mo Ran's smile grew brighter and sharper, curving into a dagger that plunged into Chu Wanning's chest, white on the way in, red on the way out, dripping with blood. Mo Ran bared a mouthful of gleaming teeth like a vicious ghost, like a venomous scorpion raising its pincers high.

"The battle of the Heavenly Rift..." Mo Ran snickered. "How wonderful that Shizun brought up the Heavenly Rift. It doesn't matter what I learned in that battle—what's important is that Shizun's finally learned to care about people."

Mo Ran watched the light in Chu Wanning's eyes falter as he tried and failed to hide the cornered look on his face. His grin was exaggerated, cavalier and cruel. He would debase Chu Wanning, tear him to shreds, bite his neck through. A shiver of delight coursed through him as he burst into laughter. "Ha ha, how amazing! What a great deal! A nameless disciple in exchange for Chu-zongshi's conscience! At last, Chu-zongshi spares a thought for whether those around him live or die. Shizun, today, I finally feel that Shi Mei's death was well and truly worth it."

Even a man as unflappable as Chu Wanning would tremble as Mo Ran's manic laughter surrounded him like a circling falcon. "Mo Ran..."

"Shi Mei's death was well worth it, a stroke of luck even—a righteous, fitting death!"

"Mo Ran, please..." *Stop laughing. Don't say any more.*

But Chu Wanning couldn't speak; he couldn't say the words. He couldn't plead or beg for mercy. Neither did he have the heart to reprimand this disciple who had nearly lost his mind. He couldn't say, *You're wrong—it wasn't that I didn't want to save him. I truly didn't have the strength. I suffered the same injury he did. Had I expended one more wisp of spiritual energy, I too would be bones in a grave, a soul beneath the Yellow Springs.*

He couldn't say it. Maybe he felt such an admission would be too pathetic. Or maybe he thought that, in Mo Ran's heart of hearts, his shizun's death would hardly merit a mention; he couldn't compare to Shi Mingjing, who had always been so kind and gentle to him. In the end, Chu Wanning steadied his quavering voice and said in a low, deliberate tone, "Mo Weiyu, it's time to pull yourself together."

Mo Ran didn't respond.

"Go back." He buried his sorrow under anger, but a bitter taste lingered in his throat. "Shi Mingjing didn't die for you to turn into a lunatic."

"Shizun, that's not quite right." Mo Ran chuckled. "Shi Mei didn't die for me at all." Like a vicious serpent, he struck for the jugular. "The person he died for was clearly *you*, Shizun."

Fangs sank into flesh.

An acrid satisfaction surged in Mo Ran's heart as he watched Chu Wanning's cheeks drain of color. He'd thrown caution to the wind to taunt and torment him. If his own pain was about to tear him apart, he would make Chu Wanning hurt in equal measure. How perfect. They could go to hell together.

"I want to go back too." Mo Ran grinned, his dimples deep and brimming with poison wine. "I don't want to be wandering out here in the dead of night either. But his room is right across from mine."

Mo Ran didn't specify whom he meant—who else could it be? He knew this would only torment Chu Wanning more. "The candle in his room will never be lit again."

Chu Wanning closed his eyes.

As the moment stretched, the smile faded from Mo Ran's face. "I'll never be able to persuade him to make me another bowl of wontons."

For an instant, Chu Wanning's eyelashes quivered; his lips parted, as though to speak. But Mo Ran didn't give him a chance, or offer any encouragement. He pressed on, his tone weighted with mockery. "Shizun, the Sichuanese make the best wontons. Chili oil, dried chilis, and peppercorn—you need all three. But you hate all these things. Back then, you wanted to make me another bowl. You meant well. But I know how to describe anything you make even without tasting it."

Chu Wanning's eyes remained closed, his brows drawn together as though he could dodge the blows dealt by Mo Ran's words if he didn't see them spoken.

"I happened to hear Xue Meng use this phrase a few days ago. It seemed so fitting for Shizun's wontons."

What was it? *A lost cause? A sorry attempt?* Chu Wanning fumbled through his vocabulary like he was searching for a suit of armor, looking for the most scathing words as if guessing in advance would deaden the sting of humiliation. *Not worth a damn?*

Mo Ran was quiet, as though savoring the taste of the words between his teeth.

It had to be *not worth a damn*, Chu Wanning decided. He couldn't think of anything more cutting than that. He forced himself to calm—until he heard Mo Ran say placidly: "A piss-poor copycat."

Chu Wanning's eyes flew open in near-disbelief. He'd never thought Mo Ran could be so vicious. Within his sleeves, his hands were trembling. He had followed the instructions exactly, the pages of *Sichuan Recipes* spread out before him—kneading the dough, adjusting the seasonings, mixing the filling... His face smudged with flour, he'd kept folding until his awkwardly misshapen wontons became adorably plump. He had practiced diligently, refining his technique—only to be called *a piss-poor copycat*.

The night was dark overhead. Chu Wanning stood unmoving as Mo Ran gazed at him on that frosty silver riverbank. Without a word, he spun on his heel and strode away.

Mo Ran couldn't say why, but he'd always thought Chu Wanning's footsteps had been hurried as he left that day. They weren't as sure and steady as usual—almost as though he were fleeing a grievous defeat. Nor did he understand why he was gripped by a vague sense of unease as he watched, frowning, as Chu Wanning walked away. In the instant his figure was about to vanish, Mo Ran cried, "Wait!"

203

Shizun Shouldn't Have Spared This Ghost

B UT CHU WANNING didn't stop, nor turn his head. He couldn't. Despite gritting his teeth against the pain, tears streamed down his face.

It hurt too much.

But what else could he do? Explain himself? Lash out? After what had happened, how was he to muster up the courage to tell Mo Ran the truth? Was he to pitifully attempt an explanation while Mo Ran mocked and ridiculed him? Did he want to get labeled a *worthless pretender* on top of a *piss-poor copycat*?

So he left.

Perhaps the conversation that took place that night between master and disciple under Naihe Bridge, by the waters of the Yellow Springs, might have drifted along the surging waters down the mountain creeks, into the rivers, all the way to the netherworld. If that youth beneath the Springs, gentle as lotus petals, overheard these words, perhaps his heart would ache at the tension between these two.

Mo Ran stood alone by the riverbank. Maybe this was fate, he thought. Chu Wanning had suspected the others, but not him. Their run-in had been a coincidence—Chu Wanning had been patrolling in the backwoods, and after summoning Tianwen to dispatch a minor ghost, hadn't dispersed the holy weapon. It had been hanging coiled at his waist, glittering gold against Chu Wanning's white robes. This vine that could compel truth, this whip that could have wound around the future Emperor Taxian-jun's neck before he ever ascended, had glowed throughout their entire conversation. But Chu Wanning hadn't unleashed it to interrogate him.

So much for Tianwen. Mo Ran trudged up the riverbank. He stepped into the depths of the rustling bamboo forest, into the gloomiest crevices of the night, and let the darkness swallow him up.

After this episode, Mo Ran set about creating chess pieces with a newfound sense of purpose. Two, then four, then ten—an ever-increasing number. He planted them one after another into the bodies of Sisheng Peak disciples, turning them into his eyes and ears, his talons and blades.

Gradually, his initial satisfaction wore off. Mo Ran grew frustrated and gloomy. He was quicker than ever to lose his temper and lash out, forever impatient. This was too slow. These pieces weren't enough. He was afraid of Chu Wanning noticing, so he didn't dare expend all his energy on making Zhenlong chess pieces as he had in that first trial. He made one piece at a time, saving half his energy.

At the same time, he put aside his open hostility; he sheathed his claws and returned to learning cultivation from Chu Wanning. He had concluded after some thought that Chu Wanning was the key to improving his cultivation as swiftly as possible. Chu Wanning could help him build the first stepping stone he'd use to trample over the bodies of the living. Why look a gift horse in the mouth?

One day, he accidentally overextended himself. As he balanced on the slender tips of a tree's branches, he lost control and dropped like a stone.

In an instant, Chu Wanning leapt toward him, a streak of white robes. He caught Mo Ran but had no hand free to summon a barrier; the two of them tumbled to the ground beneath the tree, Mo Ran landing squarely on top of Chu Wanning as he grunted in pain. When Mo Ran opened his eyes, he saw that Chu Wanning's hand had been scraped in the fall, leaving a bloody gash.

Mo Ran stared at the wound. Cruel excitement welled up in him; already his personality had begun to warp, and he felt neither gratitude nor guilt. In fact, he found this blood quite pleasing—why not shed a little more?

But the time was not yet ripe. He couldn't reveal the malevolent face hidden beneath his mask, so he helped Chu Wanning clean and dress the wound. Neither of them spoke, both lost in their own thoughts. Mo Ran wrapped the snowy white bandage several times over Chu Wanning's hand. At last, he said pointedly, "Thank you, Shizun."

These words of gratitude caught Chu Wanning off guard. He looked up, gazing into Mo Ran's face. Sunlight spilled through the branches, illuminating Mo Ran's features and his dark eyes.

Mo Ran was curious—what would Chu Wanning make of his thanks? Was this errant child finally mending his ways? Was the tension between them finally easing?

But Chu Wanning said nothing at all. He merely lowered his lashes and shook his sleeve down over his injured hand.

A breeze brushed past, and the sun warmed the earth.

In his past life, Mo Ran had never understood his shizun, and likewise, his shizun had gravely misread him.

Time marched on. Mo Ran's spiritual energy grew by leaps and bounds. His innate talent was extraordinary, and the number of chess pieces he could refine with half of his energy multiplied from one, to two, to four. But it still wasn't enough. What he needed was the power of millions of soldiers, enough to crush Sisheng Peak in one blow, enough to grind Chu Wanning under his heel.

Math was not one of his talents. When Xue Meng came to visit him, he beheld the man who would one day become Emperor Taxian-jun clutching an abacus, beads clacking as he calculated sums. Curious, he sidled close. "Hey, what are you working on?"

"Balancing the scales."

"What kind of balance?"

Mo Ran paused, eyes shadowed. "Guess," he said with a smile.

"No clue." Xue Meng walked over, picking up the notebook and mumbling as he read, "One...three hundred sixty-five days...three hundred sixty-five...four...three hundred sixty-five... What the heck is this?"

"I want to buy candy," Mo Ran said expressionlessly.

"Candy?"

"The best candy from Moonlight Confectionery is one copper apiece. If I saved one copper every day, I could buy three hundred sixty-five candies in a year. If I can save four coppers a day, that would be..." He lowered his head, counting on his fingers, but he couldn't arrive at the sum. Shaking his head, he returned to clacking on the abacus beads. "That's a thousand..."

Xue Meng was far nimbler at mental math. "One thousand, four hundred sixty candies," he offered.

Mo Ran looked up, his smile brightening. "You did that awfully quickly."

Xue Meng wasn't used to praise from Mo Ran. He blinked, then burst into laughter. "Of course. I've been helping Mom measure out medicines since I was little."

Mo Ran pondered in silence a moment. He grinned. "I can't figure it out. Do me a favor and help me out?"

He had rarely been in such a good mood since Shi Mei's death. As Xue Meng watched him sitting there with the sun at his back, a wave of pity rose in his heart. He nodded and pulled a chair beside Mo Ran. "Okay, go ahead."

"If I saved enough for ten candies a day, how many would I have in a year?"

"Three thousand, six hundred fifty. You don't need the abacus to calculate this one—that's too easy."

Mo Ran sighed. "What about more? Fifteen…" He reconsidered; maybe making that many chess pieces was too much. Mo Ran amended, "Twelve a day. How many would that be?"

"Four thousand… Four thousand, three hundred eighty."

"If I wanted five thousand, how many more days would that take?"

"You'd need…" Xue Meng scratched his head, struggling with the question. "Why do you want so much candy? It's not like you could eat them all."

Mo Ran lowered his lashes, hiding the darkness in his eyes. "Sisheng Peak's thirtieth anniversary is next year. I want to give everyone a piece of candy, so I need to start saving today."

"*That's* what you're thinking about?" Xue Meng was stunned.

"Mn." Mo Ran smiled. "Are you surprised? You'll get one too."

"I don't need one." Xue Meng waved his hands. "I don't need candy from you. Here, I'll help with the math. Let's see how long it'll take for you to buy five thousand candies."

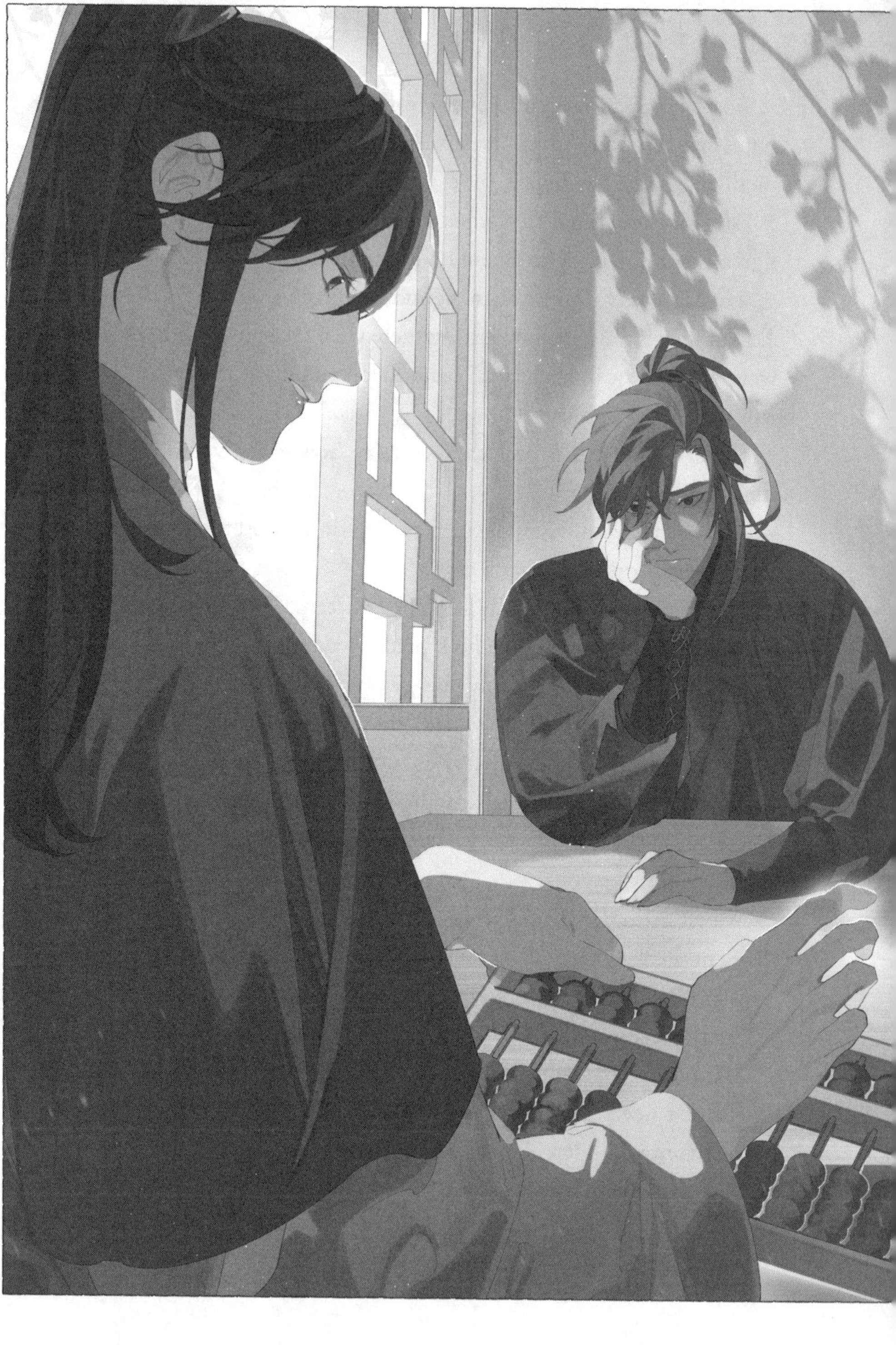

In the shade of the flowering trees by the window, Xue Meng took up the abacus and earnestly helped Mo Ran do the calculations. Mo Ran watched with a cheek propped in his hand, eyes flickering. After a spell, he chuckled and said, "Thank you."

Xue Meng scoffed, too engrossed in his task to pay Mo Ran much mind. His eyes followed those black abacus beads flicking past his fingers, like black chess pieces piling up one by one.

How was Xue Meng to know his calculations weren't for candy, but for human lives—the number of souls it would take to topple Sisheng Peak. Nor could he know it was the sight of him sitting by the windowsill and lending a hand that caught at the last wisp of kindness in Mo Ran's heart. It was on account of this lingering sentiment that Mo Ran refrained from making Xue Meng one of those five thousand pawns.

When Xue Meng wrote down the final number, Mo Ran shook his head. "It's going to take *that* long? That's too much."

"Why don't I lend you some money?" Xue Meng asked.

Mo Ran smiled. "No thanks."

After Xue Meng left, Mo Ran sank into thought. As he rifled through his scrolls, a plan took shape in his heart. This was the plan that would become a prototype of Taxian-jun's Shared-Heart Array.

That night, Mo Ran refined ten chess pieces. They were imperfect and unfinished. He hadn't put much into them, so they couldn't control the living; even corpses with some power would prove difficult.

Taking these chess pieces in hand, Mo Ran set off down the mountain toward the outskirts of Wuchang Town. He hummed as strode along, and soon arrived at his destination: Crane's Return Hill. Folktales had it that when a person died, a crane would take flight, winging them into the heavens. Commoners clung to this beautiful illusion, but in frank terms, the hill was a graveyard. The dead of Wuchang Town were buried here, their bones laid to rest in the dirt.

Mo Ran wasted no time. He stalked between rows of graves, his gaze raking across the names on top. Presently he stopped before a gravestone with fresh fruit and steamed buns arrayed before it, its inscriptions still stark. He extended a hand, fingers curling into a fist. Earth cracked, and the ground parted to reveal a simple coffin lying within the sandy soil.

Owing to an experience he'd had in his youth, Mo Ran had no fear of corpses, nor any veneration for dead bodies. He hopped down from the mound of dirt and summoned his holy weapon, prying open the lid and kicking it aside.

Moonlight shone down on the face of the deceased. Mo Ran craned his neck, studying the corpse as if judging pork at a butcher's. It was an old geezer, freshly interred, his face shriveled and sunken within his burial clothes. The graveyard wasn't in the best location, and his family hadn't the money to embalm him, so the coffin stank profoundly. Some of his flesh had already begun to rot, writhing with maggots.

Mo Ran frowned, ignoring the stench as he slipped on a pair of chain mail gloves. He grabbed the old man's neck and lifted him out of the coffin. The corpse's head lurched stiffly forward. Eyes cold, he reached out with a lightning-quick flourish and planted that Zhenlong chess piece into the old man's chest.

"Behave, behave." Mo Ran patted the corpse's cheek almost tenderly, then backhanded it hard across the face. "Why so glum?" he asked with a grin. "Stand up straight, sweetheart."

The defective black chess piece couldn't take control of a strong corpse, but it was more than capable of puppeteering a skinny old geezer. The corpse twitched to life, limbs creaking. Those tightly closed eyelids stretched open to reveal rheumy pupils.

"What is your name?" Mo Ran asked.

"My name is not mine to say."

"Where are you?"

"My location is not mine to say."

"How old are you?"

"My age is not mine to say."

Mo Ran narrowed his eyes, weighing the nine remaining chess pieces in his hand. If he made pawns of corpses like these, there would be no need to expend so much spiritual energy making those pure black chess pieces. He grinned, dimples deepening as his face split into a mesmerizing smile. Slowly, he asked the final question. "What do you want?"

"I want to serve as your pawn, sparing no effort, on pain of death."

Mo Ran burst into laughter. He was wholly satisfied by this result. Palming the remaining chess pieces, he made nine more corpse puppets. He chose only freshly buried corpses with flesh that was unspoiled and not eaten away.

These bodies were old and weak, and would topple at the slightest breeze. They had no power, but as Mo Ran watched them, his eyes sparked with madness and delight. He produced a dozen-odd small boxes from his qiankun pouch and opened one. Two crimson bugs curled within, one male and one female. They were biting each other's tails, locked in an inseparable loop.

"All right, you've had your fun. Could you two please give it a rest—it's high time you made yourself useful," Mo Ran drawled, pulling the two mating bugs apart. He picked up the male insect and turned to the first pawn he'd made, the old man. "Good sir, please open your stinking mouth."

The old man obediently did so, revealing its putrid tongue. Mo Ran tossed the male insect into his mouth. "Swallow."

Without hesitation or resistance, the corpse swallowed the soul-eater.

Mo Ran fed the remaining male insects to the corpses in the same way. "All right, now lie back down and rest."

The next day, Mo Ran refined another ten black chess pieces, all defective, none requiring much spiritual energy. He stuck the female soul-eaters on these pieces and secretly planted them inside some lower-level disciples. Those disciples merely felt some itchiness in their lower back, nothing too alarming. Now Mo Ran had to wait—but he wasn't impatient. Soon the female soul-eaters would lay eggs, hatching larvae in the disciple's hearts that would resonate with the male insects in the corpses.

In this way, two chess pieces that weren't linked at all would become a matched set of parent-child puppets. It was like flying a kite: the feeble corpses had become the kite strings, with one end in Mo Ran's hands and the other in the stronger disciples. Command the corpses with the male insects, and the living pawns containing their larvae would perform the exact same movements as if they were one—this was the meaning of "shared heart."

Mo Ran himself had invented this masterful technique. Those who had attempted the Zhenlong Chess Formation before him had been great zongshi who neither lacked for spiritual energy nor were insane enough to create thousands or tens of thousands of pawns. They had no need for such underhanded tricks.

Back then, Mo Ran, infatuated as he was with dark magic, had no notion that he'd accomplished something terrifying, something no one in the cultivation realm had done in all the years of its history—he had taken a fiendish technique that could level mountains and turned it into something anyone could attempt. Anyone could use it for their own ends.

"Ge!"

A shout from beside him—Mo Ran snapped back to his senses. Bloody light flashed before his eyes. The vines of the evil phoenix spirit nestled within Mount Huang had multiplied again; they hurtled toward him in a whirl of death. The phoenix was a beast of the air, fast as the wind. Mo Ran dodged a moment too slowly; a cut opened on his arm, spraying blood.

"Are you okay?!" Xue Meng shouted.

"Don't come any closer!" Mo Ran panted, eyes cold and sharp as he stared at those scarlet vines swaying like tentacles as they readied for another attack. "Go to Shizun, hurry!" he snapped. "Tell him to stop! Tell him to get everyone to stop!"

Blood trickled down his arm as he gripped the corpse's heart and that chess piece tighter in his hand. His mind was spinning, a thousand thoughts vying for his attention. There was no doubt anymore that this was the Shared-Heart Array, employed to much greater effect than he had done in the past life. Despite the improvements, the concept was the same. The larval body would only answer commands if the parent vessel was maintained.

Mo Ran held that Zhenlong chess piece, trembling minutely—not from the pain in his arm, but the coldness and terror crawling up his body. Someone else had been reborn, he was certain now. But did this reborn person know he, too, was a ghost who had clawed his way back to life? If they did, then...

A chill spiked up his spine; despair threatened to engulf him.

Taxian-jun's pale face seemed to swim before his eyes, the imperial bead crown rustling above a malicious leer. He sat high on the dais, staring down from the throne with his cheek in his hand. Cold and mocking, he said, "Go on and run, Mo-zongshi. Where could you flee to?"

Ghostly silhouettes rose like the tide. All the people he'd slaughtered in the past life, all the debts he'd racked up. He saw Shi Mei, covered in blood; he saw Chu Wanning, pale as ice; he saw hanged women dragging their white silk nooses, disemboweled men with their intestines spilling across the ground.

They wanted his life.

"You can't hide forever. Someone else knows—you're merely a shell hiding a despicable soul. You will never be redeemed."

Mo Ran closed his eyes. If the one behind all this knew he'd been reborn, if that person revealed everything he'd done in the past, then...what would he do?

He didn't dare to think.

Shizun Protects Me

XUE MENG had already sprinted over to the chaotic center of the fighting. "Stop! Everybody stop!" he shouted, waving his arms frantically. "Stop fighting! It's no use!"

Even before Xue Meng arrived, some of the cultivators had begun to suspect something was wrong. On the surface, accomplished cultivators cutting down a horde of corpses with no spiritual abilities made for a heroic-looking spectacle. But those fighting grew increasingly confused—they had expected an arduous battle on the mountain, not a scene like this. Only two cultivators had sustained minor injuries, the rest not a single scratch.

As soon as they heard Xue Meng's shouts, everyone stopped and turned to look at him.

"I..." Xue Meng had never felt the weight of so many eyes on him, to say nothing of the distinguished figures and elders among the crowd. The words caught in his throat.

"What's wrong?" Chu Wanning asked.

The sound of his shizun's voice relaxed Xue Meng enough to point toward Mo Ran battling the vines. "Mo Ran seems to know what's going on. He says there's no point fighting these corpses."

The cultivators in the crowd exchanged glances. Many of the sect leaders had high opinions of themselves; what youngster thought his words so valuable? Their expressions grew ugly. Jiang Xi spoke first, his face sullen. "Mo Ran is barely twenty and still wet behind the ears. What could he know?"

If anyone else had spoken, Xue Meng might have responded with some courtesy, but since it was Jiang Xi, his temper flared. "Maybe *you* were still drinking milk when you were twenty!" he cried. "That doesn't mean everyone's like you! So damn narrow-minded!"

Now he'd done it—Xue Meng had embarrassed Jiang Xi in front of the entire group. Guyueye's disciples couldn't remain silent in the face of such impertinence.

"What nonsense are you spouting!"

"Xue Meng, you'd better wash your mouth out!"

Xue Meng couldn't bear the awkwardness of everyone staring at him in silence, but now that insults were being hurled, he was in his element once more. He and Mo Ran had been squabbling for years; there was nothing he knew better than riling others up and getting riled up in turn. Shapely brows drawn low into a scowl, he snapped, "What, am I wrong? Your Jiang-zhangmen is the one who doesn't understand priorities! Look how things are going! Yet you're judging whether someone's qualified to speak based on their *age*?"

Jiang Xi's temper was no better than Xue Meng's. This esteemed head of the cultivation realm narrowed his eyes to verbally spar with a boy young enough to be his son. "Of course age and qualifications are related—once you reach your father's age, you'll understand this. Etiquette comes first when you're talking to your elders."

"Oh, so even someone of Jiang-zhangmen's character counts as an elder?" Xue Meng shot back.

"Meng-er," Xue Zhengyong cut in with a frown. "That's enough. Where's Ran-er? Take us to him."

This put an end to Xue Meng's mouthing off, so Jiang Xi had nothing left to pick at. He swept his sleeves aside and remarked, "Xue Zhengyong, you've raised your son so well."

Xue Zhengyong's face turned ashen. He looked for a moment as if he would speak, but perhaps he didn't want to offend the cultivation realm's leader. In the end, he held his tongue and hurried after the crowd.

When they reached the saddle point halfway up the mountain, they saw Mo Ran rushing toward them, black robes billowing. One sleeve was soaked in blood, and he was gripping a chess piece in his hand. Behind him, the mass of vines had been burned away; no new tendrils were snaking out of the ground for the moment.

Chu Wanning and Xue Zhengyong both paled at the sight of Mo Ran's injury. "Ran-er, are you okay?" Xue Zhengyong asked urgently. "Healers... Healers, come quick! Shi Mei! Come help out!"

Shi Mei was taken aback by Mo Ran's bloodied arm. He blanched visibly, rooted to the spot. It was Guyueye's Hanlin the Sage who stepped forward first, brushing his sleeves aside. Within seconds, Mo Ran felt the harsh sting of his wound subside. He nodded at Hua Binan. "Many thanks to the sage."

"No need for such courtesy," Hua Binan replied, his voice cool and mild. "Now tell us, what discovery does Mo-zongshi wish to relay?"

Mo Ran was deeply conflicted. If he revealed the truth of the Shared-Heart Array, many would doubt and suspect him. But he had far greater concerns—should the Zhenlong Chess Formation be deployed throughout the jianghu, neither he nor Chu Wanning would wish to see the bloody tide that followed.

"Look," Mo Ran said, opening his hand to show the crowd the black chess piece in his palm.

"A Zhenlong chess piece?" Jiang Xi said with a derisive snort. "We've known about that for months. Is this all Mo-zongshi has discovered? How else did you imagine these corpses were controlled if not the Zhenlong Chess Formation?"

Mo Ran pressed his lips together. "Not the Zhenlong chess piece—the soul-eater." He pointed out the insect on the piece to the onlookers. "Right here."

Jiang Xi stood with his hands behind his back, watching Mo Ran in impassive silence.

Xue Zhengyong stepped up to Mo Ran and scrutinized the insect carefully, but he still couldn't make sense of it after a long while. "What's the deal with this bug? Is something wrong with it?"

"There's one on every chess piece," said Mo Ran. "This Zhenlong Chess Formation is more than it seems."

Mo Ran swept his gaze over the profusion of eyes fixed upon him. He had no illusions about the choice he made here—he would divulge everything he knew to stave off certain catastrophe. But he understood the price. The villain behind the scenes had played the cards to their advantage. If this mysterious actor was unsure whether Mo Ran had been reborn, there could be no more effective bait than the Shared-Heart Array. Mo Ran could still avoid blowing his cover—he could harden his heart and refuse to speak. In doing so, he would allow a calamity to unfold. Yet if he revealed his knowledge, his adversary would know beyond a shadow of a doubt that Emperor Taxian-jun had been reborn.

Mo Ran had no other choice. He asked carefully, "Have any of you seen a puppet show before?"

After a pause, a voice in the crowd replied. "Of course. But so what?"

"I have too," said Mo Ran, "but I was short when I was a kid, and I could never shove my way to the front. I used to stand behind the puppet theater and listen from behind the stage. The puppet shows I saw are probably different from those you've seen. You saw the story that was being told in the front of the theater, with the cloth puppets appearing on stage to chatter and bicker with each other."

"What are you trying to say?" Jiang Xi asked impatiently. "Get on with it."

"I'm afraid I can't," replied Mo Ran. "Not everyone is as sharp as Jiang-zhangmen. I want to make sure they all understand."

Jiang Xi glowered at him in silence. Mo Ran continued, "Can the puppets move by themselves on stage?"

"Of course not," answered Xue Zhengyong.

"So how do they move? It requires people crouching under the theater, controlling them with wooden sticks and strings, right?"

"Indeed."

"Very well," said Mo Ran. "I have a theory... I don't know if Xu Shuanglin thought of it this way, but it seems likely to me. The Mount Huang before us is like the backstage of the puppet theater. These revenants are the people controlling the puppets beneath the stage. They don't need any exceptional skill—they only need to raise the puppets and move."

"Continue," Jiang Xi eventually said.

"If Mount Huang is the backstage, then the real show isn't here at all, but up on the stage itself," Mo Ran explained. "Xu Shuanglin is the leader of the puppet troupe. If he wants to give an order, who will he speak to—the puppets or their puppeteers?"

"The puppeteers behind the scenes, of course," said Xue Zhengyong.

"Right. So by this logic, the puppeteers holding the strings are on Mount Huang. Xu Shuanglin gives them his orders, and they make the puppets in their hands stand up and put on a show."

Jiang Xi narrowed his eyes. "You're saying that aside from Mount Huang, there's another place piled high with corpses—that's the stage you speak of? And the bodies on that stage are the 'puppets'?"

"Jiang-zhangmen is very astute."

"Don't flatter me," Jiang Xi replied. "What I want to know is this—your explanation sounds appealing enough, but the assumptions underpinning it are pure fantasy. Mo-zongshi, your word alone is not proof. What evidence do you have to support your claims?"

"Not much," Mo Ran admitted after a pause. "This theory only occurred to me because I came across this chess piece with a soul-eater in one of the bodies."

The black chess piece in his hand was covered in gore. Freshly removed from its corpse, the soul-eater was still alive, crawling feebly on the chess piece. Mo Ran was silent a moment, then looked up. However the person he fastened his gaze on was not Jiang Xi, but Hanlin the Sage—Hua Binan—standing behind him. "The sage ought to be quite familiar with the unique characteristics of soul-eaters."

"These insects have many characteristics. Which does Mo-zongshi wish to point out?"

"Mimicry," said Mo Ran.

"I know of this, of course," said Hua Binan. "Young soul-eaters are excellent mimics. They are linked with the insect that fathered them and will copy the male insect's every movement until they mature."

"Correct. So if I were to take the young offspring of the insect on this chess piece and put it into another body, what would happen?"

Hua Binan fell silent, his expression shifting slightly. Eventually, he answered, "Whatever this body does here, that body there would do as well."

"How could one stop this from happening?"

"Only by killing the insects."

Mo Ran nodded. "Everybody, please take a step back and mind your feet. Now watch carefully."

Eyes glinting like ice, he brought his hand down, aiming for the soul-eater on the chess piece. The ground began to shake as slender vines burst from the earth and hurtled toward Mo Ran. Amid the gasps of the crowd, Mo Ran dodged the vines, withdrawing his hand that was about to strike the insect.

Breathing heavily, he stood straight once more with his hands behind his back. "You see? Mount Huang protects these soul-eaters and won't allow them to come to harm. If anyone still wants to claim it's mere coincidence that these bugs have appeared with the Zhenlong Chess Formation, or that they're decorative...then I'm afraid I have nothing more to say to you."

Silence followed. The assembled cultivators seemed to be mulling this over, trying to wrap their minds around Mo Ran's conjectures. His ideas were bold—recklessly so—but somehow, no one could find fault with them. It was a crackpot theory, but he explained it so confidently, his gaze firm and steady. As though he'd completely grasped Xu Shuanglin's thought process and was doing his utmost to lay it out before the crowd.

But this degree of confidence was disconcerting in and of itself. Everyone watching felt slightly unsettled, Chu Wanning included. He frowned, looking at Mo Ran's pale face from afar. His heart skipped a beat, a portent of he knew not what—he felt like a tiny clue had torn itself free, like he had caught a glimpse of fangs about to rip something apart.

Presented with such a complicated situation, perhaps only someone like Xue Zhengyong could get right to the point. His mind was bluff and straightforward; he didn't dwell on how Mo Ran had come up with this bizarre puppet show analogy so quickly. After following Mo Ran's reasoning to its end, he clapped a hand to his forehead. "So you're saying Xu Shuanglin isn't here at all?!"

"I don't think he is," said Mo Ran.

The Xuanji Elder's concerns were different from the rest. "We probably encountered nine or ten thousand revenants on our way up the mountain," he said, knitting his brows. "Where did he get so many corpses? The ten great sects couldn't possibly have missed it if so many people died at once."

Mo Ran sighed. "They died very recently. Have you all forgotten?"

"Where did they all die?"

Meeting the crowd's blank stares, Mo Ran's answer was clipped: "Linyi."

"No way!" A voice from the crowd rose up to refute him. "The inferno in Linyi burnt everything to ash—how could there be bodies left?"

"Because there was a rift in space," said Mo Ran. "Xu Shuanglin is working with someone who knows how to create such a thing."

This time, no one argued—not because they believed him, but because the idea was too ludicrous. After a long interval, Jiang Xi said, "That's the first forbidden technique, and it's been lost for ages..."

"The first forbidden technique creates a rift in space and time," Mo Ran countered. "Not just space."

"There are thousands of bodies here—we're not talking about Xu Shuanglin passing through the rift alone," Jiang Xi said, icy. "What kind of abilities must this mysterious rift-maker have to bring thousands of people to Mount Huang before they were swallowed by the flames?"

"Jiang-zhangmen, perhaps you are looking at it from the wrong angle," Mo Ran replied. "I doubt these people were brought here alive. They were probably transported after they died, and before they turned to ashes. It would be far easier to transport corpses than living people using such a technique."

Jiang Xi was deeply irked to be receiving a younger man's suggestions. His brows drew low, but before he could speak, a pallid, slender hand pressed on his arm. Hua Binan looked at Mo Ran with a small smile. "Mo-zongshi, you speak with such confidence one might think you saw it with your own eyes. But what proof do you offer?"

Mo Ran hadn't expected a master healer such as Hanlin the Sage would be the one to step forward. He blinked in surprise. "No one could know better than Hua-zongshi whether these corpses are burned or rotten."

Hua Binan cast a glance over a pile of corpses sprawled on the ground. Their legs had been cut off, preventing them from getting up to fight. He looked back at Mo Ran and replied indifferently, "Even if they were burned, how would it prove they are from Linyi?"

Mo Ran's dark eyes fixed unfalteringly on him. "It's a mere guess. If Hua-zongshi finds it preposterous, perhaps you could propose another method by which Xu Shuanglin could have brought thousands of corpses to Mount Huang without any sect taking notice."

Hua Binan laughed lightly. "I'm not familiar with dark techniques—I'm afraid I wouldn't know."

The crowd fell quiet. These words from Hanlin the Sage cut straight to the heart of the matter. Ever since Mo Ran had begun speculating on the purpose of the adult and larval soul-eaters, many had felt a creeping unease, the hairs on the backs of their necks rising. As the saying went, it took one to know one. Most of the cultivators present were hardly naïve or innocent. They had noticed the key problem right away—

How had Mo Ran come up with such a frightening, fleshed-out theory so quickly?

He couldn't be an ally of Xu Shuanglin—otherwise, he wouldn't put these ideas out in the open. Had the apparently upright and honorable Mo-zongshi secretly dabbled in dark magic? Had he perhaps even mastered such techniques?

Hua Binan's gauze veil fluttered. "When it comes to divining Xu Shuanglin's thoughts..." He smiled. "My intuition cannot compare to Mo-zongshi's."

Words of defense sprang to Mo Ran's lips—but he realized with sudden clarity that he had no ground to stand on. He couldn't say with conviction, *I'm just making a guess—I'm not familiar with dark techniques either.*

A cold, clear voice cut in. "Hua-zongshi, what need is there for such insinuations?"

"Ah." Hua Binan chuckled softly. "Chu-zongshi."

Clad in robes the white of snow, Chu Wanning stood indifferent beneath the moonlight. "Everyone's positions are different, and their perspectives will naturally differ as well. The audience in their seats may see the puppet show as presented, but some can only watch from the back of the stage. Of course they would see the people kneeling behind the theater. Hua-zongshi, do you take my meaning?"

"Please forgive my ignorance," Hua Binan said with a smile.

"Mo Ran's point of view is his own," Chu Wanning said coolly. "He is my disciple. I hope you will be prudent with your words and refrain from unnecessary conjecture."

Hearing Chu Wanning express such steadfast faith in him, Mo Ran tasted bitterness in his throat. "Shizun..." he muttered.

Hua Binan looked at Chu Wanning as though he would say more, but seemed to think better of it. Still smiling, he retreated into the depths of Guyueye's contingent.

Jiang Xi had recovered from his earlier embarrassment, but his expression was still unsightly. "Whether it's true or not, let's climb to the summit before we say anymore," he said coldly.

And so the crowd ascended to the top of the mountain. There, they found nothing save for a massive spell array with spheres of red light bubbling from its center. The instant Mo Ran saw it, his heart sank, and his fingers grew numb with cold. It *was* the Shared-Heart Array... The only purpose of this spell was to refine resonant chess pieces and pair soul-eaters with the pawns.

The leader of Taxue Palace furrowed her brow as she examined the array diagram. "What kind of array is this? I've never seen it before. Xue-zhangmen, you've encountered many spells—do you know it?"

Xue Zhengyong walked over to take a look. "Nope," he replied, shaking his head.

Jiang Xi's deep brown eyes flickered distantly as he scrutinized the array. Extending a hand, he probed the flow of spiritual energy; he was an expert on arrays used to refine medicine. After closing his eyes for several minutes, he drew his hand back and turned to look at Mo Ran. "Do you have any other theories?"

With this, the crowd knew: Mo Ran's guesses were almost definitely correct. "I do," Mo Ran replied after some hesitation.

"Speak, then."

"This technique is based on adult insects and their offspring. It will be just as I said before—one insect is onstage, and the other is backstage. However many Zhenlong chess pieces Xu Shuanglin made here, there should be an equal number of bodies wherever he is that obey his commands in the same way." Mo Ran paused before reaching the most important point. "There's no way the bodies 'onstage' will be those of powerless commoners. They are most likely the remains of cultivators with formidable abilities."

"*That's* why Xu Shuanglin killed so many commoners?" Xue Meng exclaimed in alarm. "So he can have an easier time controlling those cultivators?"

"I'm afraid so."

Xue Meng glanced down at the massed corpses covering the mountain. The blood drained from his face. Whether it was because the sight was abhorrent, or because they would have to face an equal number of undead cultivators somewhere else, he couldn't say—perhaps both. Xue Meng looked somewhat faint.

"Over here!" someone suddenly shouted. "There's a body!"

The mountaintop was practically devoid of cover—there was only one small, scrubby bush. And just then, an observant cultivator had noticed a scrap of white fabric peeking out from beneath it.

205

Shizun, Calamity Awaits

EVERAL PEOPLE rushed over to look, pulling the body out of the brush. The corpse was badly charred; it was obvious the victim had been through a great fire. Their face was a gory mess, completely unrecognizable, but judging from their build and the snow-silk robes they wore, impervious to flame, it was very likely the corpse of a woman.

Chu Wanning raised a hand toward the body and closed his eyes. After a moment, he announced, "There's no trace of the Zhenlong Chess Formation."

"How strange," someone muttered. "Xu Shuanglin filled the whole mountain with Zhenlong chess pieces—could he really have missed this one corpse?"

"Why would a so-called forgotten corpse be left on the mountaintop like this?" another retorted.

Mo Ran walked over, carefully studying the twisted limbs. In his past life, he had been the most accomplished practitioner of the Zhenlong Chess Formation in the world; he was more familiar than anyone with the technique's limitations. He had a guess as to who this woman was, but he was looking for proof. Soon enough, he found his confirmation. Mo Ran reached down to unclasp a blackened bracelet from around the corpse's wrist. Once he wiped off the soot, pale red spiritual stones glimmered through. He handed the bracelet to Jiang Xi. "Song Qiutong."

"How did you..." Holding the bracelet, it took Jiang Xi a moment to put two and two together. "You recognize it?"

"It was my wedding gift to her," Mo Ran said simply. "Song Qiutong is a descendant of Song Xingyi. The Butterfly-Boned Beauty Feasts defeated the evil spirit of the phoenix, so their bloodline is the key that unlocks the forbidden area on Mount Huang."

Someone called out a question. "Xu Shuanglin killed Song Qiutong, then used her to open the gate to Mount Huang?"

Mo Ran shook his head, eyes never leaving Song Qiutong's face. What he felt wasn't quite pity; it was a complicated tangle of emotions. "No—when he brought her to the mountain, she was still alive."

"What do you mean?"

Jiang Xi heard a question he could answer; he was no doubt sick of letting a brat in his twenties steal the limelight and wanted to repair his reputation. He spoke up before Mo Ran could reply. "He needed her to issue a command to the mountain," he said flatly.

Mo Ran shot him a glance. It would be wise to let someone else speak. The more he explained, the more difficult it would become to evade suspicion. He stepped aside, letting Jiang Xi take the reins.

"A command?" someone else asked. "Song Qiutong was a delicate young woman—what kind of command would she be giving?"

"She might have been delicate, but not all of her ancestors were so useless. The evil spirit of the phoenix within Mount Huang will only obey those of the bloodline that subdued it." Jiang Xi had quickly grasped the situation. "Song Qiutong was the last living member of this bloodline."

The questioner gasped. "Huh? The Butterfly-Boned Beauty Feasts subdued the phoenix's evil spirit?"

"That's right."

"I've never heard that..."

"That's unsurprising," said Jiang Xi. "The four great evil mountains don't have much use besides serving as defenses. Few are aware of how to open their barriers or who can do so. Song Qiutong was a foundling before she was captured and sold at auction. She must have had no idea she could use Mount Huang as a hideout... She had probably never even heard the story about her ancestor subduing the phoenix's evil spirit."

"So... So Xu Shuanglin brought her here?"

"Most likely," Jiang Xi said. "Everyone fled for their lives when the fire broke out in Rufeng Sect. No one went back to the hall to look for a powerless woman. The only one who took notice of her was Xu Shuanglin—or whoever is working with him behind the scenes."

Nearby, Xue Zhengyong nodded pensively. "Xu Shuanglin's accomplice can open a rift in space and bring him anywhere. He would barely need to lift a finger to transport Song Qiutong too. We can guess what happened—Song Qiutong always tried to curry favor with the powerful. When he took her along, she must have seized this opportunity like a lifesaving raft and obeyed him unconditionally. They only needed to bring her to the mountain and instruct her to give a command—she wouldn't have refused."

"Why not use the Zhenlong Chess Formation to control Song Qiutong?" someone piped up.

"Because the phoenix's spirit can tell if the person commanding it is under duress," said Jiang Xi. "The blood descendant needs to be alive and speaking of their own free will. Only then will the mountain obey."

Everyone pondered this. "So what are we doing here?" another cultivator asked with rising alarm. "Haven't we just done what he wanted by stumbling upon his backstage area? Thanks to these damned vines, we can't even destroy the soul-eaters... What do we do now?"

Jiang Xi scowled, filled with disdain at the analogy Mo Ran had come up with. Still, he replied, "We'll look for the stage, and then we'll destroy Xu Shuanglin's puppets. Mo-zongshi."

Mo Ran had taken himself off to the side, listening with his arms crossed. Now he jumped slightly. "Hm? What is it?"

"Mo-zongshi, your explanations earlier were quite logical," Jiang Xi said cryptically. "Allow me to humbly ask one more thing—where do you suppose we should look for this 'stage'?"

Mo Ran hesitated. "Shall we try Jiangui?"

"Try...*what*?"

Mo Ran cleared his throat. His palm glowed scarlet, the willow vine materializing with a flash. "This—it's called Jiangui."

Jiang Xi stared at him, at a loss.

Jiangui, like Tianwen, could interrogate living people, vengeful ghosts, and bodies left behind by their souls. There was a slight difference in technique: interrogating people and corpses involved making them physically speak, while interrogating ghosts involved communicating directly with their souls.

Song Qiutong had been dead for over a month; her souls were long gone. But as luck would have it, yin energy was abundant on Mount Huang, so her corpse hadn't yet decomposed. "Jiangui, interrogate."

In response to this command, Jiangui's leaves and tendrils shivered and lengthened into a vine that wrapped three times around Song Qiutong's body. Her corpse began to glow a dazzling red. As scarlet lit the depths of his eyes, Mo Ran ventured in a low voice, "Was Xu Shuanglin the one who brought you here?"

Song Qiutong's features, disfigured by char, didn't move.

"Is it not working?" someone asked timidly.

Narrowing his eyes, Mo Ran tried again. "Was Xu Shuanglin the one who brought you here?"

No response.

"Mo-zongshi is too green after all," Jiang Xi said. "Maybe your shizun should try."

But at that moment, Song Qiutong began to move. Her motions were stiff and slow, but the shake of her head was unmistakable.

"It wasn't Xu Shuanglin?!" Xue Zhengyong exclaimed.

Mo Ran gripped Jiangui, tendons protruding from the back of his hand. "Did you get a clear look at the person who brought you here?"

After a few heartbeats of silence, Song Qiutong opened her mouth. But instead of words, what came out was a massive, slippery-coiled snake. It dropped to the ground and slithered away, hissing.

A Guyueye disciple recognized it immediately. "There was a speech-swallowing serpent in her stomach!"

Speech-swallowing serpents were non-venomous, dark creatures covered in spiritual scales. They could live in a human's innards for more than twenty years. Many sects in the upper cultivation realm used these serpents—they fed them to their shadow guards. Such guards could only speak the truth to the serpents' master. To anyone else, they must lie, or speak in a mixture of lies and truth. A word out of line and the serpent would awaken from slumber to rive their faces, break their necks, and devour their tongues.

Jiangui's red light winked out. Song Qiutong was shaking her head repeatedly, trembling from head to toe. Chunks of bloodied flesh poured from her mouth: shreds of viscera, and pieces of her tongue and throat. She could never speak another word of truth.

The crowd looked on, stricken. Someone yelled, "If she can't talk, can she write it out?"

Mo Ran knew the instant he saw the speech-swallowing serpent that the person behind this had been exceptionally thorough. But he still stepped forward to examine Song Qiutong's hands.

"How does it look?" asked Xue Zhengyong.

Mo Ran shook his head. "Her tendons have been cut. She won't be able to write anything."

Everyone fell silent. An ominous breeze whistled across the mountaintop; the forest's rustling leaves seemed to snicker, and the mournful wails of corpses filled the air, saturating the summit with a heavy dread. At last, the leader of Taobao Estate, Ma Yun, broke through the eerie stillness. "S-so we've lost the trail?"

No one answered.

Mo Ran recalled Jiangui, and Song Qiutong's body slumped to the ground. Within seconds, vines snaked out of the soil to wind around their mistress's corpse. When they covered her completely, they dragged her into the bush again as if to protect her.

Why had Xu Shuanglin and his collaborator not simply destroyed Song Qiutong's body after killing her—why had they gone to the trouble of severing her tendons and feeding her a speech-swallowing serpent? Once he saw the vines, Mo Ran understood. Mount Huang obeyed Butterfly-Boned Beauty Feasts in life and death. As long as the corpse of its mistress remained on the mountain, the phoenix's evil spirit wouldn't allow anyone to destroy it or burn it to ashes.

Mo Ran didn't know what to feel. He thought of how he had died in the past life. No one had been left to tend to his remains—he had lain himself down in the coffin within that freshly dug grave. On reflection, this had been rather pointless. The rebel army that had stormed up the mountain would never have left his corpse intact.

His death in the past lifetime had been even more miserable than Song Qiutong's; he hadn't even had a single vine to protect him in the end.

Some of the assembly had begun to chatter amongst themselves, frowning and debating on how to proceed. Others, such as Jiang Xi and Chu Wanning, were lost in thought with their eyes closed.

Mo Ran, too, closed his eyes, mentally sorting through what he'd seen. This ruthless approach reminded him too much of his past self—perhaps that was why he found it easy to guess what Xu Shuanglin would do next. In his mind's eye, he seemed to see Xu Shuanglin pacing barefoot in his courtyard, Farewell to Three Lifetimes, brooding over a problem: without sufficient spiritual energy, how could he control a massive army of undead cultivators?

Suddenly, an idea—the Shared-Heart Array. He could kill an equal number of commoners and yoke them to the cultivators. It was no different from making puppets dance—they would all do his bidding.

Where was the safest place to execute such a plan? One of the four great evil mountains. What if he couldn't open Mount Huang's barrier? He would bring Song Qiutong with him.

The clues linked up, one after another. Mo Ran's eyes darkened as he followed them to the end. Where would he get the commoners' bodies? He would burn Linyi to the ground.

These were only guesses, yet every piece fell into place. Flecks of light dispersed and gathered in his eyes. He felt like he *was* Xu Shuanglin, and Xu Shuanglin was him, standing at the summit of Mount Huang, eyes roving frantically over the sea of corpses below. The picture grew sharper and clearer—until he hit a snag.

If he were Xu Shuanglin and had accomplished all this, wouldn't he then build his stage and put on the puppet show he had been working so hard to bring to life?

Where would this stage be?

Where could he find an untold number of corpses belonging to the strongest cultivators? Where could he find protection if he weren't discovered...?

The sky, slowly brightening with the light of dawn, seemed to go dark once more. "Mount Jiao..." he mumbled.

Jiang Xi cast him a sidelong glance. "What?"

Mo Ran's face had gone pale. He looked to the east, fury burning through him. "Mount Jiao! The heroes' tomb! His stage is the heroes' tomb on Mount Jiao. Look how many commoners' corpses Xu Shuanglin obtained from the calamity in Linyi. There's no other way for him to get his hands on the same number of high-level cultivators. It has to be the heroes' tomb!"

Jiang Xi instantly picked up the thread of his thoughts. "You're saying Xu Shuanglin's puppet counterparts are the bodies buried within Rufeng Sect's heroes' tomb over the centuries?"

Mo Ran didn't bother to respond. Cursing under his breath, he flew like the wind toward the bottom of the mountain.

Xu Shuanglin was *insane*! Generations of Rufeng Sect's leaders were buried within that tomb, including their founder who had ascended to immortality after his death. It was one thing to use the Shared-Heart Array to control run-of-the-mill cultivators, but to use it on *those* corpses? If Xu Shuanglin lost control of his spiritual energy flow for even an instant, those powerful revenants would struggle free and go berserk. The backlash would swallow Xu Shuanglin, dealing him a sudden and horrible death—leaving that fearsome army of centuries of Rufeng cultivators to run amok.

It would be no less of a calamity than the Heavenly Rift to the Infinite Hells.

Shizun, Who Am I Really?

MO RAN FLEW over the roiling sea of corpses, racing toward the base of the mountain.

The moment he exited the barrier, his gaze fell upon Nangong Si. The confinement curse he used on himself had already been lifted. Ye Wangxi was on one knee next to him, helping him bandage his wounds as Mei Hanxue sat calmly on the ground between Jiangdong Hall and the two of them, his expression chilly. A zither sat before him, notes flowing like water as he plucked its strings.

Mei Hanxue was a senior direct disciple of Kunlun Taxue Palace's leader. He was known as an elusive figure, with strange martial skills and unpredictable tactics. One moment, he was perfectly upright and proper, and in the next, he would pull out some bizarre dark technique. Such was the power of his reputation that the mob from Jiangdong Hall had no choice but to sit upon the rocks glaring daggers, though they wanted nothing more than to skin Nangong Si alive.

As soon as Mei Hanxue spied Mo Ran, he lifted his fingers from the strings. He stowed the instrument, rose to his feet, and nodded respectfully. "How are things on the mountain?"

"The whole thing was fake," Mo Ran replied.

"Fake?" Mei Hanxue frowned slightly.

The Jiangdong Hall contingent, overhearing, made their way over. Huang Xiaoyue had been lying down within a nearby pavilion, having ordered several disciples to massage his legs and shoulders. He was making a great show of his frailty, but when he heard Mo Ran and Mei Hanxue's exchange, he couldn't resist peering through half-lidded eyes and straining to listen in.

"Xu Shuanglin isn't on the mountain," said Mo Ran. "He's probably on Mount Jiao. I—"

"Xu Shuanglin is on Mount Jiao?" Nangong Si didn't wait for him to finish. His face was ashen as he stared at Mo Ran.

"Maybe. It's not for certain."

Nangong Si gaped for a moment. "That's not possible, Mount Jiao only answers to the Nangong bloodline," he mumbled. "Xu Shuanglin..." The words stuck his throat. Nangong Si fixed his dark eyes on Mo Ran, the last bit of color draining from his face.

For a moment, he had forgotten that Xu Shuanglin was also a Nangong.

Many years ago, Nangong Liu and Nangong Xu had been lauded as a pair of promising young heroes. Many had speculated that Rufeng Sect would reach unparalleled heights of glory in the hands of the Nangong brothers, its future brighter than the noonday sun. Who could have foreseen the ending of these brothers, or the ending of their sect?

Nangong Si hung his head in silence.

By now, the rest of the expedition had made its way down the mountain. The thousand-strong crowd was like a migrating shoal of fish as it flowed into the clearing at the base of the mountain.

Chu Wanning strode straight over, Xue Meng and Shi Mei close behind. He looked at Nangong Si. "How did you hurt your hand?"

"It's not a problem; I cut myself," Nangong Si replied. "Thank you for your kindness, Zongshi."

Xue Meng sighed. "Why do you call him *zongshi* when you should be calling him *shizun*? Sheesh, Shizun said all that just for you to refuse it, you..."

"I never took a teacher," Nangong Si said through dry and cracking lips. "None of my education has come from studying with Zongshi. You needn't take my mother's request to heart."

Chu Wanning looked at him in silence.

"My apologies. But I don't even remember those three bows."

Before Chu Wanning could reply, he spotted Jiang Xi and several other sect leaders approaching with their retinues. Chu Wanning was unaccustomed to speaking of such private matters in public; he pursed his lips and didn't press the issue. Reaching into his qiankun pouch, he handed a small jar of salve to Nangong Si. "Put this on every day. In three days, your wound should heal."

By the time he finished speaking, the others had arrived. Huang Xiaoyue had also stumbled over from the pavilion, leaning on the arms of his disciples. Jiangdong Hall wasn't about to miss out on this piece of action.

Guyueye was currently the top sect of the cultivation realm, and thus it fell to Jiang Xi to speak first at crucial moments. But as he gazed at Nangong Si, he found himself at something of a loss as to how he should approach this young man. Rufeng Sect had abused its power for so many years, accumulating grudges too numerous to count. Now there was no ready target for vengeance—these grudges fell onto Nangong Si alone.

But what sin had Nangong Si committed? It wasn't him who had taken Bitan Manor's sword manual or set those sky-high prices. He didn't even know where that sword manual was. His father,

Nangong Liu, had a thousand crimes to his name, yet he had gone off and died without answering for any of them. A son, people said, ought to shoulder his father's debts—but if they took this principle seriously, how many could count themselves as innocent?

Besides, this young man before them now was the very last descendant of the Nangong bloodline. He was the singular key to opening the gate to Mount Jiao.

"You..." Jiang Xi began in a measured tone.

But before he got any further, a tremulous voice rose up from nearby. "Nangong-shizhu, you must come with us. The originator of these troubles should be the one to resolve them. You mustn't ignore or brush off the scandals Rufeng Sect has left behind."

Jiang Xi glanced sidelong at the owner of the voice: the abbot of Wubei Temple, Master Xuanjing. Inwardly, he sneered. This old monk was so embroiled in earthly pursuits even he was angling to reap some benefits for himself. Whatever—Jiang Xi wasn't keen to talk anyway. He shut his mouth without protest and merely watched as Master Xuanjing, leaning on his staff, gave Nangong Si an earful on principles like he was reciting sutras.

Nangong Si cut him off, "Okay, I'll go to Mount Jiao with you."

Master Xuanjing hadn't expected him to agree so readily. Blinking in surprise, he put his palms together. "Amitabha, surely Buddha will forgive some of your sins upon seeing that you readily accept reason."

Nangong Si looked as though he wanted to speak, but held his tongue. From his quiver, Naobaijin let out a whimper and tried to clamber out; Nangong Si expressionlessly shoved him back in. "I will go to Mount Jiao in hopes that I can prevent centuries of Rufeng Sect's disciples from suffering the indignity of becoming puppets to serve another's evil whims," he said, restrained. "Nevertheless, I appreciate the master's kind intent in pointing me down the righteous path."

Thus did the group acquire the living key to Mount Jiao.

Each of the four great evil mountains had its quirks. If one wished to approach Mount Jiao, they had to meet two criteria, regardless of whether they were of the Nangong bloodline themselves or accompanied by a Nangong descendant. First, they had to fast for ten days. Second, they had to proceed on foot once they arrived at the Panlong Range surrounding Mount Jiao. They couldn't ride swords or horses; in order to demonstrate their sincere intent, they had to traverse the three peaks preceding Mount Jiao on their own two feet.

Xue Zhengyong did some mental math. "It'll take about ten days to get from here to the Panlong Range on horseback. We can fast on the way. If none of you have urgent matters to attend to, I see no reason we need to return to our own sects beforehand. We can all head out together."

"That's a good plan," said the Taxue Palace leader. "If we travel together, we can discuss our strategy for the next stage."

"The only thing is, there must be at least three thousand people here," Xue Zhengyong pointed out. "It might be tricky to find enough horses..."

"I should have enough horses in my estate for everyone." A frail voice called out from the crowd, and a hand shot into the air. All eyes converged on a slight, mousy-looking man with a shrewd look about him, attired in luxurious crimson robes with a scrolling black cat motif embroidered onto the hems.

"Ma-zhuangzhu?" Jiang Xi's brows shot up.

The man who had spoken up was none other than Ma Yun, the master of Taobao Estate, one of the nine great sects of the upper cultivation realm. In that copy of the *God-Knows-What Rankings* that Xue Meng had once bought, he was named third-richest—though he was due for a promotion to the second spot now that Nangong Liu was dead.

As rich men went, Ma Yun seemed much more down-to-earth than Jiang Xi, with the solicitous demeanor of a salesman. These two men had acquired their fortunes through quite different means. Jiang Xi was ruthless and undaunted, with many priceless treasures to his name; his domain was the black market.

Master Ma, on the other hand, had established a network of delivery outposts large and small throughout the cultivation realm. Every sort of parcel and shipment passed through these outposts, and they also leased spiritual horses, boats, and carriages. Taobao Estate specialized in manufacturing various swift vessels and vehicles, and breeding herds of spiritual beasts of burden. Because he dealt in so many areas, people liked to call Ma-zhuangzhu a jack-of-all-trades, or, for short, "Jack Ma."

As their gazes met, Jack Ma quailed a little at the aloof, icy expression on Jiang Xi's face. Meekly shrinking back, he said, "Or...perhaps we should go to Rainbell Isle? I'm sure Jiang-zhangmen has more horses than me in his manor, heh heh."

Everyone stared.

Jiang Xi was momentarily speechless as he took in Ma Yun's wrinkled smile. "I was just expressing my gratitude for Ma-zhuangzhu's generosity, that's all," he eventually replied. "We're not far from Taobao Estate. If Ma-zhuangzhu is willing to play host, we would be much obliged."

Master Ma let out a breath of relief and grinned. "Then let's all head toward my humble estate! The hour is late; we might as well stay the night and set out in the morning."

Taobao Estate was located atop Gu Mountain on the shores of Hangzhou's West Lake. Despite its name, Gu Mountain was better described as a sloping hill; it took less than an hour to reach the summit.

"Here we are!" Master Ma crowed. He walked up to the main gate, brilliant with red lacquer, and dispelled the protective barrier with a wave of his hand. "Welcome, one and all!"

The various sect leaders were consumed by worry and impatience after the events on Mount Huang. Only Master Ma had recovered his easy demeanor so quickly, flashing a warm smile at all his guests. Many exchanged glances and snorted, but no one said anything much. The crowd poured through the great barrier into Taobao Estate. The sect leaders went first, then the elders, then their direct disciples, and finally the rest like a massive tide.

"What the hell is up with Jack Ma?" Xue Meng muttered to Mo Ran. "His smile gives me the creeps—do you think he might be working with Xu Shuanglin? Is he leading us into a trap?"

Mo Ran paused. "He's not."

"How are you so sure?"

"The leaders and top cultivators of the nine great sects are all here, and everyone's on guard. If he's really working with Xu Shuanglin, he'd accomplish exactly nothing by bringing us here—he'd only blow his own cover."

"Then why's he so giddy?"

Mo Ran heaved a sigh. "Because he's about to make a fortune."

"A fortune? Won't he be in the red after this?" Xue Meng asked, bewildered. This son was just like his father: he had no business acumen to speak of. Everyone on Sisheng Peak knew the story of how Madam Wang had once asked the young Xue Meng to get change for a silver leaf from a roadside peddler. The child had come back with only a kite and three greasy copper coins—in other words, he'd been painfully ripped off. But Xue Meng thought the little kite very pretty and was highly pleased with his transaction. How could a young master like him understand the workings of Jack Ma's opportunistic mind? He was still baffled even after thinking it over for a while. "Did you mishear? He said he'd let us *borrow* horses, not rent them to us. If he's giving out stuff for free, then—"

They were approached by a low-level disciple in charge of guiding the guests to their rooms. Mo Ran waved a hand in Xue Meng's direction, signaling for his silence. The two allowed the beaming disciple, outfitted in a short pink coat, to lead them to the courtyard where they would stay the night.

The guest courtyards were all at the periphery of the compound and housed six people each. As dusk fell, Mo Ran stood before the window in his room, gazing out at the cool umber of the distant mountains and the ripples grazing the surface of West Lake.

Since coming down from Mount Huang, Mo Ran had been consumed by anxiety. Now, with the door closed, he finally let that fretful energy rush out. As he gripped the window ledge with one hand, his other subconsciously fidgeted with a small, warm object he had picked up somewhere.

The Jiangnan scenery was lovely as ever, but Mo Ran found himself unable to appreciate it. Had anyone else caught sight of his face in that moment of sunset, they would never have believed the man they saw was the righteous and honest Mo-zongshi. That face belonged to the past life's Emperor Taxian-jun. It was etched with malice, irises pierced by the red light of the dying sun. As the sky darkened, Mo Weiyu's features began to warp.

The existence of another reborn person working with Xu Shuanglin sent tremors down his spine. He felt as though a knife was pressed to his throat so tightly the edge had broken skin, cutting into his flesh, letting blood seep out. But the wielder didn't press the blade down, and Mo Ran couldn't turn to look at them. He couldn't see who stood behind him, ready to take his life at any moment.

Mo Ran was on the verge of a breakdown. It seemed he couldn't keep the matter of his rebirth a secret for much longer. If the truth came out when they got to Mount Jiao, what should he do? What would his aunt and uncle think of him? What about Shi Mei? Xue Meng?

And Chu Wanning? What about Chu Wanning...?

If the sins he'd committed in the past life came to light, how much would Chu Wanning despise him? Wouldn't he be unwilling to even look at Mo Ran ever again?

Mo Ran's heart twisted in an awful knot. He felt colder and colder, encased in a bone-chilling freeze—

With a crisp *click*, the trinket in his hand fell onto the floorboards. He bent down in a daze to pick it up. It was gray with grime—no one had stayed in these rooms at Taobao Estate for ages. They hadn't been cleaned carefully, and the floor was dusty...

Wait. Mo Ran blanched.

He suddenly realized what he had been playing with. Nestled in his palm was a smooth, jet-black little stone—a Zhenlong chess piece.

The blood drained from his face.

During the last two years of his previous lifetime, he had developed a habit of funneling spiritual energy into his palm whenever he was feeling overwhelmed or stressed, concentrating it into a tiny black chess piece to fidget with. This new quirk had struck fear into the hearts of the palace servants. Mo Ran had once overheard a whispered discussion of how he must be making chess pieces in fury so he could kill people and make them into puppets.

"Aren't you terrified His Majesty might use those Zhenlong chess pieces he's always playing with?"

"To tell you the truth, I'd rather see him play with human skulls than those things."

"*You're* afraid? What about me? I'm His Majesty's personal attendant—heaven knows how many times my knees have nearly given out. Each of those chess pieces costs His Majesty a great deal of spiritual energy—he'd never make them idly. He must have a goal in mind, or maybe he needs to vent his temper... What if he vents it on *me*? What will I do..."

This conversation had left Mo Ran speechless, yet on second thought, it was quite amusing. What were these gossipy servants going on about. How were they so confident in dissecting his motives? In truth, there was no reason behind all those chess pieces—it was just one of Emperor Taxian-jun's many peculiarities. But after overhearing that conversation, he would now and again lunge forward without warning, Zhenlong chess piece in hand as if ready to plant it in one of the servant girls, then watch his attendants tremble in fright and beg for mercy. His face invariably remained cold as he surveyed such scenes, but a glimmer of amusement surfaced in his heart. This had been one of his sole sources of joy in those final two years of his life.

Many years had passed since he had last refined a Zhenlong chess piece. Since his rebirth, Mo Ran had been unwilling to touch this technique, as though trying to make a clean break with his past self. Eight years had passed in the blink of an eye. He thought he would've forgotten the technique by now, that his lips would no longer know the shape of those incantations.

But he saw now that he couldn't escape. There was evil sown within his very soul. As he stared at that black piece, his hand shook uncontrollably. He was swallowed by despair—

All of a sudden, he didn't know who he was. Was he Taxian-jun? Or was he Mo-zongshi? He didn't know *where* he was. Was he on

the banks of West Lake? Or the hall of Wushan Palace? He couldn't
tell dreams from reality. He couldn't stop trembling. That tiny black
chess piece was as heavy as a nightmare, like a spot of filthy blood the
color of soot. Manic laughter echoed in his skull as a voice shrieked,
"Mo Weiyu! Mo Weiyu! You can't escape! You can't run away! You'll
only ever amount to evil, only ever be a vengeful ghost! You're a
scourge upon this world! A scourge!"

Someone rapped on the door.

Mo Ran came back to the present with a jolt—he was drenched
in cold sweat. Fingers closing around the chess piece, he snapped,
"Who is it?"

"It's me," called the voice outside. "Xue Meng."

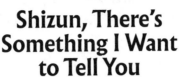

Shizun, There's Something I Want to Tell You

MO RAN PUSHED the door ajar. Through the crack, he saw Xue Meng bathed in the last glow of the setting sun, along with Shi Mei, clad in robes of green.

"We got some medicinal salve for you..." Xue Meng trailed off. "What are you doing? Open the door and let us in."

Mo Ran hesitated, then let the door swing open so Xue Meng and Shi Mei could enter the room. Xue Meng paced over to the window and craned his neck out to gaze at the sunset over the lake. "Your room has such a nice view. There are a whole bunch of camphor trees right outside mine, so I can't see a thing."

"We can switch if you like," Mo Ran offered absentmindedly.

"Nah, I've already unpacked all my stuff—I was just saying." Xue Meng waved a hand, walking back to the table. "Let Shi Mei put some salve on that wound you got from the vines. You don't want your shoulder to get infected."

Mo Ran fixed his dark brown eyes on Xue Meng. If Xue Meng knew the things he'd done in the past life, if he knew what kind of soul was hiding within his cousin's shell, would he still grin at him and bring him medicine like this...?

His focused gaze unsettled Xue Meng. "What's wrong? Is there something on my face?"

Mo Ran shook his head and sat at the table, lowering his lashes.

Shi Mei stepped up beside him. "Can you pull your robes aside so I can take a look at the wound?"

Preoccupied, Mo Ran reached up to loosen his collar. "Thanks a lot."

"Oh, you." Shi Mei shook his head and sighed. "When will you learn to be careful? You've picked up all Shizun's bad habits—always running headfirst into danger and coming out covered in injuries. My heart hurts for you."

His hands moved as he spoke, taking his supplies from the medicine chest. He carefully cleaned Mo Ran's wound, applied the salve, and bandaged his shoulder.

"Don't get it wet or move around too much for the next few days. Those vines were poisonous, so the wound may give you some trouble. Also—give me your hand; I'll check your pulse."

Mo Ran extended his arm for Shi Mei.

Shi Mei pressed slender fingers, pale as the whitest jade, to the pulse at Mo Ran's wrist. Worry flitted across his gaze—it was gone in a flash, but Mo Ran caught it. "What's wrong?"

Blinking, Shi Mei came back to himself. "It's nothing."

"Is the poison serious?"

Shi Mei shook his head. He smiled wanly at Mo Ran. "Just a little—remember to rest. Otherwise there might be side effects." He lowered his head and busied himself collecting everything back into the medicine chest. "I'll be heading out now—I have some more medicines to organize. See you two later."

He closed the door and was gone.

Staring after him, Xue Meng frowned. "Is it just me or has he been in a weird mood lately—he's acting off, like something's on his mind."

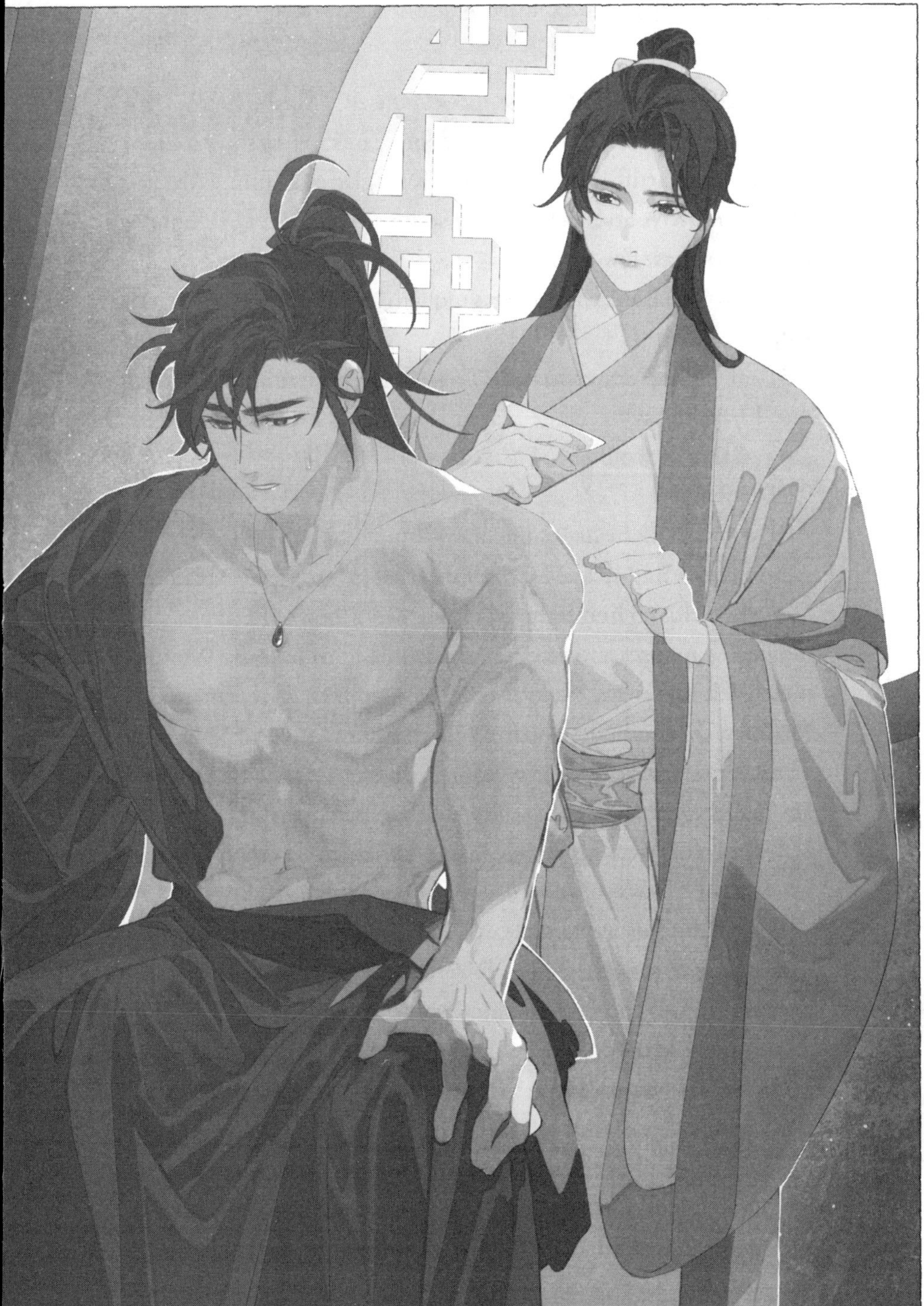

Mo Ran wasn't in the best mood himself. "Maybe he took my pulse and discovered I'm on death's door, so he's feeling sorry for me?"

"Don't say stuff like that." Xue Meng glared at him. "Are you trying to jinx yourself? I'm being serious—Shi Mei's been pretty down these past few days."

Finally Mo Ran's concern was piqued. "Really?" he asked, hands stilling.

"Really," Xue Meng insisted. "I'm telling you, he's always spacing out. I have to say his name two or three times before he responds. Do you think it could be..."

"Be what?"

"Do you think he likes someone?"

Mo Ran stared at Xue Meng. Shi Mei, liking someone? Had Xue Meng said this to him eight years ago, Mo Ran would've probably jumped to his feet and started cursing in a fit of jealousy. Now, he merely felt somewhat taken aback. He sifted through his memories for clues, only to find he hadn't paid much attention to Shi Mei at all these past few years. He was coming up blank. "Don't ask me—at any rate, the person he likes wouldn't be me," said Mo Ran. He pulled his robes back over his shoulder and put them in order. "Besides, why are you always so worried about other people's feelings?"

Xue Meng flushed and cleared his throat. "I'm not! I was just making conversation!" As he glowered at Mo Ran, pulling clothes over his stupidly perfect physique, something niggled at him. His roving gaze landed on Mo Ran's sculpted chest and stopped—

"What are you staring at?" Mo Ran quipped, though he didn't much mind. "Like what you see?"

Xue Meng didn't respond.

In that same insufferable tone, Mo Ran added, "Keep your eyes to yourself; I'm afraid our love could never be."

Xue Meng paled and turned his face aside. "Psh—you *wish*," he snapped, feigning calm. But his heart was pounding like a drum— for around Mo Ran's neck, he had seen a scarlet crystal pendant hanging right next to his heart. It looked so familiar, as though he'd seen an identical pendant once before. For some reason, although he couldn't put his finger on where or when, gooseflesh rose all over his body and a low drone filled his ears.

Where had he seen that pendant?

Mo Ran smoothed his lapels. He looked down and spotted a few droplets of medicine on the table. "Do you have a handkerchief?"

"Huh?" Xue Meng blinked. "Oh. Yeah." He rummaged through his pockets and proffered a handkerchief to Mo Ran. "You never remember to carry your own."

"I'm not in the habit."

"Yet you were still insisting Shizun would make you one," Xue Meng said stiffly. "What a dumb flex."

Only then did Mo Ran remember he had begged Chu Wanning for a haitang handkerchief like his own. Whether Chu Wanning had forgotten about it or simply couldn't be bothered, Mo Ran was still waiting. Somewhat embarrassed, he cleared his throat. "Shizun's been busy lately; he hasn't had time..."

"Even if he did have the time, he wouldn't make one just for you," Xue Meng scoffed. "I'd definitely get one too. And even...even that Nangong Si would probably get one."

At the mention of Nangong Si, Mo Ran's grim mood grew more dismal still. "Have you gone to see him?"

"Nah, why would I?" said Xue Meng. "He and Ye Wangxi are staying next to that old coot Jiang Xi. I'd rather stay a million miles away from *him*."

Mo Ran nodded. "That's good then. Jiang Xi's got a bad temper and plenty of other issues, but at least he's a reasonable person. He won't make trouble for them."

"Him?" Xue Meng's voice rose with annoyance. "If *that* stupid bastard could be called reasonable, I'd take his surname. Don't call me Xue Meng—it's Jiang Meng from now on."

Mo Ran didn't know what to say. Xue Meng had always had a gift for insulting people in every way imaginable when anger got the better of him. But with him here chattering away, Mo Ran felt some of the warmth of the living had returned to his room. Those nightmares from his past life finally began to recede.

"Speaking of," Xue Meng continued, "you don't think Shizun's really going to take Nangong Si on as a disciple, do you?"

"In those days, he certainly wouldn't have," Mo Ran replied. "But these days, neither of us can stop him."

Xue Meng stared. "Why not?"

Mo Ran let out a sigh. "Let me ask you a question. Li Wuxin was always respectful to Nangong Si. Even though he was his elder, he never dared to contradict the young master of Rufeng Sect. Why is that?"

"Because Nangong Si's dad was powerful—the leader of the cultivation realm's number one sect. Obviously."

"Okay, let me ask you another question. These days, people like Huang Xiaoyue and others not even worth mentioning don't hesitate to make Nangong Si's life difficult. Why?"

"Because...of their grudges against him?"

Mo Ran found himself momentarily speechless. *Only Xue Meng could come up with this kind of answer,* he thought. All of a sudden, he felt a prick of envy—Xue Meng was already in his twenties, yet his mind was childishly pure sometimes. There was always some nuance in describing someone as childish. Childish could mean innocent, simple, and straightforward, but it also implied that someone hadn't grown up, that they were still immature and unrefined.

As far as Mo Ran was concerned, it was nothing short of a miracle for someone to have lived two decades yet still look upon the mortal realm with pure eyes. Gazing at the miracle before him, Mo Ran laughed bitterly. "Why would they have that many grudges against him?"

"Rufeng Sect exposed so many of the upper cultivation realm's scandals…"

"But that was Xu Shuanglin's doing—what does it have to do with Nangong Si?" asked Mo Ran. "Wasn't Nangong Si the person hurt most deeply by the first secrets he revealed? He learned his father killed his mother with his own two hands. Nangong Si is the farthest thing from a perpetrator. He's a sacrificial lamb, a victim."

Xue Meng opened his mouth, and Mo Ran waited in silence for him to speak. But nothing emerged from Xue Meng's parted lips; after a while, he indignantly pressed them together once more. He didn't know how to refute it. After a long beat, he said reluctantly, "Then why do you think that is?"

"Two reasons. For the fun of it, first of all," Mo Ran said. "Those people couldn't be more thrilled at Rufeng Sect's demise. It's vastly more satisfying to bully a disgraced gongzi than a random beggar."

Xue Meng had suffered the same fate in his previous lifetime. When the son of the phoenix had hit rock bottom, he had encountered every kind of prejudice. The present Xue Meng was none the wiser, but Mo Ran knew this well. Afraid of falling afoul of Emperor Taxian-jun, not a single sect had been willing to take Xue Meng in or cooperate with him. In the first year of Mo Ran's reign, Xue Meng had run to the ends of the earth, entreating the leaders of sects large and small to join forces with him and bring an end to Mo Ran's tyrannical rule before he did anything more monstrous. Xue Meng had walked the lands for nine years, but no one had listened to him. In the end, only Kunlun Taxue Palace was willing to shelter him, and only Mei Hanxue was willing to wholeheartedly aid his cause.

Mo Ran was glad that this lifetime's Xue Meng would never have to endure such indignities.

"What about the second reason?" Xue Meng asked, wholly oblivious to Mo Ran's thoughts.

"The second reason is that they think they're upholding justice."

"What does that mean?"

"Tianyin Pavilion is ruled by the descendants of the gods. Do you know what they do with criminals from the cultivation realm?"

"After the execution, they string up the condemned for three days and three nights to publicize their crimes," Xue Meng muttered. "Why are you asking me? It's not like you haven't witnessed it. Don't you remember? When you first came to Sisheng Peak, there was a criminal about to be put to death. Dad had to go there for the trial anyway, so he took us both with him. You even watched the execution. Though you were a real scaredy-cat back then—you came down with a fever for four or five days afterward..."

Mo Ran laughed. After a moment he said, "Couldn't help it—that was the first time I'd ever seen someone get their spiritual core dug out."

"What were you so scared of—it's not like someone's gonna come and dig out *your* spiritual core."

"Hard to say," Mo Ran replied.

Startled, Xue Meng reached out to feel Mo Ran's forehead. "You don't have a fever—what are you babbling about?"

"I had a dream once that someone stabbed me in the chest with a sword. Just a few inches to the side and both my heart and spiritual core would've been gone."

Xue Meng stared at him. "Enough already," he said, waving a hand. "You're annoying, but you're still my cousin. If anyone wants to dig out your spiritual core, I'll be the first to give them a piece of my mind."

Mo Ran grinned. His pitch-dark eyes were depthless, light and shadow flickering within, holding a million thoughts and emotions. Why was he reminding Xue Meng of those bygone events at Tianyin Pavilion? Perhaps Xue Meng hadn't thought much of them, but those scenes had cast dark shadows in Mo Ran's mind.

The defendant had been a young woman in her twenties. A large crowd had assembled in Tianyin Pavilion's public square—men and women, young and old, cultivators and commoners alike. They whispered and craned their necks to look up at the woman upon the execution platform, held down with immortal-binding ropes, soul-fixing locks, and demon-subduing shackles.

"Isn't that Madam Lin?"

"Didn't she just marry into a rich family? What crime did she commit to catch Tianyin Pavilion's attention?"

"You guys don't know? She's the one who set fire to the Zhao manor! She killed her own husband!"

"Ah...?" This revelation drew gasps from the crowd.

"Why'd she do it?" someone piped up. "I heard her husband was always good to her."

As the crowd muttered and murmured, the master of Tianyin Pavilion emerged to greet the spectators with a scroll held aloft. Slowly the scroll unfurled and the charges against the Lin woman were read out; the accusations were so numerous it took an hour to list them all.

In summary, the accused wasn't actually the maiden from a distinguished clan who had been betrothed to the Zhao family. She was in fact a puppet wearing a human-skin mask, who had taken the true daughter's place with the objective of getting close to Zhao-gongzi in order to murder him for revenge. As for the betrothed maiden, she had long met a sorry end by this Miss Lin's blade.

"Quite the tale of deception," the pavilion master remarked coolly when finished. "None can escape the will of heaven. Miss Lin, it's about time you took off that mask and showed everyone your true face."

Before the watching crowd, hands tore the human-skin mask off and tossed it to the ground like the shed skin of a snake. A deathly pale and alluringly pretty face was revealed beneath the woman's wild tangles of hair. A disciple of Tianyin Pavilion grabbed her chin, forcing it up so the crowd could see.

Jeers broke out below. "Poisonous bitch!" someone yelled.

"You killed an innocent girl and destroyed the family that took you in, all for your personal grievances?"

"Beat her to death!"

"Dig out her eyes!"

"She deserves death by a thousand cuts! Peel her skin off inch by inch!"

The crowd was made up of individuals, but they behaved as though they shared a single, savage mind. They were a colossal beast weighed down by its own size, drooling and snarling. This unsightly creature seemed to think it was an auspicious beast, that its very existence reflected the will of the heavens and earth, its presence in the mortal realm righteous in and of itself.

The shrill cries from the onlookers became a roar that pierced the teenaged Mo Ran's ears. The fury of these people astonished him—as though the long-dead woman and the young Zhao-gongzi were not complete strangers, but their family or friends, their own son, their own lover. They cried out as if they wanted more than anything to get justice for those dear to them, to personally tear this criminal limb from limb.

Mo Ran's eyes were wide with confusion. "Shouldn't Tianyin Pavilion...be the ones to decide the punishment?" he asked.

"Don't be scared, Ran-er," Xue Zhengyong said soothingly. "Yes, Tianyin Pavilion will decide—everyone is just angry, that's all. All they can do is talk. Tianyin Pavilion will use its holy implements to decide the punishment. Everything will be fair and impartial, don't you worry."

But this business didn't unfold as Xue Zhengyong said. The shouts from the crowd grew more absurd, more extreme.

"This stupid bitch killed without a shred of remorse! You can't allow her an easy death. Pavilion Master Mu! You are the cultivation realm's arbiters of justice! You must try her properly—she needs to suffer! Make sure she gets her just deserts! Give her the punishment she deserves!"

"First, tear open her mouth, then pull out her teeth one by one, then cut her tongue into a hundred pieces!"

"Cover her in mud! After it dries, rip it off so her skin comes off too! Pour chili pepper water on her and make her suffer! Let her die!"

A brothel madam had also come to watch the commotion. She spit out her melon seed shells and smiled sweetly. "Aiya, tear her clothes off—doesn't someone like her deserve to be stripped? Stick some snakes and eels in her cunt and get a hundred men to take their turns with her—now *that's* a punishment that fits the crime."

Was this fury really born from their own righteousness? Back then, Mo Ran had trembled as he sat next to Xue Meng, stricken and overwhelmed.

Eventually even Xue Zhengyong noticed his unease. Just as he was about to bring them away from the stands, a loud *boom* echoed from the platform. A hand in the crowd had thrown an Exploding Talisman onto the platform, right at the woman's feet. This was against the rules, but whether because Tianyin Pavilion wasn't quick enough to intervene or because they didn't wish to, the talisman detonated. Instantly the woman's legs were a gory mess—

"Uncle!" The hand that gripped Xue Zhengyong's sleeve was shivering uncontrollably.

Loud whoops came from the audience, and the assembled heroes clapped in delight.

"Nice! She had it coming! Let's see another one!"

"Who threw that? Stop it!" the Tianyin Pavilion disciple shouted from the platform. But that was all—they did nothing else to control the crowd.

It didn't take long for people to start tossing all sorts of things onto the platform—vegetables, rocks, eggs, knives. The disciples cast a barrier in front of themselves and watched from the sidelines. As long as no one killed the defendant outright, they wouldn't step in. Tianyin Pavilion had always been high-minded and aloof. They wouldn't obstruct a group of concerned citizens upholding justice.

Recalling this episode, Mo Ran's heart sank like a stone. He didn't want to remember any more. He closed his eyes, then opened them again. "You'll see, Xue Meng. If Nangong Si refuses to say he's Shizun's disciple, he'll have no one in the entire cultivation realm to protect him. And if Tianyin Pavilion really does interrogate him after we leave Mount Jiao, the outcome will be the same as we saw all those years ago."

"But at the trial back then," Xue Meng said, "everyone was mad because that woman killed someone. So..."

"So whoever holds the knife can turn it on whomever they want, isn't that right?" Mo Ran was more and more despondent. He had thought to say more but found he couldn't go on. How many people in this world used the pretense of upholding justice to do evil? They took all the dissatisfaction in their day-to-day lives—all the indignation, fury, and resentment in their chests—and poured it out this way.

They finished their tea and chatted a while longer. The sky grew dark, and Xue Meng took his leave. Mo Ran walked to the window and retrieved the Zhenlong chess piece from his sleeve. He glanced at it one last time; with a flash of spiritual energy at his fingertips, he pinched it to dust.

The wind picked up and the leaves shuddered in the trees. The man at the window, too, shuddered. Slowly, he raised his hands and hid his face behind them. He stood in a daze for a long, long time, elbows propped on the window frame. Eventually, he turned away and walked into the dimmest corner of the room, letting the darkness swallow him.

Mo Ran sat in his lightless room for hours, losing himself in his thoughts until he felt shattered, broken beyond repair. He didn't know what he ought to do. There were things he thought he should speak of, but he didn't know if doing so would be a help or create yet more chaos. Either way, once he spoke there would be no going back.

What to do? He didn't know...The more he thought, the more frustrated he grew, and the greater his confusion. Anxiety and bitter pain swept through him.

336 o—• THE HUSKY & HIS WHITE CAT SHIZUN

He thought of the mysterious villain holding the knife behind him.

He thought of the cultivation realm's worshipful reverence and blind faith in Tianyin Pavilion.

He thought of that woman on trial, her legs blown to bloody rags.

He paced in his room like a caged beast, like a lunatic. The shadows of Taxian-jun and Mo-zongshi flitted across his gallant features, one swallowing the other in an infinite cycle.

When he could take it no longer, his footsteps halted. He pushed the door open and left the room.

Night had fallen. Chu Wanning was preparing to sleep when he heard a rap at his door. When he opened it to see Mo Ran standing outside, he was slightly taken aback. "What are you doing here?"

Mo Ran felt he was on the brink of madness; this calamity that might descend at any moment was like a sword hanging over his head—it was about to drive him crazy. He had screwed up all his courage, intending to confess the entire, absurd truth of his existence. But the instant he saw Chu Wanning's face, his gathered courage splintered into a million pieces, turning to dust, into fragile selfishness.

"Shizun..." Mo Ran's voice was pinched. "I can't sleep. Can I come in and sit with you a while?"

Chu Wanning stepped aside to let him in; Mo Ran closed the door behind him. He emanated an unease so strong Chu Wanning could tell his heart was in turmoil before he said a word. "Did something happen?"

Mo Ran didn't respond; he only stared at Chu Wanning. Then he strode to the window and pulled it firmly shut, cutting the room off from the outside world.

"There's..." Mo Ran began, his voice terribly hoarse. Anguish surged in his chest, seeming to rouse his desperate impulse to confess. "There's something I need to tell you."

"Is it about Xu Shuanglin?"

Mo Ran shook his head. But after a moment's hesitation, he nodded, only to shake his head again.

The candlelight flickered in his eyes like a viper's scarlet tongue, weaving and swaying. His expression was so distraught and the light in his eyes so scattered that Chu Wanning couldn't bear to merely look; he reached up to touch Mo Ran's face.

The moment Chu Wanning's fingertips brushed his cheek, Mo Ran's eyes snapped shut as though viciously stung. His lashes quivered and the jut of his throat rolled; turning away, he said thickly, "I'm sorry."

Chu Wanning didn't know what to say.

"Can we put out the light?" He hesitated. "If I see your face, I can't say it."

Chu Wanning had no idea what had happened; he'd never seen Mo Ran like this. Goosebumps rose on his arms. It was a devastating sight, as if some great object had fallen from the sky and crushed everything beneath it. He stilled for a moment, then nodded.

Mo Ran went to the candle, gazing into the flame. Then he reached over and snuffed out that last bit of light. The room was plunged into darkness, but the afterimage of that flame danced across his vision. Its vivid orange faded into flashing colors, its outline bleeding from crisp to blurry.

He didn't move, his back to the room. Chu Wanning didn't rush him; he waited quietly for Mo Ran to speak.

208

Shizun, Are You Sure You Want Me to Hide Under the Bed?

SEVERAL TIMES, Mo Ran's lips parted, only for him to close them in silence. His temples throbbed and ached as his pulse rampaged through his veins. But his blood seemed to carry no heat—it was cold, cold as ice. As he wrestled with his thoughts, even his fingertips seemed to freeze over.

"Shizun." A long pause. "Actually... I..."

He only managed three words before falling apart again. Did he really have to confess it? All those deeds belonged to the past life. He had already killed himself at Wushan Palace; he had died a long time ago. All that remained from that past life were his memories...

Did he have to confess it? If he spoke, his conscience would be clear, but was it really the correct choice? Things were so good right now—Xue Meng smiled at him, Chu Wanning was his, his uncle and aunt were healthy and well, and Shi Mei was alive... Nothing could be more important than this. Even if he spent the rest of his life consumed by guilt, living like a fugitive, he couldn't bear to destroy everything before his eyes.

But still he felt he should confess.

He was certain the villain behind the scenes had also been reborn. He was the only one who could tell the world the truth and prepare them. This was an opportunity for him to atone for his crimes. Perhaps the heavens had allowed him to keep his memories after death for just this moment: so he might step forward and prevent this crisis from unfolding, even if he paid with his life.

Mo Ran closed his eyes. He was shaking from head to toe, his lashes damp.

He didn't fear dying—after all, he had died once already. But there were things in this world more terrifying than death, and he'd had his fill of them in the past life. He had chosen suicide to escape those things. In the present lifetime, especially after Chu Wanning's death, he had been running as fast as he could, trying to throw that invisible monster off his trail. Yet it had chased him into a corner, its talons an inch from his throat. In the end, this was his destiny, eternal loneliness and revilement—he couldn't escape...

Mo Ran was crying, tears rolling silently down his face and dripping onto the floor. Trying desperately to suppress the quaver in his voice, he choked out, "I'm sorry... I... I don't know where to begin... I actually... I..."

A pair of strong arms encircled him.

Mo Ran's eyes flew open. Chu Wanning had stepped over and embraced him from behind.

"If you don't want to say it, then don't." Chu Wanning's voice floated over his shoulder. "Everyone has their secrets... Everyone makes mistakes."

Mo Ran froze. Chu Wanning already understood.

But of course—how could he fail to catch on? He had seen Mo Ran admit to so many mistakes, both phony and sincere, evasive and earnest. He didn't know what wrong Mo Ran had committed, but he was certain he meant to come clean about something from his past—something he didn't wish to speak of.

"Shizun…"

"If it's bothering you and you want to tell me about it, go ahead. I'm listening," said Chu Wanning. "But if it's too painful to say, you don't have to tell me, and I won't ask further." He paused. "I know you won't do anything like it ever again."

Mo Ran felt like a dagger was twisting in his chest. He shook his head minutely. *No… It's not as simple as that… It's not nearly so simple… It's not like picking a flower I wasn't supposed to—I killed; I covered the land in blood and bones. I ruined most of the cultivation realm; I ruined you.*

He broke down again.

I ruined you, Chu Wanning! You comfort your executioner… You comfort the man who stabbed a knife into your heart! Why did you use your dying breaths to tell me to spare myself? Why didn't you just kill me at the very beginning…

He was trembling, shaking uncontrollably. Chu Wanning felt a warm droplet on the back of his hand and flinched. "Mo Ran…" he murmured.

"I want to tell you."

"Go ahead, then."

Mo Ran's thoughts were a mess. Shaking his head, he said haltingly, "I… I don't know how to say it…" Up till now he had managed to speak clearly, but sobs finally began to choke his words. "Really… I really don't know where to begin…"

"Then don't say it." Chu Wanning pulled Mo Ran around to face him. In the darkness, he reached up to touch his cheek. Mo Ran flinched away, but Chu Wanning was insistent—he cupped his face in his hand. It was wet, drenched with tears.

"Don't say it," Chu Wanning repeated.

"I…"

As Chu Wanning leaned in to kiss him—the first time he'd ever taken such initiative—the only warning Mo Ran had was the faint scent of haitang growing stronger. Chu Wanning pressed his mouth against the agonized twist of Mo Ran's, moving clumsily to deepen the kiss. Bit by bit, he guided Mo Ran's mouth open, tongue slipping in to slide against Mo Ran's.

Despite the chaos, the fear, the madness, Mo Ran found himself returning the kiss, though he couldn't say why. Perhaps love was the harbor that gave him shelter from his pain. Or perhaps humans were not so different from beasts in the end; sex could force just about anything to the back of one's mind. In abandoning oneself to desire, pleasure became the only reality. It was mercy to the helpless, a moment of respite for the desperate.

Neither said any more. As their kisses grew more passionate, Chu Wanning felt Mo Ran's arousal through their clothes, hard against him. He hesitated for a moment, then reached down.

Mo Ran grabbed his hand, lacing their fingers together. "This is enough." He held Chu Wanning close. Here was the only person who could soothe his pain, who could cleanse his soul. "You don't need to do anything more. This is enough..."

Chu Wanning reached up to caress Mo Ran's face. His heart ached. "Why are you such a fool?"

Mo Ran took his other hand, all their fingers now tightly linked. He pressed his forehead to Chu Wanning's. "If only I'd always been such a fool."

Chu Wanning saw persuasion was futile. He didn't know any more sentimental words; he clumsily nuzzled Mo Ran's cheeks and the tip of his nose, and then gently captured his lips once more. Even as the tips of Chu Wanning's ears burned, he strove to maintain his composure. He'd moved first to kiss and hold Mo Ran, doing all these things he wasn't at all accustomed to doing.

"Shizun..." Mo Ran tried to squirm away, his breathing ragged from their kisses. "Enough... Don't do this."

"You're always the one taking the lead." Chu Wanning tugged a hand out of Mo Ran's grip and looped it around his neck. "Let me do it this time."

"Shizun..."

Chu Wanning looked into Mo Ran's puppy eyes, warm and shining, and reached up to pat him on the back of the head. "Be good," he said, voice steeped in tenderness.

In the darkness, they kissed against the wall, the movements of their lips and hands going from gentle to urgent, to hungry, to insatiable, overflowing with desire and impatience.

"Shizun... Wanning..." Mo Ran chanted his name—tenderly, ardently, madly, ruefully. For him, the tiniest scrap of love from Chu Wanning was the world's most potent aphrodisiac. At last he stopped thinking. He pinned Chu Wanning to the wall, kissing him fiercely, dragging his hands over his body. They panted for breath, hearts pounding. Mo Ran was almost mad with desire, the corners of his eyes scarlet.

"The candle..." Chu Wanning gasped as they broke apart, brows knitting slightly.

"It's been put out, hasn't it?" Mo Ran trailed kisses along his earlobes, his neck.

He heard Chu Wanning say into his ear, voice heavy with suppressed moans, "No, light it..."

Mo Ran froze.

"I want to see you," said Chu Wanning.

The candle flared to life, chasing away the darkness.

Chu Wanning's phoenix eyes were bright and clear, resolute yet misted with desire. His features yet carried a hint of their usual frost, but his ears were a vivid scarlet. "I want to see you," he repeated.

Mo Ran's heart ached so sharply he felt he might die. How could his filthy, ailing, once-coldly-unfeeling heart survive beneath this gaze? As he folded Chu Wanning into his arms and kissed him, Mo Ran took Chu Wanning's hand and pressed it to his own throbbing chest. "Remember this place," he said.

Chu Wanning blinked at him, uncomprehending.

"If there comes a day when my sins can no longer be pardoned," Mo Ran mumbled, brushing his nose against Chu Wanning's. "Then kill me. Right here."

A shudder ran through Chu Wanning. He stared at Mo Ran in disbelief. "What are you saying?"

Mo Ran's face broke into a smile—one that held both Mo-zongshi's gallant sincerity and Taxian-jun's wicked madness. "My spiritual core was formed because of you, and my heart is yours too. If a day comes when I must die, they should both belong to you. Only then can I..."

He stopped. Never had he seen such shock and fear in Chu Wanning's eyes; it dragged him to a halt. He lowered his lashes and offered Chu Wanning a wry smile. "Just kidding. I'm only saying all this because I want to tell you..."

Mo Ran drew Chu Wanning more tightly into his arms.

I don't know how many more chances like this we'll have.

"Wanning..."

I love you; I want you; I can't be without you.

He so badly wanted to tell him all this—but just like the events of his past life, he couldn't say any of it aloud.

Chu Wanning was caught between confusion and astonishment. He didn't know how grave a mistake had to be for someone to say something like this. But as Mo Ran kissed him, his consciousness frayed. Mo Ran's kisses weren't entirely to blame; Chu Wanning didn't lack for self-control. He was also unwilling to follow this train of thought to its end.

Desperation colored their passion, like roiling oil tossed into flames. Their entanglement grew wilder as their restraint slipped away. Before they reached the bed, most of their clothes had been shed. Mo Ran pinned Chu Wanning down on the mattress, no longer so shy and cautious as he had been the first time, that lustful male craving a simple and brutish need.

Pulling open Chu Wanning's underclothes, Mo Ran bent to kiss the hardened tip of him and take him into his mouth, glancing up as he did to drink in Chu Wanning's slack gaze in the candlelight, his head thrown back as he gasped.

How many more times could they be together like this? One? Two? In the morning they would set off for Mount Jiao, where they might immediately run into the villain orchestrating everything. If that person could really use the Zhenlong Chess Formation, only Mo Ran would be able to defuse the situation. The truth would inevitably come to light.

But as they lost themselves in each other, he tried to convince both his shizun and his despairing self—they would have many, many more chances like this. They would always be together. Just as love and desire entwined endlessly from the dark of the night to the brilliance of day, he wanted to have Chu Wanning countless times until they fell asleep with limbs tangled, until the blush of dawn painted the horizon. Then he would awaken in his warm embrace and again take him between the sheets, surrendering themselves to indulgence beneath the bright sun, drowning in filth, love, and want.

Mo Ran pressed his own heavy length to Chu Wanning's, stroking them off together, chasing release. Chu Wanning's phoenix eyes were overflowing with hazy desire. His lips were lightly parted, soft sighs escaping to the rhythm of Mo Ran's hands, his gaze going scattered and blurred.

Drowning in intoxication, they suddenly heard a knock at the door.

Chu Wanning started, color draining from his face as Mo Ran clapped a hand over his mouth to silence him. It was quiet in the room, but Mo Ran's other hand didn't slacken its frenetic pace, driving himself and the man in his arms to the brink.

Chu Wanning tried to shake his head, but Mo Ran's grip was unrelenting, pinning him in place. He only had use of his phoenix eyes, caught between rapture and suffering, protestation and despair.

"Shizun, are you there?"

Chu Wanning glared at Mo Ran, fury kindling in his gaze. He rapped his knuckles lightly against the headboard.

Mo Ran swallowed, the jut of his throat bobbing—an alluring sight. "Mn. I know, it's Xue Meng," he rasped.

"Shizun?" A minute later, after getting no response, Xue Meng mumbled, "Weird, the candle is lit… Shizun?"

But how would Mo Ran heed him? He was still on top of Chu Wanning, lost in the throes of lust. Even with the candle, the room was dark enough that he had mistaken the indignation in Chu Wanning's eyes for cresting desire.

"Shizun?"

The disciple at the door had no intention of leaving, and the disciple in his bed had no plans to stop. Chu Wanning was left with little choice but to clamp his teeth down on Mo Ran's fingers. At the jolt of pain, Mo Ran released him, a wisp of hurt surfacing in his eyes.

"Ouch, that was really hard..." Mo Ran's voice was low and heated.

"Serves you right." Chu Wanning threw him a glare, then took a deep breath and called out to Xue Meng at the door, "I'm already in bed. Is something the matter?"

"Ah, no, everything's fine," said Xue Meng. "I'm just... Something's bothering me; I can't sleep, so I wanted to talk to Shizun..." Xue Meng trailed off.

Chu Wanning could practically see the little phoenix standing outside, his neck drooping piteously. Was there something in the air? How was it that *two* of his disciples were so beset with worries tonight?

Concerned, Chu Wanning patted Mo Ran on the shoulder. "Get up and put on your clothes," he whispered.

Mo Ran's eyes widened, producing exactly the look of a dejected puppy. "You're going to let him in?"

"It sounds like something's really wrong..."

"Then what about me?"

Chu Wanning paused. Weathering his embarrassment, he said, "Get dressed and hide under the bed."

209

Shizun, Isn't This Exciting?

MO RAN SPUTTERED. He had to hand it to Xue Meng—these latest antics had chased every gloomy thought of the past life from of Mo Ran's mind, leaving nothing but fury and lust. He couldn't fathom why Xue Meng had to talk to Chu Wanning at this hour—

Shit, surely Xue Meng didn't like men?

The very thought was enough to nauseate Mo Ran, but with another moment's thought, it seemed unlikely. Mo Ran shook his head, pushed himself upright, and leaned down to glance at the space below the bed. "No way," he said.

"You—"

"Don't be mad. I'm not being difficult," said Mo Ran. "There isn't enough space; I won't fit."

Chu Wanning stared at him.

"There's no closet in here, and I can't climb through a window that small. There's nowhere for me to go. Tell him to leave."

Chu Wanning thought it over and was forced to concede. "Can we talk tomorrow?" he called. "I'm about to go to sleep."

"But I'm really..." Xue Meng's voice was tearful, the words somewhat strangled. "I won't take a lot of time, okay? Shizun, I'm really confused—there are just a few things I want to ask you about..."

Chu Wanning knit his brows in silence.

"Otherwise, I won't be able to sleep..."

His pathetic whining made Mo Ran's heart stir uncomfortably. He too wondered what Xue Meng was so keen to get off his chest tonight. He sat up, looked around, and had a sudden idea. Leaning over, he whispered into Chu Wanning's ear.

Chu Wanning's expression darkened. "Don't be ridiculous."

"Then tell him to leave."

Chu Wanning opened his mouth, then stopped. He could hear soft rustling from outside the door as Xue Meng kicked at the leaves on the ground. It was rare for Xue Meng to be so clingy; if he really sent him away in this state...

Chu Wanning cursed under his breath and shoved Mo Ran off. "Then you'd better behave, and don't ever think this will happen a second time." Pausing, he groaned. "Wait, don't forget all the clothes on the floor! Hide everything, quick."

Xue Meng had waited outside for some time in silence. Despite his sinking heart, he ventured one more time: "Shizun?"

After a moment, he got his reply. "I heard you. Come in."

Finally receiving his go-ahead, Xue Meng pushed the door open. As soon as he entered, he frowned slightly. A faint scent hung in the room, one he didn't know how to describe—fleeting but somehow familiar.

Chu Wanning was indeed already in bed, the thick curtain let down around him. As he heard Xue Meng come in, he drew the curtain aside ever so slightly, revealing features soft with drowsiness. His eyes were heavy-lidded, as though he had just woken and was still quite tired, with a faint redness at the corners. He gave Xue Meng a long look, his expression shrouded in the curtain's shadow, nebulous and hazy in the dim light of the candle.

Abashed, Xue Meng muttered, "Shizun, I'm sorry, I've disturbed your rest..."

"It's fine. Sit," said Chu Wanning. "I'll stay where I am."

Of course, Xue Meng wasn't about to tell him to get up after he'd already lain down. "Uh-huh—Shizun, just listen to me from where you are," he hastily replied.

Chu Wanning waited for him to speak.

Xue Meng sat in confused silence at the table. After returning to his room and giving the matter some thought, he had realized why the pendant around Mo Ran's neck looked so familiar—back when they were traveling to Rufeng Sect for the wedding, Mo Ran had bought one just like it for Chu Wanning. Xue Meng even remembered grabbing it for a closer look; he'd thought it very pretty and had asked Mo Ran for one as well. At the time, Mo Ran had told him it was the last pendant of its kind.

The more he thought about it, the stranger and more disconcerting it seemed. Like Mo Ran, Xue Meng had gone back and forth about whether he ought to speak, suffering the torment of indecision. In the end, his feet took him to his shizun's door.

But as he looked into Chu Wanning's eyes, Xue Meng hesitated again. He didn't know where to start. Eventually he began in a muffled voice, "Shizun, have you noticed that...Mo Ran has been acting really weird?"

Both Chu Wanning and Mo Ran's hearts skipped a beat. Chu Wanning's face was impassive as he asked, "How so?"

"Recently, I've felt like something's *off* about him... Has Shizun not noticed...?" Xue Meng asked haltingly, struggling to string the words together. Finally he steeled himself and blurted it out. "It's like he's, uh, *pursuing* someone."

Mo Ran and Chu Wanning both went very still.

352 ○—● THE HUSKY & HIS WHITE CAT SHIZUN

Naturally, Xue Meng didn't dare to say, *It's like he's pursuing Shizun*, but he snuck a glance at Chu Wanning, his eyes filled with alarm.

"What makes you say so?" Chu Wanning asked.

"I-I'm not really sure either, so I wanted to ask Shizun and see if you had the same thought."

"You don't need to worry so much about him."

"But today..."

"What happened today?"

"Today... Today, I saw something around his neck..." Xue Meng fell silent, looking down at his hands, but Mo Ran started in surprise behind the curtain. One hand groped for the crystal pendant around his neck as his expression shifted.

Chu Wanning still had no idea what Xue Meng had seen. He gazed at Xue Meng, brow furrowed, waiting for him to finish his thought. But after a long while, Xue Meng still hadn't made a sound; instead, Chu Wanning felt a large, warm hand touch his leg.

His eyes instantly flashed. Thinking Mo Ran was about to do something truly absurd, he tore his gaze away from the oblivious Xue Meng to the corner of the curtain-covered bed. Contrary to his expectations, he saw Mo Ran pointing to the pendant around his own neck as he soundlessly mouthed the word at him. Chu Wanning at once put together what had happened.

After a moment's deliberation, Chu Wanning asked, "Did you see him wearing a pendant and think it was just like mine?"

"No no, that's not what I meant!" Xue Meng exclaimed, flapping his hands in anxiety and embarrassment. "I wasn't trying to imply anything about Shizun, I just thought it was weird, I..."

"It's fine," said Chu Wanning. "I gave that pendant back to him."

"Ah... Sh-shizun gave it back to him?"

"Why else do you think he has it?"

Xue Meng let out a breath of relief, color finally coming back into his pale face. "That makes perfect sense," he said with a smile. "Back then he told me it was the last pendant. I thought he'd..."

Chu Wanning narrowed his eyes.

"That's not what I meant... I just wanted to say... Actually, I..." Xue Meng babbled. Finally, he clapped a hand to his forehead and said plaintively, "Ah, just pretend I never said anything, Shizun. I'm so bad with words, I don't know how to explain myself. Really, I just thought he was acting weird lately. You know, his brain isn't normal—I was worried he might get some strange ideas and do something to upset Shizun." After this rambling, Xue Meng asked tentatively, "Shizun...do you get what I mean?"

"No," said Chu Wanning.

"Uh, no worries then, that's good, that's really good." The longer Xue Meng spoke, the less sense he was making. Grabbing a handful of his own hair in desperation, he groaned listlessly. "Heavens... What am I even saying..."

Chu Wanning had never been a practiced liar; he had no idea how to comfort him. There were any number of things he could've said. Although it might have gone against his conscience, he could've drawn a clear line in the sand between himself and Mo Ran with a single casual utterance. After all, Xue Meng was looking for such reassurance. If Chu Wanning had just said "That's not the case," Xue Meng would always choose to believe his shizun even if proof otherwise was laid out before him.

But this unwavering belief was precisely the reason Chu Wanning couldn't bring himself to say it. He didn't want to speak in absolutes. He watched in helpless silence as Xue Meng scratched his head and sighed, clearly vexed. At last Xue Meng fell still.

He lowered his head to stare blankly at the floorboards before he spoke again. "Shizun, you'll always be our shizun, right? That won't ever change, will it?"

There was no immediate reply.

"I'm only asking because I felt bad seeing what happened with Nangong Si... I..."

"Nothing will change," said Chu Wanning.

Bit by bit, the tension bled out of Xue Meng's stiff spine. Slumping in his seat, he sniffled a laugh. "Mn, that's enough for me."

Heartache and guilt welled up unbidden in Chu Wanning. Although his features remained as composed as the still waters of a well, he murmured, "Xue Meng..."

Xue Meng waited for him to continue. But in the candlelight, Chu Wanning only gazed at him in silence. What was he supposed to say? *Whatever happens in the future, I hope you'll acknowledge me as your shifu?* Impossible. Even on pain of death, he could never utter such sappy—such cruel—words. What right did he have to ask Xue Meng to acknowledge him regardless of what might transpire? Everyone would inevitably experience separation and reunion. Everyone would grow and change, just as a young shoot of bamboo would eventually shed its outermost layer, letting it wither and crumble to dirt. Xue Meng had many decades ahead of him. It was rare for any one person to walk beside another till the end of such a long journey. Events and companions came and went, all destined to become a snake's discarded slough, a stalk of bamboo's discarded sheath.

Xue Meng waited, but Chu Wanning didn't continue. His concerned eyes grew round as he watched him. "Shizun?" he mumbled.

"It's nothing," Chu Wanning said mildly. "You seem to have a lot on your mind. I was just going to recommend you ask the Tanlang Elder for two bottles of Tapir Fragrance Dew."

Xue Meng blinked.

"Is there anything else?" asked Chu Wanning.

He thought for a bit. "Yes."

"What is it?"

Xue Meng had been stewing on this for a while. "Shizun, are you really going to take Nangong Si as a disciple? H-he's not gonna become my da-shixiong, is he?"

Chu Wanning eyed him. "Is that what you're concerned about?"

"Mn." Xue Meng gave his hem a bashful tug. "I used to be your first disciple. If he counts, then won't I..."

Chu Wanning couldn't help it; his lips bowed in a tiny smile. Xue Meng had always sulked and whined with Madam Wang when he was little. After Mo Ran came to Sisheng Peak, he grew needier still, always trying to one-up his cousin for the spotlight. Who would've thought that even as a grown man, this habit was still so deeply ingrained that the prospect of accepting Nangong Si made the little peacock's feathers fan in agitation. Xue Meng had been brooding over this question of who would come first all day.

"It makes no difference," Chu Wanning said. "I don't put any of you first or last."

"No way, I don't want him to be my da-shixiong! Even if he pledged to you first, Shizun recognized him last. I don't *mind* that he's becoming Shizun's disciple...but can't he go at the end of the line? He can be a little shidi or whatever," Xue Meng said, perfectly earnest. "I can call him Nangong-shidi."

"Whatever you'd like."

This brightened Xue Meng's mood considerably; now he wanted to stay and chat. In the back corner of the bed, Mo Ran was increasingly agitated. How did Xue Meng have *so* much to say? Why couldn't he get the hell out, out, out.

But Xue Meng didn't budge. "There's one more thing I want to ask Shizun."

"Mn," Chu Wanning replied evenly. "Go ahead."

Mo Ran stared at him in disbelief.

"Earlier today, Mo Ran said Shizun promised to give him a handkerchief."

"Oh, that..." Chu Wanning paused. "Mn, I haven't made it yet. Do you want one too?"

Xue Meng's eyes lit up. "C-can I have one?"

"I originally meant to make one for each of you. But I've been busy, so I kept putting it off."

Xue Meng was overjoyed. Mo Ran, on the contrary, was completely stunned. Wasn't that... Wasn't that supposed to be just for him? Why did Xue Meng also...

And Shi Mei too. Even *Nangong Si*...

Mo Ran felt a spike of indignation. Unfortunately, Chu Wanning's face was turned toward Xue Meng; he entirely missed the turbulent look in Mo Ran's eyes.

Xue Meng chattered on, blithely detailing what kind of handkerchief he wanted. Not a trace of his gloomy mood remained. Mo Ran, at the foot of the bed, grew more and more irked, especially as he watched Chu Wanning's cheerful countenance as he responded to Xue Meng. Even knowing there was nothing between them, dissatisfaction gnawed at his chest.

"Pollia flowers are difficult to embroider. If you want a pollia pattern, I'll have to ask Madam Wang."

"I-is it difficult?" Xue Meng was taken aback. "Forget it, then— Shizun, you should choose something you know. What are you best at?"

"I'm...actually not familiar with any flower or animal patterns."

Chu Wanning cleared his throat in mild embarrassment. "I'm really only good at stitching the Heart Sutra."

Xue Meng blinked.

"At Wubei Temple, when I was young, I... Huaizui taught me," said Chu Wanning. "I..." His brows suddenly drew together. Cheeks pale, he pressed his lips closed.

"Shizun, are you okay?" Xue Meng asked, taken aback.

There was a slow beat before Chu Wanning replied, "I'm fine... Is there anything else?"

"Mn, yeah, one more thing, but I forgot what it was. Let me think a second..." Xue Meng dipped his head, deep in thought. The instant Xue Meng lowered his gaze, Chu Wanning sucked in a breath. Fury simmering in his eyes, he glared at the man hiding in the corner of the bed.

Mo Ran had merely been idly feeling up Chu Wanning in the hope that he would send Xue Meng packing a little sooner. But the red-rimmed glare Chu Wanning shot at him in answer, added to the fact that Chu Wanning was quite powerless to mount any meaningful resistance at the moment, fanned the embers in Mo Ran's heart into a fire.

His instincts were beastly from the start, and in certain respects, he was as savage as could be. Only his overwhelming love and guilt toward Chu Wanning shackled his primal appetites. Until this point, he hadn't done anything outrageous in bed. Now impatience and envy melted those shackles down. His dark eyes gleamed silently and dangerously at Chu Wanning.

Seized by a wild impulse, he burrowed beneath the blankets, where Xue Meng couldn't see, and crawled forward between Chu Wanning's slender, muscular legs. The bedspread blocked out all the light, but the darkness only sharpened his other senses. He could distinctly feel Chu Wanning's minute tremors.

He felt a hand grab his broad shoulder, five burning fingers digging into his flesh, pushing him away. This was all Chu Wanning could do to stop him beneath the covers. It only stoked Mo Ran's desire to tear him to shreds.

Xue Meng was still talking, but not about anything important. Mo Ran listened half-heartedly. But upon hearing Xue Meng say, "No matter what Shizun embroiders, I'll like it," Mo Ran's irritation flared. His breaths were brushing against the tops of Chu Wanning's thighs. He knew precisely where that soul-stirring desire most ached, but he deliberately left it untouched. He turned his face, lashes fluttering, and trailed kisses along Chu Wanning's inner thighs, gently sucking that soft skin, leaving behind marks that would linger for days.

Chu Wanning's trembling grew more acute. At this moment, he was deeply regretting his choice to let Mo Ran stay behind. His nails dug into Mo Ran's shoulder, but force was futile against this lunatic.

"Shizun, are you listening?"

"Mn..."

Mo Ran waited, lips hovering near the delicate curve of Chu Wanning's erection, heated breaths fanning over it. He held himself still, waiting for the most perfect, most shocking, most thrilling moment.

It arrived soon enough. Xue Meng asked some irrelevant question; Mo Ran didn't care to listen, but Chu Wanning still needed to answer. In the instant Chu Wanning was about to reply, Mo Ran slid forward beneath the covers and greedily swallowed his blazing arousal.

Chu Wanning's entire body tensed; he swallowed frantically. His fingernails had already broken skin on Mo Ran's shoulder, but

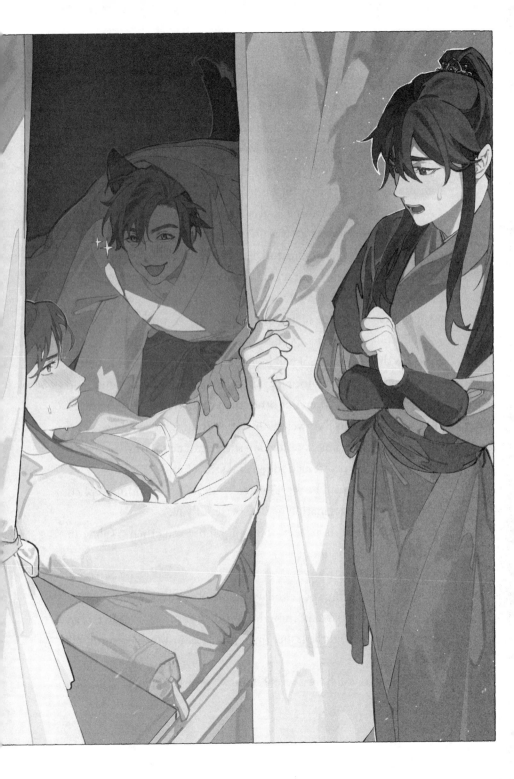

Mo Ran didn't mind a bit. His mind was a rush of exhilaration—at Chu Wanning's reaction, at the exhibitionist thrill of what they were doing in the dimness of the bed curtains. He knew Chu Wanning could bear this much; even if Mo Ran were to rip off his underclothes and fuck him right now, Chu Wanning wouldn't so much as whimper. Mo Ran cast aside his inhibitions.

Though Chu Wanning had a thousand reasons not to want this, the physical pleasure was undeniable. He was hot and hard in Mo Ran's mouth, the round, full head of his cock pressing against the back of Mo Ran's throat. It wasn't necessarily a pleasant sensation, but Mo Ran was too infatuated to care; he couldn't have been more eager.

Even in the grip of such stimulation, Chu Wanning managed to field the rest of Xue Meng's questions. Whether in this life or the past one, his sheer strength of will had ever been astonishing. He put on a commendable act of normalcy; his voice was lower than usual, and his words a trace slower, but other than that, his behavior betrayed not a thing. If Mo Ran weren't in bed with him, he would've never guessed this man was experiencing such extreme pleasure.

Eventually, Xue Meng nodded and said, "I understand."

"You should head back; it's getting late," Chu Wanning replied. "Don't let your imagination get the better of you."

Xue Meng got to his feet. "Shizun, I'll be going then... Oh yeah, should I put the light out?"

"Sure."

As Chu Wanning spoke the word, Mo Ran swallowed his entire length. His lips parted. Though he didn't gasp, he couldn't keep from frowning slightly, lashes quivering, a faint blush coloring his cheekbones.

"Shizun, do you have a fever?" Xue Meng asked tentatively.

"...I don't."

"But your face is a little red." Without thought, Xue Meng leaned down and put his hand on Chu Wanning's forehead.

Chu Wanning couldn't have foreseen that his unsuspecting disciple would touch his forehead while Mo Ran was subjecting him to such a carnal act. Xue Meng stood with a concerned gaze before him, while Mo Ran sucked him off beneath the covers, his warm mouth enveloping him, bobbing up and down in an unmistakable rhythm. His pleasure was cresting as his humiliation threatened to drown him. It took every fiber of his self-control to repress his panting and moaning.

"You don't feel hot..." Xue Meng muttered. "Shizun, are you not feeling well?"

Not feeling well? Mo Ran thought. *How could he not feel well? Your shizun is feeling pretty damn great—the fact that you're still standing here is the only thing stopping me from making him feel even better! Leave already!*

Mo Ran's resentment deepened until Xue Meng finally realized it was time for him to go. He diligently snuffed the candle, bade Chu Wanning good night, and left the room.

The second the door clicked shut, Chu Wanning exploded with rage, throwing the blankets aside and hauling Mo Ran up by his topknot. He drew back his hand and slapped him—not lightly, but none too hard either—as he snapped, "You *scoundrel*...mmph!"

The only response he got was Mo Ran's ardent, ragged breaths and his bright gaze, blurred with torrid lust. Most men were no better than animals in the heat of desire; putting them in bed with their beloved was like drugging a beast with an aphrodisiac. Mo Ran was completely unfazed by Chu Wanning's slap; he grabbed his hand and pinned him to the bed to tear off the last layer of his robes. As skin met skin, both let out a low moan.

Mo Ran didn't speak; his eyes gleamed with a feverish want. He was so hard it hurt, clear fluid leaking from the full, round head of his cock. He ground himself against Chu Wanning's abdomen as if drunk, leaving slick, sticky trails in his wake.

He had teased Chu Wanning without mercy beneath the covers; now, the flames that threatened to consume him were equally ruthless. As Chu Wanning had summoned his willpower to bite back his moans, so too Mo Ran summoned all his fortitude to stop himself from lifting Chu Wanning's legs and burying his aching hardness to the hilt.

Muscles straining, Mo Ran kissed Chu Wanning with all his might, mindlessly bucking against him. The flames of lust lapped at his heart; all he wanted was to be inside this man. All his most primal urges compelled him to fuck Chu Wanning, to claim him completely, to tear him to pieces. They demanded he make Chu Wanning take him in, accept him, swallow him; make Chu Wanning his own.

"Get up... Baby, get up..." he mumbled. "Quick—I can't wait any longer. Put your legs together..."

Mo Ran's voice was a low rasp as he clung to his last thread of rationality. He pulled Chu Wanning to his knees and, just as he had before, pressed his burning length between Chu Wanning's thighs. Hands a vise around Chu Wanning's waist, he began to move, each snap of his hips quick and brutal. His skin was sheened with sweat, the light in his eyes almost as frenzied as his movements. This incomplete consummation merely stoked the flames of his desire. He was too focused on the sensation of thrusting between Chu Wanning's legs to run his mouth with filthy words, too focused on the way his cock brushed against that hidden entrance every time, nudging against it. With each thrust, his hips met Chu Wanning's thighs, coarse hair rubbing against the soft skin there, each

SHIZUN, ISN'T THIS EXCITING? •—o 363

movement audible in the slap of his balls against the full curve of Chu Wanning's ass.

The force of it left Chu Wanning dazed; he was losing his mind, a feeling not at all helped by Mo Ran reaching down from time to time with the hand that wasn't gripping Chu Wanning's waist to curl his fingers around Chu Wanning's own straining erection and stroke him off.

"Ahh..."

Mo Ran bit down on Chu Wanning's shoulder, nibbling it before murmuring, "Not so loud. The soundproofing isn't good here, and Xue Meng might still be nearby."

Chu Wanning let no more sounds escape after that. His eyes were glassy and unfocused as Mo Ran brought him to release, as he endured the ferocious drive of Mo Ran's hips on all fours. That startlingly thick cock moved between his legs; he didn't dare contemplate how it would feel inside him. He shivered...

That night, they made love like this thrice—or, more accurately, Chu Wanning came thrice like this. By the end, his awareness was fast slipping away. He remembered clinging to the man on top of him as they kissed with abandon, and how his heart abruptly began to ache. Chu Wanning raised his head to kiss him again, somewhat clumsy, but Mo Ran was at his limit. "Don't tempt me..." he panted, disoriented.

Chu Wanning froze. *Tempt* him? Who was tempting him... Vexed, amused, and not a little helpless, Chu Wanning retorted, "Surely I can't just lie still and let you do whatever you want?"

Mo Ran dipped down to kiss the edge of his ear. "It would be great if you let me do whatever I wanted."

His tone held a hint of bitterness, betraying the disquiet still lurking in his mood. It was dark in the room, but when Chu Wanning looked up, he saw clearly the sorrow that flitted through Mo Ran's eyes.

An idea came to him in a flash of inspiration. Before Mo Ran could react, he flipped them over to straddle his strong waist. Gripping both of Mo Ran's hands, he gazed down at him from above.

"Shizun, you..." Mo Ran muttered, startled.

Chu Wanning didn't respond right away. His phoenix eyes shone, but his earlobes were crimson. "I already said—let me take the lead this time. I haven't forgotten."

Slowly, he straightened up and shifted himself down. Watching him with his scalp completely numb, Mo Ran felt his blood surge wildly. "Stop fooling around," he said. "If you really... You won't be able to make the journey tomorrow."

But Chu Wanning acted like he hadn't heard. As always, once stubbornness overtook him, he would forge his own path, never taking the words of others to heart.

Mo Ran's spine went rigid. On one hand, he longed deeply to see Chu Wanning take the initiative and ride him, to get on top of him and move his hips. But on the other, he truly didn't want Chu Wanning to do so right now. He knew that if he fucked Chu Wanning for real, Mo Ran wouldn't be able to stop after just one round, not after he had restrained himself for so long.

Besides, during their unending trysts in the past life, when had he ever been able to fuck Chu Wanning merely once? On that frenzied night when he'd used an aphrodisiac on Chu Wanning, he'd tormented that man until dawn, drinking in his helpless moans. Mo Ran was entirely wrung out toward the end, yet he refused to stop, refused to pull out, still buried himself in that wet, twitching hole. Their legs tangling, their tongues intertwining, he'd pushed himself inside him, murmuring filthy, mortifying words into his ear. "It feels good doesn't it? Shizun, look how you're still sucking me in. I came so much for you—aren't you satisfied yet?"

He had forced Chu Wanning to look where they were joined, reaching down to stroke the taut lines of Chu Wanning's stomach. "Your belly is filled with my come," he growled. "What should we do?" His eyes glinted with bestial lust as such obscenities dropped from his lips. "Will Shizun bear a child for this venerable one? Hm?" He bucked his hips, driving deeper. Come from his previous climaxes leaked out around his cock.

The aphrodisiac was still in effect. Mo Ran watched the man in his arms tremble as he shifted within him, his eyes darkening against his will as a low whine escaped from his throat. Mo Ran could no longer resist. He began to move once more, driving into him, gratifying him...

At that point, he didn't want to be the invincible emperor of the cultivation realm. His desire for Chu Wanning had always been potent and all-consuming. He wanted nothing more than to lock Chu Wanning in a room and make love to him with single-minded devotion, day and night, with no regard for anything or anyone. He wanted to take him on all fours, to take him against the wall, to fuck him with his long legs splayed open on the bed, to thrust into him as he bounced on his cock. Nothing was better than seeing Chu Wanning fucked until he babbled nonsense, until he was sobbing and begging for mercy, until his cock twitched uncontrollably, and he came. If only he could live the rest of his life sheathed inside Chu Wanning and never pull out—*that* would be the height of the mortal realm's pleasures.

Mo Ran knew what sort of beastly lust lurked at the bottom of his heart like roiling lava. His throat bobbed as he pinned dark eyes on Chu Wanning, beseeching him, warning him. "Shizun, don't do this..."

"Then I'll do something else." Chu Wanning's cheeks burned, but his gaze was unyielding.

Mo Ran had no time to consider what *something else* might be before Chu Wanning moved down and dipped his head. His movements were quick, leaving Mo Ran no opportunity to refuse, and leaving himself no time to hesitate.

He took Mo Ran's fearsome erection between his lips.

"Ah..." A jolt of electricity seemed to race down Mo Ran's spine as all the muscles in his torso tensed. He instinctively closed his eyes in ecstasy, then reached out and buried his fingers in Chu Wanning's long hair. One fine-boned hand cupped the back of Chu Wanning's head as his sculpted chest heaved.

"Wanning..."

Tears leaked from the corner of his eyes—was it from stimulation or gratitude? He couldn't be sure anymore. In his beloved's mouth, his cock grew harder yet, veins standing out in stark relief. Already imposing in size and heft before, it grew into something entirely too formidable.

Chu Wanning couldn't possibly fit the entirety of Mo Ran's length in his mouth, but he mimicked Mo Ran's motions. He licked along the shaft, trembling from head to toe with shame, even as love and desire warmed his chest from within. He strained to take both the massive head and the shaft into his mouth, but the tip was already knocking against his throat by the time his lips made it halfway down. The blazing heat at the back of his mouth coupled with the faintly musky scent of Mo Ran's arousal nearly made him retch several times.

Infinitely rueful, Mo Ran hurried to intervene. "That's enough, babe, don't..." A muffled groan swallowed the rest of his words. Chu Wanning wasn't about to give up; his obstinacy made no exception for sex. He started to move, sucking and bobbing his head.

Mo Ran had never had any issues lasting in bed, especially during his days as Taxian-jun. Back then, men and women had plied him with every manner of temptation, but his heart had never been moved. Yet when Chu Wanning leaned down between his legs, kissing him, his tongue lapping against his cock, the world turned to white nothingness in his eyes, then endless darkness, bursting with raucous color and then fading to a gentle blur.

It felt too fucking good.

Mo Ran threw his head back and panted lowly, his slender, elegant fingers tangling in Chu Wanning's hair as hoarse moans escaped his lips.

His Wanning, his shizun... Yuheng of the Night Sky, the Beidou Immortal. The loftiest man in the world—the pristine and faultless Chu Wanning—was willing to do this with him. Without drugs, without coercion, entirely of his own accord...

Mo Ran's eyes were wet, his dusky lashes quivering.

...Gladly, even.

Chu Wanning's technique was terrible, and he didn't quite know his own strength; several times, he accidentally scraped Mo Ran with his teeth, hard enough to hurt. But Mo Ran sank into Chu Wanning's ministrations with no thought of stopping.

As his climax rocked him, hot tears slipped from his eyes. He pulled Chu Wanning to his chest, gathering him into his embrace, kissing him again and again. His heart blazed with the agonies of both sorrow and affection.

"Wanning..." he murmured into his ear, over and over. "Wanning..."

Chu Wanning glanced at him, phoenix eyes wet with desire, before lowering his lashes in shame. After a long pause, he asked, voice small and hoarse, "Did you like it?"

Those gentle words pierced Mo Ran's flesh and blood, rousing a bone-deep ache. Mo Ran held him tight. "I did," he answered quietly.

Chu Wanning's ears were scarlet. After these words of affirmation, he fell silent.

Mo Ran's hand stroked his hair. "Wanning..." he murmured, voice a whisper. "I love you... It's only ever been you."

No one in the world could be better than you. No one but you will ever stir my heart.

Shizun. I love you. I love you.

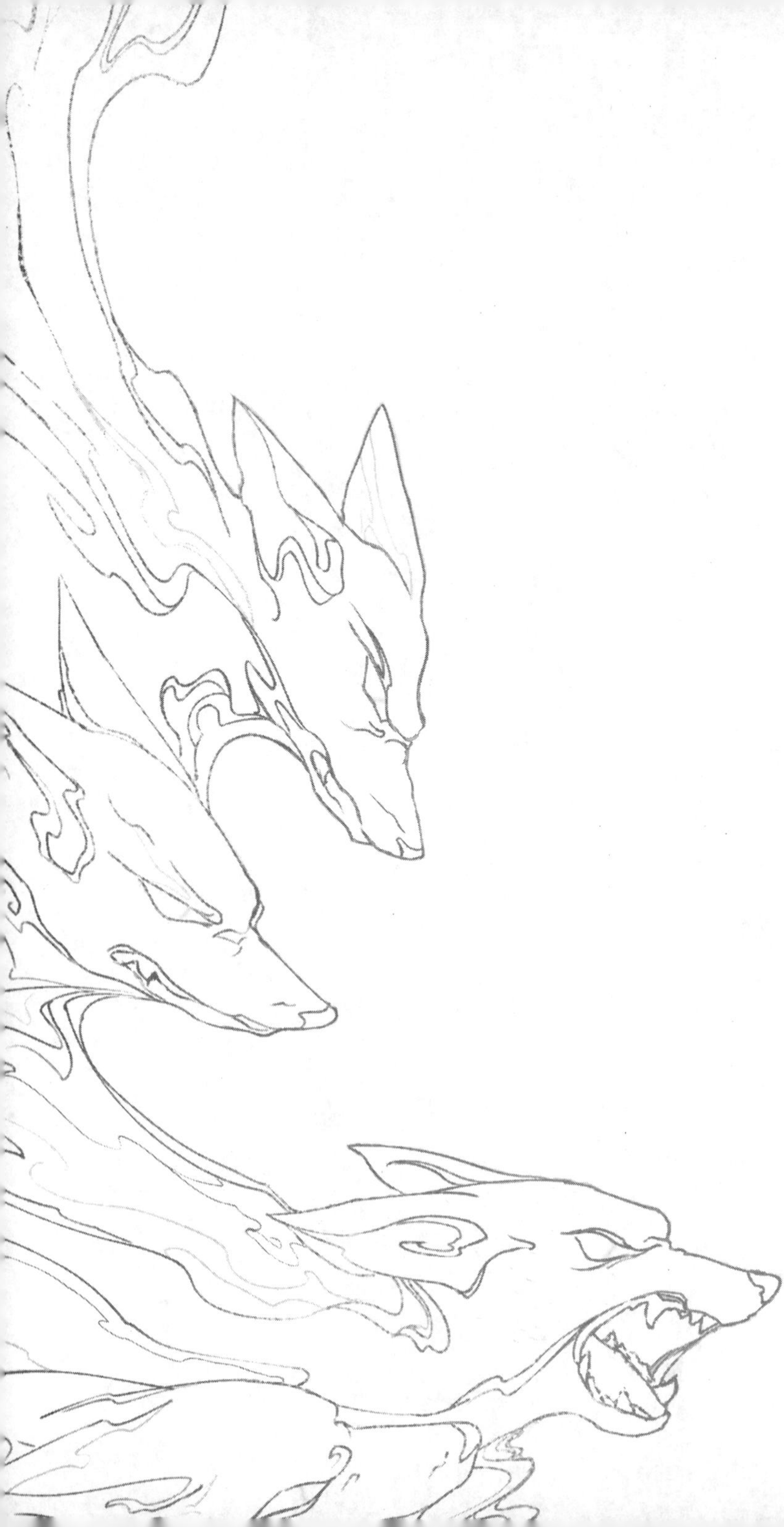

THE STORY CONTINUES IN
The Husky & His White Cat Shizun
VOLUME 7

Characters, Names, and Locations

Characters

The identity of certain characters may be a spoiler; use this guide with caution on your first read of the novel.

Note on the given name translations: Chinese characters may have many different readings. Each reading here is just one out of several possible interpretations.

MAIN CHARACTERS

Mo Ran
墨燃   SURNAME MO, "INK"; GIVEN NAME RAN, "TO IGNITE"

COURTESY NAME: Weiyu (微雨 / "gentle rain")

TITLE(S):

Taxian-jun (踏仙君 / "treading on immortals")

WEAPON(S):

Bugui (不归 / "no return")

Jiangui (见鬼 / literally, "seeing ghosts"; metaphorically, "What the hell?")

SPIRITUAL ELEMENT(S): Wood and Fire

Orphaned at a young age, Mo Ran was found at fourteen by his uncle, Xue Zhengyong, and brought back to Sisheng Peak. Despite his late start, he has a natural talent for cultivation. In his previous lifetime, Chu Wanning's refusal to save Shi Mei as he died sent Mo Ran into a spiral of grief, hatred, and destruction. Reinventing himself as Taxian-jun, tyrannical emperor of the cultivation world, he committed many atrocities—including taking his own shizun captive—before ultimately killing himself. To Mo Ran's surprise, he woke to find himself back in his fifteen-year-old body with all the memories of his past self and the opportunity to relive his life with all new choices, which is where the story begins.

Since his rebirth, Mo Ran has realized many things are not as they had seemed in the previous lifetime, a realization that came to a head after Chu Wanning's death while sealing the Heavenly Rift at Butterfly Town. During the five years of Chu Wanning's seclusion following his return from the underworld, Mo Ran wandered the land making a name for himself as Mo-zongshi.

Chu Wanning
楚晚宁　SURNAME CHU; GIVEN NAME WANNING "EVENING PEACE"

TITLE(S):

Yuheng of the Night Sky (晚夜玉衡 / Wanye, "late night"; Yuheng, "Alioth, the brightest star in Ursa Major")

Beidou Immortal (北斗仙尊 / Beidou "the Big Dipper," title *xianzun*, "immortal")

ALSO KNOWN AS: Xia Sini (夏司逆 / homonym for "scare you to death")

WEAPON(S):

Tianwen / 天问 "Heavenly Inquiry: to ask the heavens about life's enigmatic questions." The name reflects Tianwen's interrogation ability.

Jiuge / 九歌 "Nine Songs." Chu Wanning describes it as having a "chilling temperament."

Huaisha / 怀沙 "Embracing Sand to Drown Oneself." Chu Wanning uses it rarely because of its "vicious nature."

SPIRITUAL ELEMENT(S): Wood and Metal

A powerful cultivator who specializes in barriers and is talented in mechanical engineering, as well as an elder of Sisheng Peak. Aloof, strict, and short-tempered, Chu Wanning has only three disciples to his name: Xue Meng, Shi Mei, and Mo Ran. In Mo Ran's previous lifetime, Chu Wanning stood up to Taxian-jun, obstructing his tyrannical ambitions, before he was taken captive and eventually died as a prisoner. In the present day, he is Mo Ran's shizun, as well as the target of Mo Ran's mixed feelings of fear, loathing, and lust. Unaware of Mo Ran's rebirth, Chu Wanning has been acting in accordance with his own upright principles and beliefs, which culminated in his death during the events of the Heavenly Rift at Butterfly Town. With the aid of Master Huaizui and Mo Ran, he returned to the world of the living, but only after five years in seclusion.

Chu Wanning's titles refer to the brightest stars in the Ursa Major constellation, reflecting his stellar skills and presence. Specifically, Yuheng is Alioth, the brightest star in Ursa Major, and the Big Dipper is an asterism consisting of the seven brightest stars of the same constellation. Furthermore, Chu Wanning's weapons are named after poems in the *Verses of Chu*, a collection by Qu Yuan from the Warring States Period. The weapons' primary attacks, such as "Wind," take their names from *Shijing: Classic of Poetry*, the oldest existing collection of Chinese poetry. The collection comprises 305 works that are categorized into popular songs and ballads (风 / feng, "wind"), courtly songs (雅 / ya, "elegant"), or eulogies (颂 / song, "ode").

SISHENG PEAK

Xue Meng

薛蒙   SURNAME XUE; GIVEN NAME MENG "BLIND/IGNORANT"

COURTESY NAME: Ziming (子明 / "bright/clever son")
SPIRITUAL ELEMENT(S): Fire

The "darling of the heavens," Chu Wanning's first disciple, Xue Zhengyong and Madam Wang's son, and Mo Ran's cousin. Proud, haughty, and fiercely competitive, Xue Meng can at times be impulsive and rash. He often clashes with Mo Ran, especially when it comes to their shizun, whom he hugely admires. His weapon is the scimitar Longcheng.

Shi Mei
师昧   SURNAME SHI; GIVEN NAME MEI, "TO CONCEAL"

COURTESY NAME: Mingjing (明净 / "bright and clean")

EARLY NAME(S): Xue Ya (薛丫 / Surname Xue, given name Ya, "little girl")

SPIRITUAL ELEMENT(S): Water

Xue Meng's close friend, Chu Wanning's second disciple, and Mo Ran's boyhood crush. Gentle, kind, and patient, with beautiful looks to match, Shi Mei often plays peacemaker when his fellow disciples argue, which is often. Where Mo Ran and Xue Meng are more adept in combat, he specializes in the healing arts. In the previous lifetime, he died during the events of the Heavenly Rift at Butterfly Town, but in this lifetime, it is Chu Wanning who dies in his stead.

Xue Zhengyong
薛正雍   SURNAME XUE; GIVEN NAME ZHENGYONG, "RIGHTEOUS AND HARMONIOUS"

WEAPON: Fan that reads "Xue is Beautiful" on one side and "Others are Ugly" on the opposite.

The sect leader of Sisheng Peak, Xue Meng's father, and Mo Ran's uncle. Jovial, boisterous, and made out of 100 percent wifeguy material, Xue Zhengyong takes his duty to protect the common people of the lower cultivation realm very much to heart.

Madam Wang (王夫人)

Xue Meng's mother, lady of Sisheng Peak, and Mo Ran's aunt. Timid and unassuming, she originally hails from Guyueye Sect, having once been Jiang Xi's shijie, and specializes in the healing arts.

A-Li (阿狸)

Madam Wang's cat. Not pregnant, just fat.

Veggiebun (菜包)

A new addition to Sisheng Peak, a fat orange cat with a striped forehead that only eats fish and no other meat.

SISHENG PEAK ELDERS

The names of Sisheng Peak's elders vary in origin. Most of their names come from the constellation Ursa Major, such as Chu Wanning's "Yuheng." Three elders take their names from the Sha Po Lang star triad used in a form of fortune-telling based on Chinese astrology.

Jielü Elder
戒律长老   JIELÜ, "DISCIPLINE"

In charge of meting out discipline.

Xuanji Elder
璇玑长老   XUANJI, "MEGREZ, THE DELTA URSAE MAJORIS STAR"

Kind and gentle; practices an easy cultivation method. Popular with the disciples.

Lucun Elder
禄存长老   LUCUN, "PHECDA, THE GAMMA URSAE MAJORIS STAR"

Beautiful and foppish. Has a habit of phrasing things in a questionable manner.

Qisha Elder
七杀长老   QISHA, "POLIS, THE POWER STAR IN SHA PO LANG"

Very done with Lucun Elder.

Pojun Elder
破军长老   POJUN, "ALKAID, THE RUINOUS STAR IN SHA PO LANG"

Forthright and spirited.

Tanlang Elder
贪狼长老   TANLANG, "DUBHE, THE FLIRTING STAR IN SHA PO LANG"

Sardonic and ungentle with his words. Skilled in the healing arts, and on pretty bad terms with Chu Wanning.

RUFENG SECT

Ye Wangxi
叶忘昔   SURNAME YE; GIVEN NAME WANGXI, "TO FORGET THE PAST"

SPIRITUAL ELEMENT(S): Earth

A disciple of Rufeng Sect, the adopted child of Rufeng Sect's chief elder. Highly regarded by the sect leader of Rufeng Sect, and a competent, chivalric, and upright individual. Noted by Mo Ran to have been second only to Chu Wanning in the entire cultivation world, in the previous lifetime.

Nangong Si

南宫驷 SURNAME NANGONG; GIVEN NAME SI, "TO RIDE," OR "HORSE"

SPIRITUAL ELEMENT(S): Fire

The only son of Rufeng Sect's leader, who in their previous lifetime died before Mo Ran's ascension. Brash, headstrong, and volatile in temperament. He rides on his faewolf, has a hearty appetite for meat and wine, and an antagonistic relationship with Ye Wangxi. He is currently engaged to Song Qiutong. His holy weapon is the jade bow, Mantuo.

Naobaijin

瑙白金 NAO, "CARNELIAN"; BAI "WHITE"; JIN "GOLD"

Nangong Si's faewolf. Thrice the height of a human, with carnelian-red eyes, snow-white fur, and gold claws.

Song Qiutong

宋秋桐 SURNAME SONG; GIVEN NAME QIUTONG, "AUTUMN, TUNG TREE"

A Butterfly-Boned Beauty Feast who bears a resemblance to Shi Mei. After being rescued by Ye Wangxi, she joins Rufeng Sect as a disciple and eventually gets engaged to Nangong Si. In the previous lifetime, Taxian-jun took her as his wife and empress after burning Rufeng Sect. She also shares a name with a character in *Dream of the Red Chamber*.

Nangong Liu

南宫柳 SURNAME NANGONG; GIVEN NAME LIU, "WILLOW"

Leader of Rufeng Sect and father to Nangong Si. Rumored to be the second-richest person in the cultivation world. Has a gifted tongue for flattery. Seems to have some negative history with Chu Wanning.

Xu Shuanglin
徐霜林 SURNAME XU; GIVEN NAME SHUANGLIN, "FROST, FOREST"

Ye Wangxi's adoptive father, who has a carefree attitude and can never quite remember to keep his shoes on.

Rong Yan
容嫣 SURNAME RONG; GIVEN NAME YAN, "BEAUTIFUL"

Nangong Liu's wife and the mother of Nangong Si. She passed away many years ago when Nangong Si was still young.

Nangong Changying
南宫长英 SURNAME NANGONG; GIVEN NAME CHANGYING, "LASTING, HERO"

The founder of Rufeng Sect.

GUYUEYE SECT

Jiang Xi
姜曦 SURNAME JIANG; GIVEN NAME XI, "DAWN, SUNSHINE"

The aloof, haughty sect leader of Guyueye Sect. Rumored to be the richest person in the cultivation world. Despite his age, he looks to be in his twenties due to his cultivation method. His weapon is the longsword Xuehuang.

Hua Binan (Hanlin the Sage)
华碧楠 (寒鳞圣手) HUA; GIVEN NAME BINAN "JADE, CEDAR"; HANLIN, "COLD, SCALES"; SHENGSHOU, "HIGHLY SKILLED, SAGE DOCTOR"

An elder of Guyueye Sect. Highly skilled at refining pills and medicines, and renowned as the finest medicinal zongshi around. He wears a hat and veil that reveal only his eyes.

OTHER CHARACTERS

Mei Hanxue
梅含雪 SURNAME MEI; GIVEN NAME HANXUE, "TO HOLD, SNOW"

A striking cultivator with pale gold hair and jade green eyes, Mei Hanxue is the head disciple of Kunlun Taxue Palace who stayed with the Xue family at Sisheng Peak for a short time as a child. He is skilled in various arts, including dance and playing musical instruments, and is an appreciator of wine and song. Known as "Da-shixiong" to the lady cultivators who flock around him, as well as by less flattering epithets to others, namely Xue Meng and Ye Wangxi.

Master Huaizui
怀罪 HUAI, "TO BEAR, TO THINK OF"; ZUI, "SINS, GUILT, BLAME"

A monk of Wubei Temple. Renowned in the cultivation world for his choice to remain in the mortal realm despite having achieved enlightenment and being able to ascend to immortality. Master Huaizui has been in seclusion in Wubei Temple for over a century, and is reportedly able to wield the "Rebirth" technique of the three forbidden techniques. Despite his age, his physical appearance is that of a man in his early thirties. He wielded Rebirth, one of the three forbidden techniques, to bring Chu Wanning back from the underworld.

Master Xuanjing (玄镜大师)
Abbott of Wubei Temple.

Heart-Pluck Willow
摘心柳 ZHAIXIN LIU, "HEART-PLUCK WILLOW"

The spirit of the willow tree in Jincheng Lake, which shelters Gouchen the Exalted's arsenal of holy weapons.

Li Wuxin
李无心 SURNAME LI; GIVEN NAME WUXIN, "'AN EMPTY STATE OF CONSCIOUSNESS' IN BUDDHIST MEDITATION"

Leader of the recently established Bitan Manor. A man with a pair of long, flowing whiskers. Smooth-talking and somewhat condescending to those he views as beneath himself.

Mo Ran's Mother (Unnamed)

Mo Ran's mother, who raised him on her own. A talented singer and dancer, she performed on the streets to earn money to keep Mo Ran and herself fed. Compassionate and kind despite the misery of her circumstances, she is described by Mo Ran as his first moral "lighthouse."

Ma Yun (马芸)

Sect leader of Taobao Estate. Rumored to be the third richest person in the cultivation world.

Fake "Gouchen the Exalted"
勾陈上宫 GOUCHEN, "CURVED ARRAY, PART OF THE URSA MINOR CONSTELLATION"; SHANGGONG, "EXALTED")

An enigmatic figure who pretended to be the real Gouchen the Exalted, the God of Weaponry. He is in truth a corpse controlled by a white chess piece in a mysterious Zhenlong Chess Formation.

Master Tianchan
天禅大师 TIANCHAN, "HEAVENLY, MEDITATION"

Sect leader of Wubei Temple prior to Master Huaizui.

Little Mantuo
小曼陀 DIMUNITIVE PREFIX XIAO; GIVEN NAME MANTUO, "MANDALA FLOWER"

A young girl who has zero interest in Xue Meng, and a non-zero interest in Mei Hanxue.

Qi Liangji
戚良姬 SURNAME QI; GIVEN NAME LIANGJI, "VIRTUOUS, LADY"

Sect leader of Jiangdong Hall. She has a tattoo on her arm of the auspicious five-bat motif.

Third Lady Sun
孙三娘 SURNAME SUN; TITLE SANNIANG, "THIRD LADY"

The richest merchant on Flying Flower Isle, a lady in her fifties who seems to value money and little else.

Zhen Congming
甄淙明 SURNAME ZHEN; GIVEN NAME CONGMING "WATER GURGLING, BRIGHT/CLEVER"

The thirteenth direct disciple of Li Wuxin. Ignorant, and ignorant of his own ignorance. His name is a homonym for the phrase "very smart."

Huang Xiaoyue
黄啸月 SURNAME HUANG; GIVEN NAME XIAOYUE "WHISTLE, MOON"

Current sect leader of Jiangdong Hall, cousin to a former sect leader of Jiangdong Hall, and cousin-in-law to the previous sect leader, Qi Liangji.

Song Qiao; Song Xingyi (Jade-Hearted Lord)
宋乔; 宋星移 (化碧之尊) SURNAME SONG; GIVEN NAME QIAO, "TALL"; COURTESY NAME XINGYI "SHIFTING STARS"

The last zongshi from the Butterfly-Boned Beauty Feast tribe, who subdued a phoenix descended from the Vermilion Bird hundreds of years ago.

Sects and Locations

THE TEN GREAT SECTS

The cultivation world is divided into the upper and lower cultivation realms. Most of the ten great sects are located within the upper cultivation realm, while Sisheng Peak is the only great sect within the lower cultivation realm.

Sisheng Peak
死生之巅 SISHENG ZHI DIAN, "THE PEAK OF LIFE AND DEATH"

A sect in the lower cultivation realm located in modern-day Sichuan. It sits near the boundary between the mortal realm and the ghost realm, and was founded relatively recently by Xue Zhengyong and his brother. The uniform of Sisheng Peak is light armor in dark blue with silver trim, and members of the sect practice cultivation methods that do not require abstinence from meat or other foods. The sect's name refers to both its physical location in the mountains as well as the metaphorical extremes of life and death. Xue Zhengyong named many locations in Sisheng Peak after places and entities in the underworld because the sect is located in an area thick with ghostly yin energy, and he is furthermore not the sort to think up conventionally nice-sounding, formal names.

Aaaaah (啊啊啊) and Waaaah Cliffs (哇哇哇)
Where Frostsky Hall is located. Named by Xue Zhengyong as an expression of the grief he felt in the days following his brother's death.

Frostsky Hall (霜天殿)

A hall in Sisheng Peak where bodies are kept until burial.

Heaven-Piercing Tower (通天塔)

The location where Mo Ran first met Chu Wanning as well as the location where, in his past life, he laid himself to rest. It's where Sisheng Peak imprisons the spirits and demons they exorcise.

Loyalty Hall (丹心殿)

The main hall of Sisheng Peak. Taxian-jun renamed it Wushan Palace (巫山殿) when he took over the sect.

Melodic Springs (妙音池)

The communal bath of Sisheng Peak.

Mengpo Hall (孟婆堂)

The dining hall at Sisheng Peak. Named after the mythological old woman who distributes memory-erasing soup to souls before they are reborn.

Platform of Sin and Virtue (善恶台)

A platform where public events in Sisheng Peak, including punishment and announcements, are carried out.

Red Lotus Pavilion (红莲水榭)

Chu Wanning's residence. An idyllic pavilion surrounded by rare red lotuses. Some have been known to call it "Red Lotus Hell" or the "Pavilion of Broken Legs." In the previous lifetime, Chu Wanning's body was kept at the Red Lotus Pavilion after his death, preserved by Taxian-jun's spiritual energy.

Silk-Rinse Hall (浣纱堂)

The tailoring hall of Sisheng Peak, which creates and tailors clothing for members of the sect.

Three Lives Platform (三生台)

A platform in Sisheng Peak. Named after the mythological stone in the underworld located by Naihe Bridge that records a soul's past, present, and future lives.

Dancing Sword Platform (舞剑坪)

A platform in Sisheng Peak with jade railings.

Moonlight Confectionery (月晟斋)

A candy store that sells its best candy at one copper coin apiece.

Crane's Return Hill (鹤归坡)

The graveyard of Wuchang Town.

Linyi Rufeng Sect
临沂儒风门 RUFENG, "HONORING CONFUCIAN IDEALS"

A sect in the upper cultivation realm located in Linyi, a prefecture in modern-day Shandong Province. Has seventy-two cities and is known for being affluent and well-respected. In Taxian-jun's lifetime, he burned them all to the ground.

Dai City (岱城)

A mildly prosperous city by the foot of Dawning Peak. Caters to traveling cultivators on their way to Jincheng Lake.

Moonwhistle Fields (啸月校场)

Training grounds in Rufeng Sect.

Ganquan Lake (甘泉湖)

A lake located to the north of the forest behind Moonwhistle Fields.

Poetry Hall (诗乐殿居)

A reception hall in Rufeng Sect that overlooks the hunting grounds.

Flying Jade Platform (飞瑶台)

A platform in Rufeng Sect.

Golden Drum Tower (金鼓塔)

A tower in Rufeng Sect beneath which demonic spirits are locked up and suppressed.

Flying Flower Isle (飞花岛)

A modest, ring-shaped island located in the East Sea close to Linyi, Flying Flower Isle is remote and sparsely populated primarily by fishermen.

Panlong Range (磐龙群山)

A mountain range that surrounds Mount Jiao, and which can only be traversed on foot for travelers who wish to climb Mount Jiao.

Mount Jiao (蛟山)

One of the four great evil mountains of the cultivation realm, a relic of its bloody past. It also serves as the burial grounds for Rufeng disciples, earning it the moniker of Rufeng Sect's heroes' tomb.

Kunlun Taxue Palace
昆仑踏雪宫   TAXUE, "STEPPING SOFTLY ACROSS SNOW"

A sect in the upper cultivation realm located on the Kunlun Mountain range. Its name refers to both the physical location of the sect in the snowy Kunlun Mountain range and the ethereal grace of the cultivators within the sect.

Guyueye
孤月夜   GUYUEYE, "A LONELY MOON IN THE NIGHT SKY"

A sect in the upper cultivation realm located on Rainbell Isle. They focus on the medicinal arts. The name is a reference to the solitary and isolated nature of Guyueye—the island is a lone figure in the water, much like the reflection of the moon, cold and aloof.

Rainbell Isle (霖铃屿)
Not an actual island, but the back of an enormous ancient tortoise, which was bound to the founder of the sect by a blood pact to carry the entirety of Guyueye sect on its shell.

Xuanyuan Pavilion
A subsidiary operation of Guyueye, and a trading post well known in the cultivation world. Xuanyuan is a name for the Yellow Emperor, a legendary Chinese historical figure and deity, who was one of the Three Sovereigns and Five Deities alongside Fuxi.

Fragrance Inn
An inn on Rainbell Isle.

Wubei Temple
无悲寺　WUBEI, "WITHOUT SADNESS/GRIEF"

A sect in the upper cultivation realm. Disciples of Wubei Temple are monks.

Dragonblood Mountain (龙血山)

A mountain near Wubei Temple.

Bitan Manor
碧潭庄　BITAN, "GREEN POOL"

A recently established and up-and-coming sect in the upper cultivation realm. Barriers are *not* their specialty.

Taobao Estate
桃宝山庄　TAOBAO, "PEACH TREASURE"

A sect in the upper cultivation realm located in West Lake.

Jiangdong Hall
江东堂　JIANGDONG, THE SOUTH BANK OF THE YANGTZE RIVER

A sect in the upper cultivation realm. Qi Liangji became their new sect leader after the death of her husband, the previous sect leader.

Huohuang Pavilion
火凰阁　HUOHUANG, "FIRE, PHOENIX"

A sect in the upper cultivation realm.

Shangqing Pavilion
上清阁　SHANGQING, "TOWARDS HEAVEN"

One of the ten great sects, located in the upper cultivation realm. Shangqing Pavilion and Wubei Temple are the only two sects of the ten great sects to explicitly forbid sexual relationships and dual cultivation.

Tianyin Pavilion
天音阁 TIANYIN, "HEAVENLY/DIVINE SOUND"

An independent organization set up by the ten great sects that oversees trials and the imprisonment of criminals. They manage a prison that is reserved for criminals who have committed heinous crimes.

OTHER

Spiritual Mountain (灵山)

Where inter-sect meetings and competitions are held.

House of Drunken Jade (醉玉楼)

A high-class pleasure house in Xiangtan, famed for its theater, star songstress, and food. It burned down not long before the events of the current timeline.

Butterfly Town (彩蝶镇)

A town located near Baitou Mountain, noted for its relative prosperity compared to its neighbors. Its specialty exports are flowers, fragrance, and perfume powder. It also cleaves to the tradition of ghost marriages.

Dawning Peak (旭映峰)

A sacred mountain located in the upper cultivation realm, within the territory of Linyi Rufeng Sect. Known as the place where Gouchen the Exalted forged the Heavenly Emperor's sword, it is now a pilgrimage site for cultivators seeking holy weapons.

Jincheng Lake (金成池)

A lake at the summit of Dawning Peak that remains frozen over year-round. According to legend, it was formed by a drop of Gouchen the Exalted's blood, shed as he forged the Heavenly Emperor's holy sword.

Yunmeng Marsh
云梦泽   YUNMENG, "CLOUD DREAM"

A marsh that was plagued by a carp spirit for many years.

Peach Blossom Springs (桃花源)

Home of the feathered tribe, located beyond the maze of Mount Jiuhua and within the land of the immortals. *The Peach Blossom Spring* is a fable written by Chinese poet Tao Yuanming, in which the eponymous setting is an ethereal utopia where people live a peaceful, prosperous existence in harmony with nature, unaware of the outside world. In popular culture, the setting has become a symbol of an ideal world, and it has been depicted in many paintings, poems, music, and so forth.

Baidi City (白帝城)

A town in Sichuan, not far from Sisheng Peak.

Mount Huang (凰山)

One of the four great evil mountains of the cultivation realm, a relic of its bloody past.

Name Guide

Courtesy Names

Courtesy names were a tradition reserved for the upper class and were typically granted at the age of twenty. While it was generally a male-exclusive tradition, there is historical precedent for women adopting courtesy names after marriage. It was furthermore considered disrespectful for peers of the same generation to address one another by their birth name, especially in formal or written communication. Instead, one's birth name was used by elders, close friends, and spouses.

This tradition is no longer practiced in modern China, but is commonly seen in wuxia and xianxia media. As such, many characters in these novels have more than one name in these stories, though the tradition is often treated malleably for the sake of storytelling. For example, in *Husky*, characters receive their courtesy names at the age of fifteen rather than twenty.

Diminutives, nicknames, and name tags

A-: Friendly diminutive. Always a prefix. Usually for monosyllabic names, or one syllable out of a two-syllable name.

DA-: A prefix meaning "eldest."

DOUBLING: Doubling a syllable of a person's name can be a nickname, i.e. "Mengmeng"; it has childish or cutesy connotations.

-ER: A word for "son" or "child." Added to a name, it expresses affection. Similar to calling someone "Little" or "Sonny." Always a suffix.

XIAO-: A diminutive meaning "little." Always a prefix.

Family

All of these terms can be used alone or with the person's name.

BOBO: Paternal uncle (father's elder brother), but also informally a term of address for someone older than one's father.

DABO: Brother-in-law (husband's elder brother), but also informally a term of address for someone older than one's father.

DI/DIDI: Younger brother or a younger male friend.

GE/GEGE: Older brother or an older male friend.

JIE/JIEJIE/ZIZI: Older sister or an older female friend; "zizi" is a regional variant of "jieije."

MEI/MEIMEI: Younger sister or a younger female friend.

Cultivation

-JUN: A term of respect, often used as a suffix after a title.

DAOZHANG/XIANJUN/XIANZHANG: Polite terms of address for cultivators, equivalent to "Mr. Cultivator." Can be used alone as a title or attached to someone's family name. Xianjun has an implication of immortality.

QIANBEI: A respectful title or suffix for someone older, more experienced, and/or more skilled in a particular discipline. Not to be used for blood relatives.

SHIZHU: "Benefactor, alms-giver." A respectful term used by Buddhist and Taoist monks and priests to address laypeople.

XIANZHU: "Immortal lord/leader." Used in *Husky* as a respectful title for Eighteen, the leader of Peach Blossom Springs.

ZONGSHI: A title or suffix for a person of particularly outstanding skill; largely only applied to cultivators in the story of *Husky*.

Cultivation Sects

SHIZUN: Teacher/master. For one's master in one's own sect. Gender-neutral. Literal meaning is "honored/venerable master" and is a more respectful address, though Shifu is not disrespectful.

SHIZU: Grand-teacher/master. For the master of one's master.

SHIXIONG/SHIGE: Older martial brother. For senior male members of one's own sect. Shige is a more familiar variant.

SHIJIE: Older martial sister. For senior female members of one's own sect.

SHIDI: Younger martial brother. For junior male members of one's own sect.

SHIMEI: Younger martial sister. For junior female members of one's own sect.

SHINIANG: Wife of shizun/shifu.

ZHANGMEN/ZHUANGZHU/ ZUNZHU: "Sect leader/Manor leader/ Esteemed leader." Used to refer to the leader of the sect. Can be used on its own or appended to a family name, e.g., Xue-zunzhu.

Other

GONG/GONGGONG: A title or suffix. Can be used to refer to an elderly man, a man of high status, a grandfather, a father-in-law, or in a palace context, a eunuch.

GONGZI: Young master of an affluent household, or a polite way to address young men.

TAIZI: "Crown prince." A respectful title of address for the next in line to the throne.

YIFU: Person formally acknowledged as one's father; sometimes a "godfather."

Pronunciation Guide

Mandarin Chinese is the official state language of mainland China, and pinyin is the official system of romanization in which it is written. As Mandarin is a tonal language, pinyin uses diacritical marks (e.g., ā, á, ǎ, à) to indicate these tonal inflections. Most words use one of four tones, though some (as in "de" in the title below) are a neutral tone. Furthermore, regional variance can change the way native Chinese speakers pronounce the same word. For those reasons and more, please consider the guide below a simplified introduction to pronunciation of select character names and sounds from the world of Husky.

More resources are available at sevenseasdanmei.com

NAMES

Èrhā hé tā de bái māo shī zūn

Èr as in **uh**

Hā as in **har**dy

Hé as in **hur**t

Tā as in **tar**dy

De as in **dir**t

Bái as in **bye**

Māo as in **mou**th

Shī as in **shh**

Z as in **z**oom, ūn as in harp**oon**

Mò Rán

Mò as in **mo**ron

Rán as in **run**ning

Chǔ Wǎnníng

Chǔ as in **choo**se

Wǎn as in **wan**ting

Níng as in run**ning**

Xuē Méng

X as in the **s** in silk, uē as in **weh**

M as in the **m** in **m**other, é as in **uh**, **ng** as in so**ng**

Shī Mèi

Shī as in **shh**

Mèi as in **may**

GENERAL CONSONANTS

Some Mandarin Chinese consonants sound very similar, such as z/c/s and zh/ch/sh. Audio samples will provide the best opportunity to learn the difference between them.

X: somewhere between the **sh** in **sh**eep and **s** in **s**ilk

Q: a very aspirated **ch** as in **ch**arm

C: **ts** as in pan**ts**

Z: **z** as in **z**oom

S: **s** as in **s**ilk

CH: **ch** as in **ch**arm

ZH: **dg** as in do**dg**e

SH: **sh** as in **sh**ave

G: hard **g** as in **g**raphic

GENERAL VOWELS

The pronunciation of a vowel may depend on its preceding consonant. For example, the "i" in "shi" is distinct from the "i" in "di." Vowel pronunciation may also change depending on where the vowel appears in a word, for example the "i" in "shi" versus the "i" in "ting." Finally, compound vowels are often—though not always— pronounced as conjoined but separate vowels. You'll find a few of the trickier compounds below.

IU: as in **ewe**

IE: **ye** as in **ye**s

UO: **war** as in **war**m

APPENDIX

Glossary

Glossary

While not required reading, this glossary is intended to offer further context for the many concepts and terms utilized throughout this novel as well as provide a starting point for learning more about the rich culture from which these stories were written.

GENRES

Danmei

Danmei (耽美 / "indulgence in beauty") is a Chinese fiction genre focused on romanticized tales of love and attraction between men. It is analogous to the BL (boys' love) genre in Japanese media and is better understood as a genre of plot than a genre of setting. For example, though many danmei novels feature wuxia or xianxia settings, others are better understood as tales of sci-fi, fantasy, or horror.

Wuxia

Wuxia (武侠 / "martial heroes") is one of the oldest Chinese literary genres and consists of tales of noble heroes fighting evil and injustice. It often follows martial artists, monks, or rogues who live apart from the ruling government, which is often seen as useless or corrupt. These societal outcasts—both voluntary and otherwise—settle disputes among themselves, adhering to their own moral codes over the law.

Characters in wuxia focus primarily on human concerns, such as political strife between factions and advancing their own personal sense of justice. True wuxia is low on magical or supernatural elements. To Western moviegoers, a well-known example is *Crouching Tiger, Hidden Dragon*.

Xianxia

Xianxia (仙侠 / "immortal heroes") is a genre related to wuxia that places more emphasis on the supernatural. Its characters often strive to become stronger, with the end goal of extending their lifespan or achieving immortality.

Xianxia heavily features Daoist themes, while cultivation and the pursuit of immortality are both genre requirements. If these are not the story's central focus, it is not xianxia. *Husky* is considered part of both the danmei and xianxia genres.

TERMINOLOGY

BARRIERS: A type of magical shield. In *Husky*, a barrier separates the mortal realm and the ghost realm, and Chu Wanning is noted to be especially skilled in creating barriers.

CLASSICAL CHINESE CHESS (WEIQI): Weiqi is the oldest known board game in human history. The board consists of a many-lined grid upon which opponents play unmarked black and white stones as game pieces to claim territory.

COLORS:

WHITE: Death, mourning, purity. Used in funerals for both deceased and the mourners.

RED: Happiness, good luck. Used for weddings.

PURPLE: Divinity and immortality; often associated with nobility, homosexuality (in the modern context), and demonkind (in the xianxia genre).

COURTESY NAMES: A courtesy name is given to an individual when they come of age. (*See Name Guide for more information.*)

CULTIVATION/CULTIVATORS: Cultivators are practitioners of spirituality and the martial arts. They seek to gain understanding of the will of the universe while also increasing personal strength and extending their lifespan.

CUT-SLEEVE: A term for a gay man. Comes from a tale about an emperor's love for, and relationship with, a male politician. The emperor was called to the morning assembly, but his lover was asleep on his robe. Rather than wake him, the emperor cut off his own sleeve.

DRAGON: Great beasts who wield power over the weather. Chinese dragons differ from their Western counterparts as they are often benevolent, bestowing blessings and granting luck. They are associated with the Heavens, the Emperor, and yang energy.

DUAL CULTIVATION: A cultivation technique involving sex between participants that is meant to improve cultivation prowess. Can also be used as a simple euphemism for sex.

EYES: Descriptions like "phoenix eyes" or "peach-blossom eyes" refer to eye shape. Phoenix eyes have an upturned sweep at their far corners, whereas peach-blossom eyes have a rounded upper lid and are often considered particularly alluring.

FACE: *Mianzi* (面子), generally translated as "face," is an important concept in Chinese society. It is a metaphor for a person's reputation and can be extended to further descriptive metaphors. For example, "having face" refers to having a good reputation and "losing face" refers to having one's reputation hurt. Meanwhile, "giving face" means deferring to someone else to help improve their reputation, while "not wanting face" implies that a person is acting so poorly/ shamelessly that they clearly don't care about their reputation at all. "Thin face" refers to someone easily embarrassed or prone to offense at perceived slights. Conversely, "thick face" refers to someone not easily embarrassed and immune to insults.

FAE: Fae (妖 / yao), refers to natural creatures such as animals, plants, or even inanimate objects, who over time absorb spiritual energy and gain spiritual awareness to cultivate a human form. They are sometimes referred to as "demons" or "monsters," though they are not inherently evil. In *Husky*, faewolves (妖狼) are a rare and expensive breed of wolf. Similarly, the feathered tribe are beings who are half-immortal (仙) and half-fae.

THE FIVE ELEMENTS: Also known as the *wuxing* (五行 / "Five Phases") in Chinese philosophy: fire, water, wood, metal, earth. Each element corresponds to a planet: Mars, Mercury, Jupiter, Venus, and Saturn, respectively. In *Husky*, cultivators' spiritual cores correspond with one or two elements; for example, Chu Wanning's elements are metal and wood.

Fire (火 / huo)
Water (水 / shui)
Wood (木 / mu)
Metal (金 / jin)
Earth (土 / tu)

HAITANG: The *haitang* tree (海棠花), also known as crab apple or Chinese flowering apple, is endemic to China. The recurring motif for Chu Wanning is specifically the *xifu haitang* variety. In flower language, haitang symbolizes unrequited love.

INEDIA: A common ability that allows an immortal to survive without mortal food or sleep by sustaining themselves on purer forms of energy based on Daoist fasting. Depending on the setting, immortals who have achieved inedia may be unable to tolerate mortal food, or they may be able to choose to eat when desired. The cultivation taught by Sisheng Peak notably does not rely on this practice.

JADE: Jade is a culturally and spiritually important mineral in China. Its durability, beauty, and the ease with which it can be utilized for crafting decorative and functional pieces alike has made it widely beloved since ancient times. The word might evoke green jade (the mineral jadeite), but Chinese texts are often referring to white jade (the mineral nephrite), as when a person's skin is described as "the color of jade."

JIANGHU: A staple of wuxia, the jianghu (江湖 / "rivers and lakes") describes an underground society of martial artists, monks, rogues, artisans, and merchants who settle disputes between themselves per their own moral codes.

LOTUS: This flower symbolizes purity of the heart and mind, as lotuses rise untainted from the muddy waters they grow in. It also signifies the holy seat of the Buddha.

MEASUREMENTS: The "miles" and "inches" in *Husky* refer not to imperial measurement units, but to the Chinese measurement units, which have varied over time. In modern times, one Chinese mile (里 / *li*) is approximately a half-kilometer, one Chinese foot (尺 / *cun*) is approximately one-third of a meter, and one Chinese inch (寸 / *chi*) is one tenth of a Chinese foot.

MERIDIANS: The means by which qi travels through the body, like a magical bloodstream. Medical and combat techniques that focus on redirecting, manipulating, or halting qi circulation focus on targeting the meridians at specific points on the body, known as acupoints. Techniques that can manipulate or block qi prevent a cultivator from using magical techniques until the qi block is lifted.

MOE: A Japanese term referring to cuteness or vulnerability in a character that evokes a protective feeling from the reader. Originally applied largely to female characters, the term has since seen expanded use.

MYTHICAL FIGURES: Several entities from Chinese mythology make an appearance in the world of *Husky*, including:

AZURE DRAGON: The Azure Dragon (苍龙 / canglong, or 青龙 / qinglong) is one of four major creatures in Chinese astronomy, representing the cardinal direction East, the element of wood, and the season of spring.

EBON TORTOISE: The Ebon Tortoise (玄武 / xuanwu) is one of four major creatures in Chinese astronomy, representing the cardinal direction North, the element of water, and the season of winter. It is usually depicted as a tortoise entwined with a serpent.

FLAME EMPEROR: A mythological figure said to have ruled over China in ancient times. His name is attributed to his invention of slash-and-burn agriculture. There is some debate over whether the Flame Emperor is the same being as Shennong, the inventor of agriculture, or a descendant.

FUXI: Emperor of the heavens, sometimes directly called Heavenly Emperor Fuxi. A figure associated with Chinese creation mythology.

JIAO DRAGON: A type of dragon in Chinese mythology, often said to be aquatic or river-dwelling, and able to control rain and floods.

PHOENIX: Fenghuang (凤凰 / "phoenix"), a legendary bird said to only appear in times of peace and to flee when a ruler is corrupt. They are heavily associated with femininity, the empress, and happy marriages.

VERMILION BIRD: The Vermilion Bird (朱雀上神) is one of four mythical beasts in Chinese constellations, representing the cardinal direction South, the element of fire, and the season of summer.

YANLUO: King of hell or the supreme judge of the underworld. His role in the underworld is to pass judgment on the dead, sending souls on to their next life depending on the karma they accrued from their last one.

PAPER MONEY: Imitation money made from decorated sheets of paper burned as a traditional offering to the dead.

PILLS AND ELIXIRS: Magic medicines that can heal wounds, improve cultivation, extend life, etc. In Chinese culture, these medicines are usually delivered in pill form, and the pills are created in special kilns.

PLEASURE HOUSE: Courtesans at these establishments provided entertainment of many types, ranging from song and dance to more intimate pleasures.

QI: *Qi* (气) is the energy in all living things. There is both righteous qi and evil or poisonous qi.

Cultivators strive to cultivate qi by absorbing it from the natural world and refining it within themselves to improve their cultivation base. A cultivation base refers to the amount of qi a cultivator possesses or is able to possess. In xianxia, natural locations such as caves, mountains, or other secluded places with beautiful scenery are often rich in qi, and practicing there can allow a cultivator to make rapid progress in their cultivation.

Cultivators and other qi manipulators can utilize their life force in a variety of ways, including imbuing objects with it to transform them into lethal weapons, or sending out blasts of energy to do damage. Cultivators also refine their senses beyond normal human levels. For instance, they may cast out their spiritual sense to gain total awareness of everything in a region around them or to sense potential danger.

QI CIRCULATION: The metabolic cycle of qi in the body, where it flows from the dantian to the meridians and back. This cycle purifies and refines qi, and good circulation is essential to cultivation. In xianxia, qi can be transferred from one person to another through physical contact, and it can heal someone who is wounded if the donor is trained in the art.

QI DEVIATION: A qi deviation (走火入魔 / "to catch fire and enter demonhood") occurs when one's cultivation base becomes unstable. Common causes include an unstable emotional state and/or strong negative emotions, practicing cultivation methods incorrectly, reckless use of forbidden or high-level arts, or succumbing to the influence of demons and evil spirits. When qi deviation arises from mental or emotional causes, the person is often said to have succumbed to their inner demons or "heart demons" (心魔).

Symptoms of qi deviation in fiction include panic, paranoia, sensory hallucinations, and death, whether by the qi deviation itself causing irreparable damage to the body or as a result of its symptoms—such as leaping to one's death to escape a hallucination. Common fictional treatments for qi deviation include relaxation (voluntary or forced by an external party), massage, meditation, or qi transfer from another individual.

QIANKUN POUCH: (乾坤囊/ "universe pouch") A pouch containing an extradimensional space within it, capable of holding more than the physical exterior dimensions of the pouch would suggest.

QINGGONG: Qinggong (轻功) is a cultivator's ability to move swiftly through the air as if on the wind.

RED THREAD OF FATE: The red thread imagery originates in legend and has become a Chinese symbol for fated love. An invisible red thread is said to be tied around the limb or finger of the two individuals destined to fall in love, forever linking them.

REIGNING YEARS: Chinese emperors took to naming the eras of their reign for the purpose of tracking historical records. The names often reflected political agendas or the current reality of the socioeconomic landscape.

SHIDI, SHIXIONG, SHIZUN, ETC: Chinese titles and terms used to indicate a person's role or rank in relation to the speaker. Because of the robust nature of this naming system, and a lack of nuance in translating many to English, the original titles have been maintained. *(See Name Guide for more information)*

SILK-TREE FLOWERS: Silk-tree flowers (合欢花 / hehuan hua, "flowers of joyous union") symbolize love and harmonious union, as alluded to in their Chinese name.

SOUL-CALLING LANTERN: In the world of *Husky*, soul-calling lanterns (引魂灯) are lanterns embroidered with complex spell patterns, which can only be lit and maintained using spiritual energy. A lit lantern can illuminate the human soul of a person willing to return and will hold the human soul within to be brought back and reunited with the other immortal souls and corporeal spirits. If the wielder of the lantern were to give up or have second thoughts, the human soul would be devoured.

SPIRITUAL CORE: A spiritual core (灵丹/灵核) is the foundation of a cultivator's power. It is typically formed only after ten years of hard work and study.

SPIRITUAL ROOT: In *Husky,* spiritual roots (灵根) are associated with a cultivator's innate talent and elemental affinities. Not every cultivator possesses spiritual roots.

THREE IMMORTAL SOULS AND SEVEN CORPOREAL SPIRITS: Hun (魂) and po (魄) are two types of souls in Chinese philosophy and religion. Hun are immortal souls which represent the spirit and intellect, and leave the body after death. Po are corporeal spirits or mortal forms which remain with the body of the deceased. Each soul governs different aspects of a person's being, ranging from consciousness and memory, to physical function and sensation. Different traditions claim there are different numbers of each, but three hun and seven po (三魂七魄) are common in Daoism.

THE THREE REALMS: Traditionally, the universe is divided into three realms: the **heavenly realm**, the **mortal realm**, and the **ghost realm**. The heavenly realm refers to the heavens and realm of the gods, where gods reside and rule; the mortal realm refers to the human world; and the ghost realm refers to the realm of the dead.

VINEGAR: To say someone is drinking vinegar or tasting vinegar means that they're having jealous or bitter feelings. Generally used for a love interest growing jealous while watching the main character receive the attention of a rival suitor.

WHEEL OF REINCARNATION: In Buddhism, reincarnation is part of the soul's continuous cycle of birth, death, and rebirth, known as Samsara: one's karma accumulated through the course of their life determines their circumstances in the next life. The Wheel of Reincarnation (六道轮回), translated literally as "Six Realms of Reincarnation," which souls enter after death, is often represented as having six sections, or realms. Each one represents a different "realm," or state of being, a person may attain depending on their karma: the realm of gods, asura, humans, animals, ghosts, and demons.

WHITE MOONLIGHT: A romantic trope referring to a distant romantic paragon who is cherished in memory long after that person is gone. Like the moon in the sky, the memory is always present, perfect and unchanging, but like the pale light by one's bedside, it is an incorporeal shine that can only be admired, not touched. The object of admiration is out of reach, and the admiration is functionally one-way.

WILLOW TREE: Willow trees in Chinese culture have a plethora of meanings, including friendship, longing, femininity, and more.

The Chinese word for willow (柳) is a homonym for the word "stay," which has led to it being featured in many poems and stories as a symbol of farewell and a reluctance to part.

YIN ENERGY AND YANG ENERGY: Yin and yang is a concept in Chinese philosophy which describes the complementary interdependence of opposite/contrary forces. It can be applied to all forms of change and differences. Yang represents the sun, masculinity, and the living, while yin represents the shadows, femininity, and the dead, including spirits and ghosts. In fiction, imbalances between yin and yang energy may do serious harm to the body or act as the driving force for malevolent spirits seeking to replenish themselves of whichever energy they lack.

ABOUT THE AUTHOR

Rou Bao Bu Chi Rou ("Meatbun Doesn't Eat Meat") was a disciple of Sisheng Peak under the Tanlang Elder and the official chronicler of daily life at Wushan Palace. Unable to deal [redacted] after Taxian-jun's suicide, Meatbun took Madam Wang's orange cat, Cai Bao ("Veggiebun"), and fled. Thereafter Meatbun traveled the world to see the sights, making ends meet by writing down all manner of secrets and little-known anecdotes of the cultivation world—which Meatbun had gathered during travel—and selling them on the street side.

NOTABLE WORKS:

"God-Knows-What Rankings"

Top of the Cultivation World Best-Sellers List for ten years straight.

"The Red Lotus Pavilion Decameron"

Banned by Sisheng Peak Sect Leader Xue and Yuheng Elder Chu Wanning; no longer available for sale.

[redacted]

No longer available for sale due to complaints filed by Yuheng Elder Chu Wanning.

[redacted]

2019 winner of the Ghost Realm's Annual Fuxi-Roasting Writing Contest

"Twenty Years on the Forbes Cultivation World's Billionaires Ranking and Still Going Strong: A Biography of Jiang Xi"

Orig

Dumb
↓
"The Husky & His White Cat Shizun"
Also being sold in another world.

...and others to come. Please look forward to them.